# Rose Red

Sarah Biggerstaff

AOS Publishing, 2025




ISBN: 978-1-998662-67-8

Cover Design: Meredith Lindsay

Visit AOS Publishing's website:
www.aospublishing.com

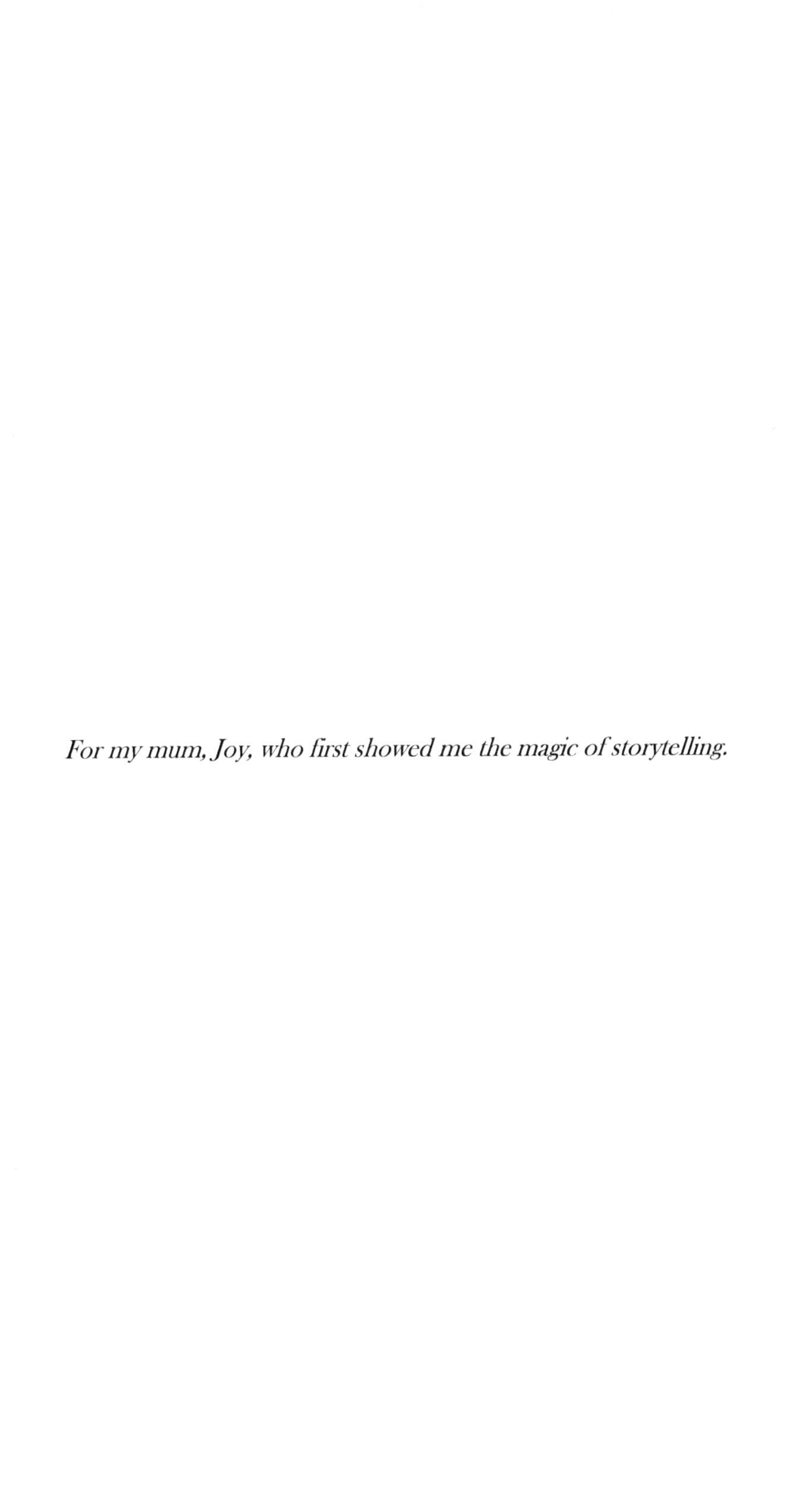

*For my mum, Joy, who first showed me the magic of storytelling.*

# Chapter One

As I stood between my older sister and my mother at the front of the enormous, drafty cathedral, all three of us dressed head to toe in black, our faces screened by long, gauzy, black veils, I was painfully aware of the gaze of the hundreds of assembled nobles and courtiers boring into my back. I felt strangely nervous, my palms sweating despite the biting cold that emanated from the old stone of the building. The crowd gathered for my father's funeral was so massive that the cathedral was filled to capacity, and mourners spilled out into the sprawling courtyard beyond. It seemed they were desperate to be as close as possible to the dead king one last time before he was laid in the royal crypt. Or perhaps they were just there to witness the spectacle of a royal funeral.

An involuntary shudder passed through me that had nothing to do with the cold. I'd thought I would need the veil to hide my lack of tears, but they came freely, flowing hotly and unchecked down my cheeks. In truth, they were tears of shame and guilt, tears of disappointment for who my father had really been, not tears of sadness at his loss. None of us, my sister, my mother, nor I, beat our breasts or wailed in sorrow, though my mother frequently dabbed at her eyes with her handkerchief beneath her veil, looking like a widow overcome by her sadness. Whispers floated up to where we stood in the very front of the church, snatches of conversation echoing strangely despite the vast crowd, people saying how terribly sad the poor queen looked, but standing just next to her, I could see that her eyes were dry. Though she could no doubt have used an enchantment or charm to induce crying, the heavy veil made it unnecessary. Besides, though it was whispered amongst the court – and probably outside of it – that she was a witch, Mother almost never used magic – not even subtle magic – in front of others, not even Lily and me. This was in part, I knew, because my father had expressly forbade it, but I also suspected she wanted to be seen as a queen first, a mother second, and a witch last. The rumours added mystique to her well-developed reputation as a woman of mystery and singular dynamism. But, as long as she never openly practiced magic, that was all they were, just rumours. At any rate, they were less confronting than the rumours which had swirled about my father before he died, which had proven true. Lecher, adulterer, predator.

I'd idolised my father for most of my life, but in the months leading up to his sudden death, I'd come to see a darker, crueller side of him. It was the first time I truly understood how contradictory people could be, how complex and inconsistent. For my father had been both kind and cruel, capricious and steady, wise and foolish. He'd just succeeded in hiding the darkness in his character for so long, I was blindsided when I learned the truth of it.

The elderly archbishop stood before what was perhaps the largest audience he had ever had, droning on about our dearly departed king, taken from us too soon, and the gathered mourners repeated his pleas for my father to be received into heaven. I murmured the words as was expected, even though I knew if there was a heaven, my father would never be admitted to it. As the bishop's proselytising drew on and on, I kept my gaze focused above his head, on the beautiful stained-glass window depicting a flaming heart against an exquisite kaleidoscope of blues, greens, purples, and pinks above the altar, feeling a strange sense of unreality. He was gone. My father, the king, was gone. Forever. What a relief.

When the mass was finally over, my mother, sister, and I were ushered out of the cathedral by a troop of guards, a stream of ladies-in-waiting and courtiers following in our wake. Those who were gathered outside the cathedral stretched out their hands to us, calling out their prayers for the dead king, for his grieving wife and daughters, as guards pressed them back, clearing a path to our waiting carriage. Some of those in the crowd had genuine tears in their eyes as they called out to us, their grief sincere and palpable. Maybe it was easier to be sad for those who didn't actually know my father.

As we drove through the streets of the city capital of Silvaner, I saw the lampposts and houses, shopfronts and statues decked out in black bunting in honour of the late king, and quickly looked away, instead focusing on my own gloved hands twisting in my lap. Even the dark grey clouds that filled the sky and blocked out the sun, the unseasonably icy wind that shrieked along the narrow streets swirling cloaks and skirts and buffeting the gathered crowds, seemed like a mark of respectful mourning for my father. No doubt he would have been pleased.

Jolting sharply with each bump and pothole the carriage wheels hit as we made our way home, I glanced at my mother and sister, both still with their veils drawn over their faces. My face was still covered, too, though I yearned to yank off the veil and draw in a full breath. But we would have to wait until we were out of sight of the crowds lining the streets to do that. Even with the veils, I could see that both of them were lost in their own thoughts.

As if she sensed me watching her, my mother's quick, green eyes jumped to mine, her gaze still piercing through the veils covering the both of us.

"It will all be over soon, Rose," she said in a reassuring tone, as though she could read the discomfort and tension in my body as it swayed unwillingly with the motion of the carriage.

The castle dominated the vista ahead of us as we drove along, a dark behemoth perched atop a hill, its high, unyielding walls and squat rounded towers forged of stone so dark it was almost black. I'd never given the ancient structure too much thought, except as a place full of dark cellars and long hallways to explore; it was just my home. Now, there was something unsettling and almost sinister about it as the carriage passed through the yawning mouth of the main gate.

The three of us made our way to my mother's sitting room for tea, each equally eager to be free of the watchful eyes that tracked our every move in almost every other part of the castle.

"I won't be needing you just now," my mother told her ladies-in-waiting, who hovered on the threshold uncertainly, looking like a brood of black chickens in their funeral dresses. "I wish to be alone with my daughters for now."

"Yes, your majesty," the most senior lady, Una, murmured, as the four of them dropped into a unified curtsey and departed, swishing their long skirts behind them as my mother closed the door.

I yanked off my veil and kicked off my too-tight new black shoes, longing for some comfort and the chance to relax a little, my mother and sister likewise removing the uncomfortable parts of their mourning attire.

Tea was brought in, and we all partook as much as we could manage. I found I was ravenous after the long day. I'd been up early to dress, then there had been the funeral procession, the interminable mass, and the unusually slow progress of the carriage through the streets clogged with mourners and spectators – and ate several slices of hot buttered toast accompanied by as many steaming cups of tea. By the third cup, the tea had gone cold, and I rose to my feet to ring for a servant to bring a fresh pot.

"What is it, Rose, dear?" Mother asked.

"The tea is cold. I was just going to ring for some more," I explained.

Mother leaned forward and touched a fingertip to the tea pot, a pretty thing of pale blue porcelain with hummingbirds painted on it.

"I think you'll find it's quite warm enough," she replied, a small smile on her full, red lips.

I was momentarily stunned by this display of magic – for indeed there was now steam issuing from the spout in a sinuous stream – then nodded, and sat back down, refilling my cup and Lily's. I couldn't remember the last time I had seen my mother use magic, even for something as simple as heating tea, but I supposed with my father gone, she no longer needed to abstain from her craft. I'd only learned of her magic quite recently, and seeing it still filled me with awe.

Lily sipped her tea and picked, birdlike, at a piece of cake, while my mother had nothing at all save a glass of wine. None of us spoke, but it was a comfortable silence, one of shared understanding and respect for each other's need for quiet introspection, broken only by the occasional crack of a log in the roaring fire.

Still, I was glad when my mother dismissed us, and Lily and I were able to retire to her sitting room. We spoke briefly about the funeral, the crawling pace of the sermon and many, many blessings, and the enormity of the crowd, but the conversation quickly turned to other topics. Neither of us wanted to dwell on our father.

"I'm so glad Mother will be regent until I'm old enough to rule," Lily said, curling up on one of the comfortable couches in her private lounge, still in her black gown, her black shoes abandoned on the carpet.

I liked this room more than most others in the castle. It had none of the comfortless spartan utility that characterised most other rooms of the ancient structure. My father had never been one for spending money on luxuries like comfortable furniture or pretty décor. But in Lily's room, the stone walls had been plastered and painted a soft blue, with brightly coloured tapestries covering much of the space, while the floors were overlaid with elaborate rugs. A matched pair of sofas were covered in powder blue damask and decorated with dark blue velvet cushions, bearing the crest of Silvaner, a silver unicorn, rearing on its hind legs, against a dark blue shield. The room was feminine and elegant without being fussy or gaudy. It was one of the few rooms in the castle where I could relax and let my feelings show, a single place of retreat and refuge in the sprawling castle that was our home.

"You know, in some kingdoms, they let royals rule much younger than twenty, especially if you're a boy," I said, nestling comfortably next to her. Lily rolled her eyes.

"I know, but then they have advisers pulling their strings anyway. At least with Mother as regent, I'll be able to get a better idea of what to expect when I take the throne in three years."

"Unless you marry before then," I teased, wiggling my eyebrows. Silvaner had an archaic rule that female heirs could not assume the throne until they were twenty years old, unless they were married. Male heirs, on the other hand, could become king any time.

"Unlikely," Lily replied firmly, looking slightly horrified by the idea. "No, I'm glad Mother is regent. I can trust her to do what's best for the kingdom, at least."

Lily had been born to our father and his first wife, who had died when Lily was less than a year old. Our father had married my mother a shockingly short time later, and I was born soon after. But Lily always referred to Queen Lorelei as 'Mother', never 'your mother' or 'my stepmother'. Lorelei was the only mother Lily remembered ever having, and she treated her as such.

"Things are going to be different with her in charge," I agreed. "For one thing, I won't have to worry about being married off to some stranger any time soon."

At fifteen, it had been something I dreaded would come all too soon, as my father sought to shore up alliances with neighbouring kingdoms, sending me wherever he pleased like some chess piece he didn't much mind losing.

"Are we terrible, heartless people for not being more sad about Father?" Lily asked, her large, bright blue eyes fixed on me with a mixture of worry and guilt.

"No," I answered without hesitation. "With the things we've learned about him since his death, I don't think we are."

My father had always been a secretive man, but I'd attributed it to the weight of his many kingly responsibilities. I had never been close to him; he'd always been a remote figure, like a character in a book or a famous painting. We knew things *about* him but did not really *know* him. He had kept us at arm's length, treating us as his subjects or possessions instead of his family, especially me. Lily had been everything to him: his heir, his beautiful, perfect daughter, a living reminder of his beloved first wife. But she had always been an object to him, too, a bargaining chip, and an assurance of the continuation of his family line.

I, on the other hand, had never mattered very much to him, except as a spare should anything happen to Lily. I was exactly like my mother, in looks at least if not in other ways, and as their marriage had deteriorated and a strange undercurrent of enmity rose up between them, my father's affection for me grew less and less. The final nail in the coffin of our relationship – before he was actually placed in a coffin, at least – had been my discovery of his assault of one of Lily's ladies-in-waiting. I'd told my mother, and the girl had been given the option to return to her family in the country, which she had taken eagerly. After that he'd avoided me like the plague, and his behaviour had become stranger and stranger, until he had died after a drunken fall sustained when he had been out hunting.

No, we had never been close, but I was certain that his death would have an impact that rippled out into every part of my future. Callous as it was, I expected things to change for the better, and they did.

* * * *

My mother, incidentally, stepped into her new role as regent with all the competence, confidence, and poise of an ideal monarch. She was a born leader, but every day I saw her deal with minor resentments and rebellions from her councillors and courtiers, who resented her new power. One man in particular, Lord Friedrich, who had been one of my father's closest companions and favoured advisers, took every opportunity to contradict and undermine her, implying that she did not know enough about agriculture, or the treasury, or the people to be able to make informed decisions. And she proved him wrong at every turn.

Now a ruler, she no longer spent her days idling away her time walking the grounds or sitting in her rooms with her ladies-in-waiting, sewing, or playing chess. Now she played a game of wits with men who continually underestimated her. Her days were spent poring over sheafs and sheafs of documents, learning everything she could, asking questions that not even her advisers knew needed to be asked. Before too long, Lord Friedrich and his cronies had aligned with her, realising that she was a true leader, a strong ruler, and not to be crossed. It was not long before the rest of the council fell into line, and my mother revelled in her victory.

Watching her work was like seeing an expert weaver at the loom, pulling in the threads of different colours as she needed them to form the design she wanted, always mindful of the bigger picture.

"Why don't you just replace the entire council?" I asked as the three of us sat gathered around a small dining table in my mother's private rooms, something we now did any time she was not required to dine with nobles and dignitaries.

"The most important part of ruling is that you have to keep your council on your side. I can replace one or two at a time, as I find legitimate reasons to remove them. But a complete overhaul of the council would outrage the lords, and I can't afford that so early in my reign, I mean, regency," she corrected with a quick glance at Lily as she cut into her roast chicken.

"I'm sure by the time I'm queen you will have assembled an excellent cabinet," Lily said with a small smile.

One morning, a few weeks after my father died, my mother summoned me unexpectedly to her study. It was, in fact, the same suite of rooms my father had conducted business from, but their appearance and atmosphere had changed dramatically now that my mother was in residence. Now the desk was positioned in front of the window, so that the sun warmed her back all morning and anyone she interviewed had to stare into the blinding light that streamed in until midday. There was a new desk, too, smaller and more manageable than the great hulk my father had used. It was made of the darkest timber I had ever seen, and its enclosed front was carved with all manner of flowers and plants. I quickly spotted a large climbing rose, my mother's favourite flower, and the one which she had named me for, forming a twining frame around the mural, the petals inlaid with rosewood. It was a botanist's dream and a thing of great beauty.

The floor was now covered with ornate, wine-coloured carpets, and a cosy couch faced towards the hearth. It felt feminine but practical, functional yet beautiful. The shield emblazoned with the silver unicorn of Silvaner against a dark blue background, which my father had prized, was still on display, though it was the only thing in the room in Silvanian blue and silver. Everything else reflected my mother's tastes.

The tapestry that dominated the rear wall was also changed. It was still a woodland scene, as it had been in my father's day, but now it depicted a forest clearing; at its centre sat a blazing fire surrounded by beautiful, naked women, with long, waving tresses flowing down their backs as they danced in the moonlight, while deer, birds, bears, and wolves stood watching from just outside the circle of light. The detailed workmanship was exquisite; the fire seemed to flicker and dance with a life of its own, just as the women did. I thought I detected my mother's handiwork in certain places, like the fire, the women, and the animals. They were all imbued with a vibrant, lifelike quality, as though a real moment in time had been captured and frozen in the many coloured threads.

Beautiful as the tapestry was, it was nothing compared to the woman who sat at the desk as I entered, scribbling away with focus and purpose. With her lovely oval-shaped face, magnificent green eyes, long, flowing auburn hair, her glowing golden-brown skin, full, red mouth, and radiant self-assurance, my mother was undoubtedly an awe-inspiring beauty. I'd inherited her dark red hair, as well as her green eyes and tanned golden skin, but I had yet to master the confidence and presence she emitted like a shimmering glow.

On seeing me, my mother rose to her feet and came towards me as I dropped into a brief but flawless curtsey.

"Hello, Rose darling. Let's sit here," she said, gesturing to the dark red brocade lounge placed before the empty fireplace. "It's much the comfiest seat," she added, settling herself into a broad, deeply cushioned corner, having removed her queen's mask so she was just my mother again.

"I need to talk to you about something," she began, a spark of restrained excitement in her bright green eyes. "Do you remember when you asked me if I was a witch, and I told you that I was, and that I would, in time, teach you the ways of magic?" Her tone was casual, almost teasingly so, as if she were baiting me.

I nodded, not trusting my voice to remain steady as my heart pounded rapidly in my chest and my pulse quickened with anticipation. I was unlikely to forget that particular conversation as long as I lived. It had been only a year ago, when things had not been going well in the kingdom: crops were failing, trade had slowed, and everyone seemed to struggle to pay their rents. The lords of the kingdom had appealed to my father en masse to request the proposed raise on taxes be postponed until their tenants could afford it. Outnumbered and caught off-guard by their coordinated entreaty, the king had grudgingly agreed.

But as he, my mother, Lily, and I sat together having dinner around the too-big dining table in the cold, oversized great hall, where my father always insisted we dine even when it was only the four of us, he brooded over the incident.

"We've not raised the taxes for two years now," he complained bitterly. His face above his beard was ruddy with discontent and too much wine. His hair, which had once been a rich, dark brown, was greying rapidly and beginning to thin, while his stomach had expanded and pulled at the front of his jacket, his body now showing the strain he was under as he dealt with the problems of the kingdom.

"That's because the last two harvests have not been as successful as hoped. A higher tax would not be supportable for many of the poorer families," my mother reminded him gently, daintily cutting up her roasted pheasant and potatoes.

"I know that," he spat at her angrily, the colour in his cheeks deepening until he was almost purple. "You think I don't know that? I'm the one dealing with supplicating nobles every other day, telling me how their lands aren't as fertile as they once were, their tenants aren't faring as well as they did. Why don't *you* do something about that?" he asked, slamming his fist on the table so hard an ewer of wine rumbled over the edge and onto the floor, dark red wine splashing and spreading across the white and black checkered marble. A servant hurried forward silently to clear away the mess and replace the wine by the king's side.

"I, dear? What do you think *I* may do about it?" my mother asked quietly. Her voice was steady, but with a steely edge, as though it held a dare, or perhaps a warning.

"How am I supposed to know? What's the good of having a witch around if you're not going to find a way to deal with these things!"

As soon as he stopped speaking, pulling himself up abruptly, a weighted silence fell over the hall. Neither Lily nor I moved a muscle or looked at our parents, frozen in apprehensive anticipation, my fork halfway between my plate and my mouth. Tension filled every space in the hall. The servants seemed to withdraw even further from us, receding into the shadows, as if sensing danger.

It was the first time I heard him call my mother a witch. Rumours had circulated about my mother having the gift of magic for years, but I had never seen anything to suggest it was true. Yet here was my father, calling her a witch right in front of us in his drunken anger. It might have been funny if it hadn't been so deeply uncomfortable to watch.

"You want me to use my skills to ensure a good harvest, my king?" she asked in a tone barely above a whisper, but firm, cold, and measured. Reasonable where he was not. "I thought you disapproved of such things."

"Well, no, damn it, I don't expect there is anything you *can* do about it. But I wish we could do *something.*" He sounded defensive, petulant, almost placating, as though he wanted to take back what he had said. It was like watching a small child throw a temper tantrum, only to be contrite and embarrassed afterwards.

"If you want me to take steps to ensure the harvest, I shall," Mother continued in the same quiet, steely tone. "Come, girls, it's time for you to practise your sewing, or reading, or something, I dare say."

Eager to get away, Lily and I rose from our half-cleared plates and walked quickly from the hall. The echo of my father's raised voice reached us again before we had gotten many steps outside down the corridor.

Alone in her room, Lily and I discussed the steadily growing hostility between our parents.

"What was that all about?" I asked, throwing myself on to the most comfortable couch and picking up one of the cushions.

Lily didn't say anything; she just paced in front of the empty hearth, a look of concern and sadness on her beautiful face.

"Lily," I said sharply. "I said, what was that all about?"

She stopped pacing and turned so that she was side on to me, not quite looking at me, her dainty, pale fingers straying distractedly over various porcelain statues and ornaments on the mantle.

"You know what people say about Mother," she murmured quietly.

"What do you mean?" I asked, knowing what she meant but wanting her to say it aloud, to talk about the rumours about our mother that had circulated the court in hushed whispers between fear and reverence for years now.

"You know that people say that she's a sorceress, that she – well, both of you – have witch's eyes," she said quietly.

"But that's just superstition and ignorance," I said, quoting my mother. For whatever reason, it was a common belief among peasants and the lower classes that emerald green eyes – like mine and my mother's – marked a woman as a witch. It was ridiculous, like so many superstitions, but persisted out of a bizarre kind of tradition and folklore. Some of the servants even went so far as to cross themselves if they saw my mother or I coming their way. As a child it had always upset me until I learned to ignore it.

Lily shook her magnificent, dark head slightly, still not meeting my eye.

"I've heard people talking – not just the servants, but courtiers as well. They say she's a witch, that before she married Father, she had a husband who died mysteriously."

"What do you mean, 'mysteriously'?" I said, trying to maintain my cynicism, but feeling my heart begin to race, afraid of what Lily might reveal next.

"Well, you know, very suddenly. Unexpectedly," she said, looking very uncomfortable, her cheeks reddening.

I just stared at her, struggling to absorb what she was saying, wondering if she truly believed any of it herself.

"People die suddenly all the time. Illnesses, accidents. It's not uncommon. Besides, are you actually suggesting she killed her first husband, Lily? People would know if that were true, they would have hanged her." I said this with certainty. I knew my mother wasn't a killer. But as to her being a witch - if enough people said it, perhaps there was some tiny kernel of truth in it.

Lily just shrugged noncommittally and continued.

"It's also said they always had the best harvests, the best livestock, that her husband had uncommonly good luck in business. People say that she made it all happen. That she used witchcraft to do it."

At this I laughed openly.

"Oh, yes, Mother has magic powers and can control the wind and the rain and the sun," I scoffed. "Not likely. She can be pretty terrifying, but I doubt even she can get the elements to do her bidding. It's all just superstition, old wives' tales, and people being jealous of her success and good luck." I sat back, assuredly, arms folded as if I'd played a trump card.

We were both silent for a minute, and with the silence my uncertainty returned. I wished Lily would look at me. Why didn't she just agree it was rubbish? The silence held a little longer before I spoke again, unable to take the tension.

"Do you believe it?" I finally asked her.

Lily hesitated, as if measuring her words carefully before she spoke. But finally, her cornflower-blue eyes met mine.

"No-o," she hesitated. "I don't believe Mother is a witch. At least not in the sense you mean, magic power over the elements and such. But I can see why people might take instances of things she's done and - I don't know - run away with the idea."

"What kind of things?" I demanded. But I knew the answer already in my heart. There had been unusual happenings, things that had been easy to miss as a child, but which became harder to explain as I grew older.

Whenever Lily, or I, or my father would get sick, Mother would give us a sticky brown tonic to drink and, almost like magic, whatever was ailing us would be gone in less than a day. She, meanwhile, was never ill or injured herself, but always in a state of perfect health. And, though she was almost forty, she looked younger than many of the women at court who were ten years younger than her.

Another time when we – I, Mother, Lily, and some ladies-in-waiting – had been out riding, a dead tree branch had snapped suddenly in a strong wind; the crack had sent my horse bolting, and my mother had chased after us. I'd been thrown from my saddle, injuring my leg when I'd fallen heavily to the uneven ground. I'd thought it was broken, the searing pain almost unbearable, but as my mother ran a hand over it, the pain eased, and it turned out to be not injured at all. Then she had whispered something I didn't hear clearly to the horse, and it calmed instantly.

There were, now that I thought about it, a half-dozen or so memories I had of things happening involving my mother that did not yield easily to explanation.

"She has unusual gifts," was all Lily said.

I went to bed but struggled to sleep, trying to remember all the times I had seen my mother do something I didn't understand. When I did sleep, my dreams were shapeless and vaguely troubling. I was trying to break through a cloud of dense, unending mist, my mother's and Lily's faces drifting in and out of sight. I called out to them, but they seemed not to hear me. Then my father's face emerged from the fog, but his eyes were white and sightless, his mouth hanging open as his head lolled to one side. I screamed in terror and his spectre vanished. Then I was alone again in the dark, with no way out.

The next day, I'd sought out my mother alone in her room and found her sitting at her writing table, a piece of paper drawn over whatever she had been working on. I marvelled again at how young she looked, with no lines on her lovely face or a single grey hair on her head. She looked like a queen, a refined, beautiful, and commanding lady, not a witch. But I still wondered.

"What is it, my scarlet Rose?" she asked with a small smile on her lips. She was in a good mood. I hesitated, not wanting to spoil things. But would there be a better time to ask her?

"I wanted to speak to you, to ask about - well, about last night."

"Yes," she said invitingly, the smile fading slightly.

"Father said, he-" I faltered, not quite knowing how to proceed. In the end I just blurted it out. "He called you a witch."

"He did." The expression on her remarkably beautiful face was neutral, inscrutable. Her green eyes, so capable of expressing anger, joy, disappointment, were shuttered now, revealing nothing. I wondered if I would ever master the skill of being so in control of my emotions as to not let a hint of them show on face. I doubted it; my feelings were always hard to contain, too big and bold to be hidden.

"Why?"

"Because he was in a bad mood. Because he is afraid that the harvest will not be bountiful this year, that we won't be able to raise the tithes on the land, that the coffers will empty and the people will revolt. Because he wanted someone he could shift the blame to."

"But - but he said you should - *could* - do something about it?"

She nodded.

"Why?" I asked again.

"Do you really not know?" She smiled again, but it was a colder smile than when I had first come into the room. She rose and walked around her table until she stood before me. She was tall, as tall as my father, and quite a bit taller than me.

I shook my head. She took both my hands in hers and looked into my eyes with her intense, penetrating gaze.

"Because I have been known to influence such things in my time. Though, since I became queen, there are certain practices I have been required to abandon. For now."

I just stared at her, not quite believing what I was hearing. I asked the question that had been trembling on my tongue from the moment I entered her room.

"Are you a witch?"

She smiled broadly at this, as if greatly amused. She let my hands drop and moved towards the window, glancing outside casually, as though she were checking the weather.

"Not in the sense that peasants would use the word. I don't cackle over cauldrons and steal children in the night. I haven't made a pact with the devil or carved out my own heart. I have skills and abilities that are commonly called witchcraft or sorcery, yes. But I dislike the word 'witch', it has such ugly, repellent connotations, don't you think?"

"Why didn't you tell me this before?" I asked, my words coming freely now, a thousand questions blooming in my mind at the acknowledgement that she possessed magical abilities, whatever term she preferred to call herself by.

"I have not kept it a secret from you. I merely didn't discuss it openly, and that is not the same thing. I hoped you would observe for yourself, observe the enchantments I cast in your presence, and ask me about it as you are asking now. I did not think it would take your father calling me a witch over our supper for you to raise the matter."

What she said seemed too fantastic to be true. She claimed to have cast enchantments right in front of me. But then I remembered the horse, the healing draughts. She had been quiet about her magic, yes, but never entirely covert. At least, not around me.

"I saw, but I don't think I ever imagined it was anything other than you. Your knowledge, your - I don't know - your personality, I suppose. I'm not expressing it right."

"You're closer than you think. Peasants think of magic as some unnatural dominion over things and people, but there is so much more to it than that. Some of it is, as you put it, personality. Or, rather, personal force - force of perseverance, of confidence, of will."

Then a thought occurred to me for the first time: could I be a witch, too? I asked and she smiled again.

"In time, with a great deal of work and training, yes."

"Will you teach me?" I asked eagerly.

"No. Or, at least, not yet."

"Why not?" I was disappointed. The idea of a special power or ability that could be just mine had seemed like such a wonderful prospect. It could be something that set me apart from Lily in a good way. But then, I thought -

"Will you teach Lily?"

"No." My mother's voice was suddenly sharp, her eyes hard. With a raised hand she stilled my next question before I asked it. "She is not my child, my blood, and so she could not become a witch, no matter how hard she tried."

"So, witches are born?" I asked, trying to understand what it was that made them, *us*, different. How did one become a witch?

"No, one must work at it, it is not a gift freely given. The ability flows in our blood, with the knowledge passed from mother to daughter, but a witch also requires a certain temperament. Certain qualities are needed: curiosity, dynamism, force, an affinity for the natural world. Your sister does not possess these. But they are strong in our bloodline. Remember how you excelled in the schoolroom when Lily did not? How you've always loved the outdoors and wanted to learn about all the plants and animals, as though you *needed* to understand them?"

I nodded.

"You and I are part of a long line of practitioners. My mother and grandmother and great-grandmother were all mistresses of Hecate's science. And in time, so shall you be."

With this, my mother turned and walked back to her table, seating herself again. It was a dismissal. I wasn't ready for the conversation to be over; I had a million more questions to ask, but I limited myself to just one.

"When will you begin to teach me?"

"Before too much more time has passed. Perhaps as long as a year. You are already much older than I was when I first began to learn. But it will depend on a number of factors. As I said, the circumstances are not yet right. I will tell you when they are. Of course, you understand that you can speak of this to no one? Not even your sister. I tell you these things in the strictest confidence for your own safety."

I nodded again and left the room.

From then on, I'd tried to observe my mother closely to see if I could detect her practising magic, but I was disappointed; as she said, she had been required to keep her practice of it to a minimum since she had become queen, only using it in special circumstances.

I'd wanted to tell Lily about our conversation, to tell her I was part of a long line of witches, that I was special, too – not a future queen like she was, but still more than just the ordinary girl I'd always felt I was. For as long as I could remember, she was the one I shared secrets with, the person I could count on to listen and take an interest in what I had to say. We were sisters, yes, but we were also the closest of friends. But I kept my word and didn't tell a soul, not even Lily, though it dulled some of the brightness of my joy to do so. For a whole year I'd kept it to myself, not even asking my mother about it, for fear that she would change her mind about teaching me if I couldn't control my impulse to talk about magic, even with her.

Now, sitting in my mother's study, she drew me sharply out of my recollections, taking my hand as we sat together, announcing, "It's time for your magical instruction to begin."

# Chapter Two

I don't know quite what I had expected. Magic wands? Flying broomsticks? Bubbling cauldrons and pointed black hats, maybe. But I was more than a little underwhelmed when Mother led me into the ante room which came off her private study and, in my father's time, had been reserved for small, private meetings and the occasional illicit sexual rendezvous. I hesitated on the threshold, uncomfortable memories of my father surfacing in my mind, but glancing quickly around the space, I saw that it was so completely transformed that it felt like an entirely different room.

The walls were all lined floor-to-ceiling with shelves, some containing tatty-looking old books with peeling bindings and faded lettering on their spines, but most housed jars of all sizes filled with herbs, flowers, seeds, stalks, and a vast miscellany of bizarre and gruesome curiosities. There were bundles of feathers, rusted nails spattered with blood, spools of what looked like human hair, a container of dried birds' feet that had curled in on themselves, numerous powders in all different shades, and all of it neatly labelled.

There was no bubbling cauldron, or even a fire. The centre of the room was occupied by a tall, unvarnished wooden table at which one would have to stand to work. On it was an array of knives, ranging from an enormous cleaver to several incredibly small, pointed knives, all gleaming brightly despite the dim lighting, along with a large, dark green marble pestle and mortar.

It looked to me like the workroom of a healer, or maybe an apothecary. It was not what I had expected of a witch's study.

My mother watched my face as I examined the room in detail, stepping up to the shelves to read the little labels on some of the bottles and jars. I read words like *Elephants' ears, Hangman's rope,* and *Areca nut.* After I had taken a lap of the room and turned to face my mother again, she asked, "Well?"

"It's not what I expected," I admitted, trying to conceal my disappointment.

"That is the truth of witchcraft: it is something the uninitiated cannot comprehend, so they tell wild stories which are taken for fact. It's not about communing with the devil, dancing naked in the moonlight, sacrificing goats, and uttering curses." Judging by this, I had to assume the tapestry in her office was some kind of ironic joke. "The truth is much more simple. Much more practical."

She walked over to a shelf, her exquisite red gown swishing on the bare marble floor, and took up a few small jars, which she brought over to the high table.

"These," she said, passing me a jar containing dried poppy flowers and another of black paste. "You already know. Poppies. Used for aiding in sleep, relaxation, and reducing stress. The paste can also promote healing."

I nodded, hoping I looked interested.

"This is vervain. It protects against evil spells. It's a kind of magical shield."

She handed the jar over to me. Inside was an unremarkable-looking dried plant stalk covered in small, pale pink flowers. She continued handing me one item and then another, explaining their uses and properties to me as she went. After seeing my mother heat the tea with a touch, I had been hoping for enchantments and spell work and was underwhelmed by this lesson in plant properties. After a while, my attention began to wander, and she noticed.

"Is this not living up to your expectations?" she asked sharply, as I stifled a yawn.

"I just thought there would be more to magic than learning the names of a few dozen herbs," I said, trying to keep from rolling my eyes.

"And so there is. But this, *this,*" she said, shaking a jar of tiny, dried mushrooms at me. "Is at the heart of it. Knowing what to use to achieve your means is essential to creating a draught or enacting a spell. Without a sound base of knowledge in plant lore, you will be lost. So, I suggest you pay attention," she added irritably.

I nodded again.

"Rose, this is where we must start. Would you teach a child how to approach complex equations if they had not yet mastered simple sums? No. If you want to be a sorceress, you must first learn the basics and you must learn patience."

She handed me an enormous, stained, and worn leather-bound volume, which provided detailed information on the properties and applications of hundreds, maybe thousands, of different plants. I nearly staggered under its weight.

"You will read this, taking in what it has to teach about the tools of this craft. Then, when you feel you have learned, and I mean really *understood* what is at play when working with plants, you will make a simple draught."

"What kind?" I asked excitedly, my enthusiasm returning instantly at the idea of concocting a potion by myself.

"I will leave that for you to determine. For now, you have a great deal to learn."

"But, you mean you want me to memorise this entire book?" I asked, incredulous, the tome in my hands feeling as heavy as a millstone.

"No. But you need to understand the science of it all."

She led the way back into her study and then towards the door, pausing before she opened it and fixing me with one of her penetrating stares.

"I ask that you keep these lessons to yourself. Witchcraft is no longer prohibited by law, but most people still fear it and will not want a witch for their queen. Do not tell anyone. It is one thing for people to call me a witch behind my back out of superstition or just the fun of gossiping, but quite another for them to hear I am actually teaching you the craft. Do you understand?"

"Yes."

"I mean it, Rose," she said, looking me gravely in the eyes. "This has the potential to be dangerous for both of us. Secrecy is essential. I need you to promise, to swear, you will tell no one about the lessons I give you. Not even your sister. I am initiating you into a long, noble tradition. I am trusting you with this most precious inheritance. Do not disappoint me." Her eyes hardened as she said this, her severe tone allowing no argument.

"I swear, Mother." I paused. "Thank you for trusting me."

"Of course I trust you, Rose. You are my own mirror image," she said, her expression softening again as she cupped my cheek for a moment before opening the door for me to leave.

Hesitating on the threshold, I asked, "Why didn't you start teaching me sooner?"

She looked surprised by the question.

"Because your father prohibited me from practising magic long ago, fearing that it would pose a threat to him. Though witchcraft is no longer a crime, many of us are still persecuted. You saw how your father grew fearful of me towards the end of his life. Imagine how he would have behaved if he knew me to be practising magic under his own roof. I was protecting us both in keeping my knowledge from you when you were too young to understand its importance. I kept my word to your father, but when he died, I was free of my promise. Besides, it was never my intention to keep the truth from you forever."

I was shocked. There was so much between my parents I'd never comprehended, so much I hadn't known about my own father. But then, how little I had known about my mother until now? In a way, my parents had been strangers to me, their innermost lives and thoughts buried too deeply for me to see. I wondered, for a moment, whether my mother could have saved my father after his fall if she had used her magic. But I decided I didn't want to know the answer.

"One more thing, Rose, if you are to learn Hecate's science from me, I must have your full focus. You will have to say goodbye to your school master."

This was an unexpected blow, for the tutor had been such an important part of my life for several years now.

Since I was ten, Lily and I had been privately educated by an elderly scholar named Tomas. He was a crotchety old man, with a bent back from years of poring over books; long, white hair growing profusely from his ears and face, his beard so long he could almost have tucked it into his belt, while his head was completely hairless, as smooth and shiny as a mirror. He was plagued by arthritis, and his crooked, thick-veined hands were often clumsy, sparking his temper. Despite his less-than-cheery demeanour, I rather liked him. He could be stern, but when he saw how much I devoted myself to my studies, he warmed to me, and we became fast friends.

He taught us a little maths and philosophy, but his knowledge and passion shone through most when he spoke of science and history. These were my own favourite subjects, and our mutual affinities made it easy for us to get along, despite our significant age difference.

As Lily and I grew older, and continued our education in both scholarly and feminine subjects, we each distinguished ourselves in different ways. I found to my delight and surprise that science, history, and languages were areas in which I excelled, as I had never excelled in anything before, except perhaps making trouble. Lily on the other hand struggled with these subjects, though her accents were flawless when she spoke languages she considered 'pretty'.

The schoolroom was one of the rare areas where I had praise heaped upon me; Tomas saw my application and intelligence and helped me to excel, never telling me to behave like a lady or mind my cuffs when I was writing hurriedly, ink splashing here and there.

It made a nice change for me to be able to shine at something which Lily did not, for even though Lily and I were as close as two sisters could be, I had always envied the way my father, courtiers, and servants fawned over my sister, praising her lovely singing voice, her flawless needlework, and her perfect, ladylike manners. Then there was the undeniable fact that Lily was spectacularly beautiful. With her snow-white complexion, oceans of long, glossy black hair, and vibrant cornflower-blue eyes, she was the loveliest girl in the kingdom. Not that I was ugly – I'd inherited my mother's unusual brand of beauty – but Lily's looks never failed to win people's heart from the moment they beheld her, and her kind and loving temperament made her quite perfect in every way.

My lessons with Tomas continued long after Lily's had ceased to allow more time for lessons in dancing, singing, sewing, and etiquette. Now, however, they were more like conversations, in which I'd ask about an event in history, or a philosophical matter, and we would debate the topic fiercely, Tomas guiding my thoughts and learning with his wisdom. I was heartbroken when my mother said I had to choose between Tomas and witchcraft; Tomas had been one of my closest companions in the last few years. He had made me feel that my curiosity and intellect were gifts, not oddities. But the truth was I didn't really need his lessons anymore, not about history and the like, anyway. I would miss his conversation, though, and the life lessons he imparted with such a generous, clever mind.

Following my mother's edict, Tomas was sent away to take up an offer to teach some nobleman's children in the north. Tears welled in my eyes as I said farewell. He took me by the shoulders and said firmly in his raspy old man's voice, "None of that now, Princess. Life is full of partings, and you must learn to bear them. I'm proud to have had you as my pupil; don't forget to keep your mind sharp."

I nodded, not trusting myself to speak without crying, already feeling the tears gathering, ready to spill at any moment.

"Good girl," he said gruffly, covering his own emotions with sternness. "Now remember what I told you: beauty is fleeting, but wisdom is forever. Now, go be wise," and with that he left.

*** * * ***

Though I applied myself to studying the behemoth book of plant lore whenever I could, other duties still required my attention. One day, my mother and I were in her bedroom examining a mountain of gowns for a dinner that was coming up, a trivial, yet necessary task, because – she explained – even though she now commanded a kingdom, she was still expected to be attractive and decorative.

"But more than that," she explained, "beauty is one of the weapons in our arsenal as women. Men underestimate us, see us as pretty things. But if they desire us, if they believe there is the least chance they can possess us, there is little they will not do. You'll find you can achieve more through subtle things like a well-cut gown or a well-timed laugh than any amount of rational argument."

I nodded, holding a dress up to the buttery sunshine that flooded in through the high, arched windows of her rooms. It was magnificent, made of golden damask that practically glowed in the sunlight.

"How about this?" I asked. She shook her head.

"I wore that to the last of these. It's silly, but people notice that kind of thing. I think, perhaps," she said, plucking a dress carelessly from the pile on her bed, "this one."

She held up a gown that was neither quite red nor purple, but the deepest shade of wine. The silk bodice was embellished with hundreds of tiny black pearls, the cuffs edged in exquisite black lace.

"It is lovely," I agreed, a little note of envy creeping into my voice. Though as a princess I wore pretty clothes every day, I longed for an excuse to wear something so ornate and sophisticated, to be part of the court social scene as my mother and Lily were.

"But," she said, stilling my hands, which were about to deposit the gold dress back on the enormous pile that now covered her large four-poster bed, "you should wear the gold gown."

My mouth fell open in surprise. I had never been to this kind of public dinner before, I'd always been told I was too young. Lily had only begun to attend them when she had turned sixteen.

"Why not?" my mother asked, smiling at the expression of astonishment on my face. "You are a young woman now, and I think it's important for you to see what these people are like at close quarters. You're an integral part of the court, and it's vital that you are prepared for every aspect of court life."

I was about to reply when Lily walked into the room, smiling as she beheld us up to our waists in the mountain of gowns.

"Lily," my mother said, appealing to her, "don't you think this gown would be perfect for Rose?" She held up the golden damask for Lily's approval.

A smile broke across my sister's delightful face.

"Oh, yes, it's perfect, and the colour!" She reached out a hand to touch the fabric. "It will look so beautiful with your gorgeous red hair."

I smiled at the compliment and Lily's enthusiasm as she gave it.

"What are you wearing to this big dinner, Lily?"

"Oh, my pale blue velvet," she said disinterestedly. I knew the one she meant; it was quite simple, but elegant and she looked lovely in it. But then, she would look pretty in a nun's garb or a hessian sack, her gloriously blue eyes and sweet smile more enchanting than any amount of lace or jewels.

At her and my mother's urging, I tried on the gold dress. I didn't expect to feel any different wearing it. And yet, when I stood before the full-length mirror, I saw something in my reflection I had not seen before: a woman. It seemed I had outgrown my awkward adolescent body almost without noticing; my breasts had sprouted and were now larger than Lily's, the stiffened front panel of the dress lifting and supporting them in place. And my hips had broadened, so I now resembled an hourglass, the full skirts emphasising my small waist and wide hips. My face had lost some of its round, childlike appearance, my pointed chin and high cheekbones now prominent, and even striking.

In this dress my eyes burned bright as emeralds and my hair gleamed, touched with red and gold in the sunlight. I looked radiant, glorious, something I had never felt before. My smile was one of pride mingled with a touch of embarrassment. In this moment, I did not envy Lily for her delicate, sylph-like beauty. For the first time, perhaps ever, I was content with my looks and did not fear comparisons between myself and my sister.

* * * *

The evening of the dinner came and went without supplying any great excitement or interest. We sat in the great hall, which felt cosier with a few dozen nobles crowded about it, collected around a single, long table. It was a relatively small dinner, considered intimate with only twenty or thirty guests. A fire roared in the broad stone hearth at one end of the hall, and tall braziers burned at regular intervals along the wall, filling the normally dim old hall with light and warmth. Bowls of flowers sat in the centre of the table in an attempt to soften the otherwise harsh-looking room.

My mother sat at the head of the table, resplendent in the wine-coloured dress, an earl or duke at either side of her, listening intently as she spoke, as though each word that fell from her mouth were a precious gem. I was seated next to Lily on one side and a Lord Manfred from the northernmost reaches of the kingdom on the other. He was elderly, slightly deaf, and dreadfully boring. He must have made an equally unfavourable assessment of me early on, as he was soon loudly chattering the ear off his neighbour on the other side. I contented myself with enjoying my food, observing the others seated around the table, and eavesdropping on the conversation Lily was having with the man next to her.

He looked considerably older than us, perhaps forty, but was quite good looking. His appeal was lessened by the fact that he was overly conscious of his appearance, and rather too proud of it. His slightly greying hair was oiled into a flawless coiffure and his goatee had been trimmed into such an unnatural design it was clear that much of his time – and money – was spent on preening, polishing, and perfecting his appearance. His hands waved about as he spoke, showing well-manicured nails and uncalloused palms.

He spoke to Lily in a continuous torrent of words, barely pausing for breath as he talked of his land, how very much land he owned. Oh, what a fine estate it was, he said, detailing the acreage and elevation, orientation and aspect. When that subject was exhausted, he talked of his horses: his many, many horses, and what remarkable creatures they were, for the breeding of horses, it seemed, was his passion. I wondered how Lily could maintain such a convincing expression of interest, when I couldn't help rolling my eyes as he spoke.

"I recently made an excellent bargain of a magnificent stallion from Malbourg. The fool selling him let him go for only five hundred gold marks, when I would have been happy to pay seven. I would be happy to teach your highness how to ride," he said with would-be gallantry, peering at Lily over the rim of his wineglass and finally pausing long enough for her to respond.

"Oh, thank you," Lily replied politely, "but I know how to ride, I've been riding since I was eight."

A look of wounded pride crossed his face for a moment, his lips puckering sullenly, but he quickly rallied and changed tack, talking of something else. I smiled and thought about something my mother had said to me once, that men needed their egos flattered or would they sulk like a small child. I snorted into my goblet in an undignified way, because that was exactly what his pout reminded me of, but luckily Lily was the only one to notice. She narrowed her brows in disapproval but couldn't completely suppress her small smile.

"I'll say this for his lordship," I remarked to Lily as we sprawled side by side on her bed after the interminable dinner. "He was entertaining. Not in the way he intended, I'm sure. I don't know how you managed to listen to him with such a serene, interested look on your face."

"These things are sent to try us," she replied with a look of exaggerated forbearance.

"Such a martyr," I teased. "I used to feel jealous when you got to do these kinds of things and I didn't. I imagined you sitting in the hall, talking to interesting people from all over the world, surrounded by adoring listeners, and dancing with handsome young men."

Lily laughed at the picture I'd painted.

"It's truly not as glamourous or fun as you'd expect. And there are way fewer handsome young men than there are homely, middle-aged ones," she agreed sleepily, stretching like a cat. "And as far as listening goes, I'm usually lucky to get a word in at all. It's like being back in the schoolroom, only the lectures are less useful".

But the dinner had been a gentle introduction, my first proper taste of the social life of the court. Before long I was attending feasts and balls with hundreds of the gentry and wealthy and important subjects in attendance.

The first ball I attended was held on a midsummer's evening and was celebrating the Feast Day of Saint Elisabeth. It was not often we celebrated Saints' days at all, let alone with such grandeur and ceremony; in fact, this was something of an anomaly. My mother confided to me that we were descendants of Elisabeth, who was famed for her miraculous transformation of bread into roses. I thought it was strange that sometimes acts of this kind were taken for miracles and other times for witchcraft. It seemed to me the distinction was arbitrary, depending on the agenda of those in power more than anything else. Miracles, I thought, were likely just magic called by a different name.

The great hall was completely transformed for the occasion, decked out in banners of pink and red, with tall urns placed about the walls filled with fresh flowers, so the room smelled like a summer garden in bloom. Each of us was dressed in the colour of our favourite roses. My mother wore a gown of blood red velvet; Lily's was a pale, delicate pink; and mine was a deep, vibrant magenta. We danced in long lines down the great hall, ladies on one side and men on the other. I liked best the dances in which we changed partners often; they were a good way to learn who danced well and who was likely to tread on your feet.

As always, Lily was the most desired lady, with men surrounding her at each break, begging for the next dance, as other ladies watched on enviously. My mother also had her share of would-be suitors, politely agreeing to dance with each of them in turn, without giving any indication that she preferred one over another. I was never without a partner, their skill ranging from indifferent to masterful, though none made my pulse quicken with excitement. Still, I danced the whole night until I wore through the soles of my dance slippers.

Afterwards my mother applauded both Lily and I, saying we had made a great success of the evening.

"I was so proud to see the two of you conduct yourselves so properly," she said, her eyes bright with motherly pride. "No one was anywhere near as beautiful as you two tonight, or as sought-after as a partner." She looked at us with a gleam in her eye but said nothing more.

For my part, I had enjoyed myself thoroughly, much more than I had at the stuffy dinner, and looked forward to partaking more in the social events of the court, provided they didn't interfere with my lessons in magic, should they ever really begin.

# Chapter Three

I had thought reading the book on plant lore would be a quick and easy task, despite its size, as I was a keen reader and a good student. I'd expected to devour the book in no time, absorbing the information in its age-darkened pages like a mental sponge. I was deeply mistaken. It was a labour of Herculean proportions. Not only did I need to know what each plant looked like and what its uses were, but I needed to learn how to harvest it, in which season, at what time of the day, and whether it needed to happen in a specific moon phase. Henbane, for instance, I learned, had to be harvested at the first new moon of autumn for it to have reached its required potency. Using Henbane collected at any other time would be worse than useless.

At times, I found reading the herb book was almost as tedious as I'd found needlework as a small child. Almost. I frequently tossed the book aside, almost sick with frustration and disappointment at my difficulty in taking it all in, and distracted myself with other, more appealing activities, like riding. I rode almost every day, and my beautiful chestnut gelding, Bastian, got more exercise in the few weeks I was wading through that damn book than he had in the previous year.

Several weeks after my mother gave me the book, I was desperate to get away from the confines of the castle, breathe fresh air, and clear my head, which swam with overwhelming amounts of information. I saddled Bastian and we set off for a few hours of freedom, no chaperones or servants in tow, just the two of us and the open air. It wasn't strictly permitted, but no one had to know. Galloping over the gently undulating meadows outside the city walls, I felt a wave of calm wash over me as the city and castle grew smaller and smaller behind me and the wide, green world filled the expanse ahead of me. I squeezed Bastian's sides with my heels and we picked up speed, flying over the grassy downs. There was a thrill in the speed, the rhythmic movement, the wind rushing past and tangling my hair, drowning out all the noisy thoughts that plagued me.

I had always had a restless spirit, even as a small child. On fine days, and even those with a chilly bite to the air or a faint drizzly haze, I would positively itch to go outside, to roam the rolling green lawns, climb trees to pick fruit, or simply wander around the beautiful, sprawling gardens. I wanted to smell every flower, learn the name of every plant. I felt somehow in my element in the garden as I never did inside. The rich, vibrant colours and the lush, fresh smells lifted my spirits before I was forced to return to the cold stone of the castle.

As a child, I was regularly scolded by our nurse, Elsa, for absconding from my lessons on sewing or etiquette to frolic about in the sunshine instead. On one such occasion, my mother had unexpectedly come to my defence, saying an interest in nature and the world around us was a gift, and that curiosity should always be admired. I felt vindicated, until she added that I needed to learn the arts expected of a princess as well, as, like it or not, that was the role I had been born into. I resolved from then on to try to better apply myself to my lessons and ignore the urges that seized me to go exploring instead.

Despite this, I never completely lost my truanting tendencies. I still seized every chance to go roaming the gardens from edge to edge and top to bottom, occasionally finding hidden secrets I shared only with Lily, like a sunken garden grotto that had been long neglected and eventually concealed by enormous shrubbery, which we came to call our secret garden. Hidden among the moss-covered stones and wild climbing plants, Lily and I had a cool, quiet refuge away from the noise and order of the castle. To us it was like a secret other world, as though we had entered the Faerie realm.

Now, away from the castle with its rules and watchful eyes, I felt the same thrill of independence I had as a child. I rode with

Bastian as far and fast as I could, revelling in the freedom and the closeness to the earth and the enormity of the sky as they stretched before me.

It all helped to clear my mind, the better for me to absorb more information when I eventually went back to the book. Because I did always go back to it, tempted as I was to give up and spare myself the frustration and tedium. But each time I considered going to my mother and saying I quit, my pride and curiosity railed against it. I still did not fully appreciate what witchcraft would allow me to do, but having seen the few times my mother used magic in front of me, I knew it would give me the kind of power that had always seemed beyond my grasp. My curiosity was awakened, and I was desperate to learn more. But first I had to master the contents of the book.

I read as much as I could each day, in all the spaces of time between dance lessons, dress fittings, parties and meals, and the time I spent with Lily. I kept my promise not to tell her that I was to learn magic, no matter how wrong it felt to have a secret from her, which meant I had to keep the book out of her sight as well.

One afternoon the two of us sat in Lily's lounge; she was putting the finishing touches on a navy blue cloak she had been working on for weeks while I sat, my hands idly tracing the unicorn on one of the cushions, as I mentally listed the properties of different herbs, sitting mesmerised as I watched Lily's needle weaving in and out of the fabric. It was one of those rare times she had sent her ladies-in-waiting away so we could talk, just the two of us, but my mind kept straying to herbs, flowers, and berries.

"Are you alright?" she asked loudly, as though she'd had to repeat herself, jolting me from my thoughts.

"Of course, why do you ask?" I said, sitting up straighter and trying to look attentive.

"You seem . . . not odd exactly, but different. Distracted. As though your mind were somewhere else."

"I'm just thinking," I said in what I hoped was an offhand way.

"What about?"

"Nothing in particular. Just, you know, life." I didn't have a better lie to hand and hoped she'd accept this very weak excuse without argument.

"How very deep of you," she said in a teasing tone, a little smirk on her pretty lips.

"Is that nearly done?" I asked, changing the subject, gesturing at the heavy cloak in her hands.

"Actually, yes." As she said this, she cut a thread from the intricately swirling crimson roses she had been embroidering around its edges. This done, she stood and held it up for me to admire.

"Do you like it?"

"It's lovely," I said honestly. The outer part was a thick, but finely woven lamb's wool, dyed a magnificent, deep blue. A trail of roses, stitched in deep crimson thread, reached all around the hem, up the front, and around the hood. Inside, it was lined with soft, pale grey rabbit fur.

"You look amazing in blue," I added appreciatively.

"It's not for me," she said, holding it out to me, an affectionate smile beaming on her face.

"For me?" I was genuinely surprised. She had been working on it for weeks, without saying a word about it being mine. But that was like her, always so generous and eager to give pleasure where she could.

"Try it on," she insisted, pressing it into my arms. I slipped into it, fastening it at the neck with the small golden clasp and pulling the hood onto my head. Lily dragged me over to a long mirror so I could see myself. The cloak was beautiful, and much as I had thought it would look good on Lily, I liked how it looked on me, too, the deep blue contrasting nicely with my red hair.

"I love it. Thank you," I said, pulling her into a tight hug, the hood sliding off my head as I did.

"You're welcome," Lily laughed and smiled in reply, clearly as happy in giving the gift as I was in receiving it. I quickly slipped it off, as summer was coming to end, but it was still warm enough for me to begin sweating in the woollen cloak.

"It will be perfect for winter," Lily said, taking the cloak from my hands and folding it carefully before placing it on the table with an affectionate little pat. "You're always getting cold".

I agreed, smiling at her thoughtfulness and imagining wearing it when I went into the woods looking for mushrooms and flowers to harvest for my potions, picturing myself, mysterious and cloaked in the misty reaches of the forest.

* * * *

The leaves of the trees in the castle gardens had turned a hundred different shades of gold and red and begun to fall by the time I felt I had mastered enough plant lore to be able to attempt making a draught of my own.

I told my mother this, and instead of leading me to her workroom to make a start as I had expected, she handed me another book, this one even older, dirtier, and more crumbling, containing instructions for concocting potions, like a recipe book for magic. Flicking through the worn and stained pages, careful not to tear or damage them, I saw directions for love potions, healing tonics, wasting draughts, an elixir to preserve beauty, a serum to cure smelly feet. It contained instructions for making every type of concoction imaginable.

"Study this," my mother instructed me. "Learn about the different types of brews. Then, you will need to gather your own ingredients."

I opened my mouth to ask why, when the walls of her workroom were almost overflowing with a cornucopia of potion ingredients, but she forestalled me. "You must collect your ingredients yourself. If I simply let you use what I have gathered by my own labour, you will not learn the discipline needed to be a successful witch. This is something you can only truly understand by doing it yourself."

I nodded, not pleased with this new information, but willing to undergo whatever tests she put to me to prove I was worthy of gaining the knowledge she had to offer. I was determined to master this skill, like I had mastered the lute, riding a horse, astronomy, and all the courtly dances. I was determined to become a witch, if for no other reason than pure stubbornness.

It took me very little time to settle on what I would attempt for my first potion. There were hundreds to choose from, but many took a long time to mature, or required ingredients I had little chance of obtaining. Where was I likely to find vipers' fangs or wolves' claws? My mother might have them, but she had prohibited me from using her stores. I would need to select a potion that required ingredients I could acquire easily and quickly.

While some of the things I needed grew in the castle's kitchen gardens, even some of the more commonplace ingredients would require me to leave the castle, something I was expressly prohibited from doing without an escort and protection. Sneaking off for a ride with Bastian was one thing, but I didn't think I would be able to just slip away by myself to gather the ingredients I needed, and I couldn't very well take a servant or guard with me without having to explain my purpose.

I visited my mother again to ask her advice. She was speaking with the master of the treasury, so I waited in the hallway as they talked over state business in tones I could hear well enough through the thick timber door, though the words were largely indistinguishable. I was struck by how funny it was that there was a man in with her speaking seriously of financial issues, and when he was done, I would go in and ask how to access the required herbs for a magical draught; the two things so completely incongruous. It didn't seem truly real to me yet, it felt like a game she and I were playing, pretending at being witches. And yet, at the same time, I took it all very seriously, eager to learn all I could and desperately wanting a way to distinguish myself and find some purpose beyond dressing nicely and dancing at balls. It wasn't that I didn't enjoy those things – I did – but there was no way they would be enough to satisfy me for the rest of my life. I knew I led a charmed, privileged life, that I'd never want for any material comforts. But magic offered me power and purpose far beyond the reach of normal court life, and I had no intention of settling for being ordinary when I could be so much more.

The treasurer, a sour-looking man with a haughty demeanour and a ridiculous wig, finally left, passing by me as he did. He stopped when he saw me, a disagreeable look on his thin, wrinkled face. But he bowed as low as his rheumatic back would allow and muttered, "Your Highness," with feigned deference all the same, then went sweeping off down the hall, eventually disappearing around a corner.

"Are all of the council as odious as that man?" I asked my mother, seating myself on the couch by the hearth.

"More or less," she replied, slamming shut an enormous ledger on her desk and coming across to me. "Some are worse."

"How do you bear them?" I asked, putting my feet up on the couch, then immediately lowering them again at a disapproving look from my mother.

"How do we bear anything? Because we must."

"You're very wise," I said ironically.

"I know. Now, what brings my lovely daughter to see me?" she asked with a warm smile.

I raised the issue of getting hold of my potion ingredients and, unexpectedly, my mother's smile widened with great amusement.

"I wondered when you would ask. Of course, you will need to roam the forest to find much of what you need. I do."

"You *do*, how? You're always with people. And aren't you recognised if you go walking about the kingdom?"

"I make time. I am a queen, but even a queen is entitled to some repose, some time alone with her thoughts. I tell my ladies-in-waiting, the servants, the council, that I am not to be disturbed or that I'm indisposed. Then I dress in common apparel, veil my identity with a spell, and leave the castle. No one suspects, and I have the kind of freedom I dream of when I am stuck for hours on end with a privy council who have never encountered a topic they are not happy to parse for hours."

I was in awe of her, even more so than I had been before. I knew she was clever and would likely not struggle with deception. I hadn't known that she was brave and reckless and willing to do things that would horrify the court were they to hear of it. My respect for her grew even greater.

"But how do you get out unseen?" I asked – then I remembered the secret tunnel Lily and I had found as children.

I'd been ten at the time and on one of my adventures around the castle, when I'd made a wonderful discovery. I'd hidden in one of the castle's several subterranean cellars, thinking no one would look for me there. It was a cavernous underground room, where wine was kept in large barrels, along with mountainous piles of grain sacks, and other food items that needed to be kept at a constant temperature. Hiding in one of the farthest corners behind a wall of wine barrels, I discovered a small, wooden slab in the earthen floor, which was, in fact, a trapdoor. It was partially covered by a vat of wine and almost entirely hidden beneath years of accumulated dirt, so that I would never have known it was there, had I not stubbed my toe on the large iron pull ring.

I attempted to prise it open, to see where it led, but the wine barrel was too heavy for me to move on my own. Then I heard Elsa enter the cellar, calling for me to come out unless I wanted to eat nothing but porridge for a fortnight. Not wanting to share my discovery with her, I hastily ran out to her before she could find me herself, facing the scolding I received as stoically as I could.

That night, I had whispered to Lily about what I had found as we lay in the darkness of our shared room. We were both curled up in Lily's bed, the blankets pulled over our heads for added secrecy.

It was rare that I could persuade Lily to join me on my adventures, but the tale of the secret trapdoor piqued her interest, and she excitedly exclaimed, "I can't wait to see what's down there, maybe a lost treasure, or a magical spinning wheel, like the one in Elsa's story of the princess and the wicked dwarf."

"Or maybe a dragon," I suggested dramatically, which she was not impressed by.

It was with hopes of a great discovery that we drifted off to sleep that night.

Having to wait three whole days before we had the chance to further investigate the mystery of the trapdoor was a test of patience tantamount to torture. During quiet moments, my mind often wandered to the trapdoor, imagining all the things we might find if we managed to open it. Then finally, one day we were released from our lesson on etiquette early because Elsa had a cold, and without hesitation Lily and I dashed to the cellar.

Lily had the sense to bring a lamp, as it was dark enough in the cellar, let alone in the underground chamber. Between us we managed to wrestle the wine barrel out of the way, pushing and straining with all our meagre might, and finally shifting the barrel enough to clear the door. Then I had to scrape away the dirt that had compacted around the trapdoor, as Lily refused to get her hands dirty. After several minutes of scratching away like a little mouse, I finally cleared away enough of the grime, freeing the door. Then, with the light to guide us, I pulled it open and began to descend the ladder attached to the wall, Lily holding the lamp over my head to help me see.

"Are you sure you don't want to go first?" I asked teasingly.

"No, thank you," she replied, looking at me as though I'd offered her a dead mouse.

It was not a very long ladder, perhaps six or seven feet, but as I went lower, a deep, damp chill surrounded me, seeming to seep into my skin, and I shivered with both cold and fear. When I reached the bottom, I called up to Lily to follow, and, seeing it was safe, she scampered down the ladder, the lamp still clasped in her hand.

When she reached the bottom, she raised the lamp high so we could better see our surroundings. It was not a room or a tomb, as we had imagined, but a hidden tunnel. The ceiling was low enough that a full-grown man would have to hunch down, but being small, we had plenty of room to stand fully upright. Just below the ladder it was quite dry, though cold, and the walls of the tunnel were covered in wispy grey spider webs, and every so often we had to duck low to avoid walking through some of the webs hanging low from the ceiling.

"I hate spiders," Lily hissed each time we had to pass one.

It was gloriously frightening down there, and as we got further down the tunnel it grew damper and colder. The flickering light from the lantern danced in menacing shapes over the dark, slick stone walls, amplifying the darkness beyond the little golden circle of the lamp's reach. Little rivulets of water trickled down the walls; moss and even little grey mushrooms sprouted from the crevices in some places, thriving in the dank, dark tunnel. Luckily there were no rats, for I don't think our courage could have endured that.

Lily and I crept along the passage, enjoying the feeling of fear tempered by excitement, and thinking that we really were perfectly safe in our own home. We continued on for what felt like hours to our young, frightened senses, before we reached an ancient iron-bound wooden door, blackened with age and the permeating damp of the place. It was locked, but the enormous iron key sat inside the lock. The real difficulty was that the lock, ring handle, and hinges were so badly rusted we could not force the door to budge. We struggled and pulled until finally the door gave way with a sharp, shrill squeal of rusted iron on stone. It only opened just wide enough for us to slip through one at a time, and even then, we had to turn sideways to be as narrow as possible.

Outside we were struck blind by the sudden watery sunshine after the darkness of the tunnel. As my eyes adjusted to the brightness, I saw just a few dozen yards away was the edge of the forest, which bordered the eastern side of the castle. I turned back to look up at the castle, but all I could see was the sheer face of its wall towering above us, seeming to reach into the sky. Behind the wall, I determined, must be the castle's forecourt, where markets were sometimes held and which visitors to the castle would have to pass through before reaching the palace proper. Beyond the forecourt stretched the city capital of Silvaner, bustling with the noise and activity of a thriving town, though this seemed strangely dimmed as we stood just outside the colossal city walls.

"Let's go!" I said, taking Lily's hand, keen to run through the forest and explore the world that had suddenly opened up to us outside of the castle.

"We can't!" shrieked Lily anxiously, tugging on my hand and yanking me back towards the door with surprising strength. Her eyes were wide with fear, sensing the trouble we would be in if we got caught. Like a sensible child, she was also afraid of the dangers that might lurk in the unfamiliar forest.

"But it's right there," I complained, breathing deeply to catch a scent of the lush firs, desperate to run between the trees, chase the rabbits, and explore the wild expanse of majestic pines.

"We would be in so much trouble if we left the castle," Lily said firmly, trying to reason with me as I still struggled to escape her grip on my hand.

"No one would know," I wheedled.

"What if someone asks where we've been? I won't lie and neither should you," she said primly, with all her elder-sister authority. Lily was always the perfect child, obedient, honest, and sensible. It grated on me sometimes that she would never bend the rules or relax her compliance just a little so we could have some real fun.

"Besides, there are probably bears," she warned, which was enough to persuade me back into the tunnel, and we made our way back to the ladder and up into the cellar. I thought it had been a first-rate adventure, but Lily saw it differently.

"We would never be trusted alone again if anyone found out. So, you must swear never to tell anyone what we did, or about the trapdoor or the tunnel, or any of it."

"Ugh, fine," I sighed, not appreciating her rational concern.

"*And*," she added pointedly, "you must also promise never to come down here again. Father and Mother would skin us alive if they ever thought we had snuck out of the castle."

This concern I could understand, having incurred our parents' wrath before for less rebellious behaviour. Lily making me promise was her way of protecting me from my own overly curious and sometimes openly defiant nature. So, we had agreed never to mention or use the secret passage again. But I could certainly not forget that it was there. I kept the knowledge of it to myself in case I should ever have need of it.

"There are hidden ways out of the castle," my mother said, recalling my attention to our conversation. "This castle is very old, with passages built to keep the royal family safe in case they needed a quick getaway. There is a secret passage that leads just outside of the castle walls from my workroom. There is also one from the king's – that is to say, what is now *my* – bedroom, which leads into the city. Your father used to sneak out to meet women that way. Between the two, I can come and go with ease."

"Are there any others?" I asked, keen to know if she had discovered the one in the cellar.

"Possibly," she said with a disinterested shrug. "But two are enough for me, especially when they are so conveniently located. I can see why your father made such liberal use of them."

She spoke so casually of my father's infidelities, but I wondered if they hurt more than she let on. I decided not to tell her about the passage from the cellar; it was mine and Lily's secret.

"I suggest you use the one in my workroom," she continued. "Go at a time of day when you are not expected in lessons or any other engagement, when you can be sure your sister will be occupied, and no one will come looking for you. Make an excuse for where you have been during this time. Do *not* say you have been out riding. It is too easy for someone to ask at the stables and catch you out."

Her face was grave as she said this, her green eyes burning with intensity. I wondered if she had ever been caught out, but I didn't dare ask.

"I understand. So, at night perhaps, would be best?"

"Yes. If you say you are retiring to bed, that you do not want to be disturbed, you can slip away. As for clothing, I will give you some things you can wear." With this, she turned and led me into her workroom. Opening a cupboard, she pulled out some dark woollen breeches, a soft, loosely woven shirt, a grey tunic, and a short, black cloak.

"Wear these; it's much easier to pass unobserved in men's clothes. You are less likely to be bothered if someone sees you, and they are far more practical for walking around the woods collecting herbs than a long dress."

She gave me a key to her study so I could come and go from the castle via her workroom as needed.

"You must also take this," she said, handing me a leather pouch containing a small knife for cutting specimens, and a bundle of vervain.

"For protection," I said, recalling what I had learned about vervain in the book on plants.

"Very good. I see you did read the book I gave you thoroughly. You will be safe from most malignant forces if you carry this. I have one on me at all times." She pulled aside the shoulder of her dress to reveal a dried green sprig tucked beside her breast. "It wouldn't hurt for you to do the same."

And that is how I came to always have a piece of foliage secreted about my person.

# Chapter Four

The potion I had selected for my first attempt was a simple healing draught, intended for coughs, colds, and other minor ailments. I wasn't going to risk failing because I was too ambitious my first time around; this was one of the more basic and easily produced potions, so I expected it to be straightforward. I would need to acquire willow bark, vervain, poppy, liquorice, borage, and potentilla. Some of these grew in the castle kitchen gardens, but borage only grew in the summer and autumn, so I hurried to gather it in the forest as soon as possible.

I readied myself for my first solo trip into the woods to collect herbs, my blood thrumming with excitement. Leaving the castle alone at night was the most adventurous thing I had ever done. I slipped out through the passage in my mother's work room and soon found myself facing the edge of the forest, the only light coming from the stars and my small lantern. The trees grew more densely the further into the forest I went, so I took care to memorise my path to avoid getting lost.

The trees were mostly evergreens, a mixture of pines, firs, and hemlocks, and I was soon surrounded by a wall of dark green shrubs and ancient brown trunks, the colours made darker by the dim light, with the stars above mostly concealed by the thick canopy of the trees.

Though it grew right by the castle, I had almost never been into the forest before, and certainly not by myself. At first, I loved the peace of it, the way the noise of the town was muffled by the trees, while the sounds of birds, foxes, and other small animals remained clear. I breathed deeply, inhaling the sharp scent of pine needles, the loamy fragrance of soil and moss, the fresh, clean smells of the forest mingled with the cool night air.

I collected some artemisia growing at the edge of the forest on my way in. I didn't need it for my potion, but knowing how many different herbs and flowers my mother had in her storeroom made me eager to collect all that I could. I liked to think myself brave, but after walking a few minutes through the deep darkness of the night beneath the trees, with their shifting shadows, the eerie calls of owls and other strange animal cries unnerved me greatly. I made my way deeper, and a hare bounded past me in the dark, making me jump at the sudden movement.

"Get a hold of yourself," I cursed aloud, my heart hammering a frantic beat.

Trying my best to shake off the incident, I raised my lantern higher and pressed on into the impenetrable darkness, my eyes scanning the ground for what I needed. There was a dim mist hanging above the forest floor, chilling my legs, and obscuring my vision, making me stumble occasionally over roots and stray branches. After what felt like hours of picking my way through the damp, cold forest, I spied a growth of mugwort, which I took cuttings of and stowed safely in the pouch hanging at my waist. A loud, shrill animal sound rang out sharply from nearby, setting my teeth on edge as I reached instinctively for my knife. I stopped for a few moments, listening for any hint of danger, but the forest had grown quiet once more. Though afraid, I forced myself to continue, lamp held aloft in one trembling hand and blade in the other.

But after the loud shriek, every little sound – the rustle of leaves, the snapping of a twig, the whisper of the wind swirling between the tree trunks – made me jump. A sort of snuffling noise and a low growl caught my attention, and looking up, I saw a dark shape emerging from among the trees ahead of me, a deeper shade of black than the trees around it. Unable to make out what it was, but not wanting to find out, I turned tail and ran as fast as I could in the other direction, slipping on moss and catching my feet on tree roots as I went.

Blood thundered in my ears and my heart hammered madly as I ran for the edge of the forest, my breath catching in my chest as my feet pounded the ground. Safely outside the gloom of the woods, I drew deep breaths, trying to steady myself. I was unused to running and had gotten winded quickly. After a while, my breath returned almost to normal, and I looked in my pouch, disappointed at my meagre bounty. All I had managed to gather was some mugwort, borage, and artemisia, of which only the borage was of use for my potion.

* * * *

The next day I told my mother of my pitifully unsuccessful excursion into the woods and my fear. It was more than just the dark and the unfamiliar forest that had troubled me, it was not knowing what I might find and whether I'd be able to protect myself if needed. I knew that it came down to being weak, my fear that should the protection of the vervain fail, I might find myself in a position where I was unable to defend myself. For all my independent spirit, I still knew no magic, nor how to fight, and had hardly ever been alone outside the castle walls. Being alone in the dark forest made me feel vulnerable in a way I never had before. My mother heard my fears with sympathy and kindness.

"It's one of the great disadvantages of our sex that we are often physically weaker than men. There are steps wiccans can take to protect themselves and those they care for, but they take time to master, and none are foolproof against other witches. Most can be overcome by other wiccans, if not by men. But I would prefer you know how to defend yourself against men as well, especially as you don't know any magic yet."

"Couldn't you just cast a protection spell over me?" I asked, feeling pathetic even as I spoke.

"I could, but would it make you feel safer? Would it teach you anything other than how to rely on the strength of others for your safety? No. I think it's time you learned what you're capable of, without magic."

The very next day I began having lessons in hand-to-hand combat, blade combat, and archery with one of the most senior castle guards, Paulus. He was the man my mother trusted most; he guarded her almost all hours of the day and was sworn to protect her.

Tall, broad-shouldered, rugged, and bearing many scars of battles long past, he was an intimidating teacher. He was not an attractive man. His fleshy, misshapen nose had clearly been broken more than once; his grey hair, which receded far back on his scalp, was shaved down to a bristly fuzz; and a few of his teeth were missing. Paulus rarely smiled, and if he did it was more of a menacing grimace than a mirthful grin, unless I had just landed on my arse during training. That usually got a chuckle out of him.

The lessons were held in one of the training rooms off the barracks at the rear of the castle. Though 'room' may be too generous a word for the spaces in which the guards and the small number of soldiers garrisoned at the castle trained. It was a large, square space with a compacted dirt floor, and was open to the elements on one side, so that in winter it was freezing, and rain often blew in sideways to soak us while we trained, while in summer it became unbearably hot by noon.

I trained with Paulus every day, telling anyone who asked that I was having fencing lessons, as the truth would have only led to more questions; princesses weren't supposed to learn how to fight.

As I bounced around the hard earth floor, dodging Paulus' fists, or swinging a sword, a trickle of curious guards and soldiers would walk by casting covert, curious looks at me while I trained. A sharp look from Paulus was enough to hurry them along, which I appreciated as I fumbled my way through the various manoeuvres and exercises.

Distracted by the soldiers who pretended to be just passing by, I failed to block Paulus' blow to my chest, and went sprawling onto the floor, landing so hard that when I rose my lip was split open and oozing blood, and I had a cut on my cheek from where I'd hit the floor. I saw stars for a moment, then rallied and got back to my feet, my hands ready to block the next hit.

"I was just making sure you were paying attention, Paulus. I see you're taking it seriously today," I taunted him, trying to cover my embarrassment at my messy spill.

"I always take the princess' safety seriously," he said, not breaking eye contact for a moment as I dusted myself off. He was frightening in his intensity sometimes, but he understood my position and taught me that my small stature did not mean I could not fight to win. Better yet, he taught me how to fight dirty.

"Use your opponent's strength and weight against them," he instructed as we circled each other, our hands held up in defensive positions. "And don't forget the weapons you were born with. Elbows! Knees! Fingers!" I struck at him, raking my fingers across his exposed wrist. "Ouch, and nails."

"Do you mean my charming personality doesn't count?"

"Always aim for where your opponent is weakest – the throat, ankles, and groin," he continued, ignoring me. "And keep an eye out for other areas they expose. Maybe they drop the left guard when they attack, and you target beneath the ribcage, or they favour one leg, so you take out their knee with a kick or swing of your sword. Find weaknesses and use them to your advantage."

Luckily, I quickly learned enough basic healing magic to repair any visible wounds after each training session in order to hide the evidence that I had been fighting with my fists instead of taking the less violent fencing lessons. But I had to live with the aches and injuries that couldn't be seen as reminders of what happened when I lost focus or was too slow. I could have asked my mother to heal me, but then she would have known how often I got injured and I wanted to avoid that at all costs. Paulus never commented on the way my injuries seemed to heal unnaturally fast, but he was far too observant not to have noticed. No wonder my mother trusted him with my safety.

We progressed from hand-to-hand combat to weapons, but even after months of training and gradually building up my strength, I was not the best with a sword; they were too heavy and unwieldy in my hands, and made it easier for an opponent to put me off balance.

"Why are all the weapons made for men?"' I complained, getting to my feet after Paulus had made me stagger back yet again.

"Because the soldiers are all men."

"If I were in charge, I'd let women enlist, too. We're just as capable of wielding a sword as men are. You'd just have to bother to make them the right size and weight so we can actually swing them."

Paulus just shrugged, unwilling to get into a debate on sexual politics with me, and handed me a set of practice daggers. Unlike swords, these suited me perfectly, and I quickly became quite deadly. Being relatively small and quick meant I could slip behind an attacker, strike low and in a blind spot. Paulus showed me the places to aim for if I wanted to immobilise an attacker, and where to strike for the kill.

The next time I left the castle to gather herbs, it was with a dagger looped onto my belt; the weight of the steel was a great comfort as I prowled the woods in complete darkness, save for the lamp I carried.

My mother had been right: no matter what protective spells she cast over me, what I needed to overcome my fear was the knowledge that if it came down to it, I would be able to defend myself without magic.

I gradually grew stronger and more skilled at fighting, though I always felt as though my legs and arms were on fire the day after an intense training session. Hot baths and salves from my mother helped, but I couldn't always hide my wince when I'd have to take one of the many flights of stairs in the castle and my muscles screamed in protest.

Lily watched me grimace and tense as I made my way awkwardly up a set of stairs, unable to keep the look of amusement off her face.

"It's not funny," I snapped, though I knew I probably looked ridiculous and couldn't suppress my smile.

"Oh, alright, I'm sorry," she replied playfully. "I didn't realise fencing was so demanding. I'm glad it's not me doing it. Why are you taking fencing lessons again?"

"So if you have any awful suitors, I can send them running," I joked, dodging her inquiry.

"Oh, well, in that case, I fully support you," she smiled. "Here," she said, taking my arm and helping me climb the rest of the stairs.

There were times when I wished I could tell Lily the whole truth about what I was up to and why. I was used to sharing every aspect of every day with her. She always knew what I was thinking, what made me happy, bored, angry, afraid. But I felt as though a veil had dropped between us when I started keeping secrets from her. I became a little removed from her life at court, as she stepped into ever-greater prominence as the future queen.

Now we were seldom, if ever, truly alone together anymore. All but gone were the nights I would snuggle down in her bed to talk over the events of the day. We were still close and would still laugh about the people we met at dinners and the various court parties. But the secret of my becoming a witch came between us and meant that our friendship had lost some of its honesty, and as a result, some of its joy.

I loved that my mother's decision to teach me magic had brought her and I closer than we had ever been, but I hated that it came at the cost of my relationship with Lily. If it had been put to me at the time that I had to choose between Lily and magic, I would have said Lily in a moment. But a part of me would have always yearned for the craft I had not fully known.

That is not to say I had an easy relationship with magic, either.

After my first abortive attempt at gathering herbs, I had rallied, aided by my increased confidence in my defensive skills.

The next few times I entered the forest, I was wary but not nearly so jumpy. I soon began to understand the odd noises I could hear, and knowing made me much less afraid. I also built a map of the woods in my mind as I walked their length and breadth over time. Where others might see nothing but a sea of trees, I began to recognise landmarks that helped guide my way. Before too long, the forest came to feel like a second home.

My confidence in that respect grew, but my first few attempts at brewing a potion were worse than fruitless; they were abject failures. The first one was too thick, the next too weak, the next too strong. Once I forgot the willow and the poppy altogether, as I obsessed over boiling the other ingredients for the exact amount of time needed. My failures seemed to mount up around me, and I often questioned if perhaps, despite what my mother said, I did not have the temperament of a true witch.

Sometimes I dreamed of quitting. I dreamed of days spent leisurely with Lily, riding, dancing, laughing at the men who wanted to marry her, strolling the grounds arm-in-arm with her, pointing out the different flowers, hiding from her ladies-in-waiting. Yet, there was something about witchcraft that always drew me back. I came to conclude eventually that it was simply in my makeup, in my blood. But, oh, how I struggled with making even the simplest of potions at first. I persisted and kept failing. I must have gotten it wrong at least a half a dozen times, but I refused to let myself be beaten by a simple brew.

Then finally, one day, a day that had nothing to distinguish it from hundreds of others, I concocted a successful healing draught. Shimmering purple vapours wafted up from the simmering cauldron as the potion sat steeping over a low flame. The different ingredients filled the small workroom with a calming smell; liquorice, peppermint, and bergamot floated to my nose as I waited for it to be ready. I knew it was right as soon as I stoppered the vial, sensing that somehow, this time I had succeeded. I ran to my mother, who was mercifully alone, and waved it under her nose. She ushered me back into her workroom, then carefully poured the vial out into a small, shallow dish to examine it.

"Well?!" I demanded anxiously, desperate to win her approval and to know that I had finally succeeded, that I wasn't a fraud.

She daintily dipped her index finger into the inky blue liquid then pressed it to her lips, and my heart seemed ready to burst with pride when she said with a small smile, "It is a good brew."

I leapt about, punching the air, flailing my arms in a wild dance of victory. I had finally, after months of trial and error, made my first potion.

"So, what now?" I asked, drunk on the elation of my success and determined to learn more.

"Now, the real fun begins," she replied with a wicked smile.

# Chapter Five

The distance between Lily and I only deepened over the following months. I was working at my craft at every possible moment, and during the times when I was forced to learn a new dance or play hostess to visiting nobles with the other ladies, I was itching to be in the workroom. Things I had enjoyed before now seemed tedious compared with spell work; it became something of an obsession. For months, my sole purpose was to study and practice magic, my abilities improving gradually over time.

As I continued to learn, I was amazed by all the secrets that gradually revealed themselves to me under my mother's tutelage. I finally became competent, if not spectacularly talented, at potion-making, and eventually learned practices from across the range of magical arts.

I learned the entire runic language, which many spells and incantations were written in, and how to use stones carved with runes for spellcasting, both major achievements. But despite this, I had barely scratched the surface of witchcraft. There were hundreds, maybe thousands, of years of magical knowledge to learn, and I could hardly begin to grasp the sheer depth of it all.

When I finally moved beyond potion-making and runes, my mother laid out all there was to learn about the different veins of the craft.

"There are ten branches of magic," she explained. "Abjuration, Alchemy, Conjuring, Enchantment, Evocation, Divination, Illusion, Transmutation, Restoration, and Necromancy.

"The practice of alchemy deals in the mixing of plants, herbs and so on, to create draughts imbued with special properties. You know it as potion-making and have already practiced it. Restoration deals with healing; it is the antithesis of necromancy. Sometimes it is achieved in conjunction with alchemy, but a gifted witch can heal with a spell alone, depending on the injury or illness. Transmutation, or more simply, transformation, enables a witch to change the physical properties of things. It can be cast over creatures, people, or objects. Objects are, of course, easier to transform than living things. Enchantment is a very diverse branch of magic. With enchantment you can affect the minds of others. For powerful witches, this extends as far as controlling their behaviour, like puppet masters. Protective spells and magical barriers are also classed as enchantments."

"Have you really mastered all these forms of magic?" I asked, astounded by the sheer diversity of what magic could do and the volume of knowledge my mother held in her beautiful head.

"Not quite. It is common for a witch to specialise in two or three branches at most. To master all ten branches of magic would take several lifetimes."

"Which are your specialties?"

"I am gifted at enchantments, alchemy, and transmutation. They are, I believe, the most practical forms of magic. Now, to continue. Conjuring. The school of conjuration is used to call objects to the summoner. It is showy but has little purpose beyond a party trick and is quite draining on the caster. Evocation allows one to control the less tangible elements of the world: wind, fire, heat, cold, etcetera. It is useful, but even skilled witches find it can be, shall we say, inconsistent? Illusion is used to manipulate others into believing things that are not true. It can deceive the senses, make others see or hear things that are not there. It is a useful skill if you need to manipulate others, but it can make a witch lazy. You must keep your wits as sharp as your knives, and over-reliance on illusions has been many a witch's downfall."

"Finally, there is Divination and Necromancy. Divination enables one to predict, or rather get glimpses of, the future. However, the future is an uncertain thing, always in motion, and one is better off forging it for oneself than relying on magic to show you the way. And Necromancy. This branch of magic is used to control the powers of death and the life force. It is the most unnatural form of magic and forbidden by many covens for this reason. I will never teach it to you. Death comes for us all in our time, and life is precious because it is finite. Only a fool would try and bend life to their will or extend life beyond its natural limits."

I let these impressive words sink in. Until now I had not fully understood or appreciated the magnitude of what magic could achieve. Brewing a mixture of herbs to alleviate illness was one thing, but my mother was suggesting I could learn to transform one thing into another, conjure objects from thin air, or trick the senses into believing a lie. It was even possible, so she said, to undo death itself. Suddenly it seemed too great a responsibility, too awesome a power for one person to possess. And how could someone do these things and not be known – and persecuted, despite the laws against it – for what they were? I asked my mother this.

"As you know, in the past, many people were killed because they were accused of witchcraft. Over the last few hundred years or so, dozens have been tried and found guilty. How many of them would you say were truly witches?"

I shrugged. I had no idea how often witch hunters had gotten it right.

"None. Granted, some of those murdered as witches had obtained potions or spells from real masters of Hecate's science, but none of them were witches themselves. I told you once that the uninitiated did not know what magic looked like. So naturally those hunting it got it wrong."

"But what happens when a witch takes things too far? Who can stop them from subjugating the whole world?"

"Other witches. There is a code, you see. The Wiccan Code. A witch may do as she likes, provided she does not exploit her powers or enslave others. The limits of the code are reasonable; a witch can acquire great wealth and power, but we may not place ourselves too far above the rest of humanity."

"People say you're a witch, though, why are you not persecuted?" I pressed.

"Because I am a queen, for one thing. For another, they rely on superstition. You and I have what are known as witches' eyes, but are green eyes so very uncommon? Could all people with green eyes be witches? Is it a reasonable assertion?"

I shook my head.

"Exactly. People know this. Our eyes alone are not enough to send the peasants to our doors with pitchforks. They also say I bewitched my own lands to ensure good harvests. But mine were not the only lands to have good harvests in those years. I made sure of it. Simple folk like to believe in magic, they like to feel the thrill of fear. They enjoy telling stories of animated corpses and fields sown with snakes' blood on a dark and stormy night. It makes their lives more exciting. But most magic can be done subtly, it does not need to be a great show of power. And smart witches know how to cover up where magic has been done, should it be necessary."

I pondered this. It made sense; no intelligent person would court persecution by parading their powers openly. And really, did people believe all the stories they told of wicked witches, or was it just as my mother had said, a way to entertain themselves, to pass the time, or stop children from being disobedient?

"So that's why no one ever realised you were doing magic, even if you did it openly, like the healing draughts you gave us?"

"That's right. The best magic is done subtly and out of necessity. Besides, if most people met a real witch and guessed what she was, they would not be brave or foolish enough to try and take her by force."

I nodded again, considering this.

"So," I asked, "what will you teach me first?"

"I think we shall have to test where your talents lie."

* * * *

After more than a year of hard study and having finally mastered the basic competencies of potion-making, I breathed more freely and was able to fall back into the normal rhythms of my life without resenting the time I spent away from magic. Knowing that I really did have the makings of a witch, I began to enjoy things again as I had before, my obsession with magic now somewhat tempered. I could patiently sit through a dinner with a prospective suitor for Lily and giggle at his absurdities or take note of his virtues. I could learn a new dance with real enjoyment, as I had used to do. I could even stand still for a whole hour at a time while new dresses were fitted to me, though I never fully lost the restless energy I had been dogged by since childhood, and the seamstress' pins pricked me more than once as I wriggled on the little raised platform.

One night, after we had sat through an interminable dinner with a prince from a remote kingdom who had been gracelessly bidding for Lily's hand in marriage, Lily and I sat on her bed in our nightgowns talking the evening over.

"And did you see," I asked, trying to repress a giggle, "he kept adjusting his breeches under the table! I thought I was going to burst a kidney trying to keep a straight face!"

Laughter bellowed out of us both. Every time we started to settle down, one of us would set the other off again.

"Stop! Stop!" I cried between shallow breaths, clasping my side. "It's making my belly hurt." I realised it had been a long time since I had laughed this hard.

"Oh," Lily gasped, trying to catch her breath, "I've missed this." She said, echoing my thoughts as she laid her hand affectionately over mine.

"What do you mean?" I asked, not quite genuinely.

"Rose, you know it's been like you aren't really here for the past year. I mean, you're here, but your mind hasn't been."

I nodded; it was true. I was bursting to tell her the truth. *Oh, Lily, I've been doing the most fantastic things. I learned how to fight and use a sword, though I'm better with a pair of daggers, and I can brew magical potions now!*

But I had promised my mother to tell no one. Besides, would Lily believe me if I did tell her? I decided it was best to just treasure the moments we had together where I could be honest and not worry about the things I couldn't tell her. I meant to keep the promise I had made to my mother, even though it hurt to keep something so important from my sister.

"I know. I'm sorry. It's just been a lot of big changes. Father died. Mother became queen. At some point we stopped being children in the schoolroom, and now there are actual grown-up men turning up wanting to marry you. Life is just moving so fast. I think I've just been struggling to take it all in, to feel like it's really real. I guess I thought if I ignored it, things might not have to change."

"You think I don't fear change? I feel as lost and unsure of everything as you do. I'm supposed to be queen when I turn twenty, or when I get married, if that's sooner. Lately it feels like there are suitors at the door every other day and I have to keep myself from yelling at them to leave me alone for a few more years."

She had just turned eighteen, and two years seemed like much too short a time for both of us to accept the major changes that would be wrought by her becoming queen. It made me regret losing any time we could be spending together, treasuring our numbered days of care-free happiness. I was suddenly overwhelmed by a feeling of selfishness. I hadn't given enough thought to how Lily must be feeling, the pressures she was under as the future queen. Instead, I'd made magic my focus, channelling my energies into my own interests. I felt guilty for it, and yet, would I now be willing to give up my magic? A small, honest voice inside me said no.

"Do you feel, you know, ready?" I asked.

Lily laughed heartily, a loud, unrestrained laugh, punctuated with snorts; an inelegant laugh no one else ever heard.

"Not at all. How am I prepared to run a kingdom? You've seen what the council are like with Mother, and she is much older and more commanding than I am."

"That's not true."

Lily raised a cynical, jet-black eyebrow at me.

"I mean," I corrected. "You are commanding, just in a different way. Mother seems to almost frighten people into doing her bidding or agreeing with her. You bring people around to your view with reason, patience, and kindness. People love and trust you. I think that is all that's really needed in a leader. There's more than one right way to do things, and I know you'll find yours."

"You're just saying that to make yourself popular with the future queen," she teased.

"Oh, yes, you have found me out your highness," I said, climbing to my knees on the soft mattress in mock reverence and imitating the affected, high-pitched tones ladies in the court often used when trying to ingratiate themselves. "Whatever my future queen doth command, I am at thy service."

We both erupted in giggles again, like we were still two little girls.

"Just promise me that when you're queen you won't try and marry me off to some dim-witted, elderly lord with half of his teeth missing, who has to listen to me through an ear trumpet," I said, laying back down on the bed beside Lily.

"I promise. How about a young, handsome nobleman, with excellent teeth and an unnatural obsession with horses?"

The laughter exploded again. When it subsided, we both had tears coursing down our faces.

"But seriously," I said, catching my breath again. "Please don't force me to marry anyone at all."

Lily looked surprised.

"What? You mean, you don't want to get married, ever?"

"I'm not sure that I do. I mean, Mother and Father weren't exactly models for a happy marriage. And I haven't met a man yet who I could imagine spending the rest of my life with. Let alone, you know, all the physical stuff," I added awkwardly, still only understanding lovemaking in the most basic anatomical sense, and associating it with my father's philandering and outright assaults.

"Oh, really? I could have sworn you were in love with that music teacher we had when we were younger. What was his name, August?"

Her words brought back memories of the handsome young music tutor we'd had lessons with for nearly a year when I had just turned thirteen. He'd had a delicate kind of beauty, the kind that is so often appealing to young girls. With his gently waved golden hair, his large, light blue eyes, and his artfully styled moustache and goatee, he seemed to me the embodiment of masculine beauty, and I wanted, desperately for him to admire me in return.

I tried applying my full attention to mastering the lute to gain his notice, and became quite reasonable at it, if not immensely talented. When he remained indifferent to me, I played poorly, in the hope that he would take a greater interest in nurturing my ability. Neither of these plans succeeded; when I played well, he simply lessened his attention to me. When I played badly, he merely instructed me to practice more. All his attention was fixed on Lily, admiring and complimenting her as she sat at her harp, a picture of beauty and elegance. There is nothing so painful as the pangs of first love, or rather, first infatuation, especially when one is a teenager.

"I did not!" I cried, hitting Lily with a pillow.

"You dare assault the future queen?" she yelled laughingly as she hit me back. It became an all-out war, each of us battering the other with a down-filled pillow until feathers floated through the air like giant snowflakes and littered the floor around the bed. In the end, we agreed to a truce, though there had been some casualties. At least two of the pillows would never be the same again.

* * * *

My mother was only able to teach me witchcraft when she was not occupied with the business of running the kingdom, which, being her job, was most of the time. Luckily there was a great deal she could delegate to reliable underlings, but still, the time available for my training was less than I would have liked. There were some skills I could pursue on my own, aided by various books on magic she kept in her workroom, including some notebooks written in her own hand. These were full of her learnings, experiments, and experiences in witchcraft. Reading them reinforced for me how magic had been passed down between the generations in my family, the knowledge only growing and expanding over time. The notebooks occasionally mentioned my grandmother, whom I knew next to nothing about, as my mother never spoke of her.

All I knew about my maternal grandmother was that she had died some time before I was born, that her name had been Mila, and that she, too, had been a witch. My mother very rarely spoke of her past and did not invite questions on the subject.

"Looking backwards rarely accomplished anything," she snapped if I asked questions about her life before she married my father.

But my curiosity regarding my grandmother had grown of late, particularly with regard to how and when she had taught my mother about witchcraft. I wondered what she had been like, if she and my mother had been close, if she and I were alike at all.

When I was tired or bored, or in quiet stretches of night while I waited for sleep to come, I often found myself imagining how different my life would have been had I not been born a princess. If I had been raised as a commoner and my mother had not been queen, perhaps I would have learned about my magical inheritance earlier, maybe even have mastered the craft by now, instead of being a seventeen-year-old novice. I could have been a very different person, with years devoted to my magical education instead of coming to it so much later than most.

As it was, my progress was not fast, but I found some types of magic easier than others; alchemy came to me more naturally because I already understood the key principles of herb lore, while divination eluded me completely. Just as in the schoolroom, I excelled best in the areas I had a keen interest in. Transformation, evocation, and healing, for instance, came to me quite easily after a short time. That is not to say I was able to do advanced magic in these fields, but rather that I seemed to be able to wrap my mind around their principles more fully than other branches. But I was determined that no matter what it took I would eventually master even the more complex facets of these branches of magic.

I tackled each branch of magic in turn, practicing and learning as much as possible, except for necromancy. I had no desire to learn it; I agreed that playing with life and death went against the laws of nature. Plus, it was creepy and gross.

Evocation was something I was desperately excited to master. I began by trying to boil water without a fire, using only magic to heat it, as my mother had done with the tea. Relatively speaking, this was a simple spell, but I was still very much a novice witch, and my first few attempts failed. I was alone in my bedroom, a clear bowl of cold water in front of me. My hand was extended above the bowl, and I uttered the words to make the water heat, but nothing happened. I flexed my fingers harder, as if that would make the water boil, and tried again. A growl of frustration escaped my lips, and I stormed away from the bowl and picked up a book, then threw myself on the bed.

But the water was just lying there, taunting me with its coolness. The book slipped from my hands, and I extended my fingers towards the bowl again, saying the words one more time.

After a few seconds, steam began to swirl from the surface of the water, bubbles slowly grew like little beads at the bowl's base, then streamed upwards and broke over the water's surface, signalling that I had managed to heat it. I dipped my fingers in, scalding my hand. It hurt, and boiling water wasn't exactly as impressive as conjuring something from nowhere, but I was pleased with myself all the same. Now at least I could reheat my tea myself.

*** * * ***

My mother and I became closer than we had ever been as she continued to teach me magic, her pride showing in her face when she watched me. I loved that it was just the two of us and I saw a side of her I had rarely seen before. Away from the probing eyes of courtiers she was relaxed, kind, funny even. We developed the sort of relationship I imagined most girls had with their mothers. Most of all, I loved to see how proud she was when I mastered some new ability.

While I busied myself with my wiccan education, Lily became more and more active in court life, regularly attending balls, grand feasts, festivals, really any celebration occurring within the kingdom.

I wasn't as removed from this as I might have been, because despite all the time I spent on magic, I still had to go through the usual rites of passage for a young noble lady. At seventeen I finally had my first kiss, though it was definitely not the romantic encounter I had pictured to myself growing up. The only good thing I could say about it was that Lily, myself, and the man were the only ones to know about it.

It was at a ball for Lily's nineteenth birthday. Nobles from across the kingdom and further afield gathered to pay homage to the young lady who would be queen in a little less than a year's time. I had an unexpected attack of nerves as Lily and I waited with Elsa, who had wanted to see the celebrations, outside the great hall where the guests were already milling about, waiting for the guest of honour.

"I can't go in, Lily," I gasped suddenly, anxious about the number of eyes that would be on me this evening, the number of strangers I'd be forced to dance with. I didn't know why this worried me; I'd been to plenty of balls before, danced with dozens of strangers already, but that night, an unfamiliar panic overwhelmed me.

"You'll be fine," she assured me, "you've done this before."

I shook my head.

"Here," Elsa said, pressing a small silver flask into my hand. "It'll give you a bit of courage."

"A bit of a buzz, more like," Lily said, eyebrows scrunched disapprovingly.

"One sip will be fine," I said, taking the flask and swallowing a good measure of the contents, which turned out to be cherry schnapps.

Unfortunately, one drink turned into several, and I was blissfully mellowed by the time we were announced, and the ball properly began. My judgement and balance were certainly a little impaired as I entered the ballroom.

Lily was resplendent in a gown of silver silk, which showed off her willowy figure beautifully. Her hair was arranged in a shiny ebony knot at the back of her head and diamonds sparkled at her throat and in her hair, catching the candlelight as she danced. My mother likewise looked magnificent, dressed in a gown of deep blue satin. I was in an elaborately embroidered crimson silk dress and felt awkwardly ostentatious. My face burned from the schnapps and awareness of all the eyes I felt on me, though it was not nearly as many as must have been on Lily, but she showed no signs of nerves.

Lily opened the evening's proceedings with a dance with a visiting prince, who was very handsome and an extremely skilled dancer. I hovered to one side of the hall, watching Lily and the many other pairs of dancers swirling through the space before me, simultaneously hoping and dreading that someone would ask me to dance. Swaying a little where I stood, I realised that the schnapps had perhaps been a misstep and hoped no one would notice I was slightly unsteady on my feet. After a few minutes, a viscount from a neighbouring kingdom approached me, dropping into a low bow and offering his hand as he asked me to dance. He wasn't exactly handsome, but he had lovely, bright blue eyes, a large moustache, and a beautiful smile. He looked to be in his mid-twenties, certainly a few years older than me, but younger than most of the other guests.

I gazed dreamily up at him as we danced, his grip and movements firm enough to make us keep time with the music, though I wasn't exactly in my best dancing form.

"Are you having a nice time?" he asked me in a deep, velvety voice.

"Mmm-hmm," I murmured in reply, only half-hearing him as we swirled about the brightly-lit hall to the gentle melody of a waltz, my eyes occasionally drifting to the people who danced around us.

When the dance ended, he whisked me off to a deserted balcony and asked if he could kiss me.

"Have you been kissed before?"

"No." I shook my head. "Not yet."

"That is a crime," he said, closing the space between us and cupping the side of my face with his gloved hand. "A girl as magnificent as you should be kissed well and often." He leaned in and gently placed his lips on mine, before kissing me deeply for what seemed like hours.

I was still tipsy enough not to be worried about the possibility of being caught kissing a stranger whose name I didn't even know, but when he put his hand on my bodice and gave my breast a squeeze, I swatted it away angrily.

"Excuse me!" I exclaimed indignantly in a very loud voice, which had him cringing and glancing about to make sure no one heard. "I am a princess, and a lady."

"Clearly not that much of a lady," he retorted, pressing himself against me again and trying to back me against the wall.

Paulus' instruction kicked in suddenly, and I punched the viscount in the throat, fast and hard. He backed away quickly, his hands on his throat as he gasped for air. Panicked, I picked up my skirts and ran back into the ballroom.

The viscount made himself scarce for the rest of the evening, which was probably for the best, because I would have died of embarrassment if I'd had to explain any of this to my mother. Cringing, I told Lily about it the next day and she was indignant, not at my behaviour, but at his.

"What a completely rapacious arse!" Lily cried, red with fury. "If it wouldn't hurt your reputation, I'd have him publicly shamed. As it is I'm going to make his life a misery if I ever get the opportunity. I hope you hit him good and hard?"

I nodded. "But what if he tells someone?"

"He won't," she assured me. "He'll be too embarrassed to share his failed conquest, especially if you got away by punching him in the throat." A smile spread over her beautiful face. "I suppose those *fencing lessons* are paying off, aren't they?"

Meanwhile, it turned out that Lily had had a lovely time at the ball, without any improper kissing or groping. The prince she had danced with at the beginning of the evening had asked for another dance later on, and another after that, and then another. His name was Prince Christian, and he was heir to the kingdom of Altenburg, with whom Silvaner shared our southern border, a range of treacherously steep mountains demarcating the boundary between the two kingdoms. He was young, only a few years older than Lily, and extremely handsome. After the ball, he stayed on at the castle with us for several weeks with a small retinue of friends and advisers.

Officially, Christian was in Silvaner to broker a more mutually beneficial trade agreement between our kingdom and his. But the court gossip said he might also find himself a wife during his visit, as a way of shoring up relations between Silvaner and Altenburg.

I liked Christian right away, and I could tell Lily did as well. I didn't blame her; he was pleasant company, with easy manners and a way of making you feel comfortable, as well as being good-looking. He had medium brown hair that fell in soft waves around his face, and sincere, grey eyes. His straight nose tended towards wideness at the bottom, and his full lips were perfectly offset by a strong jaw. He reminded me of paintings and sculptures of ancient Greek heroes, although, thankfully, he had a stronger preference for clothing than they did.

Much of Christian's time during his visit was taken up with meetings with my mother and her advisers, obligatory visits to admire the estates of various nobles, or tours of different regions, and generally sightseeing and exploring the kingdom. But during the evenings, when we had elaborate dinners and entertainments in honour of the prince and his retinue, I noticed the coy glances and shy smiles Lily and Christian exchanged, the way he would make a point of sitting near her whenever he could.

As we sat watching a new play that had been written by the court playwright especially for his visit, I watched where Christian and Lily were sitting side by side, as he leaned in and said something to her quietly. She turned to face him, ignoring the players, and replied animatedly, a smile on her lips. Moments like this, though maybe unremarkable alone, mounted up during his visit, and I was quietly confident of their mutual attraction and interest.

They were almost never alone together; between all the entertainment my mother laid on and the way each of their days seemed to be scheduled down to the minute, privacy and spontaneity were hard to come by. I did what I could, distracting Lily's watchful ladies-in-waiting long enough for her and Christian to have even a moment's private conversation. Notably, Lily now had four ladies-in-waiting who attended her at all times, hovering about her like bees around a flower bed, their chatter creating a constant buzz.

Carlotta was tall, slim, and more inclined to riding and being outdoors than sitting and sewing. But she had a lively mind, a great skill for conversation, and a truly charming, albeit toothy smile. Her profusion of mousy brown hair was always restrained in braids and buns to keep it out of her way.

Anna was small, plump, gregarious, and a bit silly. She had dark hair, dark eyes, and a surprisingly dark sense of humour.

Inge was large, loud, and took great pride in her cascades of straw-coloured hair. She had a habit of looking covetously at everything that belonged to Lily, from her beautiful black hair, to her jewels, to her sumptuous dresses. Her greed extended to food as well; at meals she would watch the spoon travel to other's mouths after she had cleared her own plate.

Finally, there was Katerina, who was the youngest of the four ladies. Katerina had a pale, heart-shaped face framed by a curtain of bright red hair. She was the embodiment of morality and good manners, but she also had a fun side to her, especially after a few glasses of champagne.

It was quite a feat, distracting all four of them long enough for Lily and Christian to exchange a few words without being overheard, something I knew they both yearned for but were too polite to say. I embarked on a campaign to give them a little privacy. One afternoon we - me, Lily, her four ladies, Christian, and the younger members of the prince's party - were enjoying an unseasonably pleasant day in the gardens. Lily and Christian walked side by side, trying to carry on a quiet conversation, while Inge and Anna hovered in their orbit, flirting with Christian's friends, and drawing Lily's attention away from Christian with inane questions and interjections.

"Don't you think Marcus is too funny," Inge trilled at Lily. "He just said that the ladies of the Silvanian court are much prettier than those in Altenburg."

Then she gave Marcus a playful shove, which almost caused him to stagger into a pond, and turned back to Lily for a response.

"How kind," Lily replied quickly before turning her attention back to Christian.

Inge opened her mouth as though she would continue, but I cut her off, crying out that I'd lost an earring.

"Oh, please, Inge. Do help me find it?" I begged, seizing her hand and hastily pocketing the pearl earring I'd surreptitiously removed a moment earlier. "You too, Anna, Katerina, Carlotta. Spread out," I ordered. "I'm not sure when I lost it, so we'll need to backtrack to the main path."

Carlotta immediately headed for the large gate that marked the beginning of the gardens, Anna trailing in her wake, both walking in a low crouch and skimming the ground with their eyes as they went. Inge and Katerina began searching in our immediate vicinity, Christian's friends helping in an awkward sort of way. Lily and Christian, meanwhile, casually kept walking, pausing a good distance ahead where they resumed talking, their faces near each other and their voices low. After about ten minutes, I 'found' the earring and we resumed our walk, small, private smiles on Lily's and Christian's lips when we eventually caught up to them.

"You're lucky I have such a devious little mind, or you'd never have two seconds alone with Christian," I half-teased Lily later. "I am so glad Mother hasn't made me take on ladies-in-waiting yet. I couldn't stand all the hovering and chatter." *Or the impossibility of practicing magic if I were constantly dodging minders,* I thought.

"Trust me, I am eminently grateful. You have earned the gratitude of your future queen," Lily answered with a wink. "But seriously, thank you for trying. It's nice being able to exchange more than banal pleasantries with Christian once in a while when we can be sure we won't be overheard."

"And what, pray, do you two talk about in these private moments?" I asked mischievously.

"None of your business," was the curt reply.

I sighed dramatically.

"Fine. Do all ladies-in-waiting hound their mistresses so thoroughly?"

"I doubt it. Actually," she paused combing her hair and looked at me with a serious expression. "I think Mother might have instructed them to make sure Christian and I aren't alone together."

"What? Why?" I asked, surprised.

"I think she wants to prevent any . . . attachment between us."

"Well, she's missed her window there," I joked. "You two look like a pair of smitten kittens," I added, flopping down on her bed as she resumed combing her hair.

"We are not!" Lily squealed, a blush colouring her cheeks a deep red. "We're just *talking*, Rose. Making conversation, being polite. You should try it sometime."

I stuck my tongue out at her in response but let the subject drop. Lily had never been in love before, but I was pretty sure she was headed that way now, and I didn't want to spook her by forcing a confidence from her too early.

What I witnessed over the next few weeks did nothing to change my opinion. Without quite gushing, Lily was profuse in her admiration and praise of Christian when she and I were alone.

"Today, Christian told me he wants to learn a skill like farming or milling, so he can better understand his subjects' lives," she would say with awe in her voice and a sparkle in her eyes. Or, "Did you know that Christian can speak three languages? Three!"

Everything he said to her was a marvel, and everything she was able to learn of him delighted her. I saw that he was as deeply impressed with her, from the way he spoke about her to me, the way he listened to her so intently, and the way he looked at her, even when they weren't seated together. A soft look of adoration crept over his face whenever they sat together talking, or listening to music, or dancing together, seemingly oblivious to the people around them. They were the perfect picture of a young couple in love, though neither of them seemed quite certain of the other.

Any time I spoke to Lily about Christian, her face glowed, but she kept her language reserved, as though unwilling to admit to being in love.

"I like him a great deal," she explained as we lay side by side on her bed late one night. "He's kind and charming; he actually asks for my opinion, then listens to my answer."

"That's a novelty in itself. And it doesn't hurt that he's extremely good-looking," I teased.

"No, it doesn't," there was a little self-conscious smile on her lips. "But I don't want to get carried away with my feelings. He hasn't said anything concrete to me, and really, I'm not even sure if we could be together, even if it was what we both wanted."

Though rumour had it that Christian had come to Silvaner with the intention of leaving with a fiancée, a relationship between him and Lily was not what anyone had wanted or imagined. Lily was heir to Silvaner and Christian would inherit his father's crown when he died, his older brother having been killed a few years earlier while out hunting. This meant a marriage between them would give rise to a mountain of bureaucratic problems, ending in the union of our two kingdoms – which was by no means simple or desirable – or a major upset to the line of succession for one of their two kingdoms.

"I think if you both really wanted it nothing could stop you," I countered. "But I know it wouldn't be easy, either."

Lily snorted and rolled her eyes.

"That's an understatement. Mother has already dropped a few not-so-subtle hints about not getting too close to Christian."

I understood why the idea of their marrying worried my mother. Silvaner was the smaller of the two kingdoms, and our prosperous farmlands and healthy trade economy offered a very attractive proposition to anyone who might rule it. And because Altenburg was very wealthy and had a large standing army to boot, it would be easy for our little kingdom to lose its identity were the two nations to merge. An alliance was desirable, but an unification was not.

"She's being strategic, that's all. If it's what you really want, I'm sure you could find a way to make everyone happy. Well, grudgingly satisfied anyway. But you'll be queen, so it'll be up to you."

"I suppose so," Lily replied meditatively. "But we're not quite there yet."

The possibility of such a union was clearly on my mother's mind, too, as she began to join us any time Lily and I were in company with Christian. She always had plenty of meetings to attend and business to manage, but suddenly she was everywhere – as we wandered the gardens, or sat listening to music; if Christian and Lily were there, my mother was as well, often with a trail of councillors behind her, seeking her approval on some matter or other. Yet I could tell Lily's courtship was the issue which concerned her most, as her eyes followed the pair closely and she listened to their conversations with great interest, often dampening any attempts at intimacy or romance.

One morning, for the first time since Christian had arrived, she and I were secreted away in her workroom, as it was a rare day when she had some free time and Christian was away visiting our northernmost province at the urging of Lord Frederick, which meant my mother had orchestrated it. She was teaching me the principles of transformation, a complex facet of magic. I asked her with would-be casualness what she thought of Christian.

"He seems a reasonably intelligent and capable boy. I think, in temperament, he and Lily would make a good match." The words were encouraging but her tone was tinged with ambivalence.

"So, you don't have an objection to their marrying?" I queried.

"Not in theory, no," she said, casting a pensive look at me. "But I cannot approve of the idea of trying to unite our two kingdoms. It's always complicated when royals marry each other if they both have their own crowns already, though it very rarely happens, as common sense usually prevails." I didn't miss this jab at Lily.

"Your sister is to be Queen of Silvaner. Christian will be King of Altenburg. I worry that their priorities may come into conflict and that such a match would not be the best thing for our kingdom. What happens to our culture, our history as a people, if the might of Altenburg subsumes our little kingdom? It would be better if he were a second son and not the heir. As it is, he stands to gain power over both kingdoms and Lily if they are foolish enough to marry. Then what your sister wants won't matter."

"They seem of the same mind on most matters," I replied hesitantly, unsure how to answer her concerns, which were valid.

"For now, perhaps. But it would mean Lily had to give up all the power, status, and independence she is entitled to as queen. A queen with a consort may do as she wants, her will is law. A queen with a king is listened to less than his advisers, if at all," she said bitterly. I knew my own father cared little for my mother's counsel, that this coloured her opinion of men in power. "Lily would be better off staying here, in Silvaner, and marrying someone of a lesser rank, like a duke or baron, or even a prince who will not inherit a kingdom, and ruling in her own right."

"But if the kingdoms unite, then surely she and Christian would rule equally?"

My mother looked at me with an expression of disbelief mingled with pity.

"Rose, child. Have you learned nothing from what I have tried to impart to you? A woman will always be subordinate to a man, to her husband, even a queen. You saw how your father treated me. I was never asked for my opinion, never consulted as to how we might improve the lives of our people. If I offered an opinion, he cut me down as quickly and easily as breathing, and told me to remember my place. I was there to give him children and to look pretty at his side, to be there in whatever capacity when he wanted me. Now, I have absolute power. Why? Because I am a queen without a king. In marrying Prince Christian, your sister would be resigning herself to a life of breeding and being little more than a figurehead. She would be giving up the freedom and power that are her birthright and willingly becoming a broodmare."

"What if Christian is different from Father?" I countered, flushing uncomfortably at the life she described too vividly and bitterly, the treatment I knew she had been subjected to all the years she had been married to my father. I could only hope that Lily would be spared that.

"He won't be. Men are all the same, in the end. Unwilling to share power. Now, remember," she continued, pointedly changing the subject. "The more alike two things are, the easier it is to transform one into the other," she said, turning from me to continue demonstrating the transformation of a frog into a fish.

I had always considered what she had to say about men to be accurate; my father had been a philanderer and even abusive, and most of the men I met at court were vain, foolish, power-hungry, or manipulative. Or some combination of those traits. There was always an agenda behind their behaviours, and everything I'd witnessed at court had always seemed to prove Mother's attitude to be right. And yet, there was Christian and his companions; they seemed to be good men, and while I knew they, too, had their own agendas and plans, I'd only ever known them to be friendly and honest. I knew the importance of being wary where men were concerned, but now I wondered about the dangers of being too cynical.

# Chapter Six

The day of Christian's departure eventually arrived, and he had not proposed to Lily, or even, she said, broached the subject. Instead, he returned home after a two-month sojourn, leaving behind a deeply besotted Lily with no answers to her questions about their future.

By then, the leaves were almost entirely stripped from the trees, and icy winds began to blow through the castle grounds. Before long, pale frost sparkled on stone and shrub alike, a deep chill settling over the castle inside and out. The chill seemed to match Lily's mood, as we had an entire winter ahead of us, with no prospect of another visit from Christian until the mountain passes had shed the perilous black ice and impenetrable walls of compacted snow that made the roads so inhospitable to travellers at this time of year.

I could sense rather than see that Lily was missing Christian. She didn't make an effort to bring him up in conversation, go off her food, or shut herself away – she was never one for histrionic displays of emotion. But I would notice her looking at a chair he had sat in with a sad little smile playing over her lips for a moment or two, or lingering over a particular dish they had enjoyed together as if savouring the memory of his company as much as the meal itself.

If she was saddened or disappointed by his departure or any part of their time together, she managed not to let it show too plainly. Instead, she busied herself more than ever, trying to learn as much as possible from our mother about the running of our kingdom, redoubling her efforts to prepare for the day that was fast approaching, with or without Christian.

I saw that my mother was resistant to this, as though she was not quite ready to loosen her grip on the reins just yet. If she feared that Lily was thinking ahead to a time when Silvaner and

Altenburg would be one, she never said anything explicitly, or showed any strong emotions, her face a mask of calm neutrality when Lily would probe her about statecraft. But sometimes I would catch a hardness in my mother's gaze for a moment or an involuntary tensing of her hands, just for a second, before she mastered herself. Lily seemed not to notice and sweetly, though insistently, asserted herself on this point, and I found myself often sitting with her and my mother as they discussed things like taxes and the shortage of housing for our poorer subjects, subjects on which they regularly disagreed.

"But wouldn't it be better to provide them houses outright and tax them a little more subsequently to recoup the cost of building, rather than have them struggle to afford a home, and be less financially stable at the same time? It would be better not to have homeless beggars walking the streets if we have the means to put a roof over their heads," Lily said in her calm, practical way.

"Possibly," my mother replied, her tone even and impassive, though her eyes glowed with something like irritation. "But what you propose would cost the kingdom more and decrease the money we received upfront, when we are still recovering from years of financial mismanagement. Besides, there is no guarantee that providing housing to the poor will ensure their ability to pay the taxes you propose in future. It is all well to do right by your subjects, but sometimes that means thinking about who would go without if you make such allowances for a minority."

They debated the matter for some time, but eventually Lily succeeded in bringing Mother around to her view. It was interesting to see how their two approaches to governing differed; my mother was a fair ruler, but she always tended more towards practicality than altruism. Lily, on the other hand, wanted to give and do more for those who had less, even if it meant the royal coffers might take a hit for a time. I knew that she would be a kind and generous queen, loved by her subjects in a way my mother was not, despite the prosperity and contentment that had seeded and grown throughout the kingdom since she had become queen.

*** * * ***

It was a pleasant break when Christmas came, a sense of frivolity and freedom pervading the castle. We celebrated with a full twelve days of holiday, with plenty of eating, drinking, and playing games. My mother, Lily, and I visited many villages, along with Lily's ladies and a stream of armed guards who accompanied the royal family almost every time we left the castle. We distributed grain, fruit, and small purses of silver, our charity always focused on the poorer families, which were luckily quite few these days.

My favourite part was giving the children toys that had been made by ladies of the court as well as some servants. They were mostly dolls fashioned from cloth or straw, balls for the children to kick and chase around, and toy horses, boats, or knights. It was heartwarming to see how such a small gesture could bring such joy, how the simplest gifts were so greatly valued.

I handed one small girl a cloth doll that I had made myself. It was far from perfect, my usual indolence where needlework was concerned rendering my effort far less successful than the other ladies'. Yet the little girl's face lit up, her big eyes full of awe and appreciation, a broad but timid smile spreading sweetly across her face.

"Thank you, my princess," she said with a thick lisp, which was accentuated by the absence of her front teeth.

I was touched by her gratitude and wondered what life must be like for the children of peasants. My own childhood, while far from perfect, had been privileged, without the concerns and dangers that these children faced. I had never been without food, or warmth, or clothing that fit, never feared sickness in the way the poor must. I had never known what it was like to spend my days unsupervised or looking after younger siblings while my parents worked to ensure that we had food and shelter.

This, I thought, seeing the lives of the people we ruled over and finding ways to better them, was what the royal family should occupy itself with. When we returned home, I still enjoyed all the festivities and extravagances of Christmas, but the pleasure was tinged with a bitter edge of guilt, the thought of others with so much less, perhaps struggling to stay warm on the cold winter nights, never far from my mind.

It snowed heavily that winter, blanketing the castle grounds and the countryside beyond in thick, white, glimmering powder, delicate icicles forming on exposed branches and hanging from the eaves. When the weather permitted, Lily and I enjoyed sleigh rides in a large sled pulled by four glossy black horses, as we sat bundled up in furs and sipping warm spiced wine, revelling in the magical beauty and quiet of the snow-kissed world. We always passed the forest on our rides, and I would think of all the plants beneath the ground, waiting for the ice to thaw and the weather to warm so they could peek their heads back above the soil. I thought about the things I could do with those herbs and plants, as my skill in witchcraft grew.

I paused my magical studies for a time, determined to relish these moments with Lily for what they were: possibly the last year I might get to spend so much time with my sister, enjoying the holiday together as we had done since we were children. I felt a presentiment of sadness when I thought of how far apart our respective futures might take us in the year to come, all the big changes that might come into our lives if she chose to marry Christian.

✱ ✱ ✱ ✱

When the last of the snow had cleared and the mountain passages opened again, a letter from Christian finally arrived for Lily, accompanied by a parcel. I'd been working with Paulus in the training arena when Lily came bursting in, a letter clutched in her hand. Her entrance distracted me for a second – she'd never come to see me when I was training before – but I still managed to block the strike Paulus unchivalrously aimed at my legs and avoid hitting the dirt in front of my sister.

"Can we just pause for a minute?" I asked, worried Lily might have received bad news.

"Battles don't pause," Paulus said heavily, panting from the exertion.

"Well, it's a good thing this is just practise, then," I said, nimbly skipping out of his circle of range and over to where Lily stood watching us with a confused expression scrunching her pretty face.

"I thought you were just fencing?" she said, eying the practise sword in my hand, which was still much heavier than an ordinary foil.

"Oh, I've, erm, moved up to some heavier weaponry. Just expanding my skills a little. What's with the letter?" I asked more to redirect the conversation than anything else.

"It's from Christian," she replied breathlessly. "Come open it with me," she urged, casting an unimpressed glance around the training room.

"Paulus will wallop me if I leave early, I'm meant to train for another hour."

Lily's eyes widened pleadingly, and her mouth formed a sad little pout. I knew she was play-acting but could still tell she was eager to open the letter together.

"I'll see if I can get an early mark."

She grinned immediately, let out a little squeal, and turned and ran back towards the castle entrance.

"I assume you heard all of that?" I asked Paulus, who was standing to the side of our arena sipping some water and blotting his face with a cloth. "Can we finish up now?"

He shrugged. "If you don't care about your training any more than gossiping, then perhaps we should stop altogether."

"Don't bait me, you big bully," I teased. "It's not ordinary gossip. Lily got a letter from a prince who wants to marry her, we think. It's a big deal."

Paulus looked unmoved.

"What if I run extra laps tomorrow to make up for it?"

He looked meditative for a few moments, drumming his fingers on his scarred chin.

"An extra twenty minutes of running tomorrow, *and* you have to train with the sandbags."

Paulus had recently gotten me to start lifting unbelievably heavy bags of sand as part of my training, because, according to him, my muscles were still too puny to move on to a regular weighted sword.

"For how long?"

"One hour."

"Thirty minutes."

"Done," he said, seizing my hand and shaking it vigorously. "And you have to tell me what was in the letter," he added in a quieter tone.

"Hypocrite," I snapped. "It's gossiping when I want to know what's going on with my sister, but for you it's fine."

He just shrugged, nonplussed, then waved me off. I turned and ran from the training room before he could change his mind.

Lily's ladies-in-waiting were hovering around her sitting room when I arrived, still dressed in my fitted pants and linen shirt from training, which they eyed disapprovingly, but she ordered them out with uncharacteristic abruptness before she would open the letter. As Carlotta pulled the door closed behind her, Lily ripped broke the wax seal with shaking hands and I settled myself down on the couch beside her.

"Christian says he will be passing through the kingdom in a few weeks and that he would like, with the Queen's permission, to stop off with us again." Lily positively glowed as she read the letter, especially as she came to the part about the parcel.

*"I have enclosed a belated Christmas gift for you, Princess, a family heirloom, which I hope you will accept with my greatest compliments,"* Lily read aloud, her cheeks suffusing with a deep flush of pleasure.

Hurriedly, she tore the paper from the parcel and revealed a black velvet jewel box. Inside was a superb necklace made up of deep blue sapphires and bright, white diamonds.

"It's spectacular!" Lily exclaimed, lifting it gently from the box and holding it out to me.

"It's heavy," I added, feeling the weight of it in my hand. I helped her put it on and we stood before a long mirror, admiring it.

She turned this way and that, wanting to see the necklace from as many angles as possible, her smile growing wider and wider with each rotation.

"It looks wonderful on you. I have to admit, Prince Christian certainly has excellent taste in jewels."

"Doesn't he?" she said breathlessly, a broad smile of pure elation plastered on her beautiful face, her eyes sparkling with happiness.

"Let's hope Altenburg has some more beauties in their treasury so he can make as good a choice of engagement ring," I teased.

Lily's cheeks coloured even more deeply.

"Do you think he will? Propose, I mean. On his next visit?" She sounded genuinely fretful and anxious, her eyes bright and her voice breathless. Her uncertainty surprised me.

"I thought there was something of an understanding between you two already?"

Lily shook her head slowly, looking as though it cost her to admit as much.

"Do you want to marry him? I mean - well - do you *love* him?"

I'd seen them together, noted how Lily's face brightened when she was with him and how everyone else seemed to fade into the background when she was with Christian. Though she'd never admitted it to me before, I expected a prompt answer in the affirmative, but Lily looked thoughtful for a moment, considering the question carefully.

"I *like* him a great deal. He is clever and handsome and good company. He is certainly very kind. And I think it would be good for the kingdom, both our kingdoms, I mean. I feel all warm and happy when I see him or think of him. But I don't think I know him well enough to love him. Yet. But I think, in time, I would."

She began pacing the room, something she only did when she was working out the answer to a problem. It was a rarity, and showed more clearly than words the upset state of her mind.

"It seems so ridiculous," she broke out suddenly. "That we are expected to make such important decisions upon so slight an acquaintance. And I am meant to be satisfied at having merely met my future husband before marrying him, when other princesses are married to total strangers!"

"You'll wear that rug out if you keep pacing like that," I said in a light, teasing manner. She flung herself into a chair, looking frustrated and unhappy.

"You know, you're in a unique position," I said more gently, taking a seat next to her so our faces were level. "You'll be queen in less than a year. You needn't marry anyone if you don't want to. Not right away."

"You sound like Mother. She just doesn't want me to marry Christian because it will disrupt her plans for the kingdom."

"Well, she *is* right. She seems quite happy ruling alone, so why shouldn't you be? And you're still so young. But if, at some point, you did meet someone whom you wanted to marry, you could. What I mean is, there's no rush. And you shouldn't marry Christian just because it might be good for the kingdom. You can wait to be sure of how you feel."

"I can't just think of myself," she said, absently scuffing the toes of her slippers on the rug, as if determined to wear it through one way or another. "I must consider what is best for everyone. That is what it means to rule."

"No one is asking you to be a martyr. And just because Christian is nice and good-looking, it doesn't mean you should marry him. I just mean, don't rush into anything," I urged her. "I'd hate to see you make a decision like this only to regret it. Like I said, you're still so young."

Lily sighed.

"I only wish Christian would tell me, truthfully, what his plans and feelings regarding me are," she said, rising and walking back towards the mirror to glance at her reflection, the jewels still sitting around her neck.

"Well, I think the necklace speaks volumes. Besides, you can ask when he comes to visit," I said brightly.

She smiled and blushed again, pulling me into a hug, then murmuring over my shoulder.

"You know I love you, Rose, but you really do smell after all that sword swinging. Go have a bath."

I smacked her on the shoulder in reply, then went off to do as she'd suggested.

Mother gave her consent for Christian to visit again. Diplomatically speaking, she couldn't refuse. But I saw that it worried her, his returning to us so soon.

"I do not want Lily to rush into a marriage without considering all of its implications," was the explanation she gave, but I sensed there were other factors at play. What would it be like for her when Lily became queen? I saw that power and independence suited my mother and thought of how she had often lamented what it was to be a woman reliant on the whims of others. I could imagine that the loss of power and the return to dependence, especially on her own child, would be a crushing blow for a woman so used to authority and freedom.

* * * *

The return of Christian and his retinue caused even more delay to my lessons in witchcraft, as it was riskier than usual to practice magic with outsiders visiting the castle. Moreover, the days and evenings were so completely taken up with balls, games, concerts, and other entertainment for our guests that I had no time for anything else. Now I was essentially another lady-in-waiting to my sister, though unofficially, chaperoning her and Christian, and socialising with the small group of men who had accompanied him, who were also his friends. It was nice to get better acquainted with people who knew Christian well, though they refused to be drawn on the subject of what the prince was truly like. Even when we all sat comfortably together, appearing at ease, the masks of diplomacy never entirely fell away.

Not that I minded for myself. It was helpful to experience every aspect of court life now that I was an adult in all the ways that mattered. Though I did not relish the thought of having to do all this without Lily, should she be required to move to Altenburg.

Of all the men Christian had with him, the one I liked best was Lucas, a trusted companion of Christian who held a privileged position in King Ludwig's court. Lucas was a few years older than Christian and had been a close friend of Christian's older brother, who had died quite young. Lucas had a calm and steady manner and was easy to talk to. He was well-read, had a broad range of interests, and was happy to discuss most subjects. What I liked most about him was that he didn't speak down to me as a woman, unlike so many other men I had met at court.

He had short, coppery-coloured hair, a broad, smiling face spattered with freckles, and clear, close-set hazel eyes. He was not what I would call handsome, but he had a charm that came from his easy way of talking and friendly personality rather than his looks. Lucas was clearly a well-trained courtier, with such a strong appearance of sincerity and good humour that he either was exactly as he seemed, or he was an excellent actor.

One afternoon, when it was too cold to be outside, despite the arrival of spring, Lily, myself, her ladies-in-waiting, and Christian and some of his men, were gathered in one of the smaller apartments, listening to some of the court musicians playing a new suite of music. Lucas sat on my right and Lily on my left, though her attention was completely absorbed in a hushed conversation with Christian, who sat on her other side.

"What is Altenburg like?" I asked Lucas quietly, not wanting to disrupt the musicians.

"Not so very different from Silvaner, I suppose," he said thoughtfully, his eyes moving from the musicians to look at me. "Although the land itself is quite different. Here you are hemmed in by mountains and woods on two sides. Altenburg is much more open."

"It's a large kingdom, isn't it?" I asked, feeling the subject flagging already and wondering at the usually-talkative Lucas being so reticent.

"Larger than here," he agreed noncommittally, "but not so large as some. Perhaps about two, maybe three times larger than Silvaner."

We fell into silence again, the lute, harp, and rebec releasing sweet melodies into the air, dispelling any awkward silences.

The chatter of Inge and Anna grew louder, as they discussed the comparative handsomeness of the men of Silvaner and those of Altenburg at an indiscreet volume. I cast them a withering look which was completely lost on them, so engrossed as they were in the subject. Lucas smiled.

"You are not interested in their conversation?" Lucas asked me quietly, but with more enthusiasm than he had shown a moment earlier.

"Not particularly. But I'm more annoyed that they have to be so loud. It makes it hard to hear the music."

"Ah, so you are a great lover of music?" he asked with an inscrutable look on his face.

"I like it, certainly. I like the way it can make you feel so many things. A sad ballad can make one cry, a swift jig makes you want to dance. It's transportive in a way. I suppose, I like how expressive it is, though I am not very gifted at music myself."

Lucas nodded appraisingly, smiling a little, then looking past me to where Lily sat.

"And your sister?" he asked. "Does she like music as much as you?"

"A good deal more, I think. Lily adores music. Although," I added, glancing at her with a smile. She was still deep in whispered conversation with Christian, the two of them taking no notice of anyone else, "not so much as she enjoys speaking with your Prince, I see."

Lucas' face became impassive again, the light and humour in his eyes dimming a little as the courtier's mask slipped back into place.

"Don't you approve?" I asked somewhat spikily.

"It's not that," he answered quietly. "I think he is quite taken with your sister. I only hope she feels the same way about him. Christian is so generous, I worry about him being the more in love of the two. Besides, there is the whole issue of how the two kingdoms would come together."

It sounded like a question, but this time, it was I who refused to be drawn on the subject.

"Time will tell," I said noncommittally. "I am sure they know their own business best."

"I see. You are her confidante and will not betray her trust; I respect that. Maybe you are better at the game than I thought," he said softly, an amused smile playing around his mouth.

* * * *

Though winter had passed, the air remained quite chilly, thick, grey mists blanketing the rolling hills beyond the city walls, and we were often compelled to stay inside in order to stay warm. But on fine days, we would ride, sometimes for hours, visiting different parts of the kingdom, a large group of us racing across the countryside. Lily and I were both very capable riders, though not all of her ladies-in-waiting enjoyed this activity, so often they would make excuses to stay behind. Usually when we rode out, my mother would remain behind, unable to justify losing a full day when the business of the kingdom never paused for a moment. These were the days I liked best; each of us more relaxed beyond the confines of the castle, the bracing cold air tugging at our clothes and hair, the pale sun breaking through the clouds weakly, promising finer days to come.

Waking one morning and seeing that it was a bright, clear day, I suggested to Lily that we take a ride and make a day of it. Christian agreed immediately, and shortly after breakfast, ten of us set off riding through the city, then out into the lush valleys where farms and great estates dotted the landscape, the only break from the green of the land and trees and sparkling blue of the lakes.

I rode beside Lucas, who was more jovial than on other occasions. The sun and air seemed to bring him out of himself, and we talked effortlessly of literature and music for most of the ride. We both stuck to these harmless topics, neither broaching the subject that had caused a brief tension between us. Lily and Christian quickly fell to the back of the group, keeping a slower pace than the rest as they rode and talked, as if unaware of the eight other people ahead of them.

After a few hours, the men began grumbling mildly that they were famished. A short while later, we stopped at a tavern on our way back to the castle for something to eat. Christian and his men led the way inside, each glancing about the taproom protectively, as though scanning for any dangers. Lucas and Christian exchanged a nod, and the innkeeper came forward hurriedly, spying our expensive attire and sensing wealth, without recognising any of us as belonging to the royal family.

"Please, sirs, this way," the stout man said, bowing obsequiously, then leading us into a private dining room set apart from the regular patrons of the tavern. We all sat comfortably at the long table, chatting pleasantly like old friends while we waited for the food and drinks to arrive.

Smaller conversations broke out around the table, and the mood was far more relaxed than it usually was at the castle. I sat between Anna and one of Christian's companions, named Hans, both of whom were speaking to other people. Unconcerned, I sat quietly, studying the others around the table, especially Lily and Christian.

They sat with their heads bent towards each other, speaking too quietly for others to hear. But I could read from their bodies that they were entirely intent on each other. Lily's face had a look of rapt attention and pleasure, while Christian looked animated and happy as he spoke. I strongly suspected that, despite what Lily had said, they were certainly well on their way to being in love, if they were not already.

* * * *

Christian and his companions stayed for a month. By the time they were preparing to leave, spring had fully arrived and all the shrubs and plants in the gardens had erupted into bloom, filling the vista with a riot of colour and a heady mixture of competing fragrances. The days were slowly growing warmer and longer, inviting us out into the gardens more and more often.

On a fine, spring day I found myself alone and decided to use the rare few moments of freedom to wander the rose garden, enjoying the sunshine, while Lucas and the rest of his friends had gone pleasure-boating with Carlotta, Anna, and Katerina. I wandered the garden paths aimlessly, enjoying my solitude, the bright sky, the fresh grass, the heat of the day beginning to radiate from the stone paths, and the rich, floral scents wafting across the garden. Rounding a corner, I almost collided with Inge, who was standing so that she blocked the entire path, her eyes darting to and fro apprehensively.

"My apologies, your highness," she said, dropping hastily into a curtsey.

"That's alright, I suspect it was my fault," I said, trying to sound gracious. I looked at her and she glanced away awkwardly, her face turning a deep shade of red.

"Why are you out here all alone? Who is with my sister?"

A look of panic passed across Inge's face, and she bit her lip as though trying to invent an answer.

"I do not know, your highness. Perhaps Anna or Carlotta-"

"They are both sailing with the prince's men."

She avoided my eye, a guilty look on her face as she began to sweat, perspiration beading on her broad forehead.

"Where is my sister?" I demanded.

Despite being a head taller and far broader than I, Inge quailed beneath my glare.

"She is with the Prince," Inge whispered.

"Where?" I snarled. A lady-in-waiting was meant to protect the princess' reputation at all costs, and here was Inge completely failing in her duty. It was one thing for me to orchestrate a few snatches of quiet conversation or a couple minutes of privacy for the pair, but another for them to be unchaperoned for who knew how long. Christian seemed like a respectful, kindly man, but I knew firsthand what happened when young girls were left alone with men. I knew how delicate a woman's reputation could be, and how readily people would gossip about Lily given the chance. I glared at Inge, and she cowered in front of me and let out a shrill little squeak before pointing at the hedge behind her.

I hurried away in the direction she had indicated and quickly came upon Lily and Christian locked in an embrace, kissing as though they meant to devour each other. Feeling awkward stumbling into such a private moment, and confident Lily wasn't doing anything she didn't want to, I made to walk away, but they noticed me and moved apart sharply.

An enormous smile broke first across Lily's face and then was mirrored in Christian's.

"Darling Rose!" Lily cried, racing towards me, and seizing my hand in a tight grip. "We're going to be married!" She held out her hand for me to admire an enormous aquamarine ring.

Christian joined us, a sheepish expression on his handsome face.

"I hope you approve," he said with a tinge of embarrassment.

I couldn't help but smile, too; I was happy for them, glad they had finally worked things out, especially seeing how tremendously happy they were. I hugged my sister tightly, then turned and hugged her future husband.

"Of course I do!" I cried. "But I'm not the one you need to worry about. What will Mother say?"

A look of trepidation appeared on both their faces. It seemed they had not yet considered this.

* * * *

My mother heard the news with a neutral expression and offered them both her congratulations, though in somewhat restrained terms. The news was announced across the kingdom and a ball was planned in honour of the great event.

Christian's parents, King Ludwig and Queen Gisela of Altenburg, were invited to come stay with us at the castle to meet Lily and our family. More importantly, the matter of how the two kingdoms would come together following the marriage had to be decided. But Queen Gisela insisted that side of things could wait. Most importantly, this was the first meeting between two families who were to be united through the marriage of their children.

The King and Queen arrived within a week of the engagement and were to stay at the castle for an entire month. Their only daughter, Sophie, who was younger than Christian, would join them a few days before the engagement ball. Lily was a bundle of nerves waiting for their arrival, and only became more anxious once she had met them. She need not have worried, of course. They were instantly charmed by her pretty face, lovely manners, and warm, welcoming attitude. Lily was deferential and gracious, and it was clear that Christian's parents thought he had chosen his bride well, despite the difficulties that were bound to arise regarding the two kingdoms coming together.

They were somehow not quite what I had expected. Queen Gisela was a short, somewhat spherical woman of about forty-five, with a pretty, round, dimpled face; kind brown eyes; and dark hair streaked liberally with grey. She was cheerful, kindly, and agreeable, much like a golden retriever. Within minutes of their meeting, she showed a warm and affectionate attitude towards Lily.

King Ludwig appeared to be about sixty years old. He was tall, but thin as a reed, and he had a look of dwindling health about him, and looked as though he could benefit from a healing tonic. While he was reasonably attractive despite his apparent poor health and age, I doubted he had ever been strikingly handsome like Christian. The king had a prominent, beak-like nose and very grey hair. He was genial enough, however, and seemed genuinely pleased to meet us all. Needless to say, he took a great liking to Lily at once – everyone always did – but I was pleasantly surprised when he also showed a strong regard for me. At times when everyone else was discussing Christian and Lily's wedding, he and I often fell into quiet conversation, discussing literature and poetry, philosophy and history. I found him a very learned, intelligent man, though I was sad to see that sometimes his face would take on a vacant, faraway look, as though his mind had wandered, and he would lose track of the conversation. I wondered how long he had exhibited these symptoms, and whether his own doctors were aware of them. I watched him closely, wondering if there was anything I or my mother could do to help him.

When the king and queen were settled, the ball planned, and all the required pleasantries were done with, discussion turned to the pressing issue of whether the two kingdoms would unite with Christian and Lily, as heirs of their respective kingdoms.

I wasn't invited to these meetings, though I was deeply interested in the outcome. Not wanting to hear about them second-hand, I listened at the door of an adjoining room, shamelessly kneeling with my ear and eye alternately pressed against the keyhole.

"Naturally, Christian and Princess Lily will live in Altenburg once Christian ascends the throne," King Ludwig said with an air of confidence and authority which brooked no argument. His usually friendly, pleasant manner evaporated when it came to negotiating the matter; instead, he became the embodiment of steely determination and pride. He was still a king and used to having his every word obeyed.

"But Princess Lily is to become Queen of Silvaner on her marriage," my mother countered coolly. "She will need to be in Silvaner if she is to rule it."

Christian spoke up in a tone of peacekeeping.

"Perhaps we could live here until, well, until I become king." He paused awkwardly, stopping before he said 'until my father dies', though the unsaid words lingered in the air. "Then, we could live between the two kingdoms."

"And leave each of them without a ruler half of the time? That is not practical," my mother's voice said tersely.

"No, of course not," I heard Lily say softly, and pressed my ear more firmly to the keyhole. "Perhaps, Mother, you could act as ruler in my place when I am in Altenburg."

"And who would look after our kingdom while you are here?" demanded King Ludwig, his voice growing louder. "Not Gisela or Sophie, as neither has any experience leading a kingdom and it would be dangerous to install anyone else as regent in your absence. It's a preposterous idea. The only solution is to unite both kingdoms under the banner of Altenburg and subsume Silvaner as one of our provinces. That eliminates the need for multiple rulers and all that needless travelling between cities. Lady Lorelei would then oversee this province as its administrator, but without the full authority of a queen."

I drew back from the keyhole for a moment, knowing what King Ludwig had said would only inflame matters more; my mother never took kindly to being told what to do, and the threat of such disenfranchisement would make her see red.

"Silvaner has stood as it does now for almost six hundred years. I cannot allow you to erase us simply for convenience." There was barely-concealed rage simmering in her voice, and I imagined her look of quiet fury and determination as she spoke. It was enough to make even the most seasoned courtiers cower. But the king was no ordinary courtier.

"We are the larger kingdom," he said coldly, not backing down.

"And we are the richer," my mother snapped back, her tone one of pure venom.

A loaded silence hung in the air, the tension perceptible even from behind my locked door.

"Couldn't we discuss all this when Christian is needed to assume the throne in Altenburg?" Lily asked gently. "King Ludwig may very well rule for many years, while I shall become queen as soon as we are wed."

There was another pregnant pause, each probably thinking this was in fact, not likely at all, given the king's visibly weakened state.

"No, I will have the issue of succession sorted out before I am on my deathbed and too weak to have any say, thank you."

"Do not overexcite yourself, dear," Queen Gisela's voice said gently, trying to soothe her irate husband.

It carried on, back and forth in this way for hours, one party suggesting a resolution and the other objecting to it, while Lily and Christian tried to foster agreement. After a long and heated debate, my mother spoke up in an even, yet tentative voice, calculated to sound respectful and conciliating.

"I would not dare propose something that might undermine your authority as your father's heir, dearest Lily. But I would be willing to continue serving as Regent of Silvaner so that you and Prince Christian could remain in Altenburg. Then we would not need to rush into assimilating our two kingdoms, and Silvaner would not lose the cultural identity of which our people are so proud. You would still be Queen of Silvaner, and live here most of the year, until King Ludwig is no longer able to serve as Altenburg's King. Then you would both take up residence in Altenburg, while I acted as caretaker here. Under your instruction, of course. You could wait until your children were of age to determine how precisely you would enact the unity of our kingdoms."

"That might work," Christian said hopefully. "It would mean Silvaner could remain independent, and our heirs would rule both kingdoms for as long as it remained feasible."

"As long as we were guaranteed support from you at any time it was needed," King Ludwig interjected in an argumentative tone. "Financial, military, whatever we might need."

"Naturally," replied my mother calmly. "And I would expect that agreement to work in both directions."

Another silence, punctuated with murmuring, as though each party were conferring amongst itself. I quickly moved my eye to the keyhole to watch the deliberations.

"It is agreeable to us," King Ludwig said eventually. "As long as Christian and Princess Lily agree as well."

"Oh, yes," said Lily, sounding relieved, eager to bring the discussions to a close.

"I think it is the only way forward for both parties. But I wonder, not wishing to offend Queen Lorelei – who would rule on our behalf at the sad time when you are no longer able to? If

Lily and I were yet to have children, I mean," I heard Christian say.

"I believe I shall be hale and hearty for many years yet to come," came my mother's voice, full of confidence and vitality. "But when I am no longer able to act as your agent here, Princess Rose would step into the position."

It was not a question. She said it as though it were an established fact.

"That seems fair; she would be my successor were anything to happen to me before we had children. I'm sure there is none better to take over from you, Mother."

With the key issue apparently decided, they moved onto discussing the finer details of financial, political, and social relations between the two kingdoms. Christian and Lily would marry in a few months' time, to allow for the wedding to be planned and for guests to make the journey to Silvaner. Then, a few days after the wedding, Lily and Christian would both be crowned as the new rulers of Silvaner, where they would live until King Ludwig died and they both became rulers of Altenburg. My mother would act as their regent in Silvaner, overseeing the kingdom whenever they were in Altenburg. Their heir would then rule both kingdoms, deferring the most sensitive issues to another generation.

Now that the most contentious point was resolved, I was amazed by how calmly they were able to discuss these matters, as though they were ordering dinner. I still sat huddled on the floor by the door, but I stopped listening, my mind wandering to the idea of my ruling Silvaner if my mother died, while Lily and Christian ruled in Altenburg.

They had all agreed amongst themselves that this was a good idea, but no one had asked me what I thought about it, if it were something I wanted. My acquiesce had been presumed. I seethed quietly as I mulled it over. Decisions had been made for me my entire life, though since my father had died, I'd thought I had at least *some* agency. But now yet again, the biggest decision of my life was being made without consulting me.

I had never thought about ruling a kingdom, because it had always been reinforced to me that Lily, not I, would be queen, and even if I was married off to some distant king, he would be the one in charge, the one to whom I was still subordinate.

But I had seen how my mother ruled for a few years now, every conversation with her a lesson in statecraft, as though she had been preparing me for this all along. My anger was not because I thought I lacked the ability to run a kingdom, but that I would have to completely rearrange any ideas I had ever had about what my life would be like. I was a little comforted by the fact that I would have plenty of time to prepare, as I was not to take on the role until after my mother's death, something I hoped would not occur for many, many years.

Still, I was angry that I hadn't even been asked about my thoughts on the matter, that my wants and needs didn't factor into anyone else's plans at all. Even Lily had not felt the need to speak to me about it before agreeing to the plan. But when she told me about it, I hid my resentment, not wanting to spoil her happiness over something that wouldn't happen for years to come.

"Isn't it wonderful?" she gushed, painting a picture of perfect connubial bliss for her and Christian as we sat on her bed talking it over as we used to do. "Christian and I in Altenburg, and you and mother here, all of us looking after our people and blazing a bright, new future together. And our children to follow after us."

I nodded and for a tight smile, not wanting to spoil her happiness with my own uncertainty and fear of losing my sister to her new life in another kingdom.

* * * *

Preparations for the engagement ball were the primary topic of discussion now that the matter of bringing the two kingdoms together was, for the time being at least, settled. Guest lists, musicians, dresses, flowers, food. Queen Gisela, my mother, and

Lily seemed to be able to discuss these things for hours. It gave me an idea of what I could expect when they began planning the wedding. My presence was mandatory for these campaign meetings, though I rarely contributed much of value. It wasn't that I had no interest in these things, so much as that I evidently was not as invested as the others were. It surprised me how quickly a debate of peonies versus lilies could become quite heated.

But finally, there was no more that could be planned, no more details that could be debated and fussed over, at least for the engagement ball. Four hundred invitations went out, with only a fortnight until the big event. Despite the short notice there was a wild flurry of replies, most advising that yes, they would be honoured to attend the engagement ball of Princess Lily and Prince Christian.

A few nights before the ball, Lily and I sat alone in her boudoir as we had of old.

"How are you feeling about it all? The engagement, the wedding, becoming a queen?"

"Honestly, I'm not *exactly* dreading all of it. I'm very excited to marry Christian, and I feel like we will rule well together. And I think we'll be very happy," she added, smiling widely.

"But I wish there wasn't so much to do beforehand. There's the engagement ball, then the wedding, which will be days and days of celebrations. Then the coronation not long after. I feel exhausted just thinking about it. I know I should feel grateful that everyone is so pleased to celebrate with us, but sometimes I wish I wasn't a royal so things could be done simply and quickly, without all the procedure and ceremony."

I laughed. It did sound excessive. I wondered whether the kingdom's coffers would have anything left at all after it was all done with. Silvaner would be paying the cost of all these proceedings, as they were taking place in our kingdom.

"But," I asked anxiously, watching her closely as I spoke, "you are happy, aren't you?"

"Oh, yes!" she exclaimed, throwing herself back onto the bed, a smile beaming on her lovely face. "I love Christian. I was hesitant to say so at first, because I was afraid of what it would all mean. I didn't quite trust my feelings. But I *do* love him."

"Then that's all that matters," I said, joining her on the bed, staring up at the ceiling. "Everything else you can work out later. How are you feeling about the wedding night?" I teased.

"Oh, don't bring that up now," she squealed, hiding her face with her hands. "I have enough to be concerned with at the moment."

*** * * ***

The day of the ball dawned bright and clear. It was now early summer, and the castle grounds were a riot of colour and fragrance. The city beyond the castle was a bustling hive of activity and celebrations; brightly-coloured bunting hung across the streets to mark the event. All the inns and wealthy estates surrounding the city were bursting with visitors from across the kingdom and beyond, some of whom were guests, but also those who had arrived simply to see the pomp and ceremony of the engagement ball and the festivities that accompanied it. It was only an inkling of what we could expect for the wedding, which would be a hundred times grander.

Our days were spent entertaining the torrent of guests who had invaded the castle, charming them with sparkling smiles plastered across our faces and our best manners on display, always. It was exhausting. In the days leading up to the ball there had already been two feasts, a hunt, a small dance, and several performances from musicians, singers, actors, and dancers from across Silvaner, with more planned for later in the week. I wondered if I would still fit into my gown or have the energy to dance a simple waltz when the ball came.

I woke late, having been up until the small hours talking to Lily. Sunshine was streaming into my room, a bright blue sky promising good weather for the day and evening ahead.

My dress for the evening was hanging on the door of my portmanteau, a delicate confection of cobalt blue taffeta, accented with gold embroidery and a golden belt. Much as I enjoyed grubbing about in the forest for herbs, riding for hours at a time and immersing myself in dusty books, I had to admit I had also come to enjoy some of the more luxurious parts of court life. I was excited to put on my lovely new dress, to dance with the men and gossip with the women at the ball.

For a long time, I had thought that to be sensible, studious, and mature somehow prohibited me from enjoying doing things that were fun and a bit frivolous. But now I was old enough and experienced enough to see that I could enjoy both, that my intelligence was not lessened by my enjoyment of a lively coranto, and wearing a pretty gown did not make me any less well-read. I refused to feel guilty or foolish for enjoying seeing my new dress hanging up in my room, or for being excited to dance and flirt at the ball.

The ball was held in the grand hall, which had been utterly transformed for the occasion. Usually spartan and unwelcoming, there were now glittering chandeliers hung from the ceiling, casting a luminescent glow over the room, and softening even the harshest faces with their warm light. The marble floor was cleared in the centre to allow space for dancing, with musicians gathered at one end, and an enormous table laden with an elaborate spread of food sat at the other.

Lords, ladies, dukes, duchesses, marquises, marchionesses, barons, baronesses, princes, and princesses whirled about the hall, all resplendent in rich silks, satins, brocade, and velvets of vibrant colour, and embellished with jewels of every shade.

The master of ceremonies announced first my mother and myself, then King Ludwig and Queen Gisela, and finally, Christian and Lily. The last were met with thunderous applause from the guests gathered, and stepping into the centre of the floor, both of them smiling with sublime happiness, they commenced the first dance of the evening.

I was asked to dance every single dance, from the gentle processional dances, like the pavane, to the fast, giddying galliards and voltas. I danced with men young and old, tall and short, handsome and ugly. I danced with a duke from Silvaner who stepped on my toes and a lord from Altenburg who lifted me off my feet. I danced until my face was red with exertion and my feet ached. Finally, I collapsed onto a bench and surreptitiously removed my slippers beneath my dress, pressing my feet to the cold marble floor in an attempt to relieve some of the discomfort.

A cup of wine appeared before me, and I looked up to see Christian's friend Lucas standing beside me, smiling.

"You look as though you need this," he said, offering me the cup.

"I do, indeed," I said, taking it gratefully and sipping the cool, fizzing liquid. "Thank you."

"I see you are the object of everyone's attention this evening," he observed with a smirk.

"What do you mean? Everyone is dancing, not just me. Besides, Lily and Christian are the stars of tonight."

"I only meant that now that your sister is engaged, you're bound to have more suitors of your own. I believe they are already circling." He nodded at a few men who passed us, each glancing briefly in our direction, then hurriedly looking away when they saw Lucas watching them.

I looked at him with an unimpressed expression. I had not long turned eighteen and had no idea of marrying any time in the foreseeable future. I told Lucas as much.

"That doesn't mean you won't have suitors lining up to court you. You have a lot to offer; you are beautiful, clever, and the sister of a queen. I doubt any other woman in the five kingdoms can match you. Any man would consider it an honour to be chosen by you."

"How flattering. Are you including yourself in that statement?" I asked coolly, only half-joking.

He smiled and looked away briefly, his eyes falling on Carlotta as she danced with one of his friends for a moment before being handed off to a new partner as the dance required.

"No, you are safe from me," he said, suddenly wistful.

"Well, thank you for the warning," I said somewhat acidly. "I was having a lovely time, but now I'll be questioning the motives of every man who asks me to dance, so thanks for that."

"I would have thought you were doing that already."

"I was, but now it will be front of mind," I said, rising to my feet, then wedging them back into my slippers, and preparing to walk away.

"I'm sorry if I ruined your evening," he said sincerely. "I was only teasing. Will you forgive me and accept my offer of a dance?" He offered his hand to me. I took it gingerly, still a little irritated by his comment.

"Only if you promise not to talk about courtship and marriage," I replied archly.

"On my honour," he said with mock solemnity.

"Then I accept."

The rest of the evening was a blur of dance and laughter. I drank more wine than I ought to have and had a marvellous time. I saw Lily dance with Christian a few times, as well as a number of obligatory dances with visiting nobles and men of importance. The rest of the time she and Christian stood to one side talking, or simply looking adoringly at each other. I noticed them disappear for over an hour at one point, only to reappear flushed and smiling.

By the time the musicians had finally stopped playing and most of the guests had shambled out of the hall, the first rosy rays of dawn were peeking their way across the mountains and forest. Servants crept about, tending to fires, or making their way down to the kitchens as I lay my head on my pillow. The world around me was waking as I drifted contentedly off to sleep.

When I awoke, the sun was high in the sky, someone having snuck in earlier to open my curtains; it must have been near noon. I sat up and stretched languidly, replaying moments from the previous night in my head, a smile on my face. Just as I was contemplating shutting the curtains again and trying for some more sleep, there was a light knock at the door and a maid entered timidly, a look of worry on her thin face.

"Please, your highness, is Princess Lily here?" she asked nervously, glancing about the room, as if expecting Lily to be standing behind the curtains or hiding under the bed.

"No, why should she be?"

The girl, Gretchen, who was only about fourteen, looked at me with an expression of terror, her brown eyes wide with alarm.

"Your highness, she is missing."

"What do you mean, missing?" I said, sitting up suddenly, my head spinning from too much wine the night before.

"She's not to be found anywhere, my lady. There are servants looking high and low, but no one's seen her all day," the girl said, twisting the corner of her apron anxiously and looking at the floor.

I sighed, covering my eyes with my hands, willing the nausea to subside. My pulse thumped sickeningly in my head and my mouth felt dry, as if I'd eaten a handful of sand.

"She's probably with Prince Christian, wherever he is," I answered irritably, reaching for the glass and pitcher of water sitting on my side table and grimacing as the light hit me again. "They're probably off riding or mooning about the gardens together."

"No, your highness. It was Prince Christian who raised the alarm that she was gone. Her maid says her bed's not been slept in and some of her things are missing."

At this I flung myself out of bed, feeling the full force of my hangover hit. Breathing deeply through my nose and willing myself not to vomit, I shucked off my night gown and began to dress quickly with Gretchen's help, anxious to learn for myself what had happened to my sister.

# Chapter Seven

My heart beat a wild tattoo of fear. I told myself it was just my hangover, that there was nothing to worry about, it was all just a misunderstanding, as I hurried to my mother's room. I didn't pause to knock before entering, I just threw open her door and stormed inside. She was seated at her desk, a quill in her hand, and looked utterly normal and unconcerned, though a little surprised at my barging into her study unannounced.

"What is this about Lily missing?" I demanded sharply.

She calmly put down the quill, got to her feet, and strode over to me.

"Prince Christian has the idea that she is. I, for one, do not think so. She has simply gone for a walk, or a ride, and not left any word."

"Has someone asked at the stables?"

"I believe Prince Christian is doing that now. He has been tearing the castle apart all morning looking for your sister. He seems quite wild about it. I hope it is not the sign of any mental weakness in our future king," she quipped.

I had no patience for her barbed commentary on Christian's behaviour and was both annoyed and a little calmed by her relaxed manner. If she was not worried, then perhaps Christian was simply overreacting and Lily really had gone somewhere to be alone and not told anyone. But that would be out of character, and if it were something more sinister, my mother ought to be doing more to find Lily.

"Are you alright, Rose, you don't look well. You're a little grey," she said gently, reaching out to touch my clammy forehead.

"I'm fine, just a little too much celebrating last night."

"You should go back to bed, and I'll send up a little remedy for you."

"Where is Christian now?" I asked, strongly tempted to do as she suggested, but only after I knew Lily was alright.

"He could be anywhere," she shrugged, nonplussed. "He's so energetic. I really don't think there is cause for concern though, dear."

"I'm going to find out what's going on."

"Very well. Do let me know when you find her," she said with a tranquil smile.

I hurried from the room and went in search of Christian, wondering where Lily's ladies-in-waiting had gone. They were always hovering when they weren't needed and now – when they could actually be useful – they were nowhere to be seen. I made for the stables and came across Christian as soon as I stepped outside, grateful for the soft breeze that played over my hot cheeks and forehead.

"What's this about Lily missing?" I asked, repeating the question I had asked my mother.

He looked worried, distraught even, his face pale and his brow furrowed with anxiety, none of his usual good humour to be seen.

"I went by her room to see her this morning, around ten o'clock. I thought she might be sleeping late, but an hour later I sent Inge to check. When she came back, she said Lily was not there and that the bed hadn't been slept in."

I bit my lip, mulling over his words.

"And you've been to the stables?"

He nodded.

"She hasn't been by there, nor has anyone seen her in the gardens today. None of the servants I've spoken to have seen her. Her ladies haven't seen her today, either. They are all looking for her, too, so far without any success." He rattled all this off impatiently, eager to go back to searching.

My panic returned – it was unlike Lily to go anywhere without letting someone know. And she was the last person I would expect to leave the castle in the night. What worried me most was that her bed had not been slept in; it suggested something very wrong to me. How long had she been missing? I tried to remember when I had last seen her at the ball, but my memory was a little blurry from the champagne, and I hadn't been paying attention to the clock.

"I remember that she said goodnight to me at some point, so she left the ball before I did," I said, pinching my aching temples, trying to dim the pounding in my head.

"Anna and Carlotta were taking her to bed when I last saw her. It was about three o'clock," Christian supplied.

"We should bring everyone together – Lily's ladies, the servants, the guards – and organise a proper search, so we know where has been checked. We can start with the castle and the grounds," I suggested, hopeful that as soon as we began searching it would become unnecessary, that Lily would just show up and we'd feel silly for overreacting.

Christian agreed, and we set off to speak to my mother. She showed more concern than when I had first spoken to her, agreed that a structured search was called for, and organised it herself with practical efficiency.

In all there were over thirty people combing the castle and grounds for Lily. I searched the special places we used to play together by myself. She was not in the secret garden grotto and there was no sign of her in the cellar tunnel, not that I really thought she would go there; the tunnel had scared her when we were children, and she may have even forgotten about it. But at least it showed no sign of having been used recently, the ground still thick with slimy muck and no footprints to be seen. None of the other secret passageways showed signs of recent use, either.

Next, I searched her room myself, hoping for some sort of sign or clue as to where she could be. On her dressing table I found her engagement ring. She must have taken it off when she was undressing and forgotten to put it back on. At least, I hoped that was the case. The ring being left behind suggested unwelcome scenarios to me, and I pushed the thoughts away despite the panic rising in my chest, as the words *where could she be?* kept repeating in my head.

With so many people looking for Lily, we managed to completely canvass the castle twice within a few hours, but by the time night fell there was still no trace of her. Christian, King Ludwig, Queen Gisela, my mother, and I sat around the dining table, the search having ceased when it became too dark to continue.

We were a grim party, King Ludwig eating dutifully in a thoughtful silence beside his wife, who made a few abortive attempts at conversation. Christian ate nothing and sat staring down at his plate, his eyes clouded with sadness and confusion. I had no appetite, either, and sat in silence playing with the food on my plate. My mother stilled my restless hands and spoke.

"We will instigate a search of the whole kingdom if we have to, starting tomorrow. The men in the stables said neither her horse nor any others were missing. She can't have gone far on foot."

"I can't believe she would leave the castle at all," Christian mumbled, an expression of despair on his handsome face.

"It's certainly odd," my mother agreed.

"She can't have been *taken,* can she?" Queen Gisela asked almost embarrassedly.

"By whom? Who do you imagine would abduct her? And how would they get out of the castle with guards at every gate?" my mother asked coldly.

"It was just a thought," the other queen replied shamefacedly.

My mother let out a sigh of frustration and continued eating her meal.

King Ludwig had not spoken for some time, but sat completely still, looking thoughtful. It was not one of the times where his wits wandered, in fact he looked like he was thinking furiously.

"Are we certain she *has* left the castle?" he said at last.

"As certain as we can be, in that we haven't found her yet, despite a thorough search," my mother replied dryly. "Why do you ask?"

"Well, it seems clear she did not leave the castle of her own volition, and no one unknown or suspicious has been seen to enter or leave since she was last seen. It appears to me that she may in fact still be here," he said reasonably.

We were silent for a few moments as this possibility sunk in.

"It's possible you are right, of course," my mother said tentatively. "But we have already had the castle searched. Feel free to search again, I shall not stop you. But I fear the fact that she left her engagement ring behind indicates otherwise."

"What are you suggesting?" Christian asked sharply, looking furiously at my mother, his face reddening.

"Well, it is possible that the ball brought home to Lily just how real all this was." She gestured around the table, her gaze stopping pointedly on Christian. "The wedding, the fact that she will become queen. Perhaps she panicked and ran away. It would not be the first time a young lady has gotten cold feet before her wedding day."

"That's not possible," Christian spat, rising to his feet so fast that his chair was knocked backwards, landing on the stone floor with bang that made his mother jump. "Lily and I love each other, and we are excited to be married."

"I hate to contradict you, your highness, but you have no way of knowing for sure what is truly in her heart. As unpalatable as it is, we must consider the possibility that she has run away."

At this, Christian turned on his heel and stormed out of the room, his face still red and his hands fisted from barely-contained rage. I thought his departure was probably wise, given he might well have said something he would regret had he remained a moment longer.

Those of us remaining at the table continued to pick at our plates in heavy, strained silence. After a time, Christian's parents excused themselves, leaving my mother and I alone, save for the servants who waited on us. In a low voice, inaudible to anyone but my mother, I asked whether there was some spell she could cast to give us any idea of where Lily was.

"There are a few such spells and charms. One for finding what you have lost, one to help you find a loved one. But I've already tried," she said grimly, looking at me with large, sad eyes.

"And?" I asked breathlessly.

"They did nothing, gave no indication of where she might be. Of course," she added, her voice lowered further so I could barely hear her, "they do not work if the person you seek is too far away. Or if they are dead."

Her words hit me like a smack in the face, making me recoil as though I had been slapped.

"You think she's dead?" It came out as barely a whisper, though I felt like screaming. "She can't be. How could she - I can't-" My mind reeled, trying to process what she was suggesting, shock and sadness filling me with a searing cold.

"I know, it's hard to take in. She may be gone. Unless she has already gotten too far for the spells to find her."

"But how-?"

"Think about it, Rose," she said, taking my hand in a comforting way. "You know there are secret ways out of the castle, ways by which no one is likely to see her come or go. She might have run away. She might have wanted some time alone to think and left the castle, and something happened to her. We will search the immediate vicinity of the town and surroundings tomorrow, and the whole kingdom if we must."

I nodded absently, only vaguely comforted by my mother's words. It was such an inexplicable thing to have happened. I didn't believe for one moment that Lily would run away. I was sure that she loved Christian and was excited to marry him. The ring lying abandoned on her table made no sense. I considered whether she might have left the castle, seeking some time with her thoughts as my mother suggested, but that seemed almost equally as unlikely. Lily followed rules, she had her ladies-in-waiting in attendance almost every hour of the day, because that was what was expected of her. It sounded far more like something I would do, and had done, than something Lily would do. It just didn't ring true. That was what I found so troubling, that every possibility went against everything I knew about my sister. I felt there was some other factor at play, something dark and malign.

"She would have told me if she was having doubts, if she wanted to call off the engagement."

"Are you so certain?" my mother asked, a frown forming between her brows. "After all, you have secrets from your sister. How can you be certain she has none from you?"

I wanted to argue against this, but she was right; however close Lily and I were, no one ever told you *everything*. I had been keeping my magic secret from Lily for years now, and we had lost some of the total transparency that had been the hallmark of our relationship when we were younger.

"You're exhausted, Rose, you need to rest. We'll continue the search tomorrow. We'll find her." Mother said confidently.

I nodded absently and made my way to my room, equal parts eager to be alone with my thoughts and anxiety at where they would lead.

Gretchen helped me undress, and I climbed into bed, leaving the candle burning on my side table, its flame flickering and casting odd shapes onto the walls, the shadows seeming deeper and darker than usual. I'd never been afraid of the dark, but my fear for Lily had me on edge and unwilling to blow the candle out.

I didn't think I would be able to sleep, as my mind raced, treading the same paths over and over again. It didn't make sense for Lily to have run away . . . someone would have seen her . . . unless she took a hidden passage . . . but that would be so totally unlike her. I spent what must have been hours tossing and turning, trying to think where she might be, refusing to seriously consider that she might be dead. That was too awful an idea to countenance. I racked my brains for a different spell to try, climbed out of bed, and pored over a spell book I'd hidden beneath my bed, searching for a way to find Lily, noting every possibility. But I didn't have much hope; my mother hadn't succeeded there, and it was unlikely that I would, as she knew so much more than me. Eventually I fell into a restless sleep, plagued by bad dreams.

✵ ✵ ✵ ✵

I woke to a grey dawn, having gotten almost no sleep, but peeled back the covers anyway and dressed myself, eager to get started on the search for Lily.

Despite my pleading, I wasn't permitted to go, but the city below the castle was searched by Christian and a team of castle guards led by Paulus, who I knew could be trusted to leave no stone unturned. They were gone the whole day, which seemed to stretch far beyond its normal limit, the time creeping by painfully slowly as I waited desperately for some news from the searchers.

When darkness had fallen, I met Christian coming in from the stables, his face ashen and his mood depressed.

"Nothing," he told me in a dejected voice before I could ask. "No sign of her anywhere. A few people claimed to have information, but it came to nothing. We'll keep searching tomorrow."

The next day was the same, and the next, until the city had been completely searched, down to every last home, shop, inn, warehouse, and stable, with no sign of my sister anywhere. Christian's hope might have started to flag, but his zeal never did; each morning he rode out with Paulus and his men, determined to search whatever new location had been chosen, until all the nearby towns and villages were searched. Weeks passed, until eventually, the entire kingdom had been scoured with no success. There was no sign of Lily anywhere, and day by day, my hope began to fade. Every day I tried casting the locator spell myself, and the summoning spell. Neither worked. I trawled through page after page of my mother's books looking for charms, spells, potions, anything to help me find my sister, but nothing I tried worked.

Sitting locked in my room surrounded by books on magic, I refused to accept that Lily had simply disappeared. I wasn't stupid, I knew young women were sometimes abducted, sold into slavery or sex work, or had awful things done to them before being dumped in the woods. But there were dozens of men looking for Lily, and she wasn't some poor, unwanted girl no one would miss; she was the heir to the throne. She couldn't have just disappeared without leaving any sign. And yet, it seemed like that was exactly what had happened.

The summer drew on, becoming unbearably hot and sultry, as the search spread wider and further away from the castle. The grass in the gardens browned and plants wilted. The heat was oppressive, draining even, and some days I struggled to do so much as leave my room, so weighed down and wretched from the heat and my grief at Lily's continued absence.

King Ludwig and Queen Gisela returned to Altenburg two weeks after Lily disappeared, unable to remain any longer when they had their own kingdom to attend to. Besides this, the King's health had undergone a sudden change for the worse, and he sought the advice of his own physician. Christian, however, remained behind, still holding out hope that Lily might be found. But his mood was low, and though the search parties still explored the furthest reaches of the kingdom, he now remained in the castle, waiting for news. With nothing useful to do, he wandered aimlessly from room to room, and had trouble settling into any activity. There were dark shadows under his eyes, showing he struggled as much to sleep as I did, and he became thinner and more withdrawn.

I understood how he felt. I felt lost without Lily, too. But I channelled my feelings into my witchcraft, returning to it with alacrity, hoping to find a way of returning Lily to us.

After a few more weeks, my mother sent out messengers, cancelling the wedding celebrations. There would be no wedding, no coronation, until we knew what had happened to Lily. The searching continued, but the longer it went on, the more hopeless we all became, as every report that came to us told the same story; Lily was still missing.

# Chapter Eight

Months passed and summer neared its end, the same feelings of anxiety, uselessness, and frustration permeating each day and sapping all my joy, all my energy, as the searches continued to turn up nothing until they quietly petered out. My eighteenth birthday passed with little ceremony; I had no heart for celebration with Lily still missing. Try as she might, my mother could not cajole, tempt, or tease me into marking the occasion beyond a small dinner with a few select members of the court. But any pleasure I felt was dampened by my grief, and any enjoyment turned to ashy, bitter disappointment because I could not share it with my sister, and worse still, I didn't know if she was even alive.

One afternoon, when there was a torrential downpour, perhaps the last summer rain, I sat in one of the small apartments with my mother and Christian. Anna, Carlotta, Inge, and Katerina were there too, as they now accompanied me most places, orbiting me now that Lily was no longer here to be their sun. It seemed that almost without my noticing, they had quietly transitioned from being Lily's ladies-in-waiting to mine. It grated on me, the idea that Lily could be so easily replaced. Now they were absorbed in conversation, glancing occasionally at Christian while paying little attention to my mother or me.

My mother had appeared a few minutes earlier, saying she needed a break from the enormous pile of documents she had been working her way through all morning, and now sat embroidering something I could not quite determine. Christian was seated near the hearth, holding a book, but his eyes were not on the page. He was staring off into the distance, lost in thought. I, too, had a book in my hands, but my mind had wandered as I watched the rain falling continuously on the windowpanes, the sound a persistent, dull drumming, still audible over the low hum of conversation. I was brought out of my reverie when my mother spoke.

"You know, at some point, we will have to declare your sister dead."

The book fell out of my hands, landing on the carpeted floor with a soft thud that belied the gravity of the moment.

"What? Why?" I exclaimed, shocked by the sudden way she brought up the matter. Lily's ladies stopped their conversation instantly to listen as my mother went on.

"The issue of succession. If she does not return soon, you will be the rightful heir. You could," she continued in a cool tone, with a quick glance at Christian, "even continue with the planned alliance with Altenburg, if you chose."

Christian stood up at this, a look of rage on his face.

"How can you suggest that? Lily has been gone a few weeks, and you expect me to marry her sister? How inconstant do you think I am? How cold do you think Rose is? Neither of us would agree to such a plan." He cast an anxious look at me, his grey eyes contracted with unease. "Would we?"

"No," I said simply. "It's too early to say Lily is dead. There's no need to rush things. You are Regent, Mother, and you will be until Lily resumes the throne. That is all there is to it."

I spoke firmly and hoped that would be the end of the conversation, at least for a little while, but my mother raised her eyebrow at me.

"It has *not* been a few weeks; it has been two months. And in two years, when you are twenty and old enough to assume the throne, will you still insist that Lily is alive?"

"There is plenty of time yet before we need to think about announcing that she is dead. As you say, there are two whole years before I would be old enough to rule. We can assess things again then, if needed. For now, there is nothing to prove she is dead, and I refuse to rush into any announcements of that kind when we have no evidence." I sounded much calmer than I felt. I could feel the sting of tears in my eyes as I spoke, my throat tight with anger.

"Aren't you at all upset that your daughter has disappeared?" Christian yelled at my mother. The heads of all the ladies-in-waiting snapped in our direction now, abandoning all pretence of not listening.

"How dare you? *Of course* I am upset," she bit back angrily. "I have lost a child. But I am at least facing the reality that she is gone. She has been gone for over two months. If she were coming back, surely she would have by now. Regardless of what her motivations for leaving were, at this point I don't know how you could possibly think she will return. I still have the good of my kingdom to think of, I don't have the luxury of acting on my personal desires. Having the succession in doubt is a vulnerability. You lost your own brother and had to take his place; you should be able to understand that the matter of succession needs to be addressed." Tears welled in her lovely eyes as her lower lip trembled.

Without saying anything else, Christian stormed out of the room, and I made to follow him. But before I did, my mother warned me to be careful of being seen alone with Christian, lest it should start people's tongues wagging.

"While you and I may know there is nothing between the two of you, the whole situation is a tinderbox that gossips will be itching to light. Don't give them any justification," she said quietly so the other ladies would not hear, fixing me with a stern look.

I ignored her and chased after Christian, catching up to him at the end of the passage.

"Christian," I called. "Don't listen to what my mother says." I quickly closed the distance between us, putting a reassuring hand on his arm, then removing it just as quickly, my mother's warning still ringing in my ears.

"Which part should I ignore? The part where she said you and I should get married, or the part where she said my fiancée was dead?"

He spoke in a trembling voice, his face red with anger, as tears began to fall down his cheeks, which he swiped away angrily.

"Forget all of it. Neither of us want to believe that Lily is dead. But we need to find out for sure. I think we should search for her ourselves," I said, voicing an idea that had been percolating for some time.

"What, you and I?" he asked incredulously. "How would that help? There have been searches already. I led a few myself." *And you're just a girl,* his expression seemed to say.

"We could search more thoroughly together, spend more time talking to people. It doesn't make sense to me that no sign of her has appeared in all the searches, which makes me think that someone missed something."

"You may be right," he said hesitantly.

"I am," I assured him, hoping rather than believing it to be true. "We'll start tomorrow."

* * * *

The next morning, I dressed in my leather breeches and a long shirt, concealing them under the blue cloak Lily had given me, a sprig of vervain pinned to its inside. It was early autumn, and the weather was still fine, but I couldn't think of how else to conceal what I was wearing. Dressing in pants when I was training with Paulus was one thing, but dressing like that outside the castle would be sure to catch people's attention, something I was eager to avoid.

Moving quickly and purposefully, I made my way to the kitchens and asked one of the boys for a loaf of bread, some cheese, fruit, and dried meat, as well as a flask of wine and one of water. He must have been newly assigned to the kitchens, because I didn't recognise him, and I knew most of the servants who worked in the castle, by sight if not by name. He looked both surprised and worried at being given instructions directly by a princess, but he did as I asked quickly, his eyes darting everywhere but me as he avoided my gaze.

With my bag packed for the journey, I went to my mother's room before setting off. Paulus was standing guard by her door, something he rarely needed to do, but he waved me through with a brief nod after knocking to let my mother know she had a visitor.

As usual, she was sitting behind her desk, a pile of papers in front of her and she held one close to her face as she read over it with a serious expression.

"Christian and I are setting off for a ride," I announced quickly, stepping forward to quickly slip into her workroom for some supplies.

"Alone?" she asked sternly, her look of disapproval on her face freezing me in my tracks.

"No-o," I said, trying to think of a lie. "Lucas and some other of Christian's men are joining us. And Anna and Carlotta too," I added quickly.

She studied me over the top of her paper with sharp eyes for a few moments.

"Sylvia told me Anna is indisposed this morning. You're going to look for your sister, aren't you?" Sylvia was my mother's maid and always seemed to know everything that went on in the castle.

I hesitated a moment too long before answering and she saw straight through my weak subterfuge.

"Obviously my earlier warnings were too subtle for you, so let me be clear," she said tersely, rising to her feet. "It is not appropriate for you two to be seen together unchaperoned – people will talk. And going into the woods to collect herbs under cover of darkness is very, very different to roaming across the countryside enquiring after your sister. There may be bandits, or one of you could be injured. It's not safe or proper conduct for a young lady, especially a *princess.* I know Christian is in denial that your sister is dead, but I thought you finally had accepted it."

"Mother, *this* is what it will take for us to accept it. Looking for ourselves, seeing for certain whether or not she can be found. If," I began hesitantly, "if we do not find her after searching the woods and the main towns, I promise I will support you in declaring her dead."

She thought this over for a few moments. I could tell she was weighing the options, assessing the dangers in her mind. When she did go to speak, I thought she might yell again, but her tone was calm, controlled.

"Very well, I shall give you one week to look. That should be enough time to satisfy even Prince Christian that your sister is gone. Afterwards, we will send out a proclamation that Princess Lily is, sadly, dead. I shall remain regent until you turn twenty, at which time you will assume the throne." Her tone was steely, leaving no room for negotiation.

I agreed, eager to get away and start searching. Part of me still believed that we would find Lily, and we would have time to talk everything over everything else later.

I hurried off to meet Christian at the stables as we had agreed. I was to ride out with him, Lucas, another of his men named Felix, Carlotta, and Katerina as far as the outer edge of the city, then they would turn back, while Christian and I progressed by ourselves. This would ensure against people gossiping about Christian and I going riding alone, and had been the only part of my plan my mother approved of, despite relenting in the end. I knew she was indulging me, that she didn't expect us to succeed, which only made me more determined.

I reached the stables and found the others were all ready to go, with the horses saddled and waiting. I did one final check of my satchel: cheese, bread, wine, water, a dagger – which I now looped onto my belt, ignoring the surprised expressions on the ladies' faces – a lantern, my runic stones, and a pouch of gold, in case we needed to motivate anyone to give us information. But the conversation with my mother had thrown me, and I'd forgotten to collect the supplies I wanted from her workroom, which had been my main purpose in visiting her - a healing draught, some more vervain for protection, and a tonic to calm the nerves. The last I planned to give Christian if he became too distressed and unreasonable. I knew he wasn't sleeping these days and didn't entirely trust him to behave rationally.

"Are you ready?" he asked me anxiously as I entered the stables. He was pacing a small distance with a raw, nervous energy, like he had been waiting for hours. The dark circles under his eyes looked like bruises, suggesting he hadn't slept in days. I knew that he was eager to go, to be doing something practical, but I urged him to wait while I ran back for something.

"It will only take a few minutes, I promise," I assured him as I hurried back towards the castle.

"It better be important," he called after me impatiently. "We're wasting daylight."

I ignored him and hurried back to my mother's room, and was surprised to see that Paulus was no longer at the door. Either she had dismissed him for some reason or had stepped out herself, which I hoped was the case, so I wouldn't have to explain myself further and keep Christian waiting longer than was essential. The study was empty when I entered, so I hurried towards her workroom, but noticed the door was ajar. I stilled for a second, surprised that it wasn't locked like usual, and as I went to push it open, I heard my mother's voice speaking to someone.

I had never known her to let anyone in her workroom apart from me. I paused, listening carefully, my hand on my dagger in case she was in danger.

"I asked you here to give me assurances that she is dead, because if she is not, I promise, you will suffer greatly. The princess and that dolt of a prince have decided to conduct their own search for her. So you best have hidden the body extremely well."

Her voice was high and as cold as death, sending a terrifying chill down my spine. I thought I could feel the man's fear – for I was sure she was speaking to a man – through the partially-closed door.

"My – my Queen, I brought you the girl's ring, I gave her the potion – just as you said," the man stammered, his voice high and shaking with fear.

"But did you cut her throat for good measure, as I also said to do?"

My blood ran cold. How could it possibly be my mother saying those things? How could she talk of killing Lily? How could she have actually ordered this man to do it? I felt dizzy at this sickening revelation and had to steady myself against a chair.

He murmured something too low for me to hear.

"Say that again," my mother ordered in the same chillingly venomous voice.

"No, my Queen."

I expected a scream of rage, a wild curse, but I only heard a sharp exhale of breath, like a hiss.

"I couldn't, my Queen. I gave her the drink, and she fell dead asleep just like you said, but I couldn't bring myself to kill her. She just looked so innocent and helpless. It wouldn't have been fair. You said she couldn't wake from it anyway, so I thought hiding her was enough."

"That was not for you to judge. I chose you for this task because you are supposed to be a hardened soldier of fortune, a cold-blooded killer, and you couldn't kill one girl? I gave you a simple task and you failed."

"Oh, please, my Queen, please do not punish me, please."

I heard what I took to be the man falling to his knees. The table grated along the stone floor, some glass bottles toppled and smashed.

"Idiot! Get up! I haven't time for your begging. I should kill you for your betrayal, but there is a way you can redeem yourself, Jurgen."

My ears pricked up at this; I had heard that name before. Jurgen had been a commander in my father's army but had been cast out for some dishonourable behaviour. I couldn't remember what it was exactly, but I thought it had something to do with giving excessive beatings to his men, being far more brutal than he needed to be. He had a reputation for enjoying violence.

"Anything, my Queen." His voice sounded thick, like he was restraining tears. He didn't sound like a hardened criminal now, but someone pleading for their life. "I will do anything, if you'll only spare me."

"You know where you left her? You can find the place again?"

"Yes, yes, my Queen, I remember well."

"Good," she replied sweetly. "Then go find her, cut her throat, and leave her body somewhere it can be found by the prince and my daughter. Nowhere too populated, but by the track that runs alongside the woods, or somewhere like that. With any luck the wolves will have gotten to her and done your job for you. But leave whatever remains of her to be found, understand?"

I felt ill listening to my mother speak this way, chunks of my breakfast beginning to rise in my throat mixed with bitter bile. But it got worse.

"And Jurgen, to make sure that this time you do as you are told, you will cut out her heart and bring it back to me. I will have hard proof this time. And if you run, I will find you; there will be no place in the world you can hide. And when I find you, I will have you torn apart slowly, painfully, in ways you cannot imagine, but first I will give you a draught to ensure you stay awake for every moment of the excruciating, horrific ordeal. Do you understand me?"

"I will not fail you again, your Majesty," Jurgen replied, his voice a quavering, barely audible rasp. He sounded as disgusted and terrified as I felt.

"I know you won't," my mother said, still using that sickly-sweet voice. "Now go. Do this now, quickly. The prince and my Rose will have set off already. And do not fail, or you will wish you were dead."

Hearing the dismissal in her voice, I rushed from the room as quickly and quietly as I could to avoid being seen. I was beyond shocked by what I had heard. My entire world ceased to make sense. My mother had ordered the murder of my sister. I felt sick and dizzy; but at least now I knew Lily really could still be alive if I got to her in time.

I stumbled down the hall, unsteady but desperate to avoid Jurgen, and found a small room nearby that was full of broken furniture and other long-abandoned rubbish. I staggered inside, my vision blurring with nausea, and shut the door behind me, pressing myself against it and sliding weakly to the floor. Overcome by everything I'd just overheard, I turned and vomited into a bucket on the floor next to me. I was shaking as though from an intense cold, but my face burned as I kept heaving until I had nothing more to bring up. My head was spinning, heart hammering madly, as I was gripped by an insane panic. How could what I had heard possibly be true?

I sat on the floor with my head in my hands trying to make sense of it all, to form a plan, aware that the whole time Christian was waiting for me in the stables, unaware of this latest vital piece of information. I decided not to tell Christian what I had overheard, not yet. He would want to confront my mother, charge her with treason, to throw her in prison, maybe even kill her. Despite what I had heard, my instinct was to protect her from this. And part of me feared what she would do if she knew she had been found out.

Besides, until I knew where Lily was, I couldn't risk exposing my mother and losing any chance of finding Lily alive. But I didn't trust Christian to be calm or reasonable, to consider all the possible repercussions if he knew what had really happened. Finding Lily had to be my first priority, and it had to be done fast. That meant doing it alone.

The man, Jurgen, was on his way to kill her, possibly right now. The immediacy of the situation hit me like one of Paulus' punches to the gut. I stood up, feeling woozy at first, but steadied myself, bracing my forehead on the cool stone wall for a moment and drawing in long, deep breaths. Feeling slightly calmer, I hurried out of the storage room and into the passageway. I didn't know how much time I had wasted panicking, so had no way to guess how far Jurgen had gotten. I'd lost precious time and was terrified he had slipped by me.

On instinct, I ran flat-out towards the stables, hoping to find him there and to be able to persuade Christian to go on as planned, but without me. When I got there, Christian and his men were gone, only Carlotta and Katerina remained, standing awkwardly to the side, waiting for me to return.

"Where's Prince Christian?" I gasped, breathless from running there.

"He left, your highness," Carlotta informed me quietly, her blue eyes bright and anxious, as if expecting a reprimand. "He said he couldn't wait any longer."

This was actually a relief, as now I wouldn't have to worry about Christian. But there was no sign of Jurgen here either. My gut tightened at the thought that I might have missed him, too.

"Has anyone else left? Has anyone come through the stables apart from us?" I asked impatiently.

"No, your highness," Katerina replied.

"No servants, soldiers, anyone like that?"

She shook her head.

"Thank God," I breathed with relief, clutching my side where I ached from my sudden run.

"Are you well, your highness?" Katerina asked, concerned. "You're terribly flushed."

"I am perfectly fine. But I would like to be alone. Will you leave me, please?"

A look of hesitation passed between the two of them, but they departed, Carlotta casting anxious looks at me over her shoulder as they made their way back to the castle.

If he hadn't already left, I miraculously still had the chance of following Jurgen when he eventually appeared. All the horses were kept in this one enormous stable, so he would have to pass through unless he was going on foot, which seemed unlikely.

Hoping he had just been delayed a little, I hid behind a screen of piled hay bales placed against the wall nearest the entrance, forcing a gap between two of them so I could see as well as hear people coming and going. Two young grooms came in and began removing the saddles, blankets, and other accoutrements from the horses Carlotta, Katerina, and I had been going to ride. They complained while they worked, about how nobles didn't care how much work they made for others, or how long it took to get the horses ready, only to have to take everything off again afterwards. I wanted to yell out to leave my horse ready to go so I could follow Jurgen when he arrived, but couldn't risk showing myself and spooking Jurgen.

I was just debating what to do, when Jurgen's wide, muscular frame appeared in the doorway, blocking out much of the daylight. He shoved his way into the stables, greeted the grooms in a perfunctory way, and began saddling a horse – a large, black stallion – for himself.

He carried no luggage, only a small saddle bag that presumably contained food and other supplies. A long knife hung from his waist. I shuddered at the sight of it, remembering how my mother had told him to cut out Lily's heart. I thought I might be sick again, but the urgency of following Jurgen steadied me. *Act now, panic later,* I thought.

I waited two minutes from when Jurgen set off from the stables before following, forcing myself to take slow, deep breaths as I itched to chase after him. He was moving quickly, clearly set on completing his mission swiftly, and I didn't want to lose sight of him. When I'd counted two minutes, the grooms had already removed Bastian's saddle, but the grey mare, which Carlotta usually rode, remained ready.

Surprising the grooms, I ran out from my hiding place and moved towards the mare, ready to mount it.

"Excuse me, miss, who gave you permission to ride this here horse? That belongs to one of the princess' ladies," the taller of the two said.

"The Queen," I replied, throwing back the hood of my cloak.

Both looked stunned for a moment, then one collected himself enough to say, "Apologies, your highness. Would you not prefer we resaddle your horse for you?"

"No, I'm in a hurry," I said, mounting the mare as I spoke. I nudged my heels into her sides and set off at a high gallop, leaving the poor grooms confused and standing in a cloud of dust, their mouths still open in surprise.

# Chapter Nine

Almost as soon as I was outside the castle walls, I was pulled up short by the crowds that lined the streets and brought traffic to a crawl. I caught sight of Jurgen's broad, leather-clad back and bald head, his horse trotting along as quickly as the busy streets allowed. We frequently had to stop where foot traffic choked the roads, or carriages and heavily-loaded wagons blocked the way. I hung back as far as I judged safe, toeing the line between keeping him in my sights and not being seen myself, not that he ever glanced back; his focus was only on what lay ahead. No one recognised me or paid me any heed as I rode along, as everyone was too busy with their own business to notice a princess dressed as a commoner, the hood of my cloak pulled up despite the bright, warming sun overhead. I might have relished the anonymity if all my attention hadn't been on the mercenary ahead of me.

Slowly, we passed through the wealthier precincts of the city, riding down street after street of busy shops, the merchants selling everything from fine clothes to exotic wines, while lavish, well-tended houses dominated the skyline. After a while, Jurgen peeled off from the main streets, wending his way through the more industrial districts, making for the direction of the forest. That he hadn't gone to the forest straight from the castle told me that he had either left Lily a considerable distance away or was taking a less direct route in case he was being followed.

Leaving the city limits and reaching a more open road, I put more distance between us, drawing back until he became a small speck on the dusty, almost empty stretch ahead of me. The road now ran alongside the dense and sprawling forest, creating a solid wall of green to my right.

We kept on like this for several miles, the only other travellers I passed being the occasional carriage or farmer's cart heavily laden with autumnal vegetables on its way to market. Glancing at the sky, I saw it was already late morning, the autumn sun beating down on me and making me sweat in my heavy cloak. But I didn't dare take it off, feeling safer with my face mostly concealed, even at a fair distance from Jurgen. I wished I'd bothered to learn some more practical magic like how to veil my identity rather than spending my time learning to magically boil water or transform a fish into a toad. I knew a concealment charm, but it would only hide me, not the mare I rode, and I didn't want anyone seeing an apparently riderless horse and trying to claim her.

Suddenly I rounded a wide bend in the road, expecting to see Jurgen still ahead of me, but the road before me was deserted for as far as I could see. I glanced up and down the road, but there was no sign of him. The ground had dried since the previous days' rain, so that his horse's tracks were indistinguishable from dozens of others that pocked the breadth of the roadway. Gazing along the edge of the forest looking for any sign of him, I spotted what looked like the rear of a horse, largely concealed by trees a few dozen yards ahead of me.

Pausing a short distance away, I strained my ears for any sign that Jurgen was still close, but all I could hear was the soft murmurings of the wind in the trees, the gentl0000e trill of bird song. I tethered my horse, then drew a deep breath, hesitating on the threshold of the forest, the sunshine at my back and the darkness of the densely-clustered trees ahead, hyperaware that I was about to willingly follow a trained killer into a dark and secluded wood. "Do it for Lily," I muttered, then pressed through the barrier of branches into the wood beyond.

I'd come up with a vague plan as I rode, trying to prepare as well as I might for facing a dangerous man who wasn't worried about killing; I wasn't taking any chances with my own safety or Lily's. Before going any further, I cast a protective spell over myself, feeling as though a thin veil of safety had dropped between my body and the world beyond. The spell wouldn't make me invincible, but it would protect me from most physical blows. Then I cast a concealment charm, for good measure. He might hear me coming, but at least he wouldn't see me until I wanted him to. As safe as I could reasonably be tracking down a killer, I hurried after him.

Moving deeper into the woods, my eyes took a moment to adjust to the comparative gloom of the forest. I prayed I wouldn't get lost, for in all my trips into the forest at night, I'd never ventured this far from home before. Walking in as straight a line as possible from the place Jurgen must have entered, I kept my steps as quiet as I could. There was no path here, but I marked the places where branches had been disturbed and snapped, continuing in Jurgen's wake for some time. Birds sang and hares bounded by happily, oblivious to any sense of menace in the air, the peace of my surroundings jarringly at odds with my own sense of fear and dread.

*Please, please let me be there in time,* I thought, moving as quickly as I dared, hoping desperately that Jurgen had not changed direction, all too aware that my tracking skills were practically non-existent. The next moment I heard noises and spotted Jurgen crashing his way through brambles and bushes just ahead of me, not making any effort to conceal his location, as though he didn't expect to have been followed, or simply had no fear of anyone he might encounter.

Jurgen had forced his way into a small clearing, well-concealed by a thick screen of trees growing so closely together around its edges that he must have squeezed through the small gap he'd forced through the verdant barrier. My heart leaped into my throat, and I strangled a cry before it could leave my mouth when I saw Jurgen kneeling in the middle of the dimly lit circle of grassy forest floor, slightly supporting the top half of Lily's body. She lay on the ground, her hair spilling loose around her shoulders like an inky puddle, while she was utterly still, as though asleep, or dead.

Jurgen had a long, thin bladed knife in his hand, poised to strike over her heart.

"Stop!" I yelled. Jurgen's head jerked up sharply in surprise, though his grip on the dagger remained firm. After a moment of calculation, he stood quickly, letting Lily's body drop limply to the ground, his eyes searching the clearing and then the woods beyond for the source of the noise, his knife ready to strike. My concealment charm held, despite the fear that had me quaking in my boots, so I remained invisible to him, though I felt sure he must have been able to hear the wild thudding of heart, beating so violently I felt like it was about to escape its bony cage.

I stared at the man, hardly daring to blink my eyes, though his own kept moving as he tried to place me. He was a large, brawny man, with an enormous, shiny, bald head, and small, beady black eyes. They darted quickly here and there, trying to determine where I was.

"Step away from the body," I ordered in my deepest voice, trying to sound as confident and menacing as possible, but cringing at how shrill and girlish I still sounded in my fear. Fortunately, Jurgen was afraid, too, and seemed not to notice, more focused on tracking the invisible threat.

"Who's there? Show yourself," he demanded in a low, rough voice, completely unlike the one he had used when addressing my mother.

"Step away from the girl," I repeated more firmly.

This time, Jurgen picked where my voice was coming from and took a step towards where I stood, just outside the edge of the clearing.

"Stop, and drop your knife, or I'll open your throat and spill your blood on the forest floor," I said in my best impression of my mother's cold, commanding tone. I was prepared to do no such thing, but I hoped Jurgen couldn't tell. He dropped his knife, then put his hands in the air in a sign of surrender.

"Are you so cowardly that you will threaten me and not even show your face?" He growled in my direction, his voice full of ire.

"I know who you are, Jurgen, and I am not foolish enough to rely on your honour."

"If *you* have any honour, you'll show yourself," he said, spitting on the ground.

I hesitated for a moment, weighing my options. Jurgen was unlikely to hand Lily over to me if he knew who I was, but even less likely if I remained hidden. In my hurry to follow him, I hadn't quite formulated plan to get past him. Reluctantly, I lowered the hood of my cloak, and so lowered the charm that had concealed me, but I kept one hand on the hilt of my blade and the other in my pocket, clutching my rune stones to help keep my protective spell strong. I had never tested it against steel or a man's brute force before and was not certain it would be enough should he decide to run at me, even without his weapon.

"Princess Rose!" he exclaimed, clearly shocked. Whoever he had thought might be threatening him, he was certainly not prepared to see me.

"Kneel," I ordered. But, his initial surprise gone, he now seemed to be assessing the situation more critically, and clearly did not think it was in my favour.

"We're not at court now, your highness, so I don't think I will." He smiled unpleasantly, his hands still up, but moving gradually lower. "So, you're a witch, too. I suppose that's no great surprise."

"Tell me why you're here, what have you done to my sister?" I asked, ignoring his comment. Though I'd overheard his conversation with my mother, I wanted to hear his account of what had happened, even if he would probably lie. I was buying time, not sure what to do next, now that I'd revealed myself, and didn't know if I'd be able to overpower him to get to Lily.

He laughed; a loud, barking laugh that made the hair on my arms stand up as a shiver raced down my spine.

"What have *I* done? Nothing. Nothing but what your mother told me to do, that is," he said with a nasty smile that revealed several broken and missing teeth.

"Tell me. Every single detail."

He laughed again.

"I assumed your highness was in on the plan," he said mockingly. "But why not? I'm a dead man either way." He dropped his hands to his sides casually, and I pulled my dagger from its sheath. He laughed again.

"Calm down, Princess. I'm just getting comfortable," he said, keeping his arms at his sides. He seemed almost at ease now. I suppose that was the difference between having lived a life as a soldier and having lived as a princess; the circumstances were not unfamiliar enough to give him much concern. Whereas this was the most dangerous situation I'd ever been in.

"Tell me," I repeated, my voice shrill, even to my own ears, as it rang through the small clearing.

He sighed dramatically.

"I was ordered by your mother to take Princess Lily from the castle, kill her, and leave her body somewhere."

"Why?"

"I didn't ask. But I'd guess it had something to do with your sister coming close to taking your mother's crown away from her. She wouldn't want that, would she?" he said, overly familiar.

"But you didn't kill her?"

"No. I might be a lot of things, but I am not, I like to think, the type of man who murders helpless girls in their sleep."

"You're very noble," I said, my voice dripping with sarcasm. "So, what did you do?"

As he spoke, I tried to think of a way to get past him, but I didn't know any spells for this kind of thing, and my training with Paulus seemed to have left my brain completely. Plus, realistically, what were my chances if I rushed a full-grown man with military training?

"As you can see, I deposited her here," he said, gesturing again to where Lily lay by his feet. I saw her chest gently rising and falling the tiniest amount. She was alive. I could hardly believe it, but she was. How well she would be when I woke her, if I could wake her, I could not tell. Sensing Jurgen moving, I quickly flicked my full attention back to him. Lily would have to wait a little longer.

"So, then I took her ring – her engagement ring – as proof I'd done the job," he continued. "The idea was that it would look like she ran away from the engagement. Your mother handed me a big bag of gold when it was all done. She didn't seem to have any suspicions then, and I'd gotten away with not killing the girl. Or so I thought at the time."

"But you're willing to kill her now? It's a miracle she didn't die from exposure, or get eaten by bears, or wolves."

He shrugged, nonplussed.

"Maybe. But now it's her or me. The Queen suspected that I hadn't quite followed through, though I don't know why. Must have gotten jumpy when she knew you were sniffing around. I wouldn't have admitted it, but she did something to me. I don't know what, but when she looked at me, I just couldn't lie. I wanted to, I tried to. But no good. When she asked me the question bluntly, the truth came pouring right out of me like honeyed mead. Damn witches. So, here we are, and it's your sister or me; frankly, I care more about me."

I lowered my guard just for a moment to look at Lily, and he lunged at me. I reacted quickly, thrusting my dagger at him instinctively, the blade piercing the palm of his hand, going straight through to the other side. An animal-like bellow burst from his mouth and, even injured, he still managed to wrestle me to the ground, pinning me with the weight of his body, my arms caught under his knees, my knife flung beyond my reach.

"You witch, that hurt," he said, before striking me backhanded in the face with his uninjured hand. My protection charm held, though, and all I felt was a glancing blow. He wound up again, preparing for another strike, when his bulk was suddenly ripped away, freeing my arms and chest. I looked up to see Jurgen and Christian fighting. I didn't know where Christian had come from or how he had found me, but all I felt was relief as I scrambled back to my feet, watching as they fought.

They looked to be evenly matched: Jurgen had the bulk, but Christian had the speed. Jurgen's knife was still on the ground, and Christian had chosen not to draw his own sword out of some misguided idea of honour. Instead, they fought hand to hand, swinging and striking madly at each other, Jurgen apparently unconcerned with the blood splashing from his injured hand with every movement. The thuds of their blows and grunts filled the clearing as I watched, still frozen in shock, worried for Christian, but unsure how to help.

Finally, Christian landed a blow to Jurgen's massive head, which sent him crashing to the ground, where he fell still. We watched him for a moment to see if he'd stir, but he seemed to be knocked out.

"What are you doing here?" I asked Christian, rising and closing the distance between us in a few steps.

"Apart from rescuing you? Looking for Lily, as we discussed." He looked me over quickly, searching for any sign of injury.

"You didn't wait for me," I said angrily, wanting to punch him.

"You took too long, I couldn't wait," he replied unapologetically.

I let out a wordless grunt of frustration, kicking at a tree root in anger and stubbing my toe. It hurt and I growled again in frustration and pain.

"Bloody men! Well, you should have," I said, my toe throbbing. "I found her, look." I pointed, directing his attention to

Lily, who still lay on the ground a short distance from where the scuffle had happened.

Letting out a moan that might have been from joy or despair, Christian dropped to her side, taking her in his arms fretfully. I picked up my fallen dagger, wiped away Jurgen's blood on the grass, and sheathed it, then I joined Christian on the ground beside Lily. I checked her pulse and was relieved by how steady it was. Miraculously she appeared unharmed, just deeply, unshakably asleep.

"Lily! Lily!" Christian cried, jostling her, trying to get her to wake.

"Stop that!" I barked, pulling away his hands. "You can't wake her like that."

"Why not?"

"She'll be fine," I said in what I hoped was an assuring tone, knowing nothing could prepare him for what I was about to say. "But it's a magical sleep. Only the correct spell or potion will wake her."

A look of horror crossed his face as the blood drained away from it.

"Witchcraft?" he whispered. "She's under the influence of witchcraft! But who–?" He left the question unfinished, a look of fury on his face. "Your mother did this! That witch did this to my–
"

"Calm down."

"Calm down?!" he shrieked. "My fiancée is in some kind of unbreakable magical sleep, and you say *calm down*?"

"Yes, because I can fix it."

Though I wouldn't have thought it was possible, his face went even paler as comprehension dawned in his eyes.

"You can fix –? Are *you* a witch, too?"

"Ye-es," I said hesitantly.

No word could fully describe the look of shock and utter disbelief on his face. I thought he might faint.

"But I had nothing to do with this; I'm here because I wanted to *find* Lily," I added quickly.

"Is - is she a witch, too?" he whispered, gesturing to Lily, looking at the woman he loved as if she were a stranger.

I shook my head. He looked intensely relieved.

"Why would your mother want to hurt Lily?"

"I don't understand it myself. I only just discovered what she had done this morning, and that was by accident. Luck, really. I overheard her speaking to Jurgen, then I followed him to find Lily and ran into a little trouble, as you saw. Thanks for jumping in, by the way. You probably saved my life."

"You're welcome," he said dismissively. "But what are we to do now? Confront the Queen? Force her to lift the spell she put on Lily?"

I shook my head again and got to my feet. I'd hoped I would have a little more time to prepare my explanation for Christian and knew he wouldn't like what I had to say now, though admittedly this was probably the worst way he could have found out.

"No, she will deny having anything to do with it, and really there is no proof. Oh, I know there's your word and mine," I added, before he could speak. "But I don't think they will carry much weight against hers. Besides, she's a very powerful witch. We don't have the strength or the power to force her to do anything. And I don't doubt she will have ways of dealing with anyone who interferes with her plan," I added bitterly.

"Do you think she would hurt you?"

I thought for a moment. I wanted to say no, but I realised that everything I had thought I'd known about my mother had been wrong, that I had no idea what she was truly capable of. She had wanted Lily dead and taken steps to ensure she died. It wasn't such a stretch to imagine she could want me dead, too, if I threatened her plans.

"I don't know," I said finally. "But it's safest to assume she would. We can't accuse her openly and we can't fight her. Neither of those things would help us bring Lily back." I began pacing up and down the width of the small clearing, trying to come up with a plan.

"We have to do something," Christian bellowed, beating his palm with his fist.

"Yes, I know, I'm working on it, so can you please shut up for a minute?"

Christian muttered offendedly and remained on the ground next to Lily's body, holding her hand, lifting her eyelids, trying fruitlessly to wake her.

"I have an idea," I said at last. "We're all safest if my mother thinks her plan has succeeded. We need to hide Lily somewhere safe, somewhere no one will expect to find her. Then I'll return to the castle and try to find a way to break the spell. We act as if everything is normal, and we have accepted that Lily is gone for good. You should return to Altenburg; there's nothing you can do here." He looked outraged and was about to speak, but I raised my hand to ask for silence, and continued.

"I know you don't want to leave Lily, but she is safe, for now. The Queen thinks she's dead, or she will if I can manage it. There is nothing you can do for her here. But you can go to your parents and ensure that they will send help, if it is needed. But don't tell them all that has happened. You must find a way to leave out what my mother has done, and the fact that we have found Lily, for it will only create more problems if it's known. It'll put my mother on her guard, then we'll lose the only advantage we have right now. Once I wake Lily, I'll find a way to deal with my mother."

"And how do you propose to do that?" he asked, a look of angry incredulity on his handsome face. He was four or five years older than me, but in that moment, he looked like a child.

"I don't know yet," I admitted. "She's a far more powerful witch than I am, and she has an army at her disposal. That will take some thinking. At least we have the advantage of her not knowing that we have found her out. We need to keep it that way, which is why I ask that you do not tell anyone what she has done until we have a way to undo it."

Christian was strongly against this plan, wanting to take immediate action, to challenge my mother despite my arguments against it. But finally, after much persuading and some light threatening on my part, he agreed to return to Altenburg, which was a relief, as I didn't trust that he would be able to maintain the façade of ignorance if he stayed in Silvaner.

"Why can't I take Lily back to Altenburg with me? She would be safest there."

"I need her close by so I can wake her as soon as I find the right spell, or potion. Me trekking off to Altenburg would raise a lot of complicated questions and decidedly would fall into the 'drawing unwanted attention' category. I'll find somewhere safe and secluded, but not too far away and keep her there."

"You could come with us. Get away from your mother's court."

"That would raise her suspicions immediately, and I need to stay at the castle as long as possible so I can access all her books on magic. It's essential that my mother stays in the dark as long as possible to give us time to come up with a plan. If we let her know she's been found out, we could start a war. We *must* avoid that at all costs."

"I don't like it. I can't just go home and do nothing."

I knew this would be frustrating for him; he was a man of action, impulsive, and used to doing as he pleased. Being given instructions by a girl, especially one younger than him, must have been galling. Worse, he was told to wait while I was the one who acted to set things right. But he took it well, all things considered. My superior knowledge of witchcraft worked in favour.

"Can you carry her? We'll put her on your horse and look for somewhere safe to keep her."

Christian nodded, lifting Lily with ease, but the second he had her in his arms, Jurgen, who it seemed had awoken during our conversation, leapt to his feet and charged at Christian and Lily, his knife once more in his hand. Still holding Lily, there was nothing Christian could do to stop Jurgen without dropping her. I saw him hesitate for a second, and so did Jurgen, as he prepared to strike at Christian with his long blade. Time seemed to slow, and I saw the dagger move towards my sister. Almost before I knew what I was doing, my dagger was in my hand, and I was thrusting it into Jurgen's neck.

He turned towards me in surprise and made to swipe at me with his knife, my blade wrenching free with the movement, unsheathing from his neck. Blood spurted from the wound, pouring in a heavy torrent, drenching his jacket with the hot, dark liquid. With a look of shock and anger on his face, he collapsed to his knees, clutching at the wound as blood continued to flow in rivulets between his fingers. A moment later, he collapsed facedown onto the ground, a sickening gurgling sound coming from his mouth as he tried to cry out, blood gushing in gradually slowing waves, while Christian and I watched in horror. Jurgen's limbs jerked for a few moments, then he was still, blood oozing from his wound, pulsing in time with his lowing heartbeats, creating a crimson pool on the forest floor, just as I had threatened earlier.

I looked at the dagger still in my hand; it was covered in blood up to the hilt, and so was my hand and half of my sleeve. I felt instantly sick, and turning away from the body, I vomited for the second time that day, though there was only bitter bile this time, and my body shuddered with every wracking heave.

Christian gently laid Lily back on the ground, away from the growing pool of blood, and came over to me.

"Are you hurt?" he asked, placing a hand on my shoulder.

"I'm fine," I said, unsure how else to reply, though I was far from fine. I felt sick with myself, horrified by what I had done.

"I can't believe I killed him," I stammered weakly, wiping sick from my chin.

"He would have killed me or Lily if you hadn't. Then he probably would have killed you as well. You had no choice. Thank you, by the way, for saving me this time," he said with a weak smile.

"I guess we're even," I laughed manically, the sound hollow and unnatural to my ears. "We should bury him," I said, changing the subject.

"He doesn't deserve it," Christian replied, a hateful look on his face.

"Perhaps not, but I don't want to risk my mother sending someone to look for him and finding his body. It would raise too many questions, and we need her to think he succeeded. I'll make it look as though he has, and then run off in the night."

Christian agreed, and even spared me from doing the thing I knew had to be done. He cut out Jurgen's heart and wrapped it in Jurgen's own shirt. I would leave it for my mother to find, hoping she would take it for Lily's heart, as the trophy she had demanded of Jurgen.

That done, we dismembered him to speed up decomposition, and between the two of us we scraped away enough earth to bury the pieces of him in a shallow grave. Neither of us had a shovel or other tool with us, so we had to work with our hands. It took a long time, and with each moment I felt like I was sullying the cold, clean earth by scraping it away, only to cover the body of a killer. But then, I was a killer now, too. When we were done, we were both dirty, with soft, dark earth smeared on our pants to the knees, and our hands stained with red blood and brown soil. Christian at least was still cleaner than me, having been spared the spray of blood from the wound on Jurgen's neck, and was far more presentable than I was.

"That will do," Christian said, pressing the soft earth over the remains as flat as possible to try and conceal it better.

"We'd better clean up," I said, glancing at the blood and dirt that stained my breeches, shirt, and hands. The smell of drying blood kept wafting up, assaulting my nose and I was desperate to wash it away.

"I passed a small stream earlier," Christian offered, lifting Lily in his arms and leading the way out of our small clearing.

It was a short walk to the little forest stream Christian had discovered, and the cool, clean water mercifully washed away the blood and filth. Standing knee-deep in the stream, wearing only my breeches and a chemise, I shivered wildly as I washed my face and hands, the shaking having nothing to do with the chilly current and everything to do with the knowledge that I had just killed a man. It had been a day of earth-shattering discoveries, and I felt as though I was beginning to shatter myself.

"Come out, Rose, or you'll freeze," Christian called warmly to me, offering me a horse blanket to dry off with as I emerged from the water feeling a little cleaner, though I hadn't succeeded in washing all the blood from my shirt.

"Here," Christian said, tossing me his mercifully clean shirt, then replacing his tunic over his bare chest. "No one is going to talk to you if you go walking around covered in blood."

I laughed feebly and thanked him, trading my blood-stained shirt for his; it was only marked a little at the cuffs, which I needed to roll up anyway to be able to use my hands. It was too big, but better than nothing. There was little I could do about my breeches, though, which were still stained despite my efforts in the stream. Now at least I could pass off as having gotten wet rather than having been in a knife fight. My shirt and cloak were almost soaked through with blood, so both were bundled up in my saddle bag. Sitting astride the grey mare and wishing she were Bastian, I shook with cold, my damp pants and light shirt doing little to protect against the chill that crept in as the sun began to make its way westward.

Christian chivalrously offered me his short green cloak, which I was too cold to refuse, and when we looked as respectable as we could manage, we set off to find a safe place to keep Lily.

****

There were a small number of small cottages around the outskirts of the forest, a good distance from the edge of the city, which Christian proposed as possible sanctuaries for Lily, but I negatived the idea. They were still too close to the town and the castle for my liking, so we rode on for some hours, the sky growing daker the further we went from the city.

As twilight settled in, we came across a cottage, which was miles away from its nearest neighbour and sat right at the forest's edge. A little ramshackle, its roof and eaves were patched with moss and its walls crawling with ivy, showing the building's age. Despite this, it looked cared for, the home of people who were not well off, but who had poured love into their surroundings. For despite the state of the building and the encroaching fingers of nature, which looked in some places like they might strangle the little house, the door and window shutters had been painted quite recently in a bright, cheerful, buttercup yellow, and in the dim light I could see a thriving vegetable garden, a pen full of fat, healthy pigs, and a small orchard consisting of some apple and plum trees around the rear of the cottage.

Sliding off the grey mare, I went to investigate, while Christian stayed with Lily. As I drew nearer, I heard someone inside singing a folk song in a dry, raspy voice. I knocked on the door, and in a few moments, it was opened the smallest crack by an elderly woman. She had grizzled grey hair, which was escaping from a bun atop her head, a thin aquiline nose, and a deeply lined face, from which intelligent hazel eyes shone out interrogatively.

"What do you want?" she asked, a slight note of fear and suspicion in her raspy voice as she studied my unfeminine attire. I drew Christian's cloak more tightly around, feeling self-conscious.

"My companion and I are travelling and have gotten lost. I wonder if you would allow us to rest our horses here a short while, and perhaps help us find our way?"

"Where's this companion, then?" she asked warily, scanning behind me with sharp eyes.

"He is with our horses, shall I fetch him?"

"What happened to you?" A nod at my stained pants, which were not quite covered by the cloak, as she kept the door open just wide enough to talk to me.

"I took a spill off my horse earlier and made a bit of a mess of myself," I replied with a shamefaced grimace.

The woman nodded, satisfied by my answer, though she still looked a little suspicious. I did not wonder at it; living where she did might make her prey for unscrupulous travellers and brigands.

"Alright then, fetch your *companion*," she said, testing the sound as though the word were a novelty. "You'll leave your weapons behind you before coming into the house," she added as I began to walk away. I nodded my agreement; my intuition told me there would be little to fear inside.

Christian returned with me to the house, while we left Lily with the horses, concealed under Christian's cloak, though I was loathe to part with it. Christian objected when I suggested this; he refused to treat her like a sack of flour. But I quickly persuaded him that we would have more difficulty making our case if we entered the house carrying an unconscious woman.

* * * *

The old woman's name was Marie, and her husband was Otto. He was even more deeply wrinkled than she was, with a cloud of fluffy white hair circling his head, and a beard that reached halfway down his chest. He seemed to be a naturally jovial, sociable type, whereas his wife was more guarded and suspicious of others.

They offered us wine, cheese, and bread, and let us rest by their burning hearth for a while, Marie's watchful eyes pinned on us the entire time. I stayed close by the fire, eager to fully dry my breeches and get some degree of warmth back into my bones. We talked of their pigs and of the weather, the harvest, of their family – of which they sadly had none, having lost a son in a war and a daughter in childbirth – before I dared broach the object of our visit. I'd been subtly sounding them out as we talked, waiting to learn more of their characters before I got around to our true purpose. Eventually, I felt confident that they were essentially kindly, trustworthy people. They had welcomed us into their home with little reason to. So, finally, I told them of our predicament, or rather, a version of it.

I told them I had a sister, who had been put into an enchanted sleep by a wrathful witch. I said we needed somewhere safe to keep her, with people who could be trusted to look after her. I left out a great many details, including the fact that my sister and I were princesses, and our mother was the witch in question. Eventually, I asked whether, in exchange for regular sums of gold, they would keep Lily safe while Christian and I searched for a cure.

Marie was hesitant, as she feared acting against a witch, but I assured her that it was in our interests to keep Lily's location a secret, too, and that no one would know they harboured her. Otto was more practical; he listed the things they could do with the gold: repairing their barn, buying more pigs, purchasing more grain to set by for the winter months. I could see he had already spent the money in his mind and saw no reason not to accept such a profitable arrangement.

"All we ask is that you keep my sister safe and hidden. She won't need food or drink, merely to be kept warm and out of sight. But it is essential that her presence remains a secret, no one can know she's here."

"And what if anyone should come looking for her?" Marie asked, her voice loaded with wary scepticism.

"They won't. Anyone apart from us who knows her believes her to be dead," Christian said, genuine sorrow in his deep, near-broken voice. It was Christian's sadness and obvious love for my sister that persuaded Marie to take Lily into their home in the end. Otto had been easy to convince, especially once he understood that all they would need to do was keep her out of sight.

The sum and mode of collection were agreed. Christian brought Lily into the house and Marie gasped when she saw her; for a moment I thought she had recognised my sister.

"But, she's so beautiful," she said with an awed sigh. I, too, sighed, relieved. I was used to Lily's beauty, but she still held great wonder for those who saw her for the first time. I smiled.

"Yes, my sister is very lovely. But more than her beauty, she has a kind heart and is greatly loved. That's why we are so anxious to ensure that she is kept safe."

Marie nodded, stroking Lily's loose black hair lovingly, her ancient, gnarled hands gentle as could be.

"Bring her in here, she may sleep in this room." Marie led us into a small but well-kept bedroom. It contained a narrow bed, with a worn patchwork quilt I suspected Marie had made herself, the once-bright flowers now faded to subdued but still pretty hues, a small fireplace, and a chest of drawers. Christian laid Lily gently on the bed, then Marie gently stroked her hair away from her face once more.

"Thank you," I said as we left Lily behind, Marie closing the door of Lily's room gently, as though afraid to wake her.

"Yes, thank you for your kindness," Christian said, laying a bulging purse of gold on the table.

Marie's eyes widened at the amount of gold, then she turned away from it before she and Otto saw us to the door. I hated to leave, having only just found Lily after believing her dead for so long. I could see Christian felt the same, his face becoming more clouded the further we went from where she lay.

"I'll be back as soon as I can. Once I've found a way to wake her," I said to the old couple as we stood at the threshold, trying to draw out the moment of departure as long as possible, as though we could spin it out forever if we just lingered long enough.

Marie nodded and smiled.

"Just as you like, dear. I promise I shall not leave the house as long as she is here."

I told her that wasn't necessary, but she just waved me away dismissively, muttering about guarding our precious treasure. The transformation her attitude had undergone since we arrived was incredible. But then, that was down to Lily. Even unconscious, she could elicit love and sympathy from complete strangers. I might have been jealous, as I had often been when we were children, had she not been lying in a cursed sleep.

Once we were a short distance from the house, I cast a protective charm over the cottage and the land for a few feet around it. Now no one who Marie and Otto did not know would be able to enter, and everyone dwelling in the house would be safe from physical harm. It would also keep Lily safe from any misdeeds on the part of Marie and Otto, in case I had misjudged their kindliness. I didn't think I had, but I had learned the hard way how deceptive people could be.

Christian watched as I cast these charms, a look of mingled interest and concern on his handsome face, which was cast whiter than usual in the light from the half-moon overhead.

"I went my whole life wondering if witchcraft was real or just a bunch of superstition, and now I find I have known two witches in the last few months."

"I'm not like my mother," I assured him. "I only want Lily to be safe. I will work every minute I can to bring her back to us."

"Work quickly. Then we will have to decide what to do about your mother."

I had wondered how long it would be before that topic came up again, and I was neither pleased nor surprised it had happened so quickly. Christian and I disagreed fundamentally where my mother was concerned. He saw her as a monster, a villain, the one who had wanted his love dead. I understood that, and I agreed that what she had done was heinous. But my feelings were complicated by my love for my mother, and some small part of me hoped there was some explanation, some detail that would somehow excuse or justify her actions, even as a more rational part of me knew it was impossible. In the last few years, we had grown so close. I felt betrayed by what she had done, but I also desperately wanted to find a peaceful resolution, though I knew in my heart that was unlikely.

Christian and I parted ways. We agreed that he would wait at an inn while I sent his men to meet him, then they were all returning to Altenburg. Deeply relieved that he had finally agreed to this plan, which kept him from encountering my mother again, I pulled on my bloodied cloak and turned in the direction of home.

* * * *

It was past midnight when I arrived back at the castle, and the guards at the side gate refused to believe I was who I said, dressed as I was in common apparel and stained from the efforts of the long, painful day, until I demanded they go for Paulus, who quickly confirmed my identity and had the gates opened for me. He then insisted on escorting me straight to my mother to let her know I had come back.

"What the hell were you thinking, leaving the castle without an escort?" He demanded in a low voice. "Anything could have happened to you. You look like a right mess. Been up to anything you shouldn't?" he asked as we made our way up the stairs.

"Who, me? Paulus, how can you suggest such a thing?" I teased, hoping to avoid answering. "Don't fret, the blood isn't mine. I can handle myself. I had a good teacher, remember?"

He let out a low grunt, and we fell silent again. As we walked, I steeled myself for the encounter, knowing I had to maintain the illusion that I knew nothing of what my mother had done. Paulus knocked and announced us before leaving me alone with her; she looked genuinely concerned when she saw me, worry furrowing her brow. Being in the same room with her was difficult; I had trouble looking her in the eye and had to press my hands into the sides of my thighs to keep them from shaking with suppressed rage and horror. When she saw me, still dressed in my stained breeches, my bloodied cloak hanging over my arm, her face paled with alarm.

"Are you hurt?" she cried, hurrying to me, anxiously inspecting my face, my arms, my legs, looking for the source of the blood.

"I am well," I said irritably. "It's not my blood; Christian fell as we were riding, and his leg was injured. Not seriously," I added in response to an inquiring look from her. "I bandaged his wound, and he will be fine. He has left, though. He returned to Altenburg this afternoon. I sent his men to follow him."

"That must have been quite the ordeal. You ought to have had some of your ladies with you," she said, with only a hint of reproach in her tone as she fussed over my dirty clothes and disarranged hair. "It wasn't very gracious of him to leave without saying goodbye to me, after all the weeks he has spent as my guest," she said dryly. "If the prince has left, I take it you did not find any sign of your sister?" she continued more gently.

"No," I said, hanging my head to avoid her gaze, my voice choked with real tears and disappointment. "No. I believe it is as you said. We will never find her; she is dead. There is no need to keep searching for her."

I lifted my eyes and saw A look of relief pass over my mother's face for the briefest moment, and I felt a surge of revulsion at it. Tears welled in my eyes, tears of anger and frustration mingled with sadness. Her face became kindly when she saw this, and I saw a warm and maternal side to her which I didn't remember seeing before, not even as a child.

"I am sorry, my darling girl, I know how you loved her," she said, taking me into a tight embrace. I resisted the urge to shove her away, to yell and scream, instead resting my head on her shoulder. I felt so, so weary, exhausted by the events of the day. Had it really only been this morning that I had overheard my mother's plan? It seemed so long ago now. A single day and my entire life had been uprooted, thrown into chaos.

"If you are not hurt, I suggest you have something to eat, then take a bath and go to bed."

It pained me to see how solicitous she was of me, knowing she had been willing, eager even, to have my sister killed. I didn't know how to reconcile these two versions of her.

However, I did as she said. I bathed, then ate, though I didn't go straight to bed. I still had a task to complete; I stole away to my mother's study in the dead of night and deposited Jurgen's heart on her desk for her to find. *Please let her believe it's Lily's,* I quietly prayed in my mind as I deposited my grim bundle. I contemplated leaving a note, disguising my handwriting, but I didn't even know if Jurgen had been literate. Hopefully the heart would be a sufficiently clear message. This done, I finally crawled into my bed. But I struggled to sleep, despite my exhaustion. Memories from the day kept surging up in my mind; Jurgen lying on top of me, pinning me and ready to strike. My dagger pierced clean through his palm. Jurgen with my dagger in his neck. Jurgen, dead on the ground, a growing crimson puddle steadily blotting out the green ground beneath him. I tried to push these thoughts from my mind and think of Lily instead.

My mind began racing in another direction then, realising how much was still to be done. I needed to find a way to wake her, remove my mother from the throne – peacefully, if that was possible – and keep her from doing any more harm. But for now, at least, Lily was safe. That was my last thought before the weight of my physical and emotional exhaustion finally pushed me mercifully over the brink, and I fell into a deep, dreamless sleep.

# Chapter Ten

Over the following days I tried to channel my energy into finding a cure for Lily, though I regularly fell into dark, contemplative moods, thinking about my mother and what she had done. My stomach twisted and my head throbbed with tension when I thought about it for too long, so I'd push myself to focus on my sister instead. I spent as much time as possible in my mother's workroom, poring over different volumes and trying to find a spell that would wake Lily.

I was able to do this with relative ease and not attract my mother's attention, though I jumped at every sound as I worked, sure that she would come in and demand to know what I was doing, foiling my plan. But I needn't have worried; preoccupied with ruling the kingdom, she thought I was burying my grief in study, which I was to an extent.

Black banners and bunting adorned the streets and houses of Silvaner, the castle echoing with a quiet grief, as everyone from the servants to the courtiers mourned the loss of the beloved princess. My mother had made an official proclamation that Lily was dead but without a body there was no funeral, only a memorial service and a bronze statue of Lily placed in the centre of the market district. It was an odd choice of location, but what grated on me most was my mother's hypocrisy in erecting a monument to the girl she had wanted murdered.

With Lily's apparent death, my mother was now assured of being regent for another two years and at times I wondered if, when I, too, was old enough to rule, she would want to remove me as well to keep her crown. Dark thoughts like this often filled my head while I searched for a cure, which only galvanised me into working harder and longer, spending hours at a time hidden away, sometimes going days were I barely spoke to anyone. Having such a cold and ugly part of my mother revealed had deeply unsettled me, and I found myself making excuses to avoid spending much time alone with her. I shunned the ladies-in-waiting too, not even bothering with an excuse, save that I wanted to be alone.

After a few days spent with my nose practically glued to the pages of the various spell books my mother had, I found a potion that would act as an antidote to the sleeping draught I suspected she had used on Lily. Though I was desperately eager to wake Lily, I stopped short of making the potion. Researching magic was one thing, but actually making a potion or testing a spell was not something I could very well do right under my mother's nose and in her own workroom without eventually attracting her attention.

Admittedly, this wasn't a difficulty I'd considered when I'd hurriedly formed my plan in the forest, and now it seemed I'd overlooked the biggest obstacle to my success. My head dropped onto the page, as the weight of my shortsightedness hit me like a wave of despair, drenching me from head to toe and soaking me with a sense of failure.

Unsure what else to do, I closed the book and left my mother's workroom. Feeling utterly useless and defeated, I paced the castle and then the gardens aimlessly, trying to think of a way around my problem and unable to admire the beauty of all the flowers and trees in bloom, which seemed to mock me with their cheery brightness. What I needed was privacy and space, so I could establish a workroom of my own; there would be nothing odd in that, I thought. I was a young woman, and the desire for my own space should not be a great surprise to my mother.

Yet realistically, how much would this solve? I would still be in the castle, under my mother's watchful eye. There would be no way to hide what I was doing if she came to see me at my work, which would only be natural; I was her pupil, and she would be curious to see what I was attempting, eager to give advice and watch my progress.

I needed a place of my own that was isolated, where I could be sure no one would come snooping at my work. But there was no place like that anywhere in the castle, and I couldn't very well go sneaking off into the city every day even if I was able to rent a safe place for my magic. I tugged on my hair until it hurt, the frustration overwhelming me until tears began to bleed down my cheeks. I'd failed my sister, and it hurt so much that I wanted to just melt into the ground and disappear.

My mother noticed my low mood and asked what was troubling me. I tried to brush off her question, telling her I was fine, just a little tired and out of sorts.

"You aren't pining for some man, are you?" she asked me, eyes narrowed suspiciously.

I assured her I was not. Chewing my lip for a few moments, I debated the best response to give to preserve my secret, but I was so dispirited at my failure, I confessed the truth of what bothered me, in part, at least.

"I just feel so trapped," I told her honestly. "I know I am lucky to be a princess, that I live in splendour and comfort. I know I have a much better life than so many others and I should be grateful. I know I probably sound like a brat, but sometimes I feel caged by court life." *By having to share my home with you.*

My mother nodded sympathetically.

"I can understand that. It's a place where we cannot all be who we truly are. We are lucky in our comforts, yes. It's a life of material privilege, but in many ways, we have less freedom than an ordinary commoner. What is it you want to do that you feel you cannot do here?"

I took a deep breath. This was the opportunity I needed. I just had to phrase it right, not raise her suspicions.

"I wish," I said, glancing about surreptitiously to check for eavesdroppers, as I always did before discussing magic. "I want to be free to cast spells unobserved, to brew potions without worrying about someone discovering what I am doing. I want to experiment, to explore my powers more fully, to see what I can do outside the confines of the castle, without having to keep one eye and ear open for fear of discovery. You've been generous in letting me use your work room, but I can't just come and go from there all the time, not without drawing attention to myself, and it feels too risky. And," I added, "it's hard to be here when everything reminds me of Lily."

She was silent for a few moments, a meditative expression on her face. After a while, she said, "There is a possibility."

I waited with bated breath for her to continue.

"You know your father kept a hunting lodge in the northern woods, many miles from here. It was where he liked to take his boon companions for days of debauchery away from watchful wives and the like. It probably reeks of dissipation, but it's quite isolated, and there are not many cottages or farms around. It hasn't been used since he died, so I can't speak to its current state. The roof could have caved in, for all I know. But if you took all the supplies you required with you, you could manage there alone for some weeks."

I wanted to leap with joy, but I forced myself to be calm, though I couldn't stop a massive smile from spreading over my face.

"It sounds ideal. But what would you say if people asked where I was?"

"That you require privacy and peace while you work through your grief at my estate in the mountains. That you are in such deep mourning for your sister you cannot bear to be at court at present. Any number of things. I am queen, no one will contradict me."

"When can I go?" I asked eagerly, my hands twitching, ready to pack my bag and set off at that very moment.

"There are still things to consider. For instance, you won't have a maid with you, as there's no one trustworthy enough. This means you will have to dress yourself, cook for yourself. You will be entirely alone."

"I can do that."

"I wonder," she said, scrutinising me, "if you can. It is one thing in principle, but in practice – well, you haven't been raised to do these things for yourself, you've never prepared a meal, or so much as drawn your own bath. It will be quite a change for you."

"I need a change. I can learn how to do those things for myself just as I have learned mathematics and science, or even witchcraft."

"And if you become ill or are injured," she continued, as though deaf to my reply. "You will have to send for assistance, and that will take time. You may be vulnerable."

"I'm not afraid. Paulus has taught me a lot and you've shown me enough protective enchantments that I'll be quite safe."

She smiled. "Brave girl. I knew you would take after me."

I cringed internally at the pride in her voice and hoped that she was wrong about that.

She saw to the arrangements quickly and efficiently. I took lessons from some of the castle cooks, learning to make a few simple dishes, how to store my food to keep it from spoiling too quickly, and how to make a fire that would burn long and hot, not fizzle out after a few minutes.

I had several new, simple, peasant-style dresses made to ensure I could dress myself and move about easily. The gowns were woollen to keep me warm at the higher elevation at which the cabin sat, and dyed the most beautiful shades of purple, green, and red. My mother also sent me off with my own small cauldron for potion-making, stores of herbs and other ingredients, spell books, books on plant lore and enchantment.

Despite my burning impatience to be away from the castle, away from my mother and finding a cure for Lily, even I could hardly complain at the speed with which everything was done. Seeing me to the stables, my mother gifted me a new silver knife for cutting herbs just before I left. It had an ornate hilt and handle, the butt shaped like the head of a wolf. The craftsmanship was beautiful, the weight wonderfully balanced. I ran my thumb over the wolf's head, feeling the smooth contours of the perfectly carved creature.

"For my little cub," she said when she handed it to me. There were tears in her eyes, but tears of pride, not sadness at my leaving her.

It was times like this when she was kind and wanted to ensure I was happy, to give me what I needed, that I struggled to believe that she had really wanted to have Lily killed. I might not have believed it at all if it were not for the evidence of my own senses. But no amount of kindness from my mother could make me forget what she had done; Lily's absence and my horribly vivid dreams of that day in the woods were constant reminders. Sometimes it seemed to me that she was two different people: one I loved, knew well, and understood, while the other a stranger, a dark, menacing, murderous stranger, whom I was wise enough to fear.

* * * *

I was escorted to the cabin by four of my mother's most trusted guards – including Paulus – and two ladies-in-waiting, Katerina and Inge. Apart from providing company for the journey, the riders all helped bear my considerable luggage to the cabin. Food stocks, books, potion ingredients, clothing, fresh linens, and, lastly, a cumbersome cage containing a large, tame crow, another gift my mother had given me. The crow was enchanted to act as a messenger and would be my sole means of corresponding with my mother whilst I was away, carrying any letters I wrote to their intended destination.

"He will always find his recipient," she had assured me, stroking his soft ebony chest with something like affection. It was an impressive enchantment, one I doubted I could have managed, but it would also enable me to communicate with Christian in Altenburg. Though I liked the crow, who was named Nox for his night-black feathers, Katerina looked at him with distaste and Inge outright screamed when he ruffled his feathers and snapped his beak at her, despite the cage keeping him quite secure. In the end, Nox was given to one of Paulus' men to convey, the cage covered and tied to the horse's saddle, shuddering with each thunderous step the animal took and often emitting a sharp "caw" of indignation.

The hunting lodge was situated in the northern reaches of the kingdom, a full day's ride from the castle. I hadn't been there before, as it had been my father's personal retreat from the court and his family. The journey, though tiring, gave me a view of all the different parts of the kingdom. The castle and capital city of Silvaner were hemmed in to the east by the sprawling, dark pine forest I usually visited when harvesting ingredients for my potions, while a lake stretched from the western side and mountains separated it from our southern neighbours, grassy flat lands and rolling meadows stretching just north of the city limits.

Further northern we passed onto undulating hills, which they were far gentler and more sprawling than the sharp, unforgiving peaks of the southern mountains. The northern half of the kingdom was home to many of the farming communities, as the land lent itself more favourably to agriculture than in the south. The climate was slightly warmer here, too, before we began the incline up to where the cabin was, and the smells of hay, grass, flowers, and soil still perfumed the air despite the briskness autumn.

"This place smells like peasants," Inge complained as we passed by rolling fields swaying with crops of wheat and rye, or covered in curling green tendrils belonging to potatoes and pumpkins. To me it smelled like freedom, nature, industry. Perhaps when I went home I'd start a small kitchen garden and insist my ladies-in-waiting help me with it. I suppressed an amused snort at the idea.

In the late afternoon we passed through the lush, green farmlands, and the distant vista became dominated by a stretch of expansive woodland. It was different from the pine forests that bordered the castle; this wood was populated with maples, oak, ash, yew, and beeches, tinged with the warm shades of the season. The temperature dropped suddenly, and we all huddled down into the cloaks we'd been advised to bring along for this very reason. I nuzzled into the soft rabbit fur that lined my hood and thought of Lily lovingly sewing the cloak herself. It had taken a long time to wash away Jurgen's blood, but eventually I'd managed to remove all traces of it.

The light faded fast once we entered the shaded reaches of the wood, but the road remained clear and wide enough for us to pass comfortably. After going a good distance into the woods, the cabin came into sight, though 'cabin' was not quite the right term, as it was a good deal larger than any of the true cottages which we had passed in the farming region. It was a solid, square building, two storeys in height. The lower level was made of large, dark grey stone blocks, similar to the ones that had been used in the castle, and the upper level was aged wood, brick, and plaster. This second level had been an afterthought added by a later generation. There were also numerous outbuildings, accommodation for horses, chickens, and servants. Though we had set off early in the morning, by the time we had arrived and unpacked all of my supplies, night had fallen, so that I could only make out the barest details of the cabin and its surroundings.

Paulus lit a fire in the hearth for me and the ladies – though I could have done it myself with a simple spell – and we sat huddled close to it as we ate cold cuts of meat, bread, and cheese that we had brought with us. The men ate outside by the light of their own fire, while Inge, Katerina, and I were accommodated inside. As the king's former hunting lodge, it was sumptuously equipped. There were eight bedrooms in all, plus the servants' accommodations out the back. I invited the men to sleep in the house with us, but Paulus insisted on maintaining the class distinctions between the men and the ladies, and advised they would be content in the servants' quarters.

Katerina and Inge seemed to find the quiet of the woods, broken occasionally by the screech of an owl or the rattle of windows in a strong breeze, unnerving, and chose to sleep in the same bedroom, while I slept in the largest and grandest bedroom. I didn't care for the style of decoration; there were too many stuffed deer and boar heads for my taste. I decided that my first order of business in the morning would be to ask the men to remove them.

The bed, on the other hand, was beautiful. It was enormous and fashioned of carved oak, with four posters supporting a green velvet canopy, with matching green velvet hangings and quilts. The large windows set into two of the four walls were hung with dark green damask drapes. A large stone fireplace was set into the wall, Silvanian unicorns carved into the stone mantle on either side. I looked forward to sitting by it when the nights became colder. But years of neglect had taken their toll on the place; the whole room was dusty, with cobwebs so thick they resembled brown rags hanging from the ceiling, the corners of the windows, and even in the fireplace itself, but it was nothing I couldn't remedy given a little time. Sadly, I didn't know any domestic magic that would clean the house for me, and cursed myself for not bothering to learn any. We had servants for everything at the castle, so it had never occurred to me I might need to learn how to clean, magically or otherwise. My mother was right, living alone would present challenges I'd never even considered before.

"I'll just have to deal with all that tomorrow," I told myself, lighting a fire in the hearth with magic and hoping it would help with the mustiness of the air.

Flinging back the bearskin furs that covered the bed sent up a cloud of hazy dust, making me choke a little. At least the bedding beneath looked clean enough, with no signs of mould or rot. I undressed myself with a little difficulty, appreciating the independence I had when I wore my breeches and simple tunic, but not wanting to bother Inge and Katerina, who were probably already asleep. I shrugged on my nightgown and slipped beneath the green coverlets, shivering against the sheets, which were cold, the kind of cold so deep it feels damp, and there was a musty, festering smell to them which felt acrid in my nostrils. I resolved that before I began doing any magic, my first task was to make the cabin, or at least the rooms I planned to use, habitable.

* * * *

The next morning Paulus, his men, and my two ladies set to helping me with my domestic woes. Old, moth-eaten carpets were rolled up and stored in one of the many extra bedrooms, along with several stuffed animal heads; bedding and curtains were washed; windows dusted and opened; and everything made generally clean. I heard Inge complain of doing servant's work and the toll it would take on her soft hands and Katerina telling her to get on with the task and stop moaning, and I stifled a little giggle. When they had done as much as possible to make the house comfortable and it no longer smelled of dust and damp, they all departed. The delay would mean they would have to break their journey at nightfall, as they'd lost a good deal of daylight while we had worked.

"You look after yourself, your highness," Paulus said solemnly. "I'd hate to hear you were slacking in your training; remember, you can practise any time, any place if you're motivated enough. And I expect you to stay motivated," he added with a growl.

"Now, now, Paulus, any more of that talk and I'll think you're worried about me," I teased.

"No, your highness. I know there's no need to worry about you. I've been meaning to say as well: I'm very sorry about your sister, she was a good girl."

That brought a stab of sadness to my chest, and I felt the pricking of tears at the backs of my eyes. To my surprise, Paulus' eyes seemed a little cloudy as well. Overtaken by a sudden impulse, I pulled him into a tight hug, which he shockingly returned, tightening his arms just a little for a few moments before letting me go.

"That's enough of that. You stay safe now," he said gruffly, turning away from me and mounting his horse. I just nodded, afraid I might cry if I spoke.

Paulus nudged his horse with his heel, and they set off. I watched their procession down the small drive that led to the road until they were out of sight, their progress swallowed up by the lush, jewel-toned forest, and for a moment I was a little sad, at a loss for what to do with myself; I had never been this alone before.

*I have never been this alone before.* The thought seized me, and I burst into manic, delirious laughter. How wonderful to be, for the first time in my entire life, utterly alone. I could do as I pleased, not adhering to anyone else's plans or rules. I could eat when I was hungry, sleep when I was tired. This felt like the greatest luxury I had ever experienced.

I was eager to set about making the potion to wake Lily, but there were practicalities to attend to first. I gave Bastian, who was in a small paddock by the lodge, a biscuit of hay, then set about ordering the house the way I wanted it, the boxes of magic books and potion ingredients still sitting untouched, as I'd instructed the men to leave them.

I lit a fire in the kitchen and made a stew from beef and vegetables I had brought with me. It wasn't nearly as good as the food I had at home, the potatoes too soft and the beef on the chewy side, all of it a little bland, but I had made it myself and was proud all the same. Next, I unpacked all my belongings and laid them away in my room. Finally, I brought out the herbs, plants, other potion ingredients, books, and tools for my witchcraft, and organised them neatly in the kitchen. This would be my workspace, for making potions was not so very different to cooking, and many of the things I needed like scales, knives, and stirring spoons were at hand there already.

The potion I planned to make to free Lily would take two weeks to mature, with each element needing to be prepared in the correct way and added exactly at the specified time. I set about it, crushing dried lavender, finely chopping dandelion roots, steeping chanterelles, shredding white sage, and generally readying all my ingredients until my fingertips were stained a ripe green and smelled like a herbalist's garden. I made a strong brew of liquorice root, fennel, and cinnamon, and when it had reduced and reached a warm golden colour, I began adding the other ingredients.

It took less time than I'd imagined to combine everything and set it to simmer, and having done all I could, I felt listless, my entire purpose in coming here now basically achieved. I paced around the cabin, absently picking items up and putting them back down somewhere else. I went from room to room removing objects that still lingered and offended my sense of taste, like paintings of ugly ancestors standing over dead animals, or fur throws with bear heads still attached to them.

The entire hunting lodge was adorned with these things, and I was quite horrified by how disrespectful it all was; celebrating killing animals for sport and displaying their hides as though they were trophies. While I ate meat and used animal parts for magic as I needed to, I never wanted to glorify their killing or mount them on walls for others to admire. The more magic I did, the more I felt connected to the land and the plants and animals who inhabited it. I was disgusted by the unnecessary killing of these creatures, the revelry in taking the life of something weaker, the blatant disregard for their right to live peacefully. How could their be pride in killing something that had no way to defend itself?

These thoughts depressed me, and to escape them, I threw on my blue cloak, and set out into the surrounding woods to explore and stretch my legs. Autumn had settled in, and the trees around the lodge were turning the most beautiful shades of gold, scarlet, amber, saffron, and burgundy, glowing jewel-bright as the sun shone through their leaves, illuminating their delicate veins.

A basket in my hand and my pouch at my waist, I set off to discover what bounty this place had to offer. Meandering between the trees, I found mushrooms to use both for magic and for eating. I also found vervain, henbane, deadly nightshade, Lady's Mantle, and artemisia, all of them used in potion making. The cabin sat in a wide clearing, but I wandered further and further from it, into the heart of the beautiful wood, unafraid of getting lost.

I had been wandering for what seemed a long time, picking berries or stopping to collect poppies, when a sharp screech of pain split the air and set my heart thumping wildly. It was a high, animal-sounding cry, and resonated with terror. I had no idea what animal it belonged to, but I drew my dagger and followed the sound quickly. The cry came again from not far off, and I quickly saw that the sound originated from a small fox, whose rear leg was caught in the cruel metal jaws of a hunter's trap.

I ran to its side and dropped to my knees, trying to free it. The poor creature had a look of sheer terror on its face when it saw me, clearly having learned to fear humans. I released the spring in the trap and the fox leapt free. It made to run away from me, but the injury to its leg was too painful and it collapsed on the ground before it had gone more than a single step, a high whine coming from its mouth. I moved towards it slowly, wanting to pick it up, and it snapped its jaws at me weakly, terror filling its wide brown eyes.

"It's alright, little one," I whispered softly. "I won't hurt you."

I took off my cloak and wrapped the fox in it so it couldn't struggle and injure itself further, then hurried back to the cabin, the little creature's cries of fear and pain making my own heart tremble and hurrying my steps. Back at the lodge, I gently unwrapped the fox and placed a calming spell over it. I saw it was a female, a vixen. Under the influence of the calming spell, she stayed still, and I was able to salve her wound with a healing balm and dress the injured leg. Mercifully, no bones appeared to be broken, and I hoped in time she would recover and I could release her back into the woods.

With the spell taking effect, she slept before the hearth, looking peaceful. After being alone for just one day, I was not longing for human company, but I liked having her there, a warm, quiet presence. As she slept, I stroked her soft, orange fur. Though I didn't plan to keep her, I had to call her something, so I named her Artemis for the goddess of the hunt and wild animals.

I kept Artemis inside most of the time while her leg healed, only letting her out under my supervision into the little enclosed garden at the back of the cabin. In the evenings she would lie on her side in front of the fire as I scratched her behind her ears or on her belly. When I went to bed she would follow me and sleep curled up next to my feet. With the care of a witch, she healed quickly and began terrorising the chickens I'd bought from a nearby farm if she got the chance, and I knew it was time to set her free. So, one day, with a tear in my eye, I opened the front door and allowed her to run outside. Leaping over the threshold, so happy to be outdoors, she bounded around and frolicked and yapped her pleasure. She dove among piles of fallen dried leaves and chased after a butterfly. At first, she stayed close to the cabin, but as she played, she moved further and further away. I watched her run out of sight, then sat on the porch and cried, my head in my hands; I'd grown attached to her. Then I felt something wet on my hand and looked down to see Artemis beside me, pressing her wet nose against my hand, her tail waving gently, her big eyes showing concern at my sobs.

It seemed she was not yet ready to part, either.

* * * *

It had taken two weeks, but my potion was finally ready. To be sure it would be safe as well as effective, I tested it on a wood pigeon I had caught. First, I gave the bird some of the sleeping draught I was quite sure my mother had used on Lily, which caused it to fall into an unshakeable sleep. Then I administered my potion, and its eyes flew open, its wings flapping wildly, as though I had startled it. Satisfied that neither potion was harmful, I tested them both again, this time on Artemis, crossing my fingers and praying that she would be alright. Again, I was able to wake her with my own brew. I felt giddy with excitement. My preference would have been to test them on myself, but I had no way of waking myself if I took the sleeping potion. I'd simply have to trust that I'd done it right.

I was as confident in my work as I could be as I set off to see Marie and Otto, Artemis chasing along beside Bastian as we rode. The ride to their cottage took several hours, but I couldn't wait until the following day, I was far too excited. I leapt from Bastian as I arrived, tying the reins to a tree and leaving him and Artemis together before I ran to the door of the cottage.

Marie opened the door and smiled when she saw me, greeting me as though I was an old friend. I was touched by her kindness – it was what I imagined it would be like to have a grandmother, never having one of my own to compare it to.

"How is she?" I asked stupidly.

"The same, dear," Marie replied in her husky voice, a sad smile on her withered lips.

"And you and Otto, are you well?"

"As well as can be. Otto's rheumatism is playing up now that it's getting colder, but that's just old age for you."

"I have a salve that would help," I said, gratefully accepting a cup of steaming tea from her.

"That would be lovely, dear," she said. I wondered whether she had any suspicions that I might be a witch; she was so sharp and observant, I wouldn't have been surprised if she guessed as much. If she did, she never let on to me.

I excitedly administered the potion to Lily, telling Marie I had convinced another witch to brew it for me. I placed a few drops on Lily's lips and waited. Nothing happened. I opened her mouth slightly and poured in more of the liquid, my pulse thrumming wildly in expectant excitement. Still nothing happened: she didn't so much as stir, even though the minutes ticked by as I waited patiently. Finally, I poured the whole flask down her throat, then sat beside her for an hour, waiting for her to wake. But she didn't.

Night had fallen by that time, and Otto was back from tending to his pigs and cattle. He and Marie sat down to a meagre dinner, which they offered to share with me, but I declined. I had no appetite and chose to keep my vigil at my sister's side instead. When they invited me to stay the night, I gratefully accepted, sleeping on a hard couch Otto and I dragged into Lily's tiny, now very crowded room. I waited all night and all morning, barely dozing, listening intently for any changes in her breathing and half-expecting her to wake at any moment, but she continued in her unshakable slumber all night long.

In the morning, having barely slept a wink, I heavily made my way out of Lily's room, closing the door behind me. I left a bag of gold with Otto and Marie for their kindness, their eyes both going round at the fat pouch filled with money. Disappointed in myself, I returned to the cabin to make another attempt at brewing a potion to wake my sister, a steady rain pounding on Bastian, Artemis, and me as we made our way home, the journey, already long and tedious was made more so by the constant downpour.

Back home, warm and dry, I once again found myself poring over the books my mother had leant me, looking for a way to wake Lily. There were charms, hexes, enchantments, potions, tonics, draughts. There were ways to curse a person to eternal sleeplessness, there were cures for sleepwalking, there were draughts to stimulate the mind and combat sleepiness. But none of these were what I needed.

The thing that vexed me was that the potion I had just tired on Lily should have been the one to wake her. It was the opposite, the antidote to the potion for deathless sleep, which I was certain was what my mother had used; all its symptoms were evident in

Lily's unshakeable sleep. Of course, my mother was a very skilled witch, with decades' more experience than me, so it was possible that I had made a mistake, or that she had done something to alter the formula of the potion. I had read that witches did, from time to time, add or alter the ingredients they used to make changes to how the formula worked. It made sense. Witches were the ones to invent potions in the first place, so why wouldn't they alter them further down the line? One witch might find a better way of doing things, and so develop her own unique brew.

The problem that faced me now was that the only way to find the right blend of ingredients to wake Lily would be by trial and error, and I had no way of knowing how long that would take. Time wore on, and most of the leaves had now fallen from the trees, littering the ground like brown ghosts of their former selves. A chill settled over the woods to match the chilliness of my mood as I continued to count the days, weeks, and months Lily had been in her cursed sleep, and the amount of time I had continued to fail her.

* * * *

One crisp morning I was walking through the forest gathering herbs, Artemis gambolling along at my side, when I heard a fierce, terrifying bellow split the air, piercing the calm quiet of the woods. Artemis' head snapped up attentively and she let out a whine, before turning tail and running back in the direction of the cabin. "Coward," I muttered under my breath, as I carried on towards the sound, just as I had the day I found Artemis, sure that another unfortunate animal had been caught in the poacher's traps.

In the weeks since my arrival at the cabin, I had come across a number of these traps, which I had destroyed each time, but there always seemed to be more, though I never encountered anyone else in my wanderings through the woods, and had never seen who set the traps. I had seen a wolf recently with only three legs and assumed it had also been caught in a trap and chosen to chew its leg off rather than be killed. I hated the things, and wished the men who set them would be caught in their own traps, the metal jaws pinning them in place without food or water until someone came to check them.

The animal had stopped its ear-splitting howling, but I could still hear it struggling, a moan of pain reaching me every so often as I searched for the trap. I soon found the source of the noise; a great, black bear, caught in a trap just as I had suspected, one of its feet pierced by the horrible trap's iron teeth. The bear was enormous, taller than any man I had ever seen and three times as broad. Up close, I saw its fur was darkest brown, almost black in colour, and it had long, black claws, huge, brown eyes, and large, sharp-looking teeth, which it bared at me when it caught my scent, hackles rising threateningly.

The bear saw me and growled, a deep, low, rumbling sound, swiping at me as I dared take a step closer. I wouldn't be able to free it as easily as I had freed Artemis, not without losing a limb myself in the process. The poor creature was frightened, trapped, and injured; no wonder it was wary of me. I closed my eyes and called up my power to cast an enchantment over the animal, making it calm, docile, and unafraid of me.

My eyes were still closed as I listened and heard the bear grow still, its breathing becoming slower, steadier. I opened my eyes and saw that its own were half-closed, as though heavy with sleep, its pupils no longer contracted in pain. I took a step closer, and it did nothing; it didn't flinch or snap or growl. I could sense his great heart beating a slow, steady rhythm. I moved another step closer, and then another, until I was almost touching it.

He stood on his back legs, one of which was caught in the trap, and his head reached almost three feet above my own. Anxiety quickened my pulse at being so close to such an enormous, dangerous animal, but I was confident that my spell had him in its grasp and that he would remain calm. For now. I had to draw my eyes away from his face as I stooped to loosen the mechanism of the trap, and it sprung open. Gently, he pulled his foot free of it, testing his weight on the foot, then he dropped down to all fours, so our faces were suddenly, frighteningly level. While he was still calm, I looked into his lovely brown eyes, like warm pools of honey and deep brown earth. He was a beautiful creature, and though a sensible voice in my head said it was unwise, I couldn't resist the urge to touch him. Slowly, I reached out, placing the palm of my hand on his snout, just below his eyes.

"Hello, beautiful boy," I murmured.

My hand still touching him, I felt as though I was knocked back by a violent wind. Though my eyes were open, I saw a different scene suddenly appear before me, but through the eyes of someone else: a man. I looked down and saw my large, long-fingered, masculine hands, my legs clad in breeches and boots. Before me stood a beautiful young woman with long, golden hair, big blue eyes, and a full, rosy mouth. But she twisted her lips to form a cruel sneer. She uttered something I did not understand, and then there was a blinding flash of light. When the light faded and I could see again, the woman was gone, and when I looked down, there were giant black paws where my hands had been only a moment before. I had been transformed into a great, black bear.

The light flashed once again, and I was back in my own body, standing face-to-face with the bear on the forest floor. During the vision, my spell to calm him had lifted, and the bear, still standing just in front of me, let loose an almighty roar that set my very bones trembling, then reared onto its back legs. Frightened, I fell back and grabbed for my blade, but knew it would not be enough to protect me from the massive animal before me. The bear dropped back to all fours, sniffed at me, pausing in an almost appraising sort of way, before it turned and sprinted off into the trees at a terrific pace.

Though shaken by the encounter, I walked around the forest for some time after that, searching and calling for the bear, but it was no use, he was gone. I hadn't really expected him to respond, but I had to try, to see if I could learn more about my vision. I returned to the cabin, where I found Artemis curled up on the porch waiting for me.

"Shall I let you inside, you big coward? What would your goddess namesake say of your running away?"

She squeaked at me in an offended way as I opened the door. She bolted inside and went immediately to hide under my bed.

"Good thing one of us isn't scared of everything," I called after her, but she ignored me.

With early winter now upon us, the cabin was icy cold, buffeted by frigid winds, and the sun only made a rare appearance through the dense grey clouds overhead. I lit a fire and helped myself to some stew, sitting close to the flames as I ate, then fell to contemplating what I had seen and felt.

The encounter with the bear had affected me deeply. Or rather the encounter with the man, who had been turned into a bear, for that must have been what I saw in the vision it had shown me. Had it been an ordinary bear, I had no doubt that I would be dead now. I wondered if the vision had been the bear trying to communicate with me, to tell me who he really was. Or perhaps it was an effect of whatever spell the witch had used on him. Whatever the cause, it was odd that I had gotten a vision from him, never having had one before.

It was unlike any magic I had ever attempted myself, though I knew that there were many stories of witches transforming people into animals, usually as punishment for misdeeds or slights against them. But the bear – or man, rather – had not seemed bad, I'd gotten no sense of evil from him.

The realisation surprised me: how did I know what he was like? It was something I had sensed unconsciously, the way I had sensed Christian and Lily were in love, the foreboding sense that I had had about Jurgen. I had never sensed anything about my mother, though, whether because my sense did not work on witches or because she had used a spell to repel me, I didn't know. Maybe there was nothing to it at all, and I had just spent too much time alone and was imagining things. That certainly seemed likely.

In any case, much as it intrigued me, the mystery of the man who was a bear was something I didn't have time to focus on right now; Lily was my priority.

I made two more new variations on my waking draught for Lily, which I planned to try on her soon, before I headed back to the castle, at least for a few weeks. I knew if I spent too long away there was a chance my mother would come looking for me herself. Plus, my supplies were beginning to run low, and I was not good enough at foraging to be able to survive here throughout the winter by myself. Besides, a small, traitorous part of me missed my mother.

Again, I visited Marie and Otto, hoping desperately one of my brews would succeed in waking Lily, but neither of the new potions wrought any change whatsoever. Just as had happened the first time, I tried first a few drops, and then more, then almost the whole flask of each. Finally, I tried mixing them together and administering them that way, but nothing happened, and Lily did not so much as stir.

She looked peaceful, but I wondered what it must be like for her, stuck in this magical sleep. Did she dream? Was she conscious of anything that happened around her? When, or if, I finally woke her, would she remember anything that had happened since she fell asleep? Would she still be my Lily? These were all questions I could ask if I ever got the potion right. Not that I needed another reason not to give up; I had already determined that I would keep trying until either I succeeded, or I died.

# Chapter Eleven

I rode back to the cabin in the dying light, and it was fully night by the time I arrived back home. Home. It was strange, but that was what the cabin had become to me now, with only Artemis, Bastian, Nox, and my magic for company. The idea of returning to the castle in which I had lived my whole life up until a few weeks ago now filled me with an overwhelming sense of dread. I wouldn't just be returning to my lying, manipulating, murderous mother, but to the continual rationing and management of my time, my meals, my clothes, and most especially, my magic.

But after my latest failure with Lily, I had determined to return to the castle for a few weeks, to prevent my mother from sending someone to come get me, or worse, her coming herself, her recent messages having subtly probed for an indication of when I would return. Winter had settled in early this year, or perhaps just in the northern part of Silvaner where the cabin was. Snow had begun to collect in little white banks on the ground, like puddles of clouds escaped from the sky. The forest smelled beautiful in the cold, the sharpness of the chill dulling the musky, loamy scent of the slumbering trees and their long-discarded leaves. But I would have to return to the castle sooner or later, with Christmas fast approaching.

I'd kept up a grudging sort of correspondence with my mother while I had been away, giving her regular, though vague, updates of my doings, many of which were fabricated to conceal my true purpose. The first time I sent off a message with Nox, it felt like the most quintessentially witchy thing I had ever done. Now that I'd determined to return home for a time, I wrote a short note asking her to send an escort to collect me in three days' time, tied this message to the crow's leg, and set him loose into the air. I'd had some doubts as to whether or not this would work the first time I tried it, but when my mother's reply came the same day, I ceased questioning Nox's reliability as a messenger.

I sent Christian updates when I had something worth sharing in the same way, though so far, I had only failures to report. The first reply I got back, he had written:

*I see the stories of animals doing witches' bidding are true! This creature fluttered at my window until I let it in to deliver your note, then would not leave until I had responded. If only humans were so loyal! Thank you for the news, though I hate to think of her still bewitched. I hope you have success soon. Be careful when you return home and take care of yourself.*

*Ever eager for your news,*

*Christian.*

My escort home arrived exactly when I'd expected it, Paulus with three of his men and Carlotta and Anna arriving a few hours after nightfall because of the short winter days. As before, they had spent the whole day journeying to me and needed to rest the night. We set off before the sun had fully risen the next morning, riding hard all day and still reaching the castle well after the sky had turned an inky black and a glowing, half-moon peered down at us from overhead. Bastian relished the chance to stretch his legs on the long ride, but Artemis did not take well to being kept in a basket for most of the journey and snubbed me for a time after we arrived, her expression accusing and disgruntled.

My mother greeted me with warmth and enthusiasm, a broad smile on her lovely face as I entered the main receiving hall.

"My darling girl, I am so pleased you are home! How have you been?" Then in an eager undertone, as she embraced me briefly, she asked, "How is your craft going?"

"I think I am progressing well. I'm learning that failure can be one of the best teachers," I replied irritably.

"Then you are wiser than most of my privy council," she said with a laugh, linking her arm through mine.

"You seem well, happy, even," I observed, trying not to sound bitter.

"It seems running the kingdom agrees with me, my daughter. And if I may say, it seems I agree with the kingdom. The harvest was a great success, the city saw a wonderful increase in profits over our summer and autumn with trade and tourism both up by a good deal, there are fewer beggars than ever, and the coffers are full, with only a slight raise of taxes. It has been, though I say it myself, a wonderful year for Silvaner." She beamed with pride.

Though it sounded like a speech she would make to her councillors, I had to admit that even though she was a would-be child-killer, she was no tyrant terrorising a kingdom. In fact, she was an excellent queen. She understood how the kingdom needed to be run and she had a kind of reserved compassion for everyone in her care, down to the humblest peasant. It seemed to genuinely matter to her that those she ruled were as happy as they could be. As always, this made it harder to believe the cruel things she had done.

"You really care for the people, don't you?" I asked, shaking my head slightly at what seemed like irreconcilable sides of her personality.

"Of course," she replied warmly, squeezing my hand affectionately. "Without them we would not have a kingdom. You must remember when you are queen, Rose, that poverty breeds unhappiness, and unhappiness breeds rebellion. To keep your kingdom prosperous, you must do your best for everyone in it."

"So, it pays to keep people happy?" I replied cynically.

She nodded her assent.

Artemis, reappeared and trotted to my side, rubbing her face against my leg. It seemed she had forgiven me for the bumpy trip in a small, enclosed space.

"Ah, you even have a *familiar,*" my mother exclaimed in a quietly thrilled tone. "That says quite a lot about your abilities, you know. Not all witches can acquire a familiar. Animals are clever, intuitive creatures, especially foxes. She must have sensed your power beckoning. Be sure to train her well." I didn't mention that I had found her in a trap, leaving my mother to think it had been some fated alliance instead.

"Have you ever had one?"

"Once, a long time ago," she said abruptly, but she did not elaborate. As always, she kept so much of her life before she became queen a secret. But then, she still kept things from me now, so I shouldn't have been surprised.

Being back at court was jarring after the freedom of the cabin. My time was no longer my own to do with as I pleased, for there were meetings to attend, ladies with whom tea had to be taken, and dances to be learned, always with Anna, Katerina, Inge, and Carlotta trailing along in my wake like baby ducklings. More than that, though, the stone walls felt claustrophobic and crowded after the quiet and solitude of the cabin, the wilderness and fresh smells of the forest. I wondered how courtiers could bear it, spending so much of their time cooped up in the castle, jostling for power and popularity, when they all had estates of their own to which they could retire in peace and privacy.

Even roaming the castle gardens did nothing to lift my spirits, as it had when I was a child. Compared to the wild beauty of the forest, the gardens were artificial, insipid, and cramped, especially with the beds barren and frostbitten in the early winter chill.

Christmas came, bringing great, smothering drifts of snow, blanketing every inch of the castle and much of the surroundings in several feet of frozen, impenetrable walls of ice. What fell in the city turned to ugly, grey slush and gave the streets and houses a grimy, unwholesome appearance. All I could think of was how different this Christmas would be because Lily was not here for it. I commissioned Carlotta to go into the town and ensure that a basket of fruit, meats, wine, and cakes was sent to Otto and Marie's cottage. I also gave her a pot of salve to include for Otto's rheumatism. She looked utterly perplexed when I gave her these instructions but carried them out dutifully nonetheless.

There was a grand Christmas ball, attended by all the nobles from across the kingdom who were not prevented by the heavy snowfalls. I wore a beautiful gown of dark amber brocade and was asked to dance at every opportunity, but I felt guilty for the enjoyment of it when Lily was many miles off, locked in a perpetual sleep.

Besides, the attention I was receiving was mostly due to my new position as heir apparent, and the knowledge irked me. Would any of the men begging for a dance have cared about me at all if I were not a princess, a future queen? Would any of the ladies have sought out my company and conversation, paid me endless streams of compliments, if they hadn't been angling for a special position in my court or the royal household? I had no way of knowing for sure, but I was confident it was my status that attracted them all to me, rather than anything about me personally.

A lord named Marco, who was reported to be very wealthy, and who was not unpleasant-looking, paid me extra-special attention, offering delicate, thoughtful compliments and appearing to listen avidly when I spoke. He suggested I step outside with him for some fresh air, but I had learned from my last such encounter and declined the offer. He looked crestfallen, but rallied quickly, asking me for another dance, which I also declined, saying I was too tired, when in truth I was just bored with his company. I watched as he slunk away, his pride wounded, and my mother appeared silently at my elbow.

"You are wise, my dear," she said quietly. "He is not so gentlemanly as he appears, and I have it on good authority his accounts are not as healthy as he professes, either."

"Do people ever tell the truth?" I asked bitterly, slumping down onto a bench and reaching for a glass of wine from a nearby table.

"Men do, sometimes, if it will work to their advantage. But I believe it is best to treat all they say as a lie until you can verify it is not."

"And what about women? Do they never lie?" I asked ironically, knowing that of course they did, and my mother was an example of the worst kind.

"Women are altogether much trickier to handle, especially noble ones, because what they want is not always so obvious as with men. With women you need to be one step ahead, so you aren't outmanoeuvred."

"So I've gathered," I replied drily. "That's not a very cheery message for Christmas." I took a large gulp from the wine glass and deposited it back on the table.

"How about this: you are a woman of power and beauty, not to mention a rather unique set of *other* skills. You need not accept a man unless he pleases you. And I have no doubt your wits are a match for anyone at court, man or woman. Your fate is in your own hands."

I smiled despite my bad mood.

"That is somewhat better," I said. "Merry Christmas, Mother."

Most of the time I was so angry with my mother I could hardly stand to speak to her, but then she would say or do something to soften my feelings again. I could never put what she had done to Lily entirely out of my mind, but I justified any warmth or affection I showed her by telling myself I was doing what was needed to preserve the ruse that I knew nothing of what she had done. But much as I felt I should, I could not bring myself to hate her.

There were the customary Christmas treats and events, twelve whole days of celebration and a holiday for the entire kingdom. There was the usual excess of eating, drinking, and playing games. Once again, I - accompanied by Carlotta, Anna, and Katerina - visited villages, distributing grain, fruit, and toys for the children.

Again, I felt the weight of my privilege, the plentiful food, comfort, and good health I enjoyed. I decided then and there that if I ever did become queen, I would not only work to comfort our kingdom's poorest at Christmas, but all year round.

I thought of Lily often, and by extension, of Marie and Otto. I hoped they were warm enough, that they had enough to eat. I knew they should be well, that the bags of gold I had given them were more than enough to see them through this harsh winter.

I thought of the bear-man, too. I wondered if he was hibernating, as real bears did, or if he was still prowling that icy forest. I debated whether I should ask my mother about him. Would she know how to reverse the spell? What were the chances that she knew the witch who had cast it?

That question birthed a host of others in my mind. Were there other witches nearby, and how many? Did she know them? It had been her mother who taught her witchcraft, but had all the women in her family been witches? These were all questions I had never thought to ask her before; I had been so preoccupied with my own magical education. I even thought there might be a chance that another witch could help me wake Lily.

One bitterly cold and snowy day, my mother and I sat in her rooms before a roaring fire. For a change, she was neither busy with royal duties nor toiling in her workroom. We sat in contented silence: she was sketching a design for a tapestry, and I was reading a book on alchemy. There were no ladies-in-waiting or courtiers hovering, it was just she and I. Taking advantage of this rare occurrence, I posed the questions I had been brooding over.

"Are there other witches?" I asked suddenly.

"Of course. Did you think it was just we two?" She laughed, as though the idea was terribly funny.

"Where? Who? Do you know any?"

"Well, they are everywhere, I imagine. Certainly all over the continent, and likely all over the world. Though, I believe witchcraft takes different forms in different places, or rather, different schools of magic are more commonly practiced, depending on where you go."

I nodded, gazing into the dancing flames of the crackling fire.

"As to who, as I told you: magic typically runs in bloodlines. Most of the women of our family have been witches, though not all have chosen to take up the craft, either out of fear or lack of aptitude. Or perhaps plain ignorance."

She was silent a few moments before she continued.

"For your final question, no. I would not say I *know* any other witches. I know *of* some, and I have crossed paths with others in my time. But I am not the social kind. I have never wanted to belong to a coven, unless you count the period of time before my mother died. Though two witches hardly makes a coven."

That tracked. She was independent, and likely thought herself above other witches, in skill and in social rank, which of course she was.

"When did your mother die?" I asked softly.

"Before I married my first husband," she said sharply, giving me a look that discouraged further questions on the subject.

"Have you ever known a witch to turn someone into an animal, like a bear, for instance?" I asked, returning to my earlier line of questioning and trying to keep my voice casual, disinterested, even.

"Not personally, but it's not uncommon for our kind to transform people into animals. Usually it's in self-defence, or if the person has offered us some great insult, broken a bargain, or something like that. That is, if they deserve it. Of course, some of the most famous witches in history have done it for their own entertainment. At least, that's what the stories would have us believe."

"Have you ever done it?" I was truly curious.

"No. Why bother? It's a waste of magic. If someone offends or threatens you that badly, just wipe them out entirely." I felt chills down my back. She said it with such casual ruthlessness.

"Although," she added, "turning someone into a beetle or a spider might be amusing. Something small and odious. Something to be crushed under your heel," she added with a malicious glint in her eye, smiling like a serpent at the idea.

There was another long silence while I processed this, thinking about what it said about her that she could talk of killing, of destroying someone's life in such a casual way. Did she think Lily had threatened her, and therefore deserved her fate? I suspected she did.

"Will you return to the cabin?" she asked, rousing me from my meditations.

"Yes."

"When?"

"As soon as is practical without arousing too much gossip," I replied, stroking the head of Artemis, who was curled up beside me.

My mother nodded, thoughtful.

"Good. I am glad to see you so invested in your craft. I remember how I felt when I was first stretching the limits of my magic. It was like a restless energy inside me that demanded to be let out. Never let that passion die, Rose. It does a witch no good to deny their magic." Her eyes took on a faraway look; I wondered how she had suffered while my father had lived, when she had been forced to suppress her magic and endure other kinds of cruelty.

* * * *

At least at Christmas I had been busy, every hour of the day filled with some activity or other. With the festivities over, I fell back into a pattern of listlessness. I had no meaningful activity to occupy me, and it was deeply frustrating. I trained with Paulus whenever our schedules allowed for it, and still spent a little time working on my magic, but as soon as I left the training rooms or my mother's workroom, I grew bored and irritable again. What I really wanted was to know more about what was happening in the kingdom, how my mother was ruling, but I was still barred from private council meetings.

She would give me a summary afterwards, but it wasn't the same as hearing their debates and arguments firsthand. It did give me a good idea of what running a kingdom entailed, the many, many facets of it. There was the obvious, of course. Taxes, harvests, law-making, and punishments for those who did not abide by law. But there was also the diplomacy needed, which I suspected had to be learned through practice rather than theory.

Silvaner was a small but wealthy kingdom. Our excellent soil yielded the best grains, fed the best cattle, and the small wine region in the west produced some of the best sweet wines on the continent, next to the kingdom of Malbourg, which was renowned for its much larger wine region. We relied so little on trade, but in a sense that only made us more dependent on good diplomacy. This was why my mother was so protective of the kingdom's independence and had been wary of brokering a union with Altenburg, why she was so diligent in her hospitality to visiting dignitaries and wealthy traders.

Of course, the winter months were quiet, as the snow prevented all but the most motivated travellers anywhere to the south from visiting Silvaner. So winter was often spent forming plans for the coming year, essential but tedious work.

It was all a learning experience, and though – provided my plans came to fruition – I never expected to rule, it was illuminating to gain a deeper insight into my mother's duties as queen.

Yet I loathed to sit about, listening to gossip, reading, or sewing, when I should be finding a cure for Lily. Even working at my craft held little appeal to me, as I could not work on developing the potion right under my mother's nose. So, I read. I read every book of magic I could lay my hands on. I even searched the royal library, though I only found what I had expected: treatises against witchcraft, accounts of the sins of witches and their persecution, stories of the unnaturalness of wiccans. I slammed shut book after dusty old book, leaving the library in disgust for the first time in my life.

By the end of January, I had reached the end of my patience. I had told my mother I would stay until the snow melted, when the journey to the cabin would be a little easier, but I grew more restless each day. Finally, I visited her in her study and told her I felt I had to leave. The journey north to the cabin was not so hard as the journey south, so my decision was not entirely unreasonable.

"I'm surprised you have stayed so long," she said, smiling enigmatically. "I thought you would be overpowered by the pull of your magic sooner. Oh, yes," she said, reading my expression. "I have known that feeling in my time. It was before I was married for the first time. I was younger than you, and still learning the depth of my abilities. I told my mother I must be freed from all other burdens, and she agreed. Of course, we were commoners then, and lived a distance from the nearest town, so I was not so closely watched as you are now. But I deeply appreciated the freedoms I had."

This was the most she had ever told me of her youth.

"You were born a commoner?" I asked, surprised.

"Oh, yes. Quite common. Quite poor. Until the wealthy Duke who owned the land on which we lived spied me walking in a field one day. He became quite besotted by me, and it was not long before he proposed marriage, with a little encouragement from me". I wondered if the encouragement had been magical, or merely physical. "Naturally, I accepted. It was a way to keep food in my family's mouths and a roof over their heads. And it made me a Duchess. Once my first husband died, it was not too far a stretch to go from Duchess to Queen. But there, I have become side-tracked. You should enjoy your magic and freedom while you can; it won't be too long before you become queen yourself, and your free time will be limited. You will go. Tomorrow, if you like. Go arrange your escort now."

I curtseyed and left, pleased to be free to return to the cabin. I wondered why she was so happy to part with me, so eager to send me on my way. Was there more to it than mere motherly care? I wondered, and not for the first time, if in time she would come to see me as a barrier to her power, as she had with Lily. What might she do then?

I pushed the thought from my mind, hoping I would not have to find out.

* * * *

Once again, I was on the road to the hunting lodge, accompanied by Katerina and Carlotta, along with four soldiers. Paulus was not with me this time; it seemed my mother had other duties for him. I burned with curiosity to know what, but I forced myself to focus on other issues. The most senior of the men escorting us was named Karl, who had a passing resemblance to Jurgen which made me uneasy. I was on edge the entire ride, my hand often going to my pocket, where my rune stones sat, as memories of being doused in Jurgen's blood, carving up his body, and burying the pieces floated, unwelcome, through my mind.

However, we made it to the cabin without incident and passed the night together quietly enough. I was sad to see Carlotta and Katerina go, as I'd become closer to them since Lily's disappearance, and even though I complained about always having the ducklings tailing me, watching them ride slowly down the sloping road away from the lodge and back towards the castle gave me a moment's sadness.

But I had enough to occupy me. As soon as they departed, I opened the front door and let Artemis out and she bolted free, streaking off into the woods for the first time in weeks. In spirit, I felt the same, finally liberated after weeks in the castle. I dressed in

185

my warmest clothes and threw my dark blue cloak over my shoulders, pressing my face into the fur lining for warmth, then wandered out into the forest. I walked aimlessly just for the sake of walking, like someone stretching their limbs after being confined in a small space for too long. I relished the sting of cold air in my nose and the crunch of snow and leaves underfoot, glad it had thawed enough for me to clear a path through the woods.

Again, I wondered what had become of the bear I had seen. I wondered if I would see him again, if I could help him. After my conversation with my mother on the subject, I had studied transformation when I had nothing else to do, and was sure I could cast a reversal spell, if only I could get close enough.

This, of course, was potentially risky. What if he attacked me in his human form? What if the spell went wrong and I only did him more harm? I weighed these factors but kept coming back to the thought that, if it was me who had been transformed into a bear, I wouldn't mind any risk if I had the chance, however slight, to be human again.

Of course, it was all moot unless I was able to track him down again. In the meantime, I practiced transforming and detransforming first objects, then creatures. I transformed Artemis into a wolf, which was easy, as they are so similar, but she had a touch of grey to her ginger fur for a few days after I turned her back. So I kept practising, doing more complex transformations each time until I felt sure I had mastered the spell. After I had successfully transformed Bastian into a snake and back again, I knew I was ready for the bear-man.

# Chapter Twelve

I developed yet another antidote for Lily and tested it yet again without success. I tried coupling spells with potions and still had no luck. I was starting to feel like the task I had set myself might be impossible, that my mother was too powerful for me to overcome her magic. Maybe I was foolish for even trying; I wasn't a fully-trained witch and my mother had decades' more experience on her side. Maybe I had set myself up for failure in even trying to beat her.

But I knew I would have no rest nor peace until I found a way to undo what had been done; for Lily's sake I had to keep trying. With another month of winter remaining the days were bitterly cold, snow or sleet falling in solid sheets, the chill seeping through my many layers of warm clothing and into my very bones. Some days I chose not to brave the elements but stayed nestled by the fire encased in a mountain of warm blankets, reading through the books on magic I had brought with me. There was still so much I didn't know about magic, and I didn't know when I would again have the leisure and freedom to study and practice in private again. So I worked my way through each of the heavy tomes one by one, practising new spells and enchantments as I went.

Defensive magic was one of my weaker subjects, but after working on them for a few days, my shield and concealment charms became much stronger, and I learned a binding spell, which could be used to freeze another witch's magic, at least for a short time. This last I thought could be useful against my mother if things became confrontational. I also worked on my transformations and illusions, growing slightly more skilled with each passing day, though I knew I was still no match for my mother.

I worked on my healing magic, eager to make sure Lily was perfectly well if I ever managed to wake her. From there, I practised more elemental magic, until I could conjure fire, wind, water, and earth with a flick of my wrist. Tired of the dried foods and meagre supply of vegetables I'd been able to bring with me, I set to growing my own vegetable garden, which soon thrived regardless of the biting cold, fed by my magic.

The more I practised, the stronger I felt, until my magic became a low thrum in my blood I could always feel, like a second pulse I'd never noticed before. I could sense that it *wanted* to be used, that if I kept it trapped for too long it might burst out of me on its own. That idea frightened me, and I made a mental note to talk about it with my mother when next I saw her.

As it was, there wasn't much time for it to reach that point, because I was now using my magic every day. I learned how to incorporate it into my physical training, too, using the wind to guide my daggers if I threw them, or conjuring a wall of fire to distance myself from my opponent.

Sometimes I felt ridiculous practising these things, with Bastian and Artemis watching on in a bemused sort of way. Even without a human audience, I got embarrassed when I'd fall or accidentally set my sleeves on fire, and threw them both dirty looks, warning them not to laugh, or to do whatever the animal equivalent of laughter was.

I kept busy, trying to keep my mind and skills sharp even as I continued to consider and test different alterations to the potion that might allow me to wake Lily.

Day by day, the snow on the ground receded further and further, and the buds on the trees began to shoot forth in tiny green bursts of life, the only thing marking the passage of time as I felt how little progress I had made in waking my sister: precisely zero. On fine days, I took long rides through the country with Bastian, Artemis trotting alongside us, or walks in the woods, in hopes of tiring my body and quieting my mind, my skin growing browner and my face lightly freckled as I spent more and more time out of doors. I thought maybe if I left the problem alone for a while, the solution might present itself to me, as often happens when one's mind is diverted. If I kept moving, Artemis gambolling along beside me, maybe I would stop feeling so utterly stuck in place.

It was on one of these walks that I saw the bear for a second time. It was splashing in a stream, trying to catch a fish. I watched it for a few minutes, frozen in place, careful not to alert it to my presence, but it must have caught my scent on the breeze because it turned sharply and looked in my direction. I was concealed behind a dense patch of trees more than twenty feet from the edge of the stream, but he knew I was there, his black nose twitching as the light breeze carried my scent towards him. Artemis ducked behind me, whining with fear at the massive bear standing so close to us.

Before he could either attack or run away, I cast the same spell as I had the first time, slowing his heart rate and calming his mind. I willed him to amble out of the river, to come towards me. I hadn't used an enchantment to control anything before, but it seemed to work, though I sensed his resistance to my will, like a puppet pulling against its strings. Slowly, still a little hesitant, I moved out of the trees, approaching him carefully despite the spell holding him. When we were about ten feet apart, I prepared to release him from the spell restraining him and started to ready myself for the transformation spell. I prayed the spell keeping him docile would hold while I also attempted to change him back, but I wasn't entirely confident in the strength of my powers. Maybe a more experienced witch could have done it with ease, but I knew the limits of my abilities, already feeling the strain of keeping such a large, powerful creature under my control.

This was the dangerous part: if he were going to attack me it would be now, when my powers were divided. When I began uttering the incantation to change him back into a human, I saw his pupils narrow and his nose quiver, sniffing the air and catching my scent again. He dropped to all fours, like his puppet strings had been cut, looking as though he meant to charge at me. Quickly, I uttered the words and cast my runic stones before me, praying that the spell would work, that I was not about to be shredded by a gigantic, hungry bear.

But I must have mastered more magic than I gave myself credit for; as soon as the words passed my lips, the bear was seized by an external force, thrown backwards, then frozen, hovering in midair for a few moments. He jerked this way and that, as though invisible ropes were attached to his limbs and head, tugging at him roughly. Then he collapsed on the ground, writhing as though in great pain, but no sound escaped him. I held my breath, fearing I'd hurt him.

In a moment he seemed to shrink, growing first shorter, then narrower. The dark fur began to recede into his body, showing pale, smooth, human skin. His long-clawed paws shortened and changed into graceful, human hands, the nails turning from black to pink. With each change of his body, I felt the magic drain from me, as if it were being siphoned off to allow the transformation to take place. I couldn't see his face, but I knew it, too, had changed, the long snout receding into a smaller, hairless face. Finally, the shuddering stopped, and he was entirely human once more. He lay on his front, face down in the grass, completely naked. At first, I thought he had died, or fainted from the pain of the transformation, but then he moved. It was just a twitch of his right hand at first, then his head turned to the side as he drew in deep, rasping breaths. Slowly, he pushed himself to his knees, marvelling at his hands, arms, chest, and legs as he did so.

He seemed not to remember or notice me, but knelt, touching his arms, feeling his face, amazed by his human form. I coughed to remind him I was there, forcing my eyes to remain on his face and not the naked body below it. I was more concerned with what he would do next than his leanly muscled body, anyway, I told myself. His eyes snapped to my face, looking hunted, fearful. Then he looked down at his body and, realising that he was naked, tried to cover himself with his hands, embarrassed and cold, the early spring air still carrying a chilling bite.

I quickly removed my cloak and tossed it to him, then turned away to give him some privacy, but only for a moment. When I heard him rise to his feet, I turned back to face him warily, my hand at my dagger, ready to defend myself in case he meant me harm. Both of us stood silent for a few moments, each assessing the other.

He tried to speak, but only a low growl came out. He cleared his throat and tried again.

"You're a witch," he said, his voice low and rough from disuse. It wasn't a question.

I inclined my head in confirmation, not trusting my voice not to shake if I spoke, deeply unsettled as I was, and a little afraid.

"And you freed me. Thank you."

I nodded again, feeling my pulse thrum quickly with an edge of fear. Not so much of the naked man who, moments earlier had been a bear, but by the magnitude of the magic I had just performed, the power I had just witnessed. I was scared of my own abilities.

Not that the naked man in any way lessened my discomfort. We stood there another few moments, an awkward silence between us.

"I'm ashamed to ask, but may I trespass on your kindness further, and borrow this cloak? As you can see," he smiled embarrassedly, "I have no clothes of my own." His voice was still a little gravelly, but he spoke clearly and eloquently enough, with no discernible accent.

"I live nearby," I said, pleased to find my voice steady and clear. "I can offer you food, a bath perhaps. Certainly, some more suitable clothes. You see, I'm rather attached to that cloak and don't mean to part with it long."

He glanced down at the cloak, which finished a bit below his knees, keeping his head down a few moments. I could see he was weighing his options, as unsure of me as I was of him. Eventually he nodded.

"Why would you help me?" His tone was sceptical, wary.

"It would be cruel to leave you wandering the woods naked and alone, and as I said, I want my cloak back," I answered sharply. "But if you'd rather I did that –"

"No, I'm sorry," he said hastily. "I didn't mean to spurn your hospitality. Please, lead the way."

I waited until he drew nearer to me before I set off, keen to keep him in my sight. I'd had little enough experience of men, and even less of it had been good, hence my cautiousness. The fact that I had lately rescued him was no guarantee that he would not harm me if he felt so inclined. Artemis, who had been hiding, now reappeared to sniff at the man's heels and tug at the edge of the cloak, urging him along, leading the way home. I hoped it was a good sign that she seemed to like him. Maybe she was a better judge of character than me.

We walked along, neither of us speaking much, the walk to the cabin seeming to take much longer than usual as the silent minutes stretched on and on while we walked, the beautiful woods and hills full of birdsong and the fresh smells of spring a harsh contrast to our brief, chilly exchanges.

"This is an impressive lodge," he said, gazing at the cabin when we came within sight of it. "Do you live here alone?"

I hesitated, unsure of how to read the question or of how honest I should be. I didn't want him to think of me as a single, defenceless woman. But I remembered another lesson from my mother: it is better to be underestimated and keep your true strength as a secret weapon.

"Yes, for the time being."

We went inside, and with a flick of my fingers, a roaring fire sprang to life in the hearth. I had gotten quite good at certain domestic spells in my time away from the castle. Though normally I would not have used magic so openly in front of a stranger, he already knew I was a witch and I wanted to remind him that I was powerful, show that I could defend myself if needed. It was a warning as well as a practical measure.

The man looked alarmed for a moment when the flames leapt up, but the look of fear passed as quickly as it had come. Despite his recent ordeal, he seemed calm, taking the oddness of what he saw in his stride. We halted before the fire, warming our hands. I knew the power of silence and waited for him to speak, to reveal more of himself, by keeping mute.

"I must look – erm – interesting in this," he said, gesturing at the cloak, which reached almost to the ground when I wore it but sat just midway between his ankles and knees. "Perhaps I could trouble you for some clothes?"

"I thought you might want a bath first," I said pointedly. "Not to be impolite, but you are quite dirty and, erm, fragrant. I don't suppose you bathed too often when you were a bear."

A bright boom of laughter burst from him unexpectedly. It was a deep, genuine laugh, warm and sincerely amused.

"When I was a bear," he said when the laughter had ceased. "You say that so calmly and matter-of-factly. But then, I suppose it's not such an unusual occurrence when you are a witch." His tone hardened a little at the word "witch".

"Actually, you are my first experience with a human-to-animal transformation. But perhaps you would have preferred that I leave you as a bear? If so, I can assure it's easily remedied," I replied tartly.

He had the grace to look abashed.

"Forgive me, I didn't mean to offend you. I am grateful for what you did and I'm much in your debt."

I nodded with what I hoped was an air of dignified indifference, like the one my mother so easily managed, but I was mollified.

I led him into the room that housed a large copper tub and began to fill it with water from a pump in the room. The water was, of course, cold, but once the tub was full, I dipped my fingers into it and warmth flowed from them until the water was nice and hot, clouds of steam rising from it. I lit the fireplace in the room as well for good measure. There was little point in saving him only to let him die from the cold.

"If you wait a minute, I'll get you some clothes. Hopefully there is something that will fit you."

When I had first arrived at the cabin, I'd come across bundles of men's clothes in various cupboards, and I assumed they were left over from some previous hunting party of my father's. I found a pair of breeches, a shirt, and tunic that I thought would be an approximate fit and took them into the bathroom. They were in good condition, though smelled a little musty from years in storage.

When I entered the bathroom, he was already in the tub, though I had told him to wait. I blushed and set the clothes on the floor quickly, averting my eyes and feeling like an intruder when he was clearly the more vulnerable of the two of us at that moment.

"Here, some clothes. I'll see if I can find you some shoes," I said, and hurried from the room. I had never seen a naked man before, and while most of him was covered by the hot water and the high edges of the tub, I still felt embarrassed being in the same room as him, not having an excuse to throw my cloak over him this time.

I looked in the cupboards of each of the empty bedrooms and finally found some boots, though I had no idea if they would fit; they looked large to me, and I had observed my guest's feet were also large, but I was by no means certain these would be a good fit. I cast an enchantment on them to make them fit any wearer, so I would not have to alter them in front of him. He had already seen me do more magic than any other person apart from my mother, and I didn't want him to get the idea that my magic was only good for domestic purposes.

I almost wished my mother was here so she could see what I had done to the boots, as it was quite a complicated little spell. But then I thought about how she would respond if she knew that I had lifted the curse from the man in the forest and was now seeing to his comforts. *Did I teach you these ancient rites so you could waste them on worthless, ordinary men? You are not a servant,* her voice said inside my head. I shook my head; a denial, but also an attempt to erase the words.

I went into the kitchen, prepared some bread and cheese, and brought out a flagon of wine, assuming he would be hungry, especially since I had interrupted him trying to catch a fish. I wondered if his time as a bear would impact his food preferences somehow. Maybe he would prefer his meat raw now? I yearned to interrogate him about what it had been like, how much he remembered, how long he had been a bear and why the witch had transformed him in the first place. But I thought some small talk would be required before I broached the subject.

He stayed in the bath a long time; I thought the water must have surely gone cold before he finally got out, despite the fire burning in the bathroom. I sat on the lounge by the fire, Artemis beside me and a book open in my hand. But I was not reading – I was listening for sounds of him moving about, a little on edge, and wondering if it had been wise to let this strange man into my home. However, when I considered the alternative, I felt there had been little choice. I couldn't very well have left him naked and lost in the woods with no money, no clothes, and no help to find his way. Although I did giggle to myself for a moment picturing it.

Despite this, I still felt the need to cast protective charms over the house, Artemis, and myself. If he did attempt to do us any harm, he would find himself frozen and unable to injure us in any way. Perhaps it was an excessive measure, but despite my abilities, I still felt vulnerable being a young woman alone in the woods. Plus, my mother's words often returned to me, reminding me that men were not to be trusted. I had always thought she was overstating the danger, her words inspired by her own bitterness as well as genuine wariness. But I chose to err on the side of caution all the same.

After what seemed an age, he finally reappeared in the lounge, washed, dressed, and altogether much more presentable. It was then I first noticed that he was handsome. Not just nice-to-look-at handsome, but a how-on-earth-are-you-a-real-person degree of handsome. I guessed he was about twenty-three or -four, which I hadn't been able to tell when I looked at him earlier, with his hair dishevelled and his face a little grubby. He had gently curly, dark brown hair that fell almost to his shoulders, a broad jaw, and a somewhat pointed chin with a small scar on it, the harshness softened by his full lips. He had a long, straight nose and large, dark brown eyes that crinkled when he smiled. When he came closer, I felt like his eyes were familiar, as though I had seen them before. With a jolt of recognition, I realised that they were the same colour as they had been when he was a bear, a deep brown with flecks the colour of honey. He was a full head taller than me, quite slim, but with a look of strength to him. I realised I quite liked looking at him. Then I realised I was staring – at least my mouth wasn't hanging open.

"Thank you for that," he said, breaking in on my meditations, though not seeming to have noticed my prolonged, intense examination of him. "I feel almost human again," he said with a small, crooked smile that made me want to giggle.

I looked at him, trying to catch his meaning.

"That was a joke," he explained, smile broadening. "Do witches not joke?"

"I couldn't say, as I don't know any others." This wasn't true, but I wanted to contradict him. I disliked the way he kept calling me a witch, as though it was an insult, and told him so.

"What should I call you, then?"

"My name is Rose."

"Rose," he said meditatively, as though testing an unfamiliar word. It sounded nice in his deep, rumbling voice.

"And you are?" I asked, trying to sound offhand.

He looked thoughtful, then frustrated.

"Don't you know?"

"I – I can't remember. I was trying, in the bath, to think, to remember about my life. But it's all kind of a blur. There are some things that are clear, but just flashes. I remember my parents, and a sister. A brother, too, I think, or maybe a close friend. The more I try to remember specific things, the more confused my memories get."

"Come, sit," I said, trying to ease his discomfort. "Are you hungry? I've prepared something for you. It's nothing special, but I thought you might need to eat."

He sat in a chair opposite me and took the plate of food gratefully.

"I'm sorry I don't have any raw fish or venison for you," I said archly.

He laughed, almost choking on the bread in his mouth.

"So wi- I mean, *you* - do joke."

"Sometimes," I said, smiling.

I let him finish eating in peace, pretending to be absorbed in my book, though I kept stealing glances at him. Artemis settled herself at his feet, and every so often she would nuzzle his knee or rest her head on his lap, receiving a gentle head scratch in return.

*Traitor*, I thought. But I was glad she liked him. It made me feel better about the warm feelings towards him that were starting to simmer in my heart, though I still didn't lower my guard.

"I won't trespass on your hospitality too long; I'll be on my way soon."

"Where are you headed?"

"I'm not sure," he said, shaking his head slightly. "I can't remember where I'm from."

"And do you know where you are now?"

"Not exactly. In a forest somewhere." He sounded defensive.

"That narrows it down," I said sarcastically. "Do you know the name of the kingdom we're in?"

He paused for a moment, then shook his head.

"Not to doubt your competence, but leaving hardly seems like a good idea. You are alone. You have no money, no idea where you are, or where you are headed, and you don't remember your name. I don't say this to be unkind, but I fear you would be quite helpless out there on your own, wandering about with no destination and no plan. The nearest town will take you a full day to reach on foot. I can't in good conscience let you go wandering off as yet."

"Why do you care?" He didn't ask meanly, but rather he seemed genuinely curious.

"I suppose I feel a sense of responsibility for you," I replied, not entirely sure of my own motivations. "I mean, I returned you to your human form, and now you're somewhat vulnerable. I'd feel a bit heartless just throwing you out into the cold with no idea where you're going."

"So, what would you suggest?"

I didn't think before I spoke, my words completely spontaneous.

"You can stay here until your memory returns. When you have a better idea of where you're from, who you are, you can set off. I'll do what I can to help you recover your memory, if you'll let me."

"That won't be an inconvenience?"

It might have been, but I could hardly rescind my offer.

"It's a large house," I shrugged, trying to appear completely indifferent as to whether he stayed or not. "We wouldn't be in each other's way."

"It's a very kind offer. I'm not sure many people would show that kind of compassion to a complete stranger. I hope you'll let me do something to repay you. I can hunt, I think. For food, I mean. If anything needed mending, I could try my hand at that."

"I appreciate that. I know how difficult it can be to be idle for too long. Who knows, maybe it would help your memory to do a few different things, see if anything seems familiar. Then maybe we can work out where you're from, or at least what you did in your former life."

As we talked, darkness had fallen, and I felt my eyelids growing heavier by the minute, my body drained by the complex magic I'd performed earlier.

"Let me show you to a bedroom," I said, rising and leading the way out of the lounge.

The room I gave him was not overly large, but it was clean and comfortable, with its own hearth, and had a pretty view of the woods in the daylight hours. But then, most rooms in the cabin had a view of the woods.

"There's wood already cut up out the front, if you wish to light a fire. Goodnight."

As I pulled away, ready to retire to my own chamber, he took my hand and held it in his.

"I don't think I have properly expressed how much I appreciate all you've done for me. You rescued me from a cruel fate, you returned me to myself."

"Not quite, I'm afraid." I grimaced. "You can't remember your own name."

"Nevertheless, I appreciate your kindness. You've done more for me than I think most people would. I owe you everything I have, even if I don't actually know what that is yet. But I will repay your generosity." He looked at me intently, his warm brown eyes bright with gratitude.

I didn't know what to say. I liked the feeling of my hand in his, the closeness in this moment. But after a few seconds I withdrew my hand, saying brusquely, "I'm sure you will.

Goodnight, then." I turned and went straight to my own room, closing the door with a snap.

I had a hard time falling asleep. I'd spent weeks thinking about the bear, wondering who he really was, if I would find him again and be able to transform him back. Now all of those things had come to pass, I still had many questions, and a strange man was sleeping just a few doors down from my own. I was restless, my thoughts continually drifting to the handsome stranger down the hall, wondering what it would be like to have him living here, even for a short time.

"Get a grip," I scolded myself. "You need to focus on waking Lily, not making doe eyes at the beautiful bear-man." But my thoughts refused to obey, and I drifted off to sleep with a small smile on my lips.

# Chapter Thirteen

I woke early the next morning and went into the small enclosure behind the cabin to collect eggs from the chickens I kept there. It was a cool, crisp morning, the scents of the forest wafting over the yard along with a chilly, thin mist, and mingling with the smell of chickens, who clucked excitedly in their pen as I approached, a basket for the eggs in one hand and a bowl of their feed in the other. The hens circled my feet, pecking at their food, and I had to be careful not to step on them as I made my way to their nests. I gathered seven eggs in all, enough for breakfast and perhaps a tart of some kind as well. My cooking repertoire was still limited, but I was getting better and more adventurous in my culinary exploits the longer I spent on my own. Though some of my experiments had resulted in positively awful outcomes.

When I entered the kitchen, my handsome guest was there, scratching Artemis behind the ear and stoking the fire burning in the stove with his other hand.

"Good morning," he said, smiling when he saw me. My insides did a strange fluttering thing when he smiled, like a bird caught in a net. I wasn't sure if I liked it, nor the flush I could feel creeping up my neck. I flicked my loose hair forward over my shoulders in an attempt to hide it.

"Good morning. I hope you like eggs," I said, brandishing my basket awkwardly between us.

"Oh, yes, boiled, scrambled, poached, fried. Any way you can think of."

"That's interesting – you can remember all the different ways of making eggs, but not your name?"

"Actually, I remembered my name last night," he said, his smile broadening until a dimple showed in each cheek. "I was just falling asleep, or maybe I was already dreaming, and I remembered a time just after I had been turned into a bear."

"Yes?" I had a ravenous curiosity about what it had been like, but tried not to show anything more than polite interest.

"I hadn't been a bear long, maybe a day or two. It's hard to tell, my sense of time is really fuzzy. But I was walking in some woods, and I heard people calling out. I knew they were looking for me, I still felt enough like myself that they were familiar. I made my way towards their voices, but when I approached, they ran from me. Of course, they didn't want to be attacked by a bear, and I had no way to let them know it was me. But I knew they were calling my name and that was how I remembered. Henri. I'm Henri."

I smiled, glad that his memory was coming back, and happy to be able to call him by something other than 'the bear man'.

"Henri," I repeated, and he smiled, his mouth tugging up slightly more on the right side than the left.

While I cooked our eggs – scrambled, because they are the hardest type to get wrong – and Henri saw to our toast, before preparing the tomatoes and mushrooms for me sauté, I asked him more about what he remembered, but the information was meagre. There seemed to be no rhyme or reason to the things he could remember and those he could not.

"How long ago were you changed?"

"I couldn't say; like I said, I had no real sense of time, not in the way humans do. I think I passed at least two winters though."

"Two years?" I was astounded. To lose two years of one's life was a horrifying thought. Lily had been in her magic sleep for over five months by this point, and it was already much too long to be without her. I dreaded to think how she would feel when she woke and realised how much time she had lost. But Henri seemed relatively unconcerned by how much time he had spent as a bear. I suppose it was because he recalled so little of his life before, so he didn't know what he might have missed during that time.

"Why did the witch transform you?" I asked a little awkwardly.

"I don't remember, it's all quite blurry. I remember I was out in the woods, hunting. Near my home, I think. I'd been with others, I think, and somehow became separated from them chasing whatever we were hunting. Then I came across this pretty young woman. She asked me something, but I don't recall what. Whatever I said must have angered her, because before I knew it, I was on all fours and covered in fur."

This tallied exactly with the vision I'd when I'd first touched him the day I freed him from the poacher's trap.

"You said you recognised the people looking for you, but you can't recall who they were now. How long did you remember things from your human life?"

"Again, I don't know. An animal's idea of time is very different to ours. I just know I felt less and less myself as time went on. I wandered a good deal, when I realised that the people who had known me as a man would have no way of knowing me for who I really was. I just kept going deeper and deeper into the forest, trying to keep away from people. I didn't want to be hunted and I didn't want to hurt anyone. It took me a long time before I found somewhere I could make my home; I had to avoid other bears' territory, and as I moved along, I forgot where I'd come from, until I had no way of knowing where my true home was. It became easy to forget things from my former life the longer I spent in a different body. I suppose the longer I spent as a bear, the more I became like one."

"Do you remember me?" I asked, trying to lead the conversation to a lighter subject.

He raised his eyebrows in surprise, the forkful of scrambled egg stopping a few inches from his mouth.

"Have we met before?"

"Sort of. You got your foot caught in a poacher's trap a few months ago and I freed you."

He shook his head.

"I remember the trap and getting away. My foot hurt for a fair while afterwards where the teeth had clamped onto it. That's all. So," he said, his face brightening as that crooked smile appeared again. "You've saved me twice now. How did you know I wasn't a real bear?"

I told him about the way his memory had burst into my mind when I'd touched him.

"Lucky for me you found me before hunters did. It seems I owe you even more than I thought."

I couldn't hide my blush of discomfort. I wasn't usually so easily embarrassed, but it seemed Henri had some kind of special ability in that way.

"There is no debt. People ought to help each other if they can," I said, trying to shrug off the awkward turn the conversation had taken.

"But when you first helped me, you thought I was a bear."

"You *were* a bear. I would never leave an animal in a trap; I think it's a cowardly, cruel thing people do, leaving them for unsuspecting animals to be caught in. I found Artemis in one, too, and that's how we ended up together. I find the damn things in the woods sometimes, and I always disable them. Lately I've taken to melting them into a big, useless lump of metal so the poachers can't reuse them."

"You rescue men and animals alike, you live alone in the woods, you use your magic to help others. Do you have no flaws? Apart from your inclination to pat stray bears, which was definitely not a good idea," he said, his tone gently teasing.

"Of course, I do," I said, almost defensive. "I'm impatient, I'm terrible at sitting still, and I get jealous of my beautiful sister." I stopped abruptly. I didn't want to talk about Lily. It was like exposing a still-raw wound.

"You have a sister?" he asked, his tone soft, sensing my sudden sadness.

"Yes. But she's unwell. Cursed, actually. I'm trying to find a way to help her."

I stood up and began to clear the table hurriedly. I'd been neglecting my duty to Lily so I could sit and talk with a handsome stranger, and I felt guilty for it. Henri sensed my anger and thought it was directed at him.

"Can I help? With your sister, I mean," he asked as he picked up dishes and followed me to the sink.

"Do you know much about making potions?" I asked, more sharply than I meant to, my anger flaring outwards even though it had nothing to do with him.

"No, but I can chop wood for your fire. I could pass you things you need. Maybe I could even help you sacrifice goats. I haven't any experience assisting with witchcraft, but I can learn. Whatever you need."

I burst out laughing.

"I don't sacrifice goats. Did you really think witches sacrificed goats?"

"It's what my nanny told me," he said, cheeks turning pink.

"Do you also think I worship the devil, dancing naked around a fire under a full moon?"

"A man can dream."

I flushed deeply at this, then chided myself for being so easily embarrassed.

"Clearly there is a lot you don't know about witches, aside from superstitions," I said, my face turned away to hide my blush.

"Clearly. I was always told witches were ugly, old hags. Imagine my surprise to find they can also be young and beautiful." He smiled, and I felt the flush creep further up my cheeks.

"I need to work," I said, curtailing the conversation abruptly. Henri paused awkwardly for a second, then made to leave the kitchen. "You can stay, if you want. You won't be in my way." I managed to make my tone gentler than before.

He did stay. As I worked compounding herbs, grating roots, and crushing moonstones to a fine powder, he watched with quiet absorption, asking me a question every so often. I'd never had any company but my mother while I worked, and I found his presence was quite welcome. I liked being able to share what I was doing with someone who was clearly interested, if a bit mystified. Someone who didn't know how much of a novice I still was.

When I'd added everything to the cauldron, which was boiling merrily over the flames, he asked if it was almost ready.

"No, it needs to sit at a low simmer for several hours. Then there is more to be added. One of the biggest parts of witchcraft is waiting for things to be ready. Magic cannot be rushed. It's an art as much as a science," I replied in my sagest voice.

He nodded.

"So, what do we do now?"

"I need to stay close by. The potion needs to be stirred at regular intervals to ensure that it's mixed properly and that all the heavier ingredients don't just stew at the bottom."

He pulled up a chair next to one he was occupying and gestured for me to sit.

"As you know, I have nowhere else to be."

I took the seat next to him, and Artemis leapt onto my lap.

"Tell me about your sister," he said gently. I hesitated, unsure if it was wise to talk about Lily. But part of me desperately wanted to talk about her, to let out all the thoughts and feelings I'd been keeping to myself for too long. But I worried that once I started, I wouldn't be able to stop, and my repressed feelings would spill over like a river flooding over its banks. I began slowly.

"Her name is Lily, and she's almost two years older than me." I paused, not wanting to say too much and reveal who my family was. "She's very beautiful and kind. Always thoughtful and obedient. When we were children, she used to stop me from doing things that were too dangerous or foolish. Actually, she still did that even when we were no longer children. She made me that blue cloak," I said, pointing to where it hung on the wall. The picture I painted of Lily, while true, was also vague, ineloquent. It didn't really capture who she was as a person, her humour and charm, the way she could put you at ease seemingly without trying. It didn't begin to express the depth of my heartbreak at losing her, my guilt at being unable to save her.

"And your parents? What are they like?" Henri asked, redirecting the conversation.

"My father is dead; he died some years ago now. I'd always thought he was a kind and good man, but something happened not long before he died that changed my mind. People aren't always who you think they are," I said, not quite meeting his gaze.

"I'm sorry," he said gently, reaching for my hand.

"Why? You didn't do anything." I smiled weakly.

"Our parents – they're the people we count on most. Or should be able to count on. I'm sorry your father wasn't that person for you."

I was touched by his sympathy and felt like I was being self-indulgent, complaining about my family when he could barely remember who he was. But he was right; when I really needed them, my parents were unable to help me.

"Do you remember any more about your family?" I asked, wanting to steer the conversation away from myself.

"I remember I have a younger brother and a sister. And my mother and father are still alive, or were when I was last with them. Anything might have happened by now." He looked sad for the first time since I'd met him; his eyes suddenly distant and his shoulders rounded by an invisible weight, as though the reality of those two lost years had finally settled on him.

"I wish I could help you remember more about your life, so you could find your family."

"Isn't there any potion or spell you can use?"

"Not that I know of. Here, you stay and stir the mixture counterclockwise every five minutes. I'm going to get something." I hurried off and returned a few minutes later with a stack of spell books and books on alchemical lore in my arms.

"There may be something in here. I certainly don't know everything about witchcraft, and I've never needed a spell for memories before. But just because I haven't seen one, does not mean they don't exist."

I passed him an ancient, leather-bound volume and started flicking through another myself, casting my eyes over spells, potions, and charms, discounting them all almost immediately. I soon tossed the book aside and took up another. Then another. And another.

"How about this?" Henri asked, holding a book out to me so I could inspect the page.

"A spell to find a loved one. Maybe, but then if you can't remember who you are I'm not sure how helpful this would be. Besides, this spell is more intended for romantic love; I'm not sure it would work to find your family."

We kept searching and I came across a healing spell I'd used many times before, usually after training sessions with Paulus that had been particularly painful, or when I'd been careless with my kitchen knife. If Henri's memory was fractured by the spell that had transformed him, perhaps this would heal any damage it had caused, or at least help his mind heal a little from the trauma of his experience. On the surface it was not an obvious solution, yet what else could his memory loss be if not a kind of magical injury or ailment of his mind?

I explained all of this to him.

"But I've never cast it on another person before. It should be safe, but I can't guarantee that, especially with something as delicate as your mind. There is a good chance it won't work at all, and very slight chance it will somehow make things worse."

Henri's face was set with a look of determination.

"I want to try, if you're willing."

"Are you sure?"

He nodded.

"I trust you."

"You hardly know me. And aren't you meant to assume the worst of witches. What would your nanny say?" I teased.

"You are so much more than a witch," he said, brushing a loose strand of hair away from my face. I felt a shiver of excitement run through me at his touch. Our faces were close together as we sat at the table, surrounded by discarded spell books. I wondered what it would be like to kiss him. *If I just leaned in a little closer-*

"So, will you do it?" he said, jolting me out of my daydream.

I laughed manically for a second while my brain caught up with his question.

"What? Yes. Yes, I will," I said, my face colouring. I consulted the book more closely, checking what was needed and how best to prepare. I tried to ignore the fact that Henri was sitting very close to me, our knees almost touching. I needed to focus on the spell if I didn't want to muddle his brains entirely.

"Are you ready?" I asked, drawing a deep breath and trying to steel my nerves.

He looked nervous, but nodded.

"Close your eyes," I instructed.

I placed my hands on his head, and took a few deep, steadying breaths, focusing on channelling my power directly into his mind, and uttered the spell. When it was done, I lifted my hands from his head and gazed into his face. His brow, which had been furrowed in concentration or fear, relaxed. After a few moments he opened his eyes and smiled at me.

"I think it worked. I'm starting to remember things. Not whole memories, just glimpses. Like a series of pictures just popping into my mind, as if some wall has been brought down. But things are clearer than they were."

"Like what?"

"I had a horse, a huge black mare. I called her Eva. I remember my parents' faces, their smiles. I remember my sister, she was several years younger than me. And my brother, too. I can see his face."

"Do you remember their names? Where you lived?" I asked, hoping to prompt memories. Since I was already questioning him, I asked casually, "Do you have a wife?"

"No, I don't remember their names, but maybe it will come back to me. It's as though they are on the tip of my tongue, but I can't quite form the words." His face tensed with concentration, and he closed his eyes. "If I push it, try to force the memory, it slips away."

"It may take some more time for the spell to fully take effect. Healing the mind is very different to healing a cut, much more complex."

This was just a guess on my part, but I was certain that any mind that had undergone the kind of trauma Henri had would take more time to heal than any ordinary injury.

"And to answer your other question; no, I don't have a wife."

"Well, that's good. That you're remembering things, I mean." I bit my lip, trying to suppress my smile.

* * * *

Over the following days and weeks, Henri's memory continued to recover, but it was a slow process. He would remember small things, like his sister's favourite food or his father's favourite song. But the big things – their names, where he lived – continued to elude him, as though the curse still lingered enough to keep him from returning to his former life.

It seemed like the more important a detail was, the harder it was to recover. At times he became irritated or even outright angry at his own inability to recall what mattered most, and I couldn't blame him. So much of his life was lost to him, and I could only imagine how difficult that must be. His very identity had been stolen from him. I couldn't hope to fully understand how painfully frustrating it was for him, but I imagined it was like trying to read a book where every other page had been torn out, so you could never know the full story.

No matter how much I wanted to help Henri, I was not sorry that every day he continued to forget these things was another day we shared a home. The more time I spent with him, the more I liked him. It was more than just him being attractive and a good listener. I liked the way he would debate things with me. I liked the way my tummy did a little flip whenever he smiled or said my name. I liked how easy it was to laugh with him and that he could laugh at himself. I liked that I never tired of his company, even though we spent hours and hours together each day. I liked that I was the truest version of myself, concealing nothing – except my family's status and the reason I had to search for Lily's cure at the cabin instead of my home. But when I spoke of myself, my thoughts and opinions, I was honest, more honest than I was with anyone else except Lily. I could tell him my faults and darker thoughts without fear of judgement.

But there were times we would be talking, and I would have to omit a detail or leave a story unfinished because I couldn't risk telling him who I really was. This weighed on my mind, especially when I was trying to fall asleep. I knew that secrets could hurt, that omissions were really just lies by another name. But I convinced myself it was for his good as well as mine. I would push the guilt from my mind and fall asleep happy in the knowledge that I would be able to spend the next day with him, too.

One morning I woke with a pounding headache and a deep, searing pain in my lower back, hips, and abdomen. My monthly cycle had arrived and was aggressively reminding me how much my own body could turn against me. I rolled onto my side and gingerly eased myself out of bed. I had to change my nightgown and clean myself up, which was all I could manage before a wave of nausea almost knocked me to the floor. I gritted my teeth and breathed deeply through my nose, willing the sick feeling to pass before I climbed back into bed. There was a tea I could make for the pain and nausea, and I had a ceramic bottle that could be filled with hot water that helped ease some of my discomfort most of the time.

The only problem was that those things were all downstairs, in the kitchen, and I barely had the will left to shift myself into a more comfortable position in the bed, let alone stand up, walk downstairs, and brew tea. Instead, I lay there for what felt like forever and no time at all, urging my body to just roll to the edge of the bed so I could get up again. But the pain was too intense and debilitating – like a dozen knives were stabbing me from the inside, as a single bass drum pounded just inside my right temple, all while I was sailing on a roiling sea in the middle of a tempest – and it was easier to lie there gritting my teeth against my discomfort than to try to force myself to rise, to even shift the position of my head. After a time, I fell asleep.

A few hours later, when it must have been nearing noon, I was awakened by a soft tapping at my door. I mumbled a soft, "come in," then Henri's head craned into the room, keeping the door still mostly closed.

"Are you sick?" he asked when he saw me lying in bed, probably looking as awful as I felt.

"No, it's, well – it's my monthly – my *women's* time," I stammered out, my face as red as a beetroot. At some point while I'd been asleep, I'd also started sweating profusely, and my nightgown clung to be in a wholly unbecoming way.

"Oh," Henri said, the door swinging further open as he released his hold on the handle. "Oh." He looked hesitant and a little awkward, his cheeks pinking slightly as he stood in the doorway, caught between coming into the room and turning away.

Artemis came bounding into the room through the now wide-open door and leapt onto the bed, curling up beside me and nuzzling in, as though she knew I needed comforting.

"Is there, I mean, can I *do* anything?" Henri asked somewhat helplessly, looking as uncomfortable as I felt, but not running away like I would have expected. "Can I get you anything to – to make things better?"

I smiled, despite the sharp cramping pains I now had in my belly, as if my insides were being wrung out like a sponge.

"Actually, there is a tea that would make me feel better. If you wouldn't mind, you just need to add a few things to some boiling water and bring it to me."

He nodded and asked for the ingredients. It was all things I already had in little labelled jars downstairs: willow bark, clary sage, lavender, peppermint, fennel, and liquorice root. Twenty minutes later Henri reappeared with a large mug of steaming tea and my heated ceramic bottle.

"Thank you," I said, taking them from him gratefully. I sipped the tea and let out a little sigh. "That will help immensely."

"I've never done magic before," he said, grinning.

I laughed loudly.

"That wasn't magic, just some healing herbs".

"It felt like magic," he retorted, smiling. His tasks complete, Henri hovered a short distance away from the bed, unsure of what to do.

"Shall I leave you to sleep?"

"No, I've been dozing all morning. You could stay, though," I said as he made to move towards the door. "If you wanted to keep me company."

He glanced about the room, then seized a large armchair, which he dragged near to the bed. We both sat in awkward silence for a few moments, before Henri suggested he might read to me. I agreed and he went to fetch a book, returning with a large volume of folktales. Settling in the chair again, Henri began reading to me: charming stories of magic and princesses, heroes and villains. I laughed at some of the renderings of witches, which were less than flattering, but it was a pleasant way to pass the day, despite my lingering pain. Henri ran back and forth, fetching me more tea and refilling my hot water bottle, his initial embarrassment at what ailed me seemingly gone.

After one of his trips downstairs to get more tea, Henri remained by the bed, and I suggested he settle by my side rather than sitting in the chair, which had a somewhat lumpy seat cushion. I thought he might prefer to keep the distance between us, but he simply removed his boots and took up a recumbent position next to me, Artemis ensconced between us, and kept reading. I dozed off again at some point, relaxed and comfortable enough to sleep, and when I next woke, it was to find Henri asleep, still above the covers, but his body had curved to fit around mine as I lay on my side. We fit together like two crescent-shaped puzzle pieces, and I smiled at the rightness of it, as if he belonged there, then closed my eyes and fell back asleep.

* * * *

Despite my wish to keep Henri to myself, I did all I could to aid his recovery; we went for long walks or rides across the land, as far as I dared to go, hoping something would be familiar and help him recall a forgotten memory. I encouraged him to go hunting and fishing to see if either of these activities felt like they belonged to his old life.

Here there was some success; one afternoon he came back from hunting with a number of rabbits to show for it. He seemed pleased, saying it had come to him naturally, as though he had done it a hundred times before.

As we sat eating a stew made from the rabbit and some vegetables I had grown in the garden, the conversation turned – as it often did – to speculations about his life before he was cursed.

"Well, that is one more thing we know about you. You are either a hunter by trade, or you are a noble, or at least wealthy enough to have the leisure to hunt for sport."

"Which would you prefer?" he asked with a sly sideways glance at me.

"My experience of nobles hasn't been the most favourable. They seem to be either vain and silly or scheming and power hungry. Or some other combination of those traits. So, I think I would prefer you to be a commoner. But," I added, "if you were unlucky enough to be high born, I could probably overlook it," I said with a smile.

"You must have known quite a few nobles, then?" His tone changed instantly from one of playful banter, becoming meditative and serious.

I bit my lip and swore under my breath. He had caught me off-guard and I had spoken without thinking. I hadn't meant to reveal so much of my other life; I had always kept my true identity a secret from Henri, for Lily's safety, for my own, even for his. I didn't know exactly how my mother would react if she found out I had a man secreted away in this secluded place, but I knew it wouldn't be good. I stood and began clearing the dinner things away, pretending I had not heard him, hoping to let the topic drop or brush it off as a throwaway joke.

"Rose? Are you on familiar terms with nobles?" Henri kept his voice even, with no anger or surprise creeping in, only genuine inquiry as he followed me into the kitchen. I placed the dirty dishes into a washing basin and busied myself with cleaning, keeping my back to him.

"Mmm," I replied.

"Why don't you want to tell me? Are you here hiding from a nobleman or something?"

"Not exactly," I said eventually, keeping my attention focused on the dishes before me as Henri took them one by one from my hands and dried them while we spoke. "I'm not hiding. I *am* here to find a cure for my sister, as I told you. I can't do that in my actual home, because my mother is the one who cursed Lily."

Henri remained silent, not pressing for details, but listening attentively. Maybe it was time to tell him the whole truth, or at least to give him a clearer idea of what I was up to and why. At any rate, I would have a much harder time keeping the secret, now that I'd well and truly let the cat out of the bag. I drew a deep breath, then pressed on in a hurry, trying to get the words out quickly.

"My mother is Queen Lorelei, regent of Silvaner, and my sister, Lily, was about to marry and succeed her as my father's heir. But my mother wanted to keep her position of power, so she put her into a cursed sleep and planned to have her murdered." I realised it sounded fantastic and a little ridiculous when I said it like that. Maybe he would think I was making it up to get out of having this conversation. There was a long silence while he processed what I had said.

"So, you're a princess?" His brown eyes widened a little as he said this, glancing at the simple peasant's gown I wore, my messy, unruly curls in a loose tangle, and a basin full of dirty dishes before me. "Why didn't you tell me sooner?" There was no anger in the questions, only surprise and perhaps a little pain, which it hurt me to see.

"I have spent months thinking of nothing but freeing my sister from her curse. It's dangerous - for her, for me. Quite literally a matter of life and death. I thought it would make things simpler not to tell you everything about me, to keep you from being involved in the situation. Then the longer I went without telling you, the harder it felt to give you the whole story. And," I hesitated, "I think part of me worried things would change between us if I told you. If you knew who I really was."

"What do you mean?"

My stomach felt as though it was tied in a knot. I wasn't ready to tell him how I felt, and I was terrified of driving him away. For all the little, comfortable intimacies that had gradually built up between us, we'd never talked about what we were to each other. It was easy to convince myself it wasn't necessary.

"I - I like your company," I said, flushing bright red and avoiding his eye. "I like how easy things are between us. I was afraid if you knew who I was, that ease would be lost. With so much risk and responsibility weighing on me to save my sister, it was nice to have something that was just good and easy."

"You didn't think it would have been better to be honest with me?" he asked, his tone a little resentful.

"I never lied to you," I said defensively. "I just omitted details, and only to keep you from getting caught up in this. Everything I told you was the truth." While this was true, it was a self-serving justification, and I hated saying it.

He was quiet for a long time. I was hesitant to break the silence and had no idea what to say in any case.

"I like your company, too, Rose. And you have been very generous with me. I owe you so much and I *do* appreciate your help. But, in future, I would prefer for you to tell me the *whole* truth of things. No omissions. Can you promise that?"

I waited a moment, thinking carefully about my response, then I shook my head. There were things I would never tell him if I could help it. How I felt about him was only one of them.

"Why not?" he asked.

"Because that kind of promise is already a lie. I don't think two people can ever honestly promise to tell each other *everything*. There are always going to be private thoughts and feelings you don't want to share. I have never told you a lie, but I think it would be foolish to believe total honesty is ever possible. But I can promise I will answer you truthfully if you ask me a question. Though sometimes the answer might be that I chose not to answer."

"That's fair," he said, extending his hand to me. "Shake on it?" I stepped closer to him, putting my hand in his, and felt my heart skip and my stomach flutter. Looking up into his face, standing so close, it would have been easy to lean in the last few inches and kiss him, which was all I wanted to do. But he released my hand and I backed away again, turning to finish washing the dishes.

Then we sat down again, and I told him everything that had happened with Lily and my mother, how I had already attempted to wake Lily several times without success. I told him that I didn't know what I would do if I ever did wake her, because the situation could only be resolved by a confrontation with my mother. All the things that had been weighing on me for months and months, the things I had been carrying around, unable to share with anyone, tumbled out in a great torrent, leaving a feeling of relief and release behind. Sharing my problems didn't solve them, but it seemed to lighten them just a little. I hadn't realised just how much tension and anger I'd been carrying until I laid it all out before him. It was strange, allowing myself to be vulnerable, to reveal things I'd never told anyone else.

I even told him about killing Jurgen. I thought he would be horrified or judgemental, or revile or fear me for what I'd done, but he simply said that I had done what was necessary to defend myself, and what any other person would have done in my place. I didn't need his approval or benediction but knowing that I was not a monster in his eyes, despite having taken a life, eased something tight and painful in my chest.

Henri listened attentively, asking questions and making the occasional remark. I realised how badly I had needed someone to talk to about the whole situation. The only other person who knew was Christian, and I hadn't seen him in months. Besides, I couldn't talk to him entirely openly; he didn't understand how I could still hesitate to wage war on my mother, to confront her with accusations of her crimes. He thought my continued love for her was a betrayal of Lily, and maybe it was. His view was clouded – or maybe it was made clearer – by the fact he had never known or loved my mother the way I had. To him, she was simply the villain in the clearest of terms.

But Henri had no agenda, no preformed opinions about the actors in my drama. I could tell him things without fear of his judgement or disgust. Maybe it was reckless to reveal so much, but trusting him with my secrets and troubles only made me feel lighter.

My heart seemed to swell almost painfully with love for him. But even as it did, I felt an ever-deepening fear of the day he would finally be well enough to leave me.

# Chapter Fourteen

When the draught Henri had helped me make was ready, I took it to Marie and Otto's house to test it, leaving Henri behind with Artemis, trying not to resent that she seemed to prefer him to me. When we were about halfway there, clouds appeared suddenly, turning the sky black and frigid rain began lashing Bastian and I as we rode along, the ground beneath us turning to mud, which Bastian churned up further under the powerful tread of his hooves. This made the already long ride feel longer and more miserable than ever before, and for a moment I contemplated turning back. But my discomfort was nothing compared to what Lily suffered, and I rode on until the little cottage came into sight. I settled Bastian in the barn and attempted to dry him with an old blanket. There were oats for him and a trough of water, and I left him as comfortable as possible.

I administered the potion just as I had several times before, waiting futilely for my sister to stir. When the potion failed to work, like all the others, I stormed out of Lily's room and threw myself down at Marie's worn kitchen table, sobbing heavily, all my suppressed rage, anxiety, frustration, and fear erupting at yet another failure, tears flooding out of me like a dam that had burst. The months and months of failure had taken their toll and finally demanded an outlet. I realised I hadn't allowed myself to cry, to sit with all my painful emotions since Lily had been cursed. I'd been so bent on trying to find a solution to save Lily that I hadn't really acknowledged my own pain and suffering, but now it demanded to be felt. Crying was cathartic, as though some of my pain was siphoned out of me along with the salty tears. But it did nothing to change my circumstances.

"Nothing works," I cried with a hiccup and a sob. "It's hopeless."

"No, dear," Marie said in her cracked, raspy voice, patting me gently on the back in soothing circular motions like a mother might. "'Hopeless' is when you give up and stop trying. It's when you decide you aren't going to keep fighting. I don't believe you're there yet."

I wiped my eyes with the sleeves of my dress, though they were already damp from the rain, and nodded. She was right; I wouldn't give up. But I was running out of solutions, and I feared that the longer Lily remained asleep the harder it would be to wake her. She had already lost nearly a year of her life, and it was my fault for failing to wake her.

"Will you stay for supper?" Marie asked kindly, shuffling back to the potatoes she had been peeling.

"No, I should get back," I said. "I have-" I paused, unsure what I meant to say. "There's someone waiting for me at home." I hadn't consciously thought of the cabin, the place I lived with Henri as home, but it seemed at that moment that it was where I really belonged, that he was who I belonged with.

Marie gave me a knowing smile and walked me to the door. The rain had finally stopped, which I took as a good sign, though the roads had turned to mud and the air was still cool.

"By the way, dear, I meant to thank you. That salve you gave Otto at Christmas has made a world of difference. He's walking and bending more easily than he has done in a long time; it's like he's ten years younger. He's almost too sprightly in some ways," she added with a twinkling eye.

"I'm glad he feels better."

"You're a good girl, Rose. I hope we see you again soon."

I rode hard to get back to the cabin, squeezing Bastian's sides with my thighs, urging him to hurry as the wind whipped against my damp clothes and left me almost frozen in place on Bastian's back, my ungloved hands grasping the reins, stinging as the cold air bit at them.

Part of me was afraid that I would come home to find Henri had gone. But my fears were unfounded. The smoke unfurling from the chimney told me Henri was still there. When I walked in, he was sitting by the fire with Artemis curled at his feet. He stood and walked towards me as I entered the room, a smile on his handsome face.

"Did it work?" he asked eagerly. I shook my head. "It will," he assured me. He followed me as I walked into the kitchen, placing my satchel on the table and unfastening my sodden cloak. "I know you will manage it."

His words were comforting, even though they weren't based on fact, merely on his faith in me. Or maybe it was *because* he had faith in me that they were comforting. Without thinking, I flung my arms around him, pulling him close, and he wrapped his around me, holding me against him.

"I hope so," I said, my voice muffled against his shoulder. "I feel so helpless."

To my surprise, he let out a low chuckle, which rumbled through his chest and made my head move involuntarily as it rested against him.

"What's funny?" I asked, still holding onto him, my face half hidden against his shoulder.

"You, thinking you're helpless. I've never met a less helpless person in my life."

"That's not saying much, seeing as you don't remember most of your life," I teased.

"You feel frozen through," he said, his mouth unexpectedly close to my ear.

"Will you warm me?" I asked, pulling away just enough to look into his face.

As I looked at him, he swallowed, once, twice, throat bobbing. I suddenly felt - not quite drunk - but the feeling one has after a glass or two of wine, when everything gets a little bit hazy and soft around the edges and one feels all warm and confident and hopeful.

I loosened my hold on him and as I moved to pull away his face came very near to mine. I cannot say who kissed who first, but in a moment, we were tangled together, our mouths reaching hungrily for each other. He pushed against me, moving me backwards until my legs connected with the table, then he lifted me onto it, moving one hand to my back while the other twined in my messy, wind-tangled hair.

The kissing turned slower, more deliberate, as he kissed my lips, my jaw, down to my neck, then my shoulder. A sound like a purr escaped me as he nuzzled at my neck, his teeth grazing against my skin, making my toes curl as a pleasurable shudder ran through me. I gripped the back of his shirt with both hands, pressing myself against him. He was unlacing the front of my dress as I tugged at his shirt, pulling it over his head, then traced my fingers over his bare chest. He pressed his mouth against mine again, his tongue stroking the roof of my mouth before he drew back.

"Do you want to stop?" he asked.

"No," I replied, pulling him closer to me again.

I felt him slowly pushing up my skirts, then his hand slipped between my legs, and when he touched me, a kind of tingling warmth filled my belly, then spread out across my body. I let out a soft moan, hyperaware of every sensation, from the uncontrollable curling of my toes to the sharp, sudden intakes of breath, like my lungs were trying to draw him into me.

Whatever he was doing, I wanted more of it. I slid my hands down to his breeches, unlacing them and sliding them past his hips. He stopped kissing me, looked into my eyes, and said quietly, "Are you sure?" I nodded and kissed him again. My legs were wrapped around him as I felt him press himself into me and my body shuddered pleasurably, despite the edge of pain. He kissed me again and I bit his lip as I climaxed, groaning rapturously.

Afterwards, he and I were both panting for breath. As we moved apart, I felt as though I had just run a mile. I was aglow with satisfaction, but he looked almost embarrassed and avoided my gaze.

"What's wrong?" I asked. "Did I – I mean, was that not – Is something wrong?" I didn't really know what I was asking, just that I felt things had suddenly gone from perfect bliss to its gut-wrenching opposite.

"No," he said, looking troubled. "No, it's me. I shouldn't have . . . let that happen."

I let out a nervous giggle. I was both relieved that he hadn't found fault with me and confused by his response.

"I'm don't think that's quite how it happened."

"I just mean . . ." but he didn't know what he meant. I did, at least I thought I did. That I was *sullied* or *ruined* for him now. A girl who gave up her virtue willingly, eagerly even. But what had we done that was so bad? It was true I had very little experience, but I knew that this kind of thing did happen outside of marriage. Was it really such a problem? I knew how to ensure there would be no baby. I was about to tell him so, when he turned away from me, adjusting his clothes, and I felt my anger rising. He had initiated it. What was I meant to have done? Screamed? Run away? Hit him with a skillet? The truth was I had wanted him, too, and we had both been equal parties to what had happened. But perhaps he felt I had some claim on him now, that I'd tricked him in some way.

"Can't you look at me now?" I asked angrily. That did make him face me, but he looked miserable. It was worse than him not looking at me at all, seeing a blend of troubling emotions I couldn't quite read on his handsome face. He opened his mouth, then seemed to rethink whatever it was he had been going to say and closed it again.

"I'm going to bed," I said furiously. "Goodnight," I spat the word out as though it were an insult or a curse. I slid off the table, straightened my skirt, and stormed off to my room. As I slammed the door, I could have sworn I heard a crack of thunder. That sometimes happened if I was in a particularly bad temper. *Good,* I thought, *let him fear the witch.* I seethed with righteous anger until I fell into a comfortless sleep. When I woke, I both hoped and feared he would be gone. I didn't honestly know which would be worse, but my face burned when I thought of facing him again.

I crept into the kitchen, where the pale dawn light was sliding quietly across the clean surfaces. I saw the table where we had been last night and flinched away, looking pointedly in the other direction. Then I saw him sleeping on the couch, looking utterly at peace and undisturbed, Artemis curled up beside him. It was odd that he had slept out here instead of in his bedroom, but I didn't ponder it long, as anger rose in my belly again and I wanted to strike out with my spite. *I could always turn him back into a bear,* I thought savagely.

Instead, I noiselessly donned my still slightly damp cloak, slipped on my shoes, and picked up my basket and herb knife. Artemis followed me out of the front door.

Dew lay heavily over everything, like tiny jewels of light, and the sun's weak early rays were only just stretching into some corners of the wood, suffusing them with a rosy pink colour, whilst most remained in darkness, cloaked by the tangled canopy of the trees.

With a light morning breeze on my face, cooling some of my anger and embarrassment, I tried to set to work in an orderly way, collecting herbs, mushrooms, and anything else that might be useful in my witchcraft or cooking. But my mind wandered as I worked, and my hands shook angrily, and I was so distracted that I unintentionally shredded some elephant's ears I had picked. Would I be brought so low in Henri's opinion that he wouldn't want to stay with me?

*Did you think he would stay forever?* the cruel voice in my head asked. *Did you think this could go on? You must go home sometime. You must free your sister. He will get his memory back eventually, and why should his life have space for you? Were you foolish enough to imagine a life for you together? What could a happy ending possibly look like?*

*No, I had no expectations,* I answered, knowing it was a lie. Why did I care so much? Because he was the first man I had been with? Hadn't my mother said that men were tools, to be used when the need arose and laid down when they were no longer wanted? She had wanted me to use men and then cast them aside, never growing emotionally attached. Men, she had taught me, were not to be trusted. I was meant to harden my heart against them, lest they break it.

But it wasn't like that; Henri meant too much to me. I cared for him, more than simply wishing him well and wanting to free him from his enchantment. More than wanting to give him back the life he had before. *You love him,* the cold voice said. *And love is the greatest weakness there is. Just look at the state you're in now.*

I spent the rest of the morning practicing in my head all of the cutting, cruel things I would say if Henri threw the fact that we'd had sex in my face. There were also kinder, dignified speeches, too, full of superior glances and grandiose language.

It must have been midday when I finally returned to the cabin. I had postponed seeing Henri for as long as possible. But the moment I was back, I worried once again that my entrance would be met with his absence. I opened the door; he was not in the hall, nor the kitchen, nor the dining room, nor any of the bedrooms. The house was empty. I felt the fluttering of panic beginning in my chest, my throat tightening and the hot sting of tears behind my eyes as I walked briskly to the back door and out into the little enclosure.

There he was, mending the chickens' hutch. I felt a weight drop from me as I was flooded with relief at seeing him, but his face clouded when he saw me.

"I'm glad you're making yourself useful, because I have lunch," I said in a clipped tone, waving my basket of foragings vaguely. "Are you hungry?"

His brow cleared, he smiled, and my heart leapt despite myself.

"Rose," he breathed, coming toward me, and almost falling over a stray wooden paling as he kept his eyes on me. "You're back."

"I am," I said, forcing a casual smile. "Did you think I'd gotten lost?"

"Something like that."

"Well, as you say, I'm back. Bring in some eggs, will you? I'll make lunch."

Inside, I busied myself with preparing the meal. I thought about how ridiculous my mother would think me, preparing food for a man with my own hands and mooning about like some common peasant girl or scullery maid. I pushed the thought away and focused instead on the omelette before me. It was something I had become especially good at making while I'd been at the cabin, and while it was by no means a fancy or complicated dish, I found the simple meal wholesome and comforting.

When we were both seated at the table and I was already tucking into my omelette, Henri said in a serious tone, "Rose, do you want me to leave?"

I almost choked in my surprise.

"What? No, why would you think that?"

"I thought, maybe, after last night, you might not want me to be here anymore."

*Of course, I want you, you big, handsome idiot,* my brain yelled, but my pride had the sense to rein in my mouth. I took a deep, calming breath and recalled one of the many speeches I had prepared in my morning's wanderings. There had been a few different versions, ranging from contrite, to reasoning, to furious. One had included the threat of turning him back into a bear. I chose to be reasonable. And honest.

"I don't feel ashamed about what we did last night, though I feel like you think I should be." He made to speak, but I gave him a look that silenced him. "I won't be made to feel guilty or embarrassed, or unworthy of respect. In my mind, we are two reasonable people, and no harm has been done to anyone. I certainly wasn't hurt – in fact, quite the opposite."

He looked relieved. Then he smiled, a small, embarrassed smile. I hated how much I loved his smile.

"I see. I'm glad you feel that way. Because I'm not ashamed, either, and I certainly don't want you to be. I just worried you might have felt – taken advantage of – or, or–" Words, apparently, failed him.

"I don't," I said with feigned nonchalance. I stood up, trying to make a dignified exit, though my omelette was only half-finished, and went to the kitchen, where I began cleaning up. I piled dishes into the basin and was about to begin washing when Henri came in behind me.

He reached around me and took hold of each of my hands, then gently turned me to face him.

"Rose," he said, "if I had nowhere else to go, would you let me stay here, with you?"

"Yes," I said, a bit breathless, not meeting his eye.

"And if I had somewhere to go, but wanted to stay here anyway, would you have me?"

I looked him in the face then, wondering if he meant what I thought he might. What a future together might look like, or if it would even be possible, I had no idea. There were so many factors in motion, so many things that needed to be resolved that making plans seemed foolish. Despite this, the word 'yes' escaped as a whisper before he kissed me and I stopped talking or even thinking.

*** * * ***

I spent the next few weeks in a kind of blissful, love-fogged daze. Almost every moment that was not spent working on a potion for Lily, eating, sleeping, or doing some other essential activity, I spent with Henri. We would lie together in bed or in front of the fire at night, while I shared stories from my childhood, Henri sometimes remembering a similar story of his own, or recalling some other memory from his past. Now that he knew everything about me, I didn't have to edit my stories, and I could tell him the whole truth. It was so freeing to be utterly honest and real in everything I said, to keep nothing back. I realised there wasn't a single other person who knew everything about me, not even Lily or my mother. I'd always had to be a different version of myself, trying to please everyone and never allowing myself to be seen in my entirety.

Talking seemed to help him remember his own life better than anything else did, so each day I was able to draw new information from him. For instance, we established that he must have been from a noble family, or possibly one wealthy from trade, because the details of his life that he described aligned so well with my own experience, I felt sure he had grown up with the same privileges I had.

He remembered his younger sister's name was Sophie, and that she was possibly as much as eight years younger than him, while his brother was younger by about two years. He remembered that he had a dog, a Schnauzer called Gus, who had followed him everywhere.

I loved hearing the little details of his life, seeing how he lit up when things fell into place, and he knew just a little more about himself. Though I was happy that he was remembering more about his past, I wondered if there would ever be a place for me in his future once he finally remembered everything. Perhaps more importantly, once I had woken Lily and found a peaceful way to restore her to the throne. Even in the idyllic world Henri and I lived in for those few months, I never forgot the responsibility that weighed on me night and day. Or if I did forget, it was only for a moment. I knew the longer he stayed with me, the greater the chance that someone would be sent to check on me, and would discover him, too, as my mother's notes continued to arrive, albeit infrequently. While she hadn't questioned me about my plans for returning home, it was only a matter of time before she did, and I would have to decide what to do about Henri. I certainly couldn't have him discovered living with me when my escort inevitably arrived. Vague plans formed in my mind, but I tried to ignore the issue as much as possible, despite knowing that one way or another, things would eventually come to a head, and we would have to say goodbye.

One day, as I was getting dressed, Henri walked up behind me and brushed aside my hair, which was hanging loose and long down my back, to place a tender kiss where my neck met my shoulder. I closed my eyes, content.

"I hope you aren't trying to distract me," I said with mock severity. "I have a lot to do today. I've thought of another variation to try with the potion."

"I would never dare come between a witch and her craft," Henri said, before kissing up my neck to just below my ear, making me go all tingly, as a current of excitement ran through my blood.

"Really, because you seem bent on drawing me from my purpose," I said, my voice hitching as I turned to kiss him back.

"Your highness," he teased. "I do not think there is a man alive who could draw you from your purpose, if you did not want to be drawn. You are as tenacious as you are beautiful, like a lioness. It's something that makes you different from most other people, your unrelenting determination. And it's one of the things

I love about you." He moved in to kiss me again. I pulled away, the beginnings of an idea suddenly illuminating my brain.

"Say that again?"

"I love you," he said, smiling and moving to kiss me again.

This time I let him distract me for a while, and when we broke apart, I said, "I love you, too. But I meant the other thing you said. What makes me *different.*"

I ran from the room, downstairs to the kitchen, and began rummaging among my books, throwing things aside in my hunt for a specific text, a particular passage I had read at some previous time, but dismissed as being irrelevant until now.

"Aha!" I yelled in triumph, throwing the book on the table with a bang. "There it is," I said, gesturing to the open page with a flourish. "What makes *us* different."

Henri had followed me downstairs and now stood beside me, a bemused look on his face.

"I love your manic energy, and you look very beautiful when you're excited, but I don't follow you. What makes you different?"

"Exactly!" I cried excitedly. "My mother has said to me often that what makes us, she and I, different from other witches is the number of generations that witchcraft goes back in our family. Magic is said to grow stronger with each practising generation, of which we have had many. She said something like two hundred years of unbroken practice of Hecate's science by witches in our family line."

Henri looked confused, and it was adorable.

"That *is* a lot. So?"

"*So,* to strengthen a potion, or to produce a certain unique effect, a witch may imbue it with her own qualities. In this case, the concentration of magic from her powerful ancestors, for added potency. I share my mother's lineage and so am also imbued with the same deep magic, if not more so. If I add a piece of *myself* to the potion – because I share blood with both the brewer *and* the victim – it should bridge whatever changes my mother made to her original potion and have the strength needed to wake Lily!"

"A piece of you? Like a chunk of flesh?" He sounded disgusted as well as worried.

"I don't think that will be necessary. Maybe some blood or hair. Or both, for good measure."

"That still sounds unpleasant. So, what do we do now?" he asked, eager to assist, and my heart swelled again at the way his first instinct was always to help.

"Now, we wake my sister," I announced with a wicked grin.

# Chapter Fifteen

After all my previous attempts at concocting a cure for Lily, I had several vials of potions lying around. All I needed was the basic antidote, the same one I had first brewed, combined with my hair and blood to strengthen it. I was sure this was the answer. Whether it was just hope, intuition, or some magical ability I didn't fully understand, I was certain that I had finally landed on the right track at last.

The potion needed twenty-four hours to mature: just enough time for me to come up with a plan and set it in motion. I rode to the nearest town and purchased another horse so Henri could accompany me to Marie and Otto's home, where I would wake Lily and then we would ride on to Altenburg the following morning. I sent Christian a message telling him when and where to meet us, ensuring we had an escort into Altenburg. I instructed him to send a reply by Nox if there was a problem, but that I would take silence as confirmation for the sake of saving time.

Once Lily awakened there would be no shelter for us in Silvaner, not as long as my mother ruled. I was sure she would know that I had set myself against her before too long; she had already asked when I would return home more than once in her messages and was certain to send someone to the cabin eventually, despite my regular replies.

My plan was to ensure Lily's safety by taking her to Christian for protection while we worked out how to dethrone my mother. To keep her from wondering where I was or sending for me, I wrote to my mother and told her I would be returning home in a few weeks' time, desperately hoping she wouldn't send someone any sooner.

Such were the broad strokes of my plan. The details were somewhat more complicated. For instance, I had written to Christian, asking him to meet us at the border of our two kingdoms in two days' time, feeling inexplicably certain that I would be able to awaken Lily and reunite them. But I had no way of knowing how we, or rather I, would be received by the King and Queen when they heard the full story. Christian had agreed to tell them only that Lily was missing and that I was working to recover her, but the truth was bound to come out when we arrived in Altenburg.

For another, I knew that magic would be my greatest resource if it came to a fight between us and my mother; but I couldn't take all of the books and supplies I needed for my work. With only two horses to carry our baggage, I had to restrain myself, packing only the most essential volumes, and taking only the potions I knew would be most useful. As for the ingredients I had collected over the last few months, most were readily available in the woods or even at markets, but the rarer and harder to come by items, such as bat's wings and snake blood, would need to come with me to Altenburg. When I woke that day, a thick mist had descended over the forest, and despite the arrival of summer, the air felt frigid as well as damp, and a sense of unease gripped my stomach like a clenched fist. As we packed our supplies for the journey, along with my cumbrous books and potion ingredients into the saddle bags hanging either side of Henri's new horse, Henri laid his hand over mine as I checked the buckle was properly fastened for the third time.

"It's going to be ok," he said gently as I turned to look at him.

"You don't know that," I replied, feeling ill from the painfully tight clenching sensation in my belly.

Instead of answering me, Henri pulled me into a tight hug and rested his chin atop my head for a few moments. The closeness was calming, and I felt my pulse slow slightly, my stomach releasing some of its tension.

Eventually, we set off for Marie and Otto's cottage, Artemis trotting along at our side, having refused to enter her basket again and bolting off like an arrow when I showed it to her.

The mist cleared as the sun grew higher, burning off the damp haze and brightening my mood infinitesimally, but the ride still felt like the longest I had ever taken, time seeming to slow to a crawl as my eagerness to reach my sister whittled away my patience to almost nothing.

When we reached the cottage, Marie opened the door to us, smiling. Then her eyes crinkled with something like caution when she saw Henri standing just behind me.

"This is my brother, Henri," I lied quickly, hoping to spare us awkward questions and explanations. Marie's face softened and she led us into the cottage. Introductions made, I hurried into Lily's room, while Henri waited with Otto and Marie at their kitchen table. They all had looks of tense expectation on their faces, as though waiting for the arrival of a baby or the delivery of some terrible news.

The sight of my sister in her unnatural slumber never failed to make my heart ache, as she lay on the bed, as beautiful as the first snowdrop of the season, her cheeks and lips still rosy even in a cursed sleep, her chest rising and falling almost imperceptibly, the only indicator that she lived. *Please, please let this work,* I thought. It had been years since I'd prayed, but in that moment I sent out prayers to any deity who might be listening. My hands shook as I unstoppered the vial. I knew this was the most potent potion I had ever made, and the strongest I could possibly make. If it failed, I would have exhausted all options, and we would be truly lost. All the surety and confidence I had felt up to now ebbed away as I sat on the edge of the bed, readying myself for whatever might happen, hoping desperately to succeed but trembling with fear of failure.

I drew a deep, sobering breath and eased the cork from the vial. I tilted back Lily's lovely head and allowed a few drops to fall into her open mouth. Then I laid her head back down on the pillow and waited.

Her eyes still closed, she drew a deep, sleepy breath and exhaled with a drawn-out sigh. My heart was in my mouth as I reached a shaking hand out to her and gently took hold of her shoulder.

"Five more minutes," she murmured in a voice thick with sleep, as she lazily swatted my hand away.

A bark of shocked laughter burst from me and startled her awake, her bright blue eyes suddenly wide open. She had the stunned, slightly annoyed look of someone who has been suddenly awakened from a deep and pleasant sleep. Tears of happiness and relief spilled down my cheeks as I threw myself onto her, hugging her tightly. She made a noise of irritation, and I sat back up to see her looking at me in confusion.

"Rose, what are you doing? You're squashing me." Then she glanced around the room, taking notice of the unfamiliar surroundings. "Where are we? Why are you dressed like that?"

I looked down at my peasant dress and let out another strangled laughed.

"You spend months asleep and the first thing you ask is about my dress?"

"What do you mean?" she asked, astounded. "I have *not* been asleep for months. I was just weary after the ball, I had to rest my eyes. You know it was a late night." She glanced around the room again, this time with a sharper eye. "But we aren't at the palace. Where are we?"

I bit my lips a moment, steeling myself to tell her what had happened.

"What I am going to tell you will sound completely mad, but I promise you it's the truth."

I told her the whole story: what our mother had done, how Jurgen had spirited her away, my discovery of her, Christian saving me, me saving Christian, leaving her with Marie and Otto, my attempts to wake her, all that had happened over the last ten months. It took a surprisingly little time to tell. When I finished, her eyes were round with astonishment, wonder, and shock.

"Mother wanted me dead? She actually ordered this man, Jurgen, to *kill* me?"

"I wouldn't have believed it myself had I not overheard her with my own ears and seen Jurgen with my own eyes," I said, squeezing her hand, reassuring myself that she was truly with me again.

"But why? Why would she-?"

"I've had more time to process this than you, and my answer is this: I think she wanted to keep the crown for herself. I think when she realised you were really going to marry Christian, she became desperate."

Lily nodded thoughtfully, worrying at her bottom lip with her teeth.

"She is very much in love with her power," Lily said, almost absently. "And you're a witch now?" There was no fear or anger in her question, only astonished curiosity.

"Yes. I've been studying with Mother for some time."

"How long?"

"A little more than four years."

"Four years?!" she shrieked. "Four years and you never told me?"

"I swore I would keep it a secret from everyone. Even you. I wanted to tell you, truly. But I promised."

Lily puffed out a thoughtful breath.

"At least now I know why you've been distant, always busy with things that didn't involve me. And telling me the most unconvincing stories of what you were up to. I thought of all kinds of reasons why you pulled away from me, but that you were a witch never crossed my mind."

"I'm sorry." It felt like an almost comically insufficient response, but it was all I could think to say.

"Well, at least there are no more secrets between us," she said with a sweet smile, rising from the bed.

"Actually," I said, gesturing for her to sit back down. "There is a man out there, who I have told our hosts is our brother. It's a long story, but you must pretend he is. I promise I'll explain all of it once we're away from here."

"But who is he? And why is here?"

"I'll tell you everything when we're on our way to Altenburg."

When I reminded Lily that we were to set off shortly to meet Christian, she agreed to do whatever I asked. I helped her to her feet and assisted her in changing into a set of clothes I had brought with me. She was still in her elaborate, fine gown from the night of the ball, and the sight of it was unexpectedly unsettling for the way it highlighted just how long my sister had been asleep. Lily was a little unsteady on her feet after several months' inactivity, and I had to help her to the door.

When we rejoined the others, Marie rushed to my sister's side, a motherly smile of affection crinkling her wizened old face.

"My dear, dear girl. I'm so happy to see you up and about. We were beginning to worry you would never wake."

Lily smiled awkwardly; Marie and Otto had watched over her for many months, growing attached to her, even. But to her they were still complete strangers; it had to be a deeply disorienting experience.

Marie insisted on giving us lunch, which we ate gratefully, though Lily confessed afterwards that she was still ravenous. Spending several months in an enchanted sleep appeared to have given her quite an appetite.

I was sad to be farewelling Marie and Otto; they'd done a great service to the kingdom, though they didn't know it. But more than that, they had been kind and cared for my sister when I couldn't. It was true that they had been paid handsomely, but no amount of gold would ever wipe out the debt, as far as I was concerned. The balance of good done was entirely on their side of the bargain.

Marie gave me a warm hug as I bade her farewell, but dissolved into a mess of tears when she said goodbye to Lily. Lily, for her part, acted very kindly and sympathetically, but looked uncomfortable at the fervour of Marie's affectionate farewell.

As we rode off, Lily and I on Bastian, and Henri on the other horse I'd purchased, she whispered to me, "Now will you tell me about the man?"

I laughed aloud and invited Henri to tell the story himself. It was bizarre to hear it all from his perspective. He made the tale of my transforming him back into his human form sound like an act of intense bravery and wonder, to the point that I asked him to talk about something else. At one or two places he paused, deciding how much to tell Lily about our relationship. Thankfully, he kept the specifics to a minimum. There were a few places I had to fill in some details, but otherwise, he told a good story.

"So you were a bear? An actual *bear*? With claws and paws and a snout and – and everything?" Lily asked, astounded.

"Yes, I was," he replied evenly, a smile on his lips.

"How incredible. Was it fun?"

Henri laughed. "Sometimes."

However, when Lily asked how long it had been since he had returned to his human form and what we had been doing in the meantime, I answered before Henri could.

"I've been busy finding a cure for you, dear sister, and Henri has been trying to recover his memory."

"I'm glad you had some company, Rose, and weren't at that cabin all by yourself all this time. I would have hated for you to be *lonely*," she said, a little too innocently. I elbowed her lightly in the ribs and she dropped the subject.

We passed the night at a wayside inn, taking two rooms, with Lily and I sharing one. As I climbed into bed next to her, an irrepressible smile spread across my face.

"I've missed this. I missed you," I said, snuggling in close, breathing her familiar scent of violets and primrose, and closing my eyes, trying to commit every detail to memory and store them away like treasures.

"It's so strange. To me, it's as though I only saw you last night. For me, the ball *was* last night. But you say it's been months. Nearly a year. You can't understand what it's like to fall asleep and then awaken to find that so much time has passed. Never mind how greatly my life has changed. It's thoroughly disorienting."

"I can only imagine. The spell essentially froze you in slumber, so really it was just one long sleep. You've taken it all much better than I'd have expected."

She ignored this remark.

"What must it have been like for Christian all this time? Have you been in touch with him?" she asked fretfully, her forehead puckering with worry lines.

"Yes, I told you. I sent him reports as often as I had anything worthwhile to tell him. Though it wasn't very often."

"And by crow, no less. You really *are* a witch." Her voice was full of wonder, not fear or disgust, which filled me with relief. She had every right to be furious with me, but she wasn't.

"I'm still me, Lily. The magic is – well – it's just a part of me now. Like my sight or smell. It's something I do, but also something I *am*. Sometimes I feel like it's always been there inside me and was just waiting," I mused. "But I'm still your sister, and I love you."

"I love you too," she said, giving my arm a warm squeeze.

I thought this was the end of our conversation and rolled over on my side to sleep. But then she spoke again.

"So, what were you and your handsome man-bear friend up to, alone together all that time in the woods?"

"I told you. I was focused on helping you."

"Every hour of the day and night? Pfft! I don't believe you. And I saw how you looked at him, like he was a little puppy you wanted to wrap up in your arms and smother with kisses. *Have you kissed him?*"

I dimmed the lamp on the small bedside table and pulled the covers over my head so she couldn't see my face.

"Be quiet, Lily, it's time to sleep," I said thickly through the blanket.

"I'm not tired. I've been asleep for months, remember? Have you done *more* than kiss him?"

She pulled the covers from my face and leant in to interrogate me more closely, looming over me in the dimness.

"Go to sleep now, or I'll curse you myself," I said, half-jokingly.

"Oh, fine," she sighed, slumping onto her back.

There was silence for a minute.

"Was it nice?" she asked, and then I hit her with a pillow.

# Chapter Sixteen

The next morning, we set off as early as we could, though we were slightly delayed by the necessity of having a sizeable breakfast at the inn, which Lily assured me she couldn't possibly do without. It was strange, seeing her eat so much and with such enthusiasm, when she had always prided herself on her small appetite.

I had told Christian to expect us around sunset, and we still had quite a distance to cover, mostly crossing the narrow pass between the mountains at the southern border. It was early summer, so there was no snow or ice to slow our progress, but the road was long and undulated significantly between steep peaks and deep troughs that made up the range which marked the boundary between our two kingdoms. Luckily it was such a well-used thoroughfare that it was well maintained, albeit overly worn in places. Our horses were burdened by carrying us as well as the magical supplies I'd brought from the cabin, but our progress was as swift as could be expected, with only the necessary breaks to rest and refresh ourselves and the horses.

Yet the anxiety burning away inside me like a well-fed fire made any delay, no matter how small, feel like an eternity. So much was dependent on our reaching Altenburg safely, on getting Lily away from the reaches of my mother's power. Once we arrived, we still had to secure support for Lily's bid for the crown and find a way to deal with my mother. With all these monumental concerns still to be addressed, I tried not to think of what would happen between Henri and I. Somehow my love life seemed like the least of our problems, and if I was honest, I was happy for any excuse to defer having to make any decisions that would lead to mine and Henri's parting, because that seemed the most likely outcome, no matter what either of us wanted.

Because of my eagerness to reach our destination, the journey passed painfully slowly, but conversation was in great supply, and between the three of us a constant stream of dialogue was maintained as we rode through the day. Though much of it I could have happily gone without.

"If Mother was desperate enough to keep the throne that she was willing to kill me, how do you propose we remove her without having to wage an all-out war?"

"I had hoped that I'd be able to persuade her to go into exile. When she knows that you're alive and married to Christian, with the might of Altenburg behind you, she will have to concede the throne to you," I said with more certainty than I felt.

"And if she refuses?"

"I suppose it will have to be war. But I hate the idea of Silvanian soldiers dying when we might resolve this peacefully. I have to hope that she can be persuaded to do what's best for our kingdom."

"And, you're certain Christian still wants me? It's been almost a year – are you sure his affections haven't. . . cooled?"

"I promise you they have not. He wrote of how desperately he missed you in every letter".

Lily let out a long, mournful sigh. I envied her assurance in a future with the man she loved. Then recalled that she had far more at stake than I did and mentally shook myself.

"It's still so difficult for me to believe that Mother could really want me dead," she said, resting her head on my back as we rode on.

"I know. I've been battling with the idea for months and I still have trouble really believing it. It must be a great shock to you." I sighed and continued, "I know there must be a confrontation, and a punishment for what she's done; there's no way around that now. But I can't help feeling miserable about it."

"I know what you mean. She's still our mother."

"Yes, she's still our mother. But I can't forgive her for what she did to you, and what more she meant to do. I feel all mixed up about it. I don't know what the best outcome would be, or how we'll live with it when it's all over. There's no version of this story where we all get what we want."

"Whether for good or bad, she'll make the choice for us. What she decides to do next is out of our hands," Lily said softly.

There was something calming about the fact that whatever happened next was beyond our influence. Try as I might, I couldn't make others' decisions for them. I could only control my own actions and do what I thought was right. I only hoped it would be enough.

"Listen to you, so wise. You already sound like a queen".

As the sun sank lower, casting the landscape in grey, while the clouds overhead glowed with shades of pink, mauve, orange, and gold, we passed through the lowest slopes on the further side of the mountain range, then out onto an open plain. Finally, we drew near the appointed meeting place, and I spotted mounted horses in the distance. We were too far away to make them out clearly, but I knew which was Christian by his princely attire, while the men with him wore soldiers' uniforms, marked with the green and gold of Altenburg. There was another figure with them, too, a woman; from a distance I couldn't tell who, but from the slim silhouette and chic riding costume, I was certain it wasn't Queen Gisela.

"There he is," Lily breathed softly, impatiently craning her neck over my shoulder for a better view. "He came for us."

"Did you doubt he would?" I asked, amused.

"Go faster," she urged.

I gave Bastian a squeeze with my heels and our pace quickened, with Henri keeping close behind us. When we were about fifty yards from the other party, the girl who was with them let out a shriek, then yelled out, "Henri!" and kicked her horse into a gallop. She closed the distance between us quickly, Christian following close on her tail, and they reached us at almost the same time.

"Henri," she called again breathlessly, as she drew her horse up beside his and threw her arms around him, the horses nickering in surprise. "*Where have you been?* We thought you were dead!"

Dread and jealousy were competing for an equal place inside me as I saw Henri warmly embrace the pretty young girl, tears streaming down both of their faces.

"I know, Sophie, I know. It's a long story, and I'll tell you everything soon. Christian," he added, seeing the prince a few feet behind Sophie.

Christian said nothing but dismounted his horse quickly before pulling Henri roughly from his saddle as well. His face clouded with a tumult of emotion; for a moment I thought he would hit Henri. Then he pulled Henri into a hug, as his sister had done, and I saw tears glistening on his cheeks.

"Oh, Brother," Christian said, his voice muffled against Henri's shoulder. "We'd lost hope that you would ever come back to us."

The full meaning of this exchange hit me like a thunderclap. Henri was Christian's brother the one who had died while out hunting. But he hadn't died at all, only been cursed and wandered very far from home, losing himself more and more the longer he spent as a bear. The brothers parted with exclamations of surprise and incredulity, then Sophie, too, dismounted and joined in, hugging her brothers and crying happily at their unexpected reunion.

Lily and I were still perched on Bastian's back throughout all of this, unobserved by the three siblings and not wanting to spoil the family's moment. But eventually Lily grew impatient and said in a clear but soft voice:

"Hello, Christian." He was instantly at her side, helping her from the horse, embracing her and kissing her, his face streaked with a fresh wave of tears.

Henri approached me, offering a hand to help me dismount. I accepted, and when I was once again on the ground, I said in a low voice that only Henri would be able to hear, "Thank you, your highness."

"I promise, I didn't know until just now. It just came flooding back to me when I saw Sophie and Christian," he said, his voice too low to be overheard, his tone full of apology and conciliation.

"It's alright. We can talk later," I whispered in a tone of false calm and forcing a smile, before turning to Christian, who stood beside us, still with a look of dumbfounded happiness on his handsome face. Now that I saw them side by side, I wondered how I could have failed to notice the resemblance before now. True, Henri was a little taller, maybe a little leaner where Christian was more heavily muscled. His hair was several shades darker, and his eyes brown instead of grey. But the shapes of their faces, the broad jaws and narrow chins, the straight, clear lines of their noses, were almost like mirror images.

"You, Rose, are truly a woman in a thousand, more even! You not only saved my love, Lily, but you've returned my brother to us as well. Our family owes you a great deal. How is this possible?" Christian said, pulling me into a suffocating hug that made explanation impossible.

"It's a long story," I gasped out, slightly strangled by his hold on me. "One we should wait to tell until we are safely in Altenburg." Though we had crossed the border a short time ago, I was hesitant to linger chatting over our histories until we had put a greater distance between ourselves and Silvaner.

"Of course," he said, suddenly releasing me. He turned to his men, who had joined us sometime during the various reunions and remained a short, respectful distance away, while keeping watch for any threats. Christian gave instructions to their captain. "Help the ladies mount up; Princess Lily shall ride with me. You will stay close to Prince Henri, Princess Rose, and Princess Sophie. I mean for us to reach the palace quickly and safely."

The captain nodded sharply, then cast a quick, surprised glance at Henri before setting the men moving on his command, and soon we were all mounted again and on our way. In the chaos of the moment, I had secured Artemis - who was frightened of so many strangers - in her basket and tied it to Bastian's saddle.

"I know, girl. It's a lot to take in," I said to her through the wicker bands. "Believe me, I'm as confounded as you are."

"Leadership suits you," Henri observed smilingly to Christian.

"Well, I've had to step in more and more of late. Father's not well."

The smile on Henri's face vanished.

"Tell me."

"His heart is weak; he becomes exhausted doing the least thing these days. And his mind wanders sometimes, like he isn't really there. All the physicians say the same thing; he doesn't have much longer."

The brothers discussed the king's health, the queen, and the kingdom in general all the way to the palace, Sophie trailing close behind them, interposing details and observations every so often. Lily sat in front of Christian, his arms banded around her, while I fell quietly to the back of the caravan, wishing Lily were still riding with me so I wouldn't have to be alone with my thoughts. With the three siblings chatting busily and Lily ensconced amongst them, I felt about as useful and welcome as a fifth wheel on a wagon.

I hadn't given much thought to what would become of Henri and I after all of this was done with; I'd hardly had time, and it was easier not to plan for a future we might not have. But in the rare moments between waking and sleeping, my mind sometimes showed me pictures of what a life together might be like. I had imagined us living in Silvaner, at the castle, or perhaps a *château* in the hills. Somewhere we were alone, comfortable, able to be ourselves, as we had been at the cabin.

Of course, there was no chance of that now. Henri would be king of Altenburg when his father died, which it seemed could be any day. Then he would be required to make a suitable, strategic marriage, one that brought his kingdom soldiers, or gold, or profitable trade agreements. While Christian would still marry Lily, and they would rule Silvaner together. But there was no place for me in that version of the future. It made me regret that I had never applied myself much to learning the art of prophecy. Maybe if I had, I would have seen this coming.

*  *  *  *

The sky was darkening when we reached the gates of the city of Bellin Stadt, the capital and beating heart of Altenburg. It was a colossal, towering city, and sprawled across a great stretch of land, a wide river coursing through its centre. We entered through the immense, towering gates into the city, passing through a large market square, then a shopping district full of tailors, cobblers, haberdashers at one end, and butchers, grocers, and bakers at the other. In between there was every kind of merchant, craftsperson, and food vendor imaginable. It was the most modern and bustling city I had ever seen; it made Silvaner look provincial, old, and insignificant by comparison.

The streets churned with tradespeople and servants going about their business. Large carriages carrying the wealthy choked up sections of the broad, cobbled road that bisected the city, the inhabitants calling out directions to their servants or crying greetings to those in passing carriages.

There was a gentle incline as we passed through the heart of the city en route to the palace, which gleamed in the middle distance. It was constructed of white stone and looked much more modern than the castle of Silvaner. It had several tall, narrow towers with pointed turrets and many levels stacked neatly each atop the other, the roof made up of dark blue tile. It was as beautiful and delicate-looking as a wedding cake.

Once we had entered the open forecourt, which instantly flooded with grooms, guards, and servants, we dismounted and prepared to go inside. Henri whispered an order to a footman who stood near the grooms waiting to take our horses to the stables. The footman gave a sharp, intelligent nod and followed after the grooms to retrieve our luggage.

"I've ensured that your things are taken to my room. No one will meddle with them," Henri said quietly.

"Thank you." I'd been anxious not to have anyone looking through my books and supplies; the fewer people who knew I was a witch, the better.

"Our parents will want to see us immediately; they'll want to know Henri has returned," Christian said as we made our way up the broad stone steps to the grand oak doors. "In the meantime, I shall have Princess Lily and Princess Rose taken to guest rooms."

He turned, speaking to a maid who had appeared at his side. A small army of other servants fluttered around the cavernous entry hall, each busily going about some task or other like a hive of active bees.

"Please take them up to the Emperor's Suite and see that they have everything they need," Christian instructed the maid. Turning back to Lily, he said, "I shall see you soon," and kissed her hand, looking at her as though leaving her side was the most painful thing he'd ever endured.

I looked at Henri, wanting to exchange a look or word with him before we were efficiently escorted away, but his mind was elsewhere, probably in the room where his parents waited for him, so Lily and I were ushered away without another word.

"I am Gerda," the servant told us in a stern tone. "Please follow me."

She was a tall, slim, intimidating-looking woman I guessed to be in her mid-forties. She had steely grey hair pulled back in a severe style, intelligent brown eyes, and a short, cherubic, snub nose that was at odds with her professional, acerbic demeanour.

Gerda herded us up numerous flights of stairs, treating us more like she was our nanny than a servant. She had the type of authoritative personality I thought would make even kings do as she told them, and had no doubt that she tyrannised the younger staff.

Several storeys up, we were shown into a suite of rooms: two bedrooms with an adjoining bath and sitting room. The sitting room was richly furnished in pale green brocades and silks, with thick, cream-coloured carpets on the floors and ivory damask drapes hanging at the windows. It was lavish but not ostentatious, and still had an air of comfort. It also had a spectacular view over the sprawling city below, now sparkling with small lights in the growing darkness.

"Makes the castle of Silvaner look like a mausoleum," Lily whispered to me, eying the elegant décor.

"Shall I have baths drawn for your highnesses?" Gerda asked in between giving orders to a number of other maids, who had materialised as we entered the sitting room.

"Oh, yes, a bath would be heaven," Lily said, sitting on the edge of a richly upholstered couch, as though she didn't dare get too comfortable. "Though I have no other dress with me to wear afterwards. Rose, did you bring any more gowns?"

I shook my head.

"I brought the bare minimum, I'm afraid. Making a fashion statement wasn't my highest priority."

"Never mind," Lily said, eyes downcast, as though she minded very much, rubbing the woollen fabric of the simple dress I'd lent her between her fingers.

"I shall have a selection of gowns brought to your highnesses," Gerda said matter-of-factly. "And tea shall arrive shortly. When you have finished that, your baths shall be ready." With a stately curtsey, she withdrew.

"What a terrifyingly efficient woman," I said, reclining comfortably by Lily on the couch, hoping my dress wouldn't leave any dirty marks behind. "But I am desperate for something to eat, and a bath."

"Oh, yes, I need a long, hot soak. I'm terribly saddle sore," Lily moaned.

I had to suppress a laugh. Lily had spent considerably less time on horseback than I had in the last few days and looked altogether much cleaner and fresher than I did.

"I know, you haven't bathed in months," I teased, and we both burst out into fits of slightly manic giggles.

We had to restrain ourselves from pouncing on the serving girl who brought our tea, and Lily almost cried with joy when she saw the cakes that came with it. They were beautiful: small cakes covered in pink icing, solid fruit cakes, simple tea cakes, bread and butter, and four different types of jam. After months of subsisting on bread, cheese, eggs, and stews, it took all my self-control not to stuff the cakes into my face whole.

After we had both sated our appetites and made our way into the twin copper tubs that sat steaming with hot water in the bathroom, Lily broached the subject of Henri's true identity.

"Isn't it the strangest coincidence? I mean, that he should be Christian's brother! I would never have thought it."

"Nor I, at first. We spent months together and I didn't spot it. But seeing them together, there is a strong resemblance."

"I suppose," Lily said, turning away from me. "But Christian is more handsome."

"He is not!" I exclaimed indignantly, flicking bath water at her.

"I was only teasing," said Lily with a mischievous smile. "I think you are quite smitten with him. Wouldn't it be funny if we married brothers?"

"Hilarious," I remarked drily, not wanting to discuss that particular issue. "You see what this means for Christian, though, don't you? He was all set to be king and now Henri is next in line again."

"It doesn't matter much, for Christian and I will marry, and he will be king of Silvaner."

"Consort, not king," I corrected automatically. "And there is rather a lot to be sorted out first, the small matter of our mother, for one. But you and he should marry. Soon. It will be essential if you are to have the backing of Altenburg in your bid for queen."

Lily uttered a deep, mournful sigh that lingered in the steamy air.

"You sound very strategic. Why is everything so difficult?"

"I believe it is the double burden of being a woman and the rightful queen."

"You know," Lily began tentatively, her hand weaving lightly through the bubbles of her bath. "I've been wondering if it's all worth it."

"How do you mean?"

"Well, you said the kingdom has been thriving under Mother's rule. And if she doesn't choose to give up the crown willingly, we'll have to go to war. I wonder if it's truly worth the cost, just so I can be queen."

I had not considered this point of view; I'd simply taken for granted that Lily was the rightful queen, and therefore we would take whatever measures were necessary to regain her crown. I said as much to her.

"I know it's my birthright and all that," she said. "I just wonder if it might not be easier to simply let Mother rule Silvaner. I don't want people being hurt for me, and we don't know how long a war might last, whether or not Altenburg decides to join on my account."

"Certainly, it would be *easier*," I replied. "But as to whether it would be *right*. Well, I don't know. Do you *want* to be queen?"

"I'm not sure how much what I want comes into it. I was born and raised with the expectation of becoming queen, and I have lived my whole life building up to that purpose. Silvaner is my home, and they are my people. I suppose I feel it's my responsibility to be queen."

"Then you have your answer."

"And what about Mother?" she asked despondently.

"No matter how often I think on the matter, I can't get past what she's done. She betrayed you, both of us, really. Maybe the kingdom, too. I don't know – we can't just let it go."

"I do agree with you. I just don't want to start a war over this."

"We'll do all we can to make sure that doesn't happen."

We would have discussed the matter further, but our conversation was interrupted at this point by the entrance of Gerda and her small army of maids.

"The King and Queen have requested your immediate presence," Gerda announced with the greatest dignity.

"I think we had probably better get dressed first," I said.

Lily giggled.

"These ladies will assist you," Gerda continued, ignoring my comment. "There are gowns for you to choose from in the sitting room. But you must make haste. I shall return in a half-hour." With that, she turned and left the room.

"I suspect Gerda may not have a sense of humour," Lily said, rising from her bath.

We were dressed hurriedly, Lily in a gown of soft mauve satin and I in one of darkest blue. The maids swiftly styled our hair – cooing over Lily's delicate white skin and glossy black locks, frowning at my mass of curls – and pinched our cheeks before declaring us ready to see the King. I had barely sat down again when Gerda reappeared and led us back down several flights of stairs into the King's receiving room.

King Ludwig looked even thinner and more fragile than he had the last time I'd seen him. His face looked almost grey; his breath rasped in his throat as he spoke, and he coughed frequently. Queen Gisela, sitting by his side, fussed over him, declaring that he should be in bed. But he insisted on greeting us with all due ceremony.

"Princess Lily, we are pleased to see you are well. We heard rumours that you had died. I am most glad that is not the case. Welcome to Altenburg. I am sorry it is not under more felicitous circumstances."

"Thank you, Your Majesty," Lily replied with an expertly executed curtsey. "I am well, thanks mostly to my sister, but also to your elder son, who accompanied us from Silvaner."

"Ah, yes," said the King before he was overcome by a coughing fit that lasted a minute or so. "I was coming to that," he continued once he got his breath back. "Princess Rose, I understand that you are responsible for restoring my heir to me. Henri has told us a most fantastic story. Almost too fantastic to be true. But he assures me it's to you we owe thanks for his return."

I curtsied and thanked him for his kind words.

"My other son informs me that he wishes to marry Princess Lily with all haste, and I confess, I should like to see him married before I go." Here he broke off into another fit of coughing. When he next spoke, he added, "It seems I am not long for this world." He was seized again by his cough, and we were excused so that the King could retire to see his physician.

A footman escorted Lily and I into a comfortable room, as beautifully decorated as the sitting room we had left upstairs. But I cared not for the room, only its occupants. Henri and Christian rose to their feet as we entered, Christian taking Lily's hand in his.

"What did Father want to see you about?" he asked anxiously.

"He only welcomed us and thanked Rose for bringing Henri back." She looked at Henri then. "I feel we need another introduction, especially as I am to call you 'brother' soon." She beamed at him as she said this, while he blushed.

"Yes, and I must introduce you to my sister as well. I'm afraid I have been very remiss in my duties. There's been rather a lot going on," Christian said with a sheepish grin. He gestured for Sophie, who had been sitting by the window, to join us.

"Princess Lily and Princess Rose of Silvaner, this is Princess Sophie of Altenburg."

"I am so pleased to meet you," Sophie squealed, flinging her arms around Lily and squeezing tightly. "Christian has told me so much about you, and you are to be married! How exciting. I always wanted a sister – please let me help you plan the wedding."

"I'm afraid it will be quite small, you see; we are likely going to be married in a hurry," Lily explained, casting a quick look at Christian.

"I know you have been through a great ordeal, and to have your crown usurped by your own mother! I cannot imagine how you must feel, my poor sister," she said, her arms still around Lily. Sophie was clearly thrilled to have a new sister in Lily, and I couldn't blame her. Lily was an excellent older sister, and Sophie had spent her whole life only knowing brothers. The princess resembled her mother quite strongly, with her brown hair and brown eyes, like her mother's and Henri's. She looked a few years younger than me, and still had a round, childlike quality about her face. But she seemed a sensible and affectionate girl, and I was pleased to see how warmly she and the rest of Christian's family responded to Lily. It made me hopeful of their support in regaining her crown.

Lily's thoughts must have followed a similar pattern, as she returned Sophie's hug, then asked her to excuse us, so we could discuss some matters in private. Sophie looked offended but left us all the same. Once she was gone, Lily said, "Your father didn't say anything about sending his men to Silvaner should we need it."

"Well, he wouldn't. He won't agree to anything until we're married," Christian replied. "He wants our alliance solidified before committing men to fight for you."

"Then you must act quickly," I put in. "Lily needs to be installed as Silvaner's queen as soon as possible. And she needs the support and protection of Altenburg recognising her as the rightful queen to do that."

Christian nodded, then turned to Henri. They looked odd, side by side, Christian in his splendid prince's attire and Henri still dressed in the simple clothes I had given him at the cabin, as though he hadn't had leisure to change yet.

"If I propose to Father that I marry Lily now, tomorrow, or as soon as we manage it, will you support me?" Christian asked his brother.

"Yes," Henri replied simply. "We owe their family, more than you know," he said, looking at me, his eyes full of warm, unspoken feelings. "I'll help in any way I can. As one future ruler to another, you have my support," he said, directing his gaze to Lily. His eyes said so much more as they lingered on my face, and I yearned to take his hand, to show him how much I appreciated his unhesitating support. But our relationship now existed in a completely different light, and it was possible we wouldn't ever even be able to hold hands in front of other people. The last time we had kissed, he hadn't been set to inherit a kingdom. Now that he was once again the future king of Altenburg, he would need to marry someone who could offer something of valuable to his kingdom: armies, trade agreements, land, or a significant amount of gold. Christian marrying Lily would already shore up ties between our two nations, meaning I had nothing further to offer as a prospective wife. I was once again reminded that my value as a princess was strategic, not personal.

"What we need is an army," I said, tearing my eyes away from Henri's and speaking to the others. "I hope to convince my mother to surrender peacefully, but there is a good chance she'll refuse; she knows she has the upper hand, and she won't give up her power without a fight. We'll most likely need to remove her by force," I said, eager to settle the matter.

"We don't want a war," Christian interposed.

"Nor do we. But we do need your bride installed as the rightful queen. And when you're married, you'll be her consort, it will be your kingdom, too. We don't want a war, but we have to be ready for one," I replied.

"I agree," Henri added. I smiled at him, feeling like my heart was going to leap out of my chest.

"As do I. But first," said Lily, her expression softening. "I would like us to be married."

# Chapter Seventeen

Lily and Christian were married a few days later in the cathedral, which sat a short distance from the palace grounds, but was far older than the pale stone castle. It was a large and beautiful church, with dark, pointed spires that rose like sharp fingers towards the sky. Exquisite stained-glass windows cast multicoloured rays of light over row upon row of aged oak pews. Lily looked radiant in a borrowed gown of violet silk, holding a bouquet of white lilies. It was a small, simple wedding by royal standards, with only Christian's parents, Sophie, Henri, and I in attendance, along with some of Christian's closest friends, including Lucas, and as many of the courtiers who were presently in the city. All told there were perhaps fifty guests – far fewer than there would have been had Lily been able to have the wedding she was meant to as Queen, with all our extended family and the Silvanian nobles in attendance.

As I helped her get ready in our suite at the castle, with several maids bustling about, straightening her train, picking wilted petals from her bouquet, and generally being useful, Lily said to me quietly, "I always thought Elsa would be here, helping me get ready on my wedding day."

I squeezed her shoulder affectionately, thinking fondly of our childhood nanny, who had almost been like a second mother to us.

"I'm sure she'll be there for all the other important things. I know it must be hard not getting married at home, like we'd always thought you would. This isn't the grand celebration it should be."

She nodded silently, looking as though she were holding back tears.

"At least Christian and I will be together," she said softly as a single tear tracked down the apple of her cheek. "That's what matters."

"We'll make everything right," I assured her, squeezing her shoulder again. "Now, no more tears, or you'll be all puffy-faced when you walk down the aisle," I added, and she answered with a brave smile.

When she stood at the doors to the church, Lily no longer seemed concerned about all those who were not there, her entire attention focused on Christian, and his on her as she made her way slowly and gracefully toward him down the considerable length of the dark carpeted aisle.

Their ceremony was long, the bishop speaking for much longer than anyone cared to listen, but I beamed as he declared them husband and wife, tears pricking at my eyes as my gaze wandered to Henri, now dressed in all the elegance of the courtly style. He looked handsome, but I had loved him when I didn't know he was a prince, when he wore whatever clothes I could find at the cabin, so the finery mattered little. I felt a pang of sadness.

He and I hadn't been alone together since our arrival in Altenburg. Between his unexpected family reunion, Lily's wedding plans, and my preoccupation with our imminent return to Silvaner, neither of us had had much leisure time. There was so much I wanted to say to him, but I also missed being able to touch him, missed the casual way he would slip his arm around my waist or how I'd brush his hair back from his brow. We'd grown so close and comfortable in our time at the cabin. Here at court, we had to maintain decorum, which kept us apart. Having lived as we did with no one else around us, it felt strange to be in a room crowded with people standing between Henri and I, unable to touch or even speak to each other most of the time. But his eyes caught mine across the chapel and he smiled, making my heart ache with love and fear. The revelation of his identity as

Altenburg's next king was another thing we would have to contend with, another potential obstacle to our being together.

Cheers and applause erupted from everyone gathered in the cathedral, and the newlywed couple glided out of the church and into the sunshine, where an open carriage waited to carry them about the city so the inhabitants crowding the streets could wave and cheer for their new princess. Back at the castle, a long reception followed, as all the courtiers paid their respects and offered their congratulations to the happy couple.

I was caught up in the throng of guests as they made their way to the magnificent throne room, which was hung with hundreds of beautiful floral garlands and decorated to look like a fairy-blessed wood. There was a feast of pheasants, ducks, boars, trays of baked vegetables, bowls of salad, mountains of the tiny, brilliantly colourful cakes we'd had when we arrived, and endless jugs of wine, beer, and sweet, fruity punch.

It was still early when the king retired to bed, looking grey and utterly drained by the day's festivities, his condition only growing worse with every exertion. But the rest of the wedding party celebrated all day and late into the night. The party was very merry, and it was after midnight when Christian declared himself tired and ready to be alone with his wife.

Lily looked exhausted but delighted as she kissed me goodnight before retiring with Christian.

"Enjoy your wedding night," I whispered as I hugged her, then winking as I let her go.

She blushed deeply, an enormous smile on her beautiful face.

After the bride and groom had left, followed by the cheers and yells of those who remained behind, I caught Henri's eye meaningfully, before pointedly leaving the dining hall myself. I loitered for a few minutes in an alcove outside the hall before he joined me, taking me in his arms immediately and almost crushing me as he held me close. I responded with my own tight hug, feeling as though I couldn't get close enough.

"Six days is far too long to go without being alone together," I said, as he took my face in his hands and kissed me urgently.

"I know. It's been a mad few days. So much has happened," he said, punctuating his sentences with kisses.

"What," I replied ironically. "You mean learning you're the future king of Altenburg, reuniting with your long-lost family, and my sister marrying your brother has been more excitement than you are used to?"

"Don't forget, not so very long ago, I was a bear."

I laughed and kissed him again, making up for lost time.

"Can I come to your room tonight?" he asked. "Lily and Christian will be in his room."

I nodded, Lily's things – mostly borrowed from the Queen and Sophie since we'd had to travel so lightly – had been moved to another suite of rooms nearer to Christian's the day before.

"Yes. Just give me ten minutes, then come to my room."

I hurried upstairs and undressed quickly, letting down my hair from the complicated *coiffure* it had been twisted and pinned into for the wedding, and slipping on a light, silk robe. A short time later there was a soft knock at the sitting room door, and Henri entered. I ran to close the space between us, kissing him and starting to undo his shirt.

"Wait a minute, I need to talk to you about something," he said, taking hold of my hands gently.

"We can talk later," I said, slipping from his loose grasp and wrapping my arms around his neck to kiss him.

"It's important. Besides, you don't want me to think you only want me for my body, do you?" he asked in a teasing tone.

"No, Your Highness," I said in a scandalised tone.

"Come here," he said, leading me to the couch and gesturing for me to sit. I sighed, then did as he asked.

He took a seat beside me.

"Rose, I've been thinking a lot since we arrived. I know there's been a great deal going on, it's been a tumultuous time, and I haven't been able to be with you as much as I want. But it's clarified something for me."

I said nothing, waiting for him to continue, but he seemed to be searching for the words, his throat bobbing slightly as he collected himself. Finally, he said, "I love you," gravely, with an unusual vehemence, as though he were speaking the words for the first time.

"I love you, too," I replied, leaning in to kiss him. He pulled away and slipped onto the floor in front of me, taking my hand.

"Marry me."

I stared stupidly at him for a few seconds before replying.

"What, now?"

"Not right now, but soon. When everything has been resolved with Lily and your mother. I don't want to wait too long, I want to be able to take your hand in public, kiss you when I want to. I hate having to steal a few minutes alone when no one is looking. I love you and I want to marry you."

"But you're going to be king," I said, as though he needed reminding.

"Yes, eventually." He rose from the floor and resumed his seat next to me, my hand still clasped in his. "Don't you want to marry me?" he asked, looking a little hurt by my hesitancy.

"Of course, I do. But things are *so* different now. I mean, are you even allowed to choose your wife just like that? Won't you have to ask for council and get approvals? You aren't just choosing a wife, but a queen. This is state business, not just a choice you can make alone."

"I don't care about any of that. Besides, you're a princess, you're a perfect choice. Add to that the fact that you saved me, returned me to my family. You're a hero, too. And I don't want anyone else. Please say yes."

"I want to - but there are other things I want, too. I want Lily's crown to be safe. I want to know that we're all going to make it through whatever happens when we go to Silvaner. And, I want-" I took a deep breath, stalling for time as I hesitated over my choice of words. "I want to keep practising magic, to be the version of myself I was in the woods. I don't want to go back to-"

"I want that, too, I want you to be happy, fulfilled. I don't want you to feel like you need to change for me, future queen or not. So, will you at least think about it?"

What could I say? Every particle of my being was screaming 'yes', even with all the things still left unsettled. With so much uncertainty in my life, he was one of the few things I was certain of. So, I agreed to think about it, and he said he would give me the time I needed to do that. Then he kissed me again.

"Shall we shake on it?" he asked, his voice light and playful.

"I have a better idea," I said, leading him to the bedroom.

* * * *

I woke the next morning as the sun was just starting to peek over the horizon, flooding the land with hazy yellow light. We had left the drapes open, and a beam of weak sunlight fell on Henri as he dressed.

"I didn't mean to wake you. But I should get back to my room, we don't want the servants talking."

"No, I know, that would be scandalous," I teased. "I wish you could stay."

"I do, too," he said, bending down to kiss me.

"Will you speak to your father today? About sending men to Silvaner?"

"Yes. You know, I sometimes think you're only sleeping with me because I have all these resources at my disposal now."

"Oh, please, I was sleeping with you when I had no idea about any of this," I replied, gesturing to the sumptuous room. "But the fact you have a standing army definitely adds to your attraction."

He laughed.

"Will I see much of you today?" I asked, stretching like a cat in the watery sunshine.

"That depends. I know Father wanted to talk over the matter of succession, his plans for the kingdom. I may be with him sometime, especially if we discuss supporting Lily's bid for Silvaner. But I'll see you at dinner, and maybe again tonight?"

"I hope so," I said, blushing, then marvelling at the fact that he could still make me flush. Then he kissed me goodbye and left. I fell back onto the pillows, wide awake despite the early hour, thinking of how best to approach my mother, worrying what Lily and I would do if the King refused to support Lily's claim. But then I remembered last night, Henri's proposal and everything else, and despite the uncertainty of the future, a broad smile spread across my face.

I didn't expect to see Lily that day; she and Christian had only married the day before. Surely, they would want to be alone for a while. They couldn't take a full honeymoon when we hoped to return to Silvaner any day now, but I expected them to at least take a few days to themselves. Yet, as I was finishing dressing, wondering about getting access to my books so I could prepare for the encounter with my mother, Lily tapped gently at the door before entering the bedroom.

"What's wrong?" I asked, seeing her face creased in sadness and worry. Her eyes were red, and she looked ready to burst into tears.

"King Ludwig is dead. He died in the small hours of this morning. Christian and Henri were both sent for, but he passed quite quickly."

I put my hand to my mouth as tears filled my eyes. I had liked King Ludwig; he could be petulant and proud, and his views were terribly outdated, but he had always shown kindness towards me. But my sorrow was more for Henri. He had only been reunited with his family for such a short time before he lost his father again.

But despite my sadness, there were other pressing concerns that forced themselves on my mind. I wondered what this meant for Lily and me. Henri had said they needed to discuss the succession – did that mean it was not certain Henri would be the next king, after two years away? I hoped whichever brother became King, we would have the support we needed to secure Lily's crown. A tinge of guilt washed over me for considering such things when the man had just died; but there wasn't anything to be done for him now, while mine and Lily's concerns were more pressing than ever.

"Have you seen Christian since he was sent for?"

Lily shook her head slightly, her tears welling as mine had done.

"Not yet, a servant gave me the news. And our presence is requested in the King's study."

It took me a moment to realise that it was not King Ludwig who would be waiting for us when we arrived, but his two sons. We hurried through the corridors, down a flight of stairs, and along another passage before we reached the King's study. When we entered, Henri and Christian were both standing by a large desk littered with papers, deep in conversation.

Lily ran to her husband and embraced him. I walked to Henri, taking his hand, and cupping his cheek with my free hand. I could see the King's death had deeply affected him; his face was drawn and taut with repressed sorrow. Yet he was forced to deal with matters of state before he would have leisure to really feel his grief. He drew me into a tight hug, bowing his head and resting his brow on my shoulder.

"I'm so sorry," I whispered.

We drew apart and the four of us faced each other.

"Our father must have known he didn't have long, he called for a scribe sometime last night to have his wishes set down. Henri is now King," Christian announced, his voice rough with unshed tears.

Lily and I automatically dropped into curtsies, murmuring, "Your Majesty," our years of courtly training taking over.

"Please stand," Henri said, grimacing. "At least when we're alone." He cleared his throat, then said in a more formal tone, "There are things we must discuss. We will have a royal funeral in a few days' time, to allow nobles and dignitaries to travel here. I know there are other pressing matters," he said looking from Lily to me, "but we cannot rush proceedings. King Ludwig deserves the funeral of a King, and we shall take our time and ensure it is all done properly."

We all nodded our agreement. Though I was eager to settle other matters, I knew we had to honour the King as he deserved. More than that, I wanted his family to be able to mourn him properly, without haste. Especially Henri, for whom the hurt had to be doubly sharp, his reunion with his father so recent. This was when the family needed to be together. Our other troubles could wait a little longer.

"In the meantime, I will write to your mother, advising that Princess Lily has the full support of the crown of Altenburg, and that she, Queen Lorelei, has one week to go into exile, or we will send in our army," Henri continued.

"I want to deliver the message to my mother," I said urgently. "It would be better if I spoke with her directly. Then we'll know what's on her mind and she won't be able to brush me off like she might a messenger."

*Or send back their head as a reply.*

"Is that wise?" Christian asked at the same time that Lily said, "Is that safe?"

"Who better to broker peace than me? If she's willing to listen to anyone, to talk terms, it will be me. I want the chance to negotiate, peacefully."

Christian shook his head, his expression dark. "It's a bad idea."

"Do you really think she'll listen to you when she finds out what you've done? Do you think she'll hesitate to imprison you? Or worse?" Henri asked, squeezing my hand anxiously.

"Never mind the fact that she should spend the rest of her life in prison for what she did to Lily," Christian said heatedly. "Even exile is being too generous."

"She's still our mother. I know she's done terrible things, and I'm not saying I forgive her, but I think we need to give her a chance. It matters how Lily starts her reign; it sends a message about what kind of ruler she will be."

Christian and Henri remained silent, but I could tell neither really approved of my idea, but it wasn't their opinions that mattered in this instance.

"Lily, what would you have us do? It's your crown, after all; it should be your decision," I said, hoping to speed an agreement.

"I think," she said tentatively, trying to mediate the hot tempers in the room, but quietly resolved in her own way. "I think Rose should go. Our mother will be more open with her than any other messenger. And as Rose said, if we are to reach a peaceful resolution, she's the best person for the job."

I smiled gratefully at her. Christian scowled and Henri frowned.

It took some more persuading, but eventually it was agreed that I would act as envoy to my mother. But Henri had only agreed on the condition that a detachment of a thousand men, along with Henri himself, would accompany me and set up a camp some miles from the city of Silvaner. I argued against this. Henri was the new King, and it would be dangerous for him to be there if fighting broke out. But in the end, this was the compromise we reached; we would both go to Silvaner, or neither of us would.

"You're being incredibly stubborn and difficult," I told him when we'd reached an agreement.

"As are you," he replied with a slight smile pulling up one side of his mouth.

Lily and Christian insisted on accompanying us, too. I hadn't expected otherwise; it was natural that Lily should be close at hand to see how things proceeded with our mother and her kingdom. But the idea of her being so close to our mother made me nervous.

When we'd talked through our plans as much as we could, Lily and Christian left to see Queen Gisela. I remained with Henri.

"I'm so sorry about your father," I said, drawing my arms around him, feeling useless that all I had to offer were words of little comfort.

"I'm not ready to be King." He looked stunned, maybe even a little afraid.

"You are. You have so much more strength and goodness than you know. And I'm here, for whatever you need."

"I love you, Rose," he said, kissing me deeply, so my reply was lost.

When we broke apart, I felt breathless, almost dizzy.

"You should go; there are bound to be councillors, and God knows who else queued at the door to speak to me." But he didn't release my hand right away; he pressed it to his lips before letting me go.

"The business of the crown, I understand. I just wanted to tell you something quickly first. If your proposal still stands, I accept." I said it quietly, uncertain if this was the wrong time, but he swept me up into his arms and spun around wildly, his beautiful smile beaming, erasing all the sadness from his face.

"Thank you," he said, kissing me. "Thank you for giving me some good news today."

I smiled tearfully and kissed him again before I left. There were about a half-dozen men milling about in the corridor as I left his study, carrying sheaves of paper, enormous ledgers, and all the accoutrements of business. They looked at me with open curiosity as I passed, but I paid them no heed, walking by with my chin raised proudly. One day soon – if our plans succeeded – I would be their queen, and now was not the time to look nervous.

* * * *

Now that he was King, Henri spent every waking hour in his study, meeting with his councillors, together and individually. The magnitude of his responsibilities meant that I only saw brief glimpses of him during the day. Even at night I rarely saw him. I imagined him staying up late, poring over papers and orders, trying to prepare for the onslaught of meetings the following day. It seemed that the business of the kingdom had been neglected of late.

This wasn't a great surprise; King Ludwig had been unwell for some time and had seemed – to me, at least – to be in denial about how sick he really was. In his eagerness to keep the kingdom going and unwillingness to ask for help, he must have left much undone.

Christian was an essential advisor, attending the same meetings as Henri, which meant I spent a good deal of time with Lily, Sophie, and her mother. I liked their company and appreciated the chance to know Henri's family better, though I felt restless and was eager to set off for Silvaner. We sat in sitting rooms, or the garden, or the long gallery, sipping tea and talking, or sewing, or engaged in some other sedentary activity that made me want to tear my hair out. Knowing we were on the cusp of something dire and dangerous but forced into passive inactivity tested my patience more than anything else ever had.

As though he knew I needed the occasional break from his family, Henri had organised for a workroom to be set up, though no one knew what I was to use it for. He handed me the key and promised I would never be interrupted when I was in my sanctuary. I almost knocked him to the ground, so fervent were my kisses of gratitude.

"Remind me to promise you peace and quiet more often," he teased.

When I could slip away to my workroom, even just for an hour, it was a welcome break from the wearying air of mourning that hung over the family when we gathered together.

I had thought that Henri would want to delay announcing our engagement until after the funeral, but he surprised me by telling his family a few days after the King's death. Christian looked utterly unsurprised and pleased with the news, while Sophie and Queen Gisela expressed their joy and amazement openly, embracing me warmly. Queen Gisela hugged me with tears of mingled joy and grief in her eyes.

"I wish Henri's father could have been here to see this, he so admired and respected you. He would have been pleased with Henri's choice of queen," she added, taking my hand affectionately.

I smiled at the compliment, happy to be so willingly adopted by their family, which was closer and more affectionate than my own had ever been, save for Lily. And now she and I would be sisters twice over. This was a bright point of happiness in an otherwise sad and difficult time.

The funeral took place two weeks after the King's death, when nobles, royals, and other dignitaries from across the continent had arrived to honour the late King. Being thrown into the maelstrom of courtly strangers and presented as the future queen of Altenburg made me grateful that I'd seen and learned so much of court life from my mother in recent years. I felt a sharp pang of sadness at the thought of her; no matter what she had done since, she had been assiduous in preparing me for the life I seemed destined to live.

# Chapter Eighteen

Two days after the King's funeral, we set off in a large caravan, Henri, Lily, Christian, and I, accompanied by one thousand soldiers of Altenburg's standing army. There were other familiar faces, too; Lucas formed part of Henri's new Privy Council, and several of Christian's companions, whom I had known in Silvaner, were also with us.

Sophie had begged to come as well, but as the only other royal child she had to remain in the safety of the palace. She would be queen if both her brothers were killed, and she and her mother would act as co-regents in Christian and Henri's absence.

Unhindered by the snows and ice of winter, our progress was quick, and we arrived at our destination on the second day, with a little daylight still remaining. We made camp a few miles from the capital, on an open plain that stretched to the west of the city, just north of the great lake.

I had planned to deliver a message to the queen the morning after we arrived, but as we were setting up camp, a scout entered the war tent and announced that a mounted messenger, and several members of the royal guard, were approaching on the road which led to the city. Henri, Christian, Lily, and I went to watch their approach, our faces tense with anticipation.

I could sense anxiety and determination in the air as we walked through the camp, the atmosphere taut as a bowstring. There was a tension among the men, all of whom were trained soldiers, but many of whom hadn't seen real conflict because the region had been at peace for so long. I saw the fear in their faces as I walked past them and felt guilty and responsible for bringing them here. Some were young, younger than me, and I dreaded the idea of any of them dying if I failed in my mission.

At least we would be safe from an assault in the night, as I had placed protective charms around the entire camp, but this was not widely known. For now, my gifts were a secret to all but Lily, Christian, and Henri.

As the messenger and his guards drew nearer, I recognised Paulus leading the way, with several of his best soldiers following. They drew up to the camp and all except Paulus dismounted. The messenger bowed before handing Henri the missive, noting the simple crown Henri now wore.

"Your Majesty," the messenger said. "A message from her Majesty, Queen Lorelei of Silvaner. I am tasked with returning with your reply."

Henri read the note quickly, then handed it to me, while Christian and Lily read over my shoulder. It said:

*Your Majesty,*

*My deepest sympathies for the loss of your father, the late King Ludwig, and congratulations on your new role as King.*

*I believe you have my daughter, Princess Rose, in company with you, and I demand you return her to me at once or I shall consider your refusal to be an act of war, especially with your host encamped at my doorstep.*

*You have until dawn to return Rose to me and I shall accept your apologies and the advice of your intended removal, along with the immediate return of my daughter as a sign of goodwill and an assurance that you don't mean me or my kingdom any violence.*

*Faithfully,*

*Queen Lorelei of Silvaner.*

I read the letter through twice, biting my lip thoughtfully. This changed little, only moving our plans up by a few hours, but it would mean I returned on my mother's terms, which I hoped would put her in a more conciliatory mood.

"Please give us some time to draft a reply," Henri said evenly to the messenger.

"This changes nothing," I said when we were all gathered along with Henri's advisors and generals in the largest tent. "The plan stays the same; I go to my mother and try to negotiate a peaceful surrender."

There was a general outcry against this.

"That note was not the work of someone looking to surrender," Christian said, arms crossed and scowling.

"If we agree to the Queen's terms by sending Princess Rose to her so soon, we won't have any grounds on which to bargain," an older, balding man, with a stooped back said. I recognised him as one of Henri's council members, but couldn't recall his name.

"Her Highness is the future Queen of Altenburg, you can't possibly think it's wise to send her in," Lucas said. I threw him a glare.

"Can we stop talking about me as though I'm not here?" I demanded. "This is what we agreed on," I continued, speaking only to Henri. "I can keep myself safe," I added more quietly. My magic wasn't something to discuss in the present company, but Henri, Lily, and Christian knew what I meant. "Please".

"Very well," he said, speaking to the council as well as me.

"But, Your Majesty-" the balding man began.

"I trust our future Queen's judgement," Henri said firming, cutting off further debate.

Frowning, he sent everyone away, even Lily and Christian, then drew me close as we talked over the plan one last time. Though he had agreed to me meeting with my mother before the rest of the war council, now that we were alone he tried to talk me out of it. We went over the same arguments for and against, me insisting I was the only person who could go safely, while he urged me to take an extensive guard.

"I hate the idea of you being in this dangerous position, while the rest of us are safely at camp."

"What happened to trusting my judgement?" I asked sharply.

"It's not *your* judgment I don't trust".

I let out a frustrated sigh.

"Do you remember when you told me I was the fiercest and most capable person you had ever met?"

"Yes," he said, sensing where this conversation was headed.

"Do you still think that?"

"Yes." His voice was low, conceding the point.

"Then you have to trust me enough to let me go. Besides, when my mother says she will take a refusal as an act of war, she isn't bluffing. There's no choice but for me to go."

He had no rebuttal to this.

"Just be careful, my love," he whispered pressing a kiss to my forehead.

My mother's envoys waited as Lily helped me dress in a fine gown of dark, burnt orange silk, provided by Queen Gisela and hastily altered to fit me before we'd left Altenburg. I had thought it more practical for me to wear breeches and a tunic, but I was to appear as an emissary, a guest. There was to be no threat in my arrival; I had to look like a future queen, not a bandit. Once dressed, I bid farewell to Lily, Christian, and finally Henri.

"I'll be alright," I said, forcing a smile.

The truth was that my spells would be of little use against my mother if she truly meant to harm me, but didn't tell Lily or Henri this. I tried to downplay the dangers of my mission as much as possible, fearing they might try to prevent me from going if they knew how out of my depth I truly was. But Henri didn't try to persuade me again; he simply held me tight and kissed me in full sight of Lily, Christian, and most of his men. It felt like a goodbye, and my throat ached with unshed tears as I walked away from them all.

Without further delay, I mounted Bastian and allowed the guards to escort me back to the city, none of them, not even Paulus, saying a word to me, or even so much as glancing my way. Though it was now fully dark, as we rode through the lower town there were still merchants going about their work, people walking the streets without any cares in the world. In the upper town, lights and music poured from the windows of the large, beautiful houses, the wealthy inhabitants dining, dancing, and who knew what else, just beginning their night. The city looked as it always had: prosperous, happy, and safe. If I had any doubt as to the wellbeing of the kingdom under my mother's rule, it was put to rest; whatever else she might be, she was clearly a good Queen. This knowledge didn't make me feel any better about the coming confrontation or the possibility of unleashing war on these innocent people.

We passed through the high-walled forecourt, reaching the vast wooden gates into the castle proper. The men who were guarding the gate looked surprised when they saw me but remained silent, opening the gates on Paulus' order.

A groom waited to take Bastian's reins as I dismounted, and I was shown into the castle with all courtesy and haste, escorted by Paulus and two other guards. I wondered what, if anything, the inhabitants of the castle knew of my visit to Altenburg. Did they see me as a traitor, or only as the Princess returning from her sojourn in the country? Either way, my mode of arrival would be enough to set tongues wagging, except that Paulus deliberately led me through smaller, less commonly used passages and corridors.

I was escorted to my mother's study, where she had first begun to teach me about magic. She smiled when she saw me, though it was cold – not quite her normal smile, but strained – and there was some other emotion in her face I could not quite name.

"Leave us," she said to the two men who had been sitting with her. It seemed as though I had interrupted an important meeting with the treasurer and the court scribe. Looking offended as they gathered their books and notes, they hastily left the room. "We won't be needing you, either," she said to Paulus. He gave her a brief, questioning look, then nodded before stepping out and closing the door behind him.

When we were alone, the smile fell from my mother's face.

"Where have you been?" she demanded in an even, if slightly raised tone. "Do not say at the cabin, for I sent men to fetch you a week ago and they returned to tell me the place was quite abandoned. They thought you had been abducted, but I knew you were too strong a witch to have been taken forcibly."

"It's true, I left the cabin some weeks ago. I went to awaken my sister."

This was clearly not what she had expected me to say. Her face showed surprise, but she quickly recovered.

"I thought we had agreed that your sister was dead. That was some months ago, in fact." The slightest movement of her fingers as she fidgeted with her skirt was the only indication that she was anything less than perfectly at ease.

"I was *almost* ready to believe it until I followed your man, Jurgen, into the woods and discovered that she was very much alive, albeit in an enchanted sleep."

Her face took on a look of defiance.

"Whatever that wicked man told you was a lie. He was as untrustworthy as any man I have ever met. Why, he absconded just afterwards and has not been seen since."

"While I share your low opinion of him, he didn't abscond. He's dead."

"Dead? Well, that's no great loss. There's no one to mourn him. But you say Lily is alive?"

"This will go much more quickly if we drop the pretense. I know you tried to have her killed," I said firmly, mimicking her stern, precise way of speaking.

I told her everything: how I had found Lily, and searched night and day for months for a way to revive her, how I had finally succeeded. I told her that Lily and Christian were now married, that they had the full support of Altenburg's new King, my fiancé, and that we sought to place Lily on the throne as Silvaner's rightful Queen.

"So, there is a man in the mix. I might have guessed it. And you expect me to, what? Step aside? Give up the throne without a fight?"

"I hope that you will. Altenburg is ready to go to war over this, but I had hoped to avoid that. And this isn't about Henri, it's about the fact that you tried to have Lily killed and stole her throne. I'm here to set things right. There's no need for good men to die when we might resolve this peacefully, and I had hoped you might agree with me on that."

"'Is that what you thought, my daughter?" She looked at me pityingly, disappointed, as though I had made some trivial mistake, as though I was a silly child. "Well, you shall be disappointed. I have no intention of giving up the crown. The kingdom has known peace and great prosperity during my reign."

"And you have known great power. But it isn't your kingdom to rule, and you know it. If you don't agree to go into exile, we will take the city by force if we have to," I said.

"So it's 'we' now, is it?" she shook her head. "It takes a powerful leader to rule a kingdom as I have done. Your sister is not fit to rule; she is a child and a simpleton. Your boy king and his friends may fight me if they wish, but they will all die. My magic protects this castle. My magic gives my soldiers courage and strength. And your magic is no match for mine."

"I know that," I said quietly but firmly. "So, you will not agree to peaceful terms?" I asked, giving her one last chance to do the right thing.

"I did not say that. I shall tell your boy king if he withdraws his troops and takes your sister with him, he shall have no trouble from me. If he refuses, I'll defend my kingdom to the last man. But it is not men alone he will have to contend with."

"And what of me?"

"You will stay here. It seems I cannot trust you out of my sight. You will stay here, and in time you will see I have acted for the best, and one day far, far into the future, you, too, shall be queen. You and I will have the power that we deserve, that I have spent my life fighting for. I think that is quite generous of me given all the difficulties you've caused. Of course, if you insist on making trouble, I will have to keep you somewhere you can't cause any mischief."

I was amazed by how calmly she said all of this. She showed no fear, no remorse. Her facial expression barely changed from that of smooth, unruffled resolve. She was simply a woman in power, setting out the terms of a business transaction. I saw now the hardness, the coldness I had seen in her when I was a small child and she refused to comfort me if I was sad. I also saw that she had no love for me; she had only seen me as an extension of herself, a conduit of her own power, maybe her legacy. She would not agree to peace. She was ready, perhaps even hoping, for war.

"Are you really going to imprison me, your own daughter? Do you really care for your power more than me?" I asked, my voice shaking a little with emotion.

"I am doing this *for* you, for us. How many times have I told you that women have no power in this world, except that which we can take by force? I am giving us a kingdom, freeing us from the bedrooms and the sitting rooms where men would have us confined until they have need of our beauty or our bodies. We have no control over our lives but that which we take for ourselves. Why can't you see that?"

"And Lily? What about her? You were willing to kill her, a girl you helped raise from a small child."

"She is no child of mine. There is nothing extraordinary or strong about her. She is the legacy of an antiquated system that gives power to those whose only achievement was to be born into the right family. You are the one that matters. Yes, as I said, I am doing this for *you*. You will stay here, with me. In time, you will even forget your little King."

"If I am not returned tomorrow, they will come for me," I lied. The plan had been for them to wait at least two days before attacking.

She shrugged her shoulders, indifferent to the threat.

"As I say, it is no matter. No army can defeat me. You should know that I am not to be trifled with; my power is greater than you can imagine. But there's no point discussing this further if you are going to keep acting like a spoiled child. Guards," she called loudly, and two armed men opened the door. One of them was Paulus. "Take Princess Rose to her room. She is under great threat by outside forces and must be protected at all costs. Alas, she does not appreciate the danger and may try to resist. Lock her in her room, do not let her out under any circumstances, and keep an armed guard in place all night. Oh, and hold her while I search her for concealed weapons. We don't want her hurting herself."

The two men seized me, one on each arm, and though I struggled, their hold remained tight.

"Paulus," I pleaded, looking up into his face. "Let me go. She wants to hold me prisoner. Help me."

But he did not speak, nor did he meet my eye. I could see there was conflict in him, the way his cheeks reddened in shame. But always the good solider, he obeyed his Queen.

As they restrained me, my mother removed the pouch that hung at my waist containing a few small vials of various potions. Then she took a small knife from my garter and another – the wolf-headed blade she had given me before I first left for the cabin – from up my sleeve. After checking my hair for concealed pins, she seemed satisfied, and ordered me to be taken away.

I had anticipated this response from my mother, and I had prepared for it. Though I'd hoped the others were wrong, that she could be reasoned with, I'd also made allowances for things turning out this way. Sadly, now I knew beyond a doubt that the only way to remove her was by force. It hurt, deeply, that she had chosen power over love, over me. But then, maybe she had never really known love.

The way she spoke about her power and about how hard she had fought for it, I thought she must have been unhappy for much of her life, always fighting tooth and nail for every inch of ground she gained. That was it; life was a struggle for her, and she had resolved to fight her hardest no matter the cost, unwilling to cede even a modicum of her hard-won power.

The moment I was locked in my room I began planning my escape. There were guards posted outside the door, so I would have difficulty getting out that way, even with a concealment charm. Fortunately, I knew the castle well, as I'd scoured every inch of it many times over since I was a child.

I planned to go out via the window and didn't want to tumble to my death because of my long skirts clinging to me. Luckily, I was in my own room, and all my things were still there. Quietly, I changed out of my dress into an old set of clothes I wore when I roamed the forest. It would have been a lot harder if Mother had put me in a dungeon or even another room.

I had a small knife concealed in my bodice, which I now put in my boot. I had expected to be searched; the potions and other knives were a decoy, intended to create a sense of security. It would have been suspicious if I'd been unarmed. Now dressed in breeches and equipped with my spare dagger, I undid the latch on my window. There was no balcony, only a narrow ledge with a fifty-foot drop below, and visibility was poor in the darkness of the night. I placed a concealment charm on myself, as I had done the day I followed Jurgen, so should anyone look up or pass me at a window they wouldn't see me. Still, I had to make sure I was quiet.

Clinging desperately to the tiny gaps between the stones where time had worn away little niches and any little protrusions I could get hold of, my fingers ached and my nails shredded as I gripped tightly, clinging on for dear life. I crept along the outside wall, praying not to fall, until I reached a window that opened onto an empty, dimly-lit corridor. Using my knife, I lifted the window latch from outside and the window swung open, screeching slightly as it went. I paused for a few moments, listening for approaching footsteps or voices, but no one seemed to have heard anything. Once safely back inside, I thanked Hecate for my safety and made my way to my mother's bed chamber.

# Chapter Nineteen

The corridor outside my mother's room was deserted, no guards or servants to be seen, so it was safe to assume she was not there. At this time of night, she was likely taking her evening meal or was still in her study, with no reason to suspect I had gotten past her guards. Silently praising myself for the success of my plan, I slipped into her room, quiet and unseen. It looked as it always had; the large, four-poster bed hung with crimson drapes, plush crimson carpets covering the floor, beautiful, detailed tapestries adoring the walls, and directly opposite the door, a walnut vanity table with elaborately turned legs, a large mirror positioned above it. I approached, noting where her various hairbrushes, perfumes, oils, and cosmetics lay. I took a small vial, which I had also concealed in my bodice, and emptied its contents into a bottle of lavender scent. I knew she would apply it before going to bed, as part of her evening ritual, to help her sleep. How right she was, for the potion I had added was the same one she had given Lily, and it was just as effective when applied to the skin as it was when ingested. After she rubbed the oil on her hair or skin she would not wake until I chose to wake her. There was a sense of poetic justice to this, and it would buy me time while we decided how to deal with her treachery.

My mission complete, I crept down the corridor, still concealed by my charm but eager not to make any noise or otherwise attract attention. Moving slowly and carefully, I got as far as the great hall, where my mother sat with two of her advisors, half a dozen or so servants milling about, carrying dishes of meat or carafes of wine.

"I understand that Princess Rose has returned to us," said Lord Wilhelm, a former lackey of my father's and now a devout follower of my mother. His tone was even, almost bored-sounding, as though he was hesitant to ask an actual question.

"Yes," my mother replied pleasantly, smiling a little. "She is still very much grieved by her sister's death and, I fear, will require some more time in quiet solitude to recover her spirits. But I have high hopes that she will return fully to court life. Eventually."

I wasn't surprised that my mother was already paving the way for me to remain isolated from the court until I agreed to cooperate with her. After all, I had already laid much of the groundwork myself in spending so much time away at the cabin over the last twelve months, little thinking I was giving her ammunition to use against me if I refused to do as she asked. I wondered how calculated it had all been; her agreeing to my spending so much time away, encouraging it even. Had she been anticipating this turn of events, preparing a contingency plan just as I had done? The idea made my stomach clench with anger and bitterness.

The other advisor murmured something about Altenburg's forces being camped a short distance from the city.

"You don't need to worry about that, Lord Marlon, I have already entered into parley with the young King, and I expect they will be gone in a day or two."

"But why are they here at all?" he asked roughly. "It's hardly a friendly gesture to arrive on our doorstep with a small army in the dead of night. We ought to convene a war council right away."

"They didn't arrive in the dead of night," my mother answered coldly. I couldn't see her face, but I sensed her rolling her eyes as she spoke. "And as to why they are here, the young King has some notion of marrying my daughter, to force the alliance that would have been achieved through the marriage of Princess Lily and Prince Christian. It seems as though that family has something of an obsession with marrying into my own. I suspect it's a ploy to take over our kingdom and make it part of their own. Some elaborate scheme to start a new empire." I bristled at the blatant lie, moving slowly to where I could see her expression.

"But there is no need to call a war council," she continued calmly. "I shall send them packing before too long."

"But–" Lord Marlon continued, only for his speech to be halted by the raising of a single eyebrow on the Queen's part. It was a small, almost lazy action, but it quelled the man's speech in an instant. "Yes, Your Majesty."

The conversation moved on to a less inflammatory subject, and while they were preoccupied, I was able to slip past, unnoticed, the sound of my footsteps lost in the noise of their talk and the servants lifting and replacing the great domed covers on the various dishes.

When I reached the stables, I ran into a problem. Two grooms, the same who had been there the day I found Lily, were working, one busy brushing down one of the horses, the other raking up horse dung as they talked and laughed.

I waited, hoping they would leave to have their supper soon. But of course, when I wanted them to shirk their duties, they remained diligent. I wished in that moment I had learned how to compel people with enchantment, but it had never occurred to me before that I would find myself in a situation where such a spell would be useful. A half-hour passed, and I grew tired of waiting, eager to get back to the camp, and fearful my escape would be discovered every minute that I lingered there. As quietly as possible, I crept to the stall that held a stallion I knew to be particularly bad-tempered, and let myself in, lifting the latch ever so quietly. He was enormous, and though very beautiful, with the glossiest black coat and mane, he was as wild and wicked as the devil. I made sure his stall door was ajar, then I pricked him very slightly with the tip of my blade. I didn't even break the skin, but it was enough; he kicked backwards, and when he realised the stall was open, he bolted from the stables, the two shocked and frightened grooms pursuing him, swearing and dismayed at his escape. Hastily, I saddled Bastian and set off, slipping out a side gate no one was monitoring, the guards' attention drawn by the runaway horse.

* * * *

I rode only by the light of the moon until the campfires came into view, not lifting the concealment charm from myself until I could see the flags attached to the tops of the white, peaked tent roofs. As the spell lifted, soldiers at the entrance startled to see me suddenly appear as though from thin air. They drew their swords with practiced speed, but recognised me a moment later, re-sheathing them just as fast. Dismounting and handing Bastian's reins off to one of them, I went straight to the tent that served as a war room and found Henri, Christian, and Lily seated around a large table, along with high-ranking officers, all clad in the green and gold of Altenburg. Henri was also dressed in the kingdom's colours, the crest, which, ironically, depicted a large bear on all fours emblazoned across his chest. He rose to his feet as I entered, and the others followed suit.

"What happened?" Lily asked, voice strained with anxiety as she and Henri rushed to my side, looking equal parts relieved and worried.

"She will not surrender," I said simply. I told them everything that had happened after I arrived at the castle. When I got to the part where I was locked in my room, Henri broke in angrily.

"How dare she. Her own daughter."

"She's done worse," I said drily, looking at Lily.

The conversation turned to what we would do next. There had already been ample discussions of what tactics would work best, how many men would be needed, whether we should strike openly or find another way in.

"I think it would be best if a small group of men and I sneak into the castle," I said, loudly enough to heard over the cacophony of men's voices.

"How do you propose to do that?" said one of the men, whose regalia showed him to be a general, sounding cynical.

I explained about the secret tunnel that ran under the cellar and how it would allow us to enter the castle by stealth.

"Once inside, the men will subdue any guards they came across, then open the forecourt to allow the rest of your forces into the castle. There are usually a few hundred soldiers and guards stationed at the castle at most," I explained. "All going well, the guards will be overrun by your soldiers before they have time to raise an alarm".

I thought it was a good plan; it would mean we could take the castle quickly and quietly, without loss of life.

"I can't let you come along," Henri said, his face flushed in a way that suggested he knew a fight was coming, and it wasn't the one against my mother.

"You won't *let* me?" I said angrily. Complete silence fell in the tent as the others seated at the table looked anywhere but at Henri and me. "You aren't my King, I'm not one of your subjects, and you don't get to tell me what to do. I am a Princess and I'll do what I want. Besides, does anyone have a better idea?"

The other men in the room shuffled awkwardly but remained silent.

"It's not safe," Henri said quietly, taking my hand. "I don't want to put you at risk."

"I'm the only one who knows where the entrance to the tunnel is and how to find my way around the castle. Without me there is no plan. Your men would be discovered the second they got inside and would be lucky if they could even find the forecourt from the cellar."

"So, you *need* to be one of the party?"

"It's unavoidable," I replied, chin angled upwards with determination.

"Then I'm coming with you," he said stubbornly.

"That's stupid, you're the King, you can't be in the thick of it if fighting breaks out," I argued heatedly.

"Your Majesty," Lucas spoke up, reminding me that Henri and I had an audience. "Princess Rose is right, you're too valuable to be going into enemy territory."

"If we were fighting in open battle, I'd be leading the charge like any other useful king. I wouldn't hide behind my men then, so I why should I now? Besides," he added, looking at me again. "If she's going, I'm going," Henri said, obdurate resolve written all over his handsome face.

"Fine," I said, eager to settle things. I was confident I could keep him safe with my magic if it came down to a fight, though I hated the idea of him being in a dangerous situation, especially if it was a confrontation with my mother. But clearly, he felt the same about me, so we were at an impasse. This finally agreed upon, the commanders all approved to the key points of the plan. We would enter the castle by stealth and be as subtle in our invasion as possible.

"But no killing," Lily reminded them all loudly, her eyes bright and her tone commanding. She had barely spoken the entire meeting, but she made herself heard now. "The people in the castle are my subjects and I do not want my reign to begin with bloodshed."

"It might be unavoidable, Your Majesty," Henri said gently, speaking to my sister as one monarch to another. "If your mother doesn't use the potion Rose placed in her room, we may have to fight in earnest. And even if she does, it will still be risky for my men entering the castle. I doubt the castle guards will take an invasion lightly. But," he continued, addressing the men gathered, "instruct your troops to only kill if it is absolutely unavoidable. We want as few casualties as possible, on *both* sides."

It was decided that Christian would join the main host, waiting to strike until the castle had been breached, while Lily remained safely at the camp. She argued against this at first, saying that if I went then she should as well. Eventually, Christian convinced her that she was too important to send into danger, while I argued she would be needed most when the fighting was done with. But she put up a good fight, showing more strength and resistance than was usual for her. She was warming to her role as Queen and did not take dissent lightly.

"I could have just put her to sleep again," I joked as we left the tent, attempting to lighten the mood.

"Maybe next time," Christian replied, managing a strained smile.

✳ ✳ ✳ ✳

It was well after midnight by the time we said our goodbyes to Lily. The commanders went to speak to their troops, while Henri introduced me to the men who would accompany us inside the castle.

"Lucas you already know," he said, as his red-haired friend embraced me briefly.

"Here we have Felix, Max, and Hans." I shook their hands in turn. Normally I would have curtsied when I met new people, but it felt out of place here. Besides, tonight I was a soldier, not a Princess. We talked through the plan once more and then we were ready to begin.

As we rode silently towards the castle, I surreptitiously placed protective charms over our companions, Henri, and myself, as I had done to Christian before we left camp. They weren't impenetrable, but they would at least prevent them from being seriously injured. I would have cast charms over the entire army if I could, but I knew my magic wasn't strong enough for that, and settled for protecting those I knew would be in the most danger.

Night had dropped its shawl of inky blackness across the castle and the city beyond, and we had only the half-moon and starlight to see by. Lanterns would have given us away, so we rode on in darkness, skirting around the city completely, keeping to the shadows at the edge of the forest for cover and adding over an hour to our journey. Leaving our horses hidden in the shadows of the forest, we moved silently and stealthily towards the door concealed by ivy.

We proceeded cautiously; there was a chance I wasn't the only one who knew about the tunnel, and perhaps guards would be placed here, anticipating our arrival. However, as I listened at the door for noises on the other side, there was no sign that the passage was protected. Tensing with nerves, I pushed my magic through the door and outwards, like invisible hands feeling for any human presence on the other side of the door, but there was nothing. Gently, I turned the enormous ring handle of the door, cringing when it released an ear-splitting squeal as the rusted metal grated against the stone wall, but it refused to open. The door was now more overgrown with vines than ever, and appeared to have swollen from all the moisture in the passage; the iron handle and hinges were rusted almost beyond movement, and it resisted all my force, but Max and Felix managed to wrench it open just wide enough for us to pass through. I could have forced it with my magic, but I was conserving what power I could for any real obstacles or threats. In the darkness of the tunnel, Felix lit a lamp, which he passed to Henri before lighting a second one he held himself.

"Remember," I whispered, my voice distorted in the long, damp tunnel, "you go straight past the great hall, and find the main entrance, then you open the gates to Christian and his men from the forecourt." They nodded. We'd been over this a dozen times already, but I didn't know what else to say to them; going over the plan one final time was all I could think to do. I led the way along the damp passage to the trapdoor. Hans went up first to make sure the cellar and stairs into the castle were clear.

"Come on," he said, waving us up from the top of the ladder.

As the lid of the trapdoor closed, we set off up the stairs and into the passage that led to the kitchens. When we came to a corridor that ended in a fork, Lucas, Felix, Max, and Hans set off down the left hand passage, making for the forecourt, while Henri and I took the one to the right, headed for my mother's bed chamber.

"Good luck," Henri called softly to his men.

"And you," Lucas replied before disappearing down the corridor.

Henri and I set off, making as little noise as possible.

"You don't need to come with me; surely you should be with your men," I said for what seemed the hundredth time. But he was steadfast.

"Christian and Felix will manage on their end. I'm where I need to be," he said, giving my hand a quick squeeze.

I turned my face away so he wouldn't see my smile. I was pleased he was with me, not because I needed protecting, but because his presence was a balm to my nerves. It was strange to be prowling around my own home in the darkness like a thief in the night, terrified of meeting someone at each corner we approached.

I used the concealment charm again, hiding us from anyone who might be wandering the halls. We hurried up flights of stairs, pausing at corners to check for guards, servants, or courtiers paying late-night calls, but my spell kept us from being seen, and we encountered no real obstacles before reaching the corridor that led to my mother's room. When we rounded the last corner, I saw Paulus standing guard outside her door. He turned towards us as he heard the soft sounds of our footsteps, but we remained invisible to him.

"What now?" Henri asked quietly, his lips close to my ear.

"Stay here," I whispered back. Henri frowned at me but nodded.

I had two choices: speak to Paulus or put him into a trance and slip by him quietly. I knew what I should do, strategically, but it felt wrong to use my magic against someone I respected as much as Paulus. I lifted the spell to reveal myself to Paulus, but kept Henri concealed. His hand went for his sword when I first appeared, but on recognising me, he became still.

"Your Highness, what are you doing here?"

"I've come to speak to my mother, Paulus, let me by," I said quietly but forcefully.

"I'm sorry, Your Highness, but I can't do that. The Queen is not to be disturbed. And you're meant to be in your room. My men should have raised the alarm – what did you do to them?" he asked, his brows furrowing with worry for the first time.

"Nothing. They don't know I left. Now, Paulus, you must let me pass. It's important." I tried to make my voice light and easy as I took a step towards him, but he drew his sword. I felt Henri tense behind me, his hand likely on his own sword.

"I can't allow you to pass, Princess," Paulus said, his voice strained. He seemed caught between his loyalty to my mother and whatever affection he held for me.

"Would you kill me?" I asked softly as I edged closer and closer, my hands nowhere near the daggers strapped to my belt.

"Only if you made me." His voice broke and there was a sheen to his eyes.

I sighed, hurt by how easily I had gone from friend to enemy in his eyes.

"Very well," I said, twisting my right wrist as I uttered a spell that sent Paulus crashing to the floor. I leapt forwards to try to prevent his fall, but I was too late. He lay sprawled on the floor, a dazed look on his face. I had only stunned him, and it wouldn't last long. At least there would be no long-term damage.

I waved Henri over to the door. "Let me speak to her alone."

"No, you tried that, and she put you in chains. We go together."

"She's very powerful, it's not safe for you," I pleaded.

"It's not safe for you, either. It's not safe for *anyone,* and we don't have time to argue. I'm coming with you."

"Fine. But let me do the talking." He nodded in agreement. "With any luck, she'll have used the oil and be asleep."

"Then there's nothing to worry about," he said with his cocky grin. I wanted both to punch him and kiss him. As I leaned in to kiss Henri, I said, "I'm sorry," and placed a freezing spell on him, then a concealment charm, making him invisible and unable to follow me. He would be safe.

I reached for the door and tested the handle; it was unlocked. Without looking back, I opened it and let myself in, leaving Henri safely behind.

# Chapter Twenty

I opened the door to find my mother standing by her bed, still fully dressed, and looking at me expectantly, the hint of a condescending smile on her scarlet lips.

"Well daughter of mine, this is a surprise. For you, I imagine. I dare say you thought I'd be sleeping," she said, her lips broadening into a wider, openly mocking smile.

I was stunned; how could she have known about my plan? She must have read the question on my face.

"Did you think your childish attempt to stop me would succeed? My daughter, I have been using magic since before you were born; I could smell your pitiful potion a mile away. I had hoped I had taught you better. If you really meant to stop me, you should have gone with something more *lethal.*"

"I wanted to do this peacefully, to give you the chance to walk away safely," I said, refusing to cower before her, though my heart raced anxiously, fear crawling up my throat.

"You sound like your simpleton sister, all peace and love and no backbone or good sense. I will *never* walk away. I told you; this kingdom is mine now, I have worked too hard for too long to let it go. Do you think I removed your useless father for nothing? I should have done it much sooner. Did you think I would give up my crown to your milksop of a sister? That girl isn't fit to lead a parade, let alone a kingdom."

I almost gasped aloud – the way she so calmly revealed that she had killed my father, no remorse, no shame, only irritation at her plans being interrupted. My father hadn't been a good man, or even a moderately estimable one, but that was not justification for murder.

"And me? Am I worthy in your esteem?" I asked, unsure how to proceed, playing for time. While the potion hadn't worked, there was still a chance for Henri's men to overpower the castle if I kept my mother busy for long enough.

"I thought so, once. That's why I trained you to be my *true* heir. But you've shown yourself to be ungrateful for my teachings and a mediocre witch. Although," she paused as though genuinely considering, "I admit, I was impressed you were able to wake your sister. I thought that spell was quite unshakeable with the blood lock, which you clearly figured out how to overcome. Still, you've been a disappointment, Rose. You could have had unlimited power, security, and independence, and you're throwing it away for your sister and a boy you've just met". She shook her head, dissatisfied. "But enough pleasantries. If you leave now, I will let you and the boy you've frozen outside – who is clearly under the delusion that he can protect you – go. But that's my final offer."

I didn't dare glance at the door, Henri on the other side, like she wanted. She was trying to use Henri to distract me, but I wouldn't let him be brought into a witch fight.

"We aren't leaving," I said, throwing out a spell to bind her powers. She flicked it aside with a bored, disappointed look. I'd known she was much more powerful than I was, but was still surprised by how easily she out-manoeuvred me. All my plans and even my contingencies were crumbling away under the weight of her power.

"Very well, you have left me no choice," she said, her eyes narrowed with loathing. She didn't look like my mother anymore, but a fierce, cruel enchantress, bent on keeping her power by any means. Her eyes burned with fire and a maleficence I wouldn't have thought possible. It was like she wasn't even human anymore.

"Let me show you what *real* power looks like," she said in a venomously cold voice that made my flesh creep.

She raised her arm in the air, and with a brief wave, she had Henri entering the room, seemingly moving against his own volition.

"Please don't," I rasped, turning back towards her, my voice suddenly hoarse with fear. "Don't hurt him".

Ignoring me, her hand formed a fist, and I heard Henri gasp. I turned and saw him clawing at his throat, fighting for air, his feet hovering a few inches above the floor. She was using her magic to suffocate him, to rip the air from his lungs. She was killing him, without touching or even looking at him. I looked from him to her, racking my brain for a way to help him, but I didn't know enough spells; I was utterly useless against her.

"Stop it," I begged her, rushing to Henri's side and watching him slowly redden with the strain.

"Your little charm might have stopped my men from hurting your Prince," she said, ignoring my pleas, "but it's no match for my powers. Your love for him makes you weak, vulnerable. Here is a final lesson for you, daughter, though I'm sure you don't deserve my wisdom. If you want to wield real power, to truly reach the limits of your abilities, you cannot keep your hands clean. You must be prepared to fight, to kill for it. True freedom always comes at a cost."

I watched, horrified and motionless as she wrung the life from Henri. His head drooped to the side, and he stopped moving – dead or unconscious, I didn't know, but he was still dangling in the air, borne aloft by her spell. I let out a yell of rage and fury, feeling like I would raze the whole room to rumble in my anger. With no plan and no thought in my mind except to save Henri, I threw out both my hands towards my mother, crying, "No. You can't take him from me."

I cast no spell, uttered no charm; I just cried out in my fear and frenzy, throwing my arms out towards her as though to shield Henri from her magic, even though I was too late. I felt the strength of my power explode from my fingertips, filling the room with a blinding, white light, before it struck my mother like a tidal wave.

Then the light was gone, and for a moment it seemed nothing had happened, like it had just been a flash of light and nothing more. My mother smirked at me, amused. Then her face changed from smug superiority to pain and shock. She staggered, clutching her hands to her neck, her chest, her arms, where blood suddenly ran from a thousand slashes, some small and shallow, others deep and gaping. Bright red blood gushed hot and sticky between her fingers as she tried futilely to stem the flow from a deep wound that had suddenly opened at her throat as she collapsed to the floor. I rushed to her side, wanting to help, to stop the blood that was falling into a fast-growing pool on the floor beside her. There was so much of it, more than I would have thought she could possibly hold, and it just kept coming.

I knelt beside her, my breeches instantly soaked in her blood, trying every spell I could think of to close the wounds. But each time I managed to heal one, several more appeared, all oozing blood more slowly now, as if the well were beginning to run dry. Nothing I could think of helped, so I pressed one hand to the wound at her neck, scrabbling wildly in the pouch at my belt for a salve to heal her, but it was too late. The damage my power had wrought could not be undone by any magic I knew; I had wounded her with an unspoken curse I couldn't undo. Not knowing what else to do, I held her in my arms, trying to comfort her, to let her know that I hadn't meant for this to happen.

"I'm sorry, I'm sorry, I'm sorry," I muttered, as though it could make any difference.

My mother opened her mouth, but no sound came from her lips except a horrible rasping noise, as small drops of blood flecked my chest as she tried to speak. Her skin had gone pale and waxy, a sheen of perspiration on her brow. Her magnificent, fiery green eyes spoke shock, anger, and then took on an odd faraway look before the light left them, and I knew she was gone. It all happened so quickly. I gently slid her lids down to close her eyes, but there was no pretending she might be sleeping, for there was no peace in her unnatural pose or the puddle of blood we were lying in, which now covered most of my clothes while my hands were stained completely red. I felt chilled and hollow, like a gaping cavern had opened inside me. No tears came to my eyes, and my throat felt dry as I turned to face Henri.

He was bracing himself against the wall, watching silently as he rubbed at his throat. I thought he would be afraid, seeing what I had just done, but he merely looked concerned, and moved to embrace me, arms outstretched and ready to comfort. I was so utterly relieved that he was alive, he was unharmed, but I couldn't bear the thought of him touching me in that moment, my hands and clothes drenched in my mother's blood.

"Not now," I snapped, my voice cold as I cringed away from him. I wanted his embrace more than anything, but I was angry at what I had just witnessed, what I had just done, and I didn't deserve to be comforted. And there were still things I needed to do if my mother's death was to serve any purpose.

Quickly, I rose and led the way out of the room, pausing at the door to seal it with a protective spell to prevent anyone but myself from entering, so no one could touch or desecrate my mother's body. Paulus was nowhere to be seen, but I could hear the sounds of fighting coming from the passage ahead of us. It sounded as though Christian's men had entered the castle and a battle was raging in the halls below us. The clang and crash of iron sword on iron shield echoed through the passage, and as we moved along towards the main hall, we passed pools of blood, broken bodies, men dying, and those already dead. I saw Altenburg green and Silvanian blue, but I tried not to look too closely, afraid of recognising their faces. I broke into a run and flew along the passage, trying to think of what to do next. No one seemed to notice Henri and I as we ran along, or if they did, one look at my blood-soaked clothing was enough to send them in the other direction.

"Where are you going?" Henri called after me, parrying a blow from a Silvanian guard as we kept running.

"To stop this," I yelled back, slowing slightly to turn a corner and dodging two men locked in close combat.

As we reached a walkway that overlooked the great hall where the fighting was fiercest, I stopped, no plan in my mind, only instinct. Not pausing to think, I called out to the men below, those from Silvaner and Altenburg alike.

"Stop! Put down your weapons." I spoke to all those not only in the hall, but throughout the castle, my voice unnaturally amplified and ringing with power, not royal, but magical. An unseen force projected my voice so it could be heard by all those who were fighting, as if my magic compelled all to listen and obey. A sudden, eerie silence met my ears. The men stopped fighting, and no one spoke, as hundreds of faces now looked up at me, swords hanging limply at their sides and hands pressed to injuries.

"Queen Lorelei is dead," I said in my new, terrible, thundering voice, trying to keep it from trembling. "King Albrecht's true heir, Princess Lily, is now your Queen. You have no need to fight anymore. Our kingdoms will have peace. We will gather our dead, tend to our wounded, and those who are able will lend assistance to anyone who needs it, no matter what colours they wear, or they will have me to deal with." As I spoke, I felt a halo of warmth envelop my body, and glanced down to see I was wreathed in golden light that did not burn but soothed me, drying the blood that still clung to me and burning it away in some places. I must have looked like a saint in a stained-glass window, wreathed in fiery light, except there was nothing holy about me now.

Those who were gathered in the hall stared at me with wide eyes, some looking fearful and some simply awestruck, some dropping to their knees. I knew they had all heard and obeyed, even beyond the hall, though I could not say how I knew. A fragile peace had fallen over the castle.

*** * * ***

With the fighting ceased, the wounded were collected together in the great hall so they might be treated, the dead laid in a place of quiet repose to await their funeral rites.

"We should send for Lily," I told Henri, men from both sides of the battle now working around me to do as I had ordered. "The people will want to see her. It will help establish order."

Henri nodded and turned on his heel, off to dispatch my command, as though I were the Queen or a general, not the killer and witch that I was. But he'd always been like that, willing to do whatever I asked, trusting me even when he had little reason to. I felt a burning despair in my throat as I watched him out of sight, feeling as though I were somehow letting him go for good, remembering what I had done for him, what I would do again in a heartbeat. But I knew what I had done was monstrous and would kill any love he felt for me. He'd known I was a witch, but he had never seen the worst my power could do, until now. I hadn't even known what I was capable of, and looking down at my hands, now stained with the blood of the wounded as well as my mother's, a wave of sickening fury and shame washed over me. I pushed my feelings down, focusing instead on what needed to be done.

The dead were, sadly, many. The wounded, even more. I had hoped to prevent bloodshed with my plan of infiltration and avoid an all-out conflict. But I had failed. I, and others from the castle, including ladies and servants, ministered to the wounded as best we could. Healers were summoned from the city. Elsa appeared in the hall and, after fussing over me for a few moments, began to help those who were in far worse states than me. There were so, so many injured, and I worked as quickly as I could, uttering healing spells under my breath and applying reparative salves where possible. But for some of them, there was nothing to be done, save hold their hands as they passed into the next world. All told almost one hundred men had died – very few, I was told, compared to most battles – but I felt the weight of them all. One of the bodies I passed by was that of a boy wearing what was clearly borrowed armour. He couldn't have been more than fifteen, yet from his wounds I could tell he had managed to hold his own for a while. I recognised him; he was the kitchen boy I'd spoken with the day I'd gone to find Lily. I didn't even know his name, but said a silent prayer and passed on, unable to keep the tears from my eyes.

As I went in search of Christian and Henri, I came across Paulus half propped up against the wall, his face, arms, and chest covered in blood.

"Paulus," I cried, falling to my knees beside him. "I'm sorry. I'm so sorry."

The same words I had said to my mother, useless now as they had been then. His breathing was ragged, shallow, his whole body shaking with the effort. He tried to focus his eyes on me. I examined him to find the source of his pain, but with the deep, wide wound across his gut, there was nothing I could do to help him. So instead, I took his hand in mine, crying silently.

"Princess," he gasped, his breath laborious and shallow. "Don't cry. All is well." Then his eyelids fell closed and he breathed no more. Someone covered his body with a stained blanket, prising my hand from his. I rose in a daze and wandered off, not wanting to see anymore carnage.

I made my way to the forecourt, where I found Christian giving orders to various soldiers, seeing to the removal of the dead and wounded, the resumption of order. He turned, and seeing my tear-stained face, pulled me into a brotherly hug.

"So many, Christian. So many died," I said thickly through renewed tears.

"It could have been so much worse, Rose. It might not feel like it, but you saved a lot of lives tonight."

"Not enough," I said as he released me. I wasn't even sure if he'd heard me.

He had just opened his mouth to speak again at the moment Lily arrived on horseback, escorted by a half-dozen soldiers from the encampment. The moment the horse came to a halt, she launched from its back and threw herself into Christian's waiting arms.

"Are you hurt? I was so afraid, I was certain something terrible would happen to you," she cried frantically.

They clung to each other tightly for an age before their hold slackened.

"I'm alright," he assured her. "Mostly thanks to Rose. She called a stop to the battle before we had really got started. And whatever that charm was, it worked. There's barely a scratch on me." This was not strictly true; he had a great gash on one of his forearms where some of his armour had come away and an ugly bruise emerging below his left eye. But he would heal. I suppressed a shudder; if this was the aftermath of a minor skirmish, I never wanted to see a full-scale battle.

Lily threw her arms around me, pulling me into the tightest hug of my life.

"Darling Rose, thank you. Are you injured?" she asked, stepping back to look me over. "You're covered in blood!"

"It's not mine. The Queen's," I replied to her questioning look. I didn't want to say it was our mother's.

"Oh, Rose. Are you alright?" Concern was etched on every inch of her face.

I knew she didn't mean physically, that she'd guessed to an extent what had happened. I gave a half-shrug, not wanting to discuss it, and willed myself not to cry there. The pain was too fresh to let it consume me just yet.

Lily turned back to Christian, asking for details of the battle, and once she was distracted, I turned and left them alone. With no one I could help in that moment, I made my way back to my mother's room. I hesitated outside the door, my gut roiling with guilt and horror at the knowledge of what awaited me inside.

Somehow it was more ghastly seeing her dead a second time, how she lay at an unnatural angle, her deeply red blood pooled and congealing around her, soaking into her dark red hair, her skin so white it was almost blue, so unlike the rosy, healthy glow she'd had in life. I fell to my knees, my breeches quickly becoming further steeped in blood, somehow not yet saturated. I held her as I had when she lay dying, as I had not been able to hold her in life.

"I'm sorry," I whispered again, unshed tears making my voice thick and rough in my throat. "I'm sorry. I love you, I wish you had chosen me. I know I disappointed you, but I couldn't let you kill him. Or Lily. I love them, too."

There was a gentle knock on the door, then a soft voice; "It's me." Lily. She was the one person I could bear to see in this moment, the only one who might understand what the cost of our victory had been, and that whatever our mother had been, no matter how wicked or malign, she was still our mother.

"Come in,'" I called hoarsely. The door swung open silently and she came to my side, kneeling on the floor with me. She said nothing but embraced me in a tight hug, the blood clinging to the pale skirt of her dress as it clung to me, slowly staining her gown a dark red. With my head against her chest, I released my grasp on my grief, unleashing the pain that I'd been fighting to keep walled up since the moment I'd known we had won, and let out deep, wracking, horrible sobs. I sobbed harder than I had since childhood, deeply sorry for what I had done, my very bones shaking with the convulsive force of my sobs.

"I didn't mean to," I gasped out.

"I know," Lily said gently, rubbing her hand in slow, soothing circles on my back.

"Was it the right thing?" I pleaded through tears, wanting her to absolve me, tell me it had been right, that it had been necessary.

"Yes. This was her choice," she whispered. "How else would it have ended?"

It was rhetorical. I knew how it would have ended; with Lily's death, perhaps mine, Henri's certainly. Seeing my mother choking the life from him before my eyes again, I knew I would never regret the decision to save him, though I would regret her death, brutal and shocking as it was, for as long as I lived.

"I need to speak to them," Lily said after a long time, beginning to rise from the floor.

She meant her subjects, those who had fought against Henri's men, the servants in the castle, courtiers, everyone. She extended her hand and helped me to my feet, both of us now soaked in our mother's blood, yet somehow Lily managed to still look regal and unruffled. I sealed the room again as we left. We would tend to our mother's body later.

Everyone who could still walk was gathered in the great hall; soldiers, servants, nobles, everyone in the castle, from the humblest kitchen boy to the grandest duke, though most of the nobles had fled when the fighting broke out. One or two had taken up arms and been caught in the skirmish. Lily made a speech; she spoke of the loss that had been suffered on both sides. She spoke of the death of the Queen, how she had refused to abdicate and had chosen war. Lily promised she would never allow war to touch her people again, that there would be peace.

"The aftermath of a battle, no matter how short, is never easy. I see here women without husbands, children without parents, parents without sons. I know it will not be easy to forgive or forget all that has happened. But I hope that you will believe me when I say that now we shall have lasting peace, with Altenburg as our ally. Those you have fought against tonight you will learn to call friends. And in time, we will heal all the wounds that have been opened. I promise you, as your Queen, that no plea will go unheard by me, no call for justice ignored. I am young, but I trust that I can lead this kingdom to a brighter future, by looking to the resilience, bravery, and goodness of our people, of all of you, to be my guiding light."

It was an excellent speech, one that moved many to tears. Seeing her standing before her people, speaking these words, I knew she would be a wonderful Queen.

* * * *

The next day Lily and I had our mother buried quietly in the earth outside the chapel. We had asked no one else to join us, save for the priest who uttered the funeral rites. This was something we had to do alone, each other's grief something only we could understand. Neither of us wore black; it would have felt false, since I'd been the one to kill her and she in turn had tried to kill Lily. As we stood by her grave saying our farewells, I marvelled, not for the last time, at the conflicting elements of her personality. She had been a witch and a queen; a mother and a murderer. She had been loved by her daughters and her people. She had been many things. And now, in spite of all her darkest deeds, she would be missed.

"Goodbye, Mother," I said, laying a small bundle of red roses on her grave. "I hope wherever you are now, you are at peace."

# Chapter Twenty-One

A few days later the army of Altenburg departed, and Henri along with them. Lily's coronation was held a few weeks later. It was a grand, stately affair, attended by nobles and royalty from across Silvaner, Altenburg, and beyond. This was her presentation to the kingdom as the new Queen and a chance to show the world who she was, what kind of leader she would be. It was a step towards healing the hurt done to many because of my mother.

Henri would be attending the coronation, and I both yearned to see him and feared it. I had only seen him a few, brief times since the battle, before he returned home. We hadn't been alone together since that night.

The fact that he was now a King seemed to loom larger than it had done before. When we were planning how to regain Lily's crown, it didn't seem to matter; he was an ally, the brother of Lily's husband, the man I loved, that was all. Our engagement had seemed natural and easy enough, if somewhat hurried. Now, the fact that he had a kingdom to rule and many demands upon him kept him away from me.

A cowardly part of me welcomed the distance, the time apart, as I wondered if he could still love me after what he had seen me do, now that he knew what I was capable of. He had seen me kill my own mother, without even meaning to, and I was not sure our love could survive that. I was afraid of my powers, of the way I'd wrought destruction with so little effort, my control vanishing in my fear for Henri's life. It was reasonable that he should be afraid of my magic as well. Our engagement had not been formally announced; there was still time for him to change his mind.

I hadn't done any magic since the night we reclaimed the castle. I was afraid to, a sense of revulsion coming over me if I imagined so much as heating the bath water by magic. At night I would awaken, drenched in sweat, screaming from dreams of the night I'd killed my mother, dreams in which I was covered head-to-toe in her blood, and her pale, blank face swam before my vision.

I dreamed of the things she had said to me before I killed her. *Pitiful, weak, ungrateful.* Maybe I was those things.

"Does this dress look right?" Lily asked for the hundredth time, as she tried on gowns for the coronation ceremony, the reception, and the ball to follow. The dress she had on now was a pale silver, overladen with ruffles and trimmings and pleats. It looked more like a wedding cake than a gown.

"Which event is this one for?" I asked, trying to recall where we were up to in our preparations. It hadn't taken long for me to lose interest and forget which dresses I'd already seen, and which were new.

"The coronation ceremony, where I shall officially become Queen," she said, her voice deep with feigned snootiness.

"You want my true opinion? Honestly?" I asked, rising from the chaise on which I'd been reclining and daydreaming.

"Of course."

"Well. . . You would be better served by a more vibrant shade, something to play up your colouring. The silver – while lovely – kind of washes you out."

"Go on," Lily urged, despite the outraged look that had appeared on the seamstress' face.

I stood up and crossed the room to stand behind Lily in the mirror.

"You are notoriously the most beautiful woman in the land – you don't need something extravagant to shine. You could wear something simpler. A royal blue, to highlight your eyes and set off your skin and hair. Less of this–" I said, pointedly fluffing a small mountain of fabric at her behind, "and more simple, clean lines. What's the point of being spectacularly beautiful if everyone is distracted by the wrappings?"

She looked a little embarrassed at the compliment. I'd never known anyone to be as dismissive of her own beauty as my sister, nor as happy to heap praise on others. She meditated on my words for a few moments.

"Lisette," she called to the dressmaker, who was standing disapprovingly to the side of us, throwing glares in my direction, no doubt concocting hideous gowns for me as a mode of revenge. "You heard what my sister said. Get to work, please. Royal blue . . . satin, I think. And nice, clean lines. Nothing so busy as all this." She shook the oceans of fabric at her hips and sleeves.

* * * *

The day of the coronation dawned bright and warm. The sweet scents of summer were in the air. It was almost exactly one year since Lily had disappeared.

Lily glowed with an unmatched incandescence and was the most beautiful she had ever been in her happiness. While Christian had accepted Henri's return and inheritance of the crown with dignity and gallantry, I thought it must have stung at least a little, but Christian never showed it. Now, he would be Lily's consort, without the power of a King. The kingdoms would be united, it seemed, if not by a marriage between the two sovereigns, then at least by ties of blood and affection. My thoughts turned naturally to Henri. I hadn't spoken to him before the coronation; he had been busy in various meetings, and I had been attending to many details for the ceremony and all the events accompanying it. Still, I wondered if he was avoiding me, unable to deny I had taken some steps to avoid him, too.

The ceremony seemed to run on for hours, filled with protracted readings and speeches. The temperature in the chapel soared, draining those gathered of their energy and for much of the time, we sat there, a stupefied mass in the high heat. I wore a beautiful dress of dark burgundy and gold silk, but was soon sweating through it, which I thought would ruin the effect a little. But finally, the moment came when Lily and Christian, seated on their thrones, were handed their sceptres and rods, and crowns were placed on their heads, Christian's a good deal smaller than Lily's. Despite the heat, the crowd erupted into loud applause as my sister was crowned Queen Lily the First, of Silvaner.

There was a formal reception afterwards, which mostly entailed Lily and Christian standing for hours, as the many, many nobles and dignitaries in attendance wrung their hands, offered their congratulations and their loyalty, maybe broached an issue of trade policy, then were speedily moved on by the master of ceremonies, who managed the steady flow of traffic. I felt sorry for Lily and Christian; after meeting the new Queen and her consort, the guests were guided through to the great hall, where refreshments awaited them, while Lily and Christian were stuck to their spot with nothing to eat or drink for what seemed an age.

I searched the crowd for Henri, and eventually spied him speaking with an ambassador from the kingdom of Malbourg, an important trading partner of Altenburg. My eyes continued to scan the crowd until I saw Lucas standing with Carlotta. I approached them and Carlotta beamed.

"Your Highness," she said, brimming with excitement when I reached them. "Lord Lucas and I are engaged!"

"My congratulations," I said, genuinely pleased for them. I gave them both a hug and kissed their cheeks. "Where will you live?"

"The Queen has asked that I remain as one of her ladies-in-waiting, so we shall live here."

"How lovely. How is his majesty taking the news of your leaving Altenburg?" I added to Lucas in an undertone. Lucas just grimaced by way of reply and Carlotta went on to tell me exactly how and when Lucas had proposed, effusive and smiling her sweet, toothy grin, while Lucas stood beside her, also smiling and uncharacteristically quiet. She had begun to talk of plans for their wedding when Henri appeared beside me.

"Your Majesty," the three of us said, dropping into curtsies and a bow.

"I heard congratulations are in order. Well done," he said, shaking Lucas warmly by the hand. "Sorry to interrupt, but I need to speak to Princess Rose for a moment."

"Of course, Your Majesty," Carlotta gushed, her cheeks turning pink, dropping into another deep curtsey.

Without another word, Henri took my hand and led me out of the crowded hall and into the quiet garden. The sun was beating down on us, so I suggested we walk along a shaded path, bordered by hedges; it was private as well as cool. I hoped the sweat stains on my dress would dry quickly in the light summer breeze before Henri noticed them. Glancing down, I was relieved to see the darkness of the fabric concealed them quite well. That was some consolation at least.

"Have you been avoiding me?" Henri asked suddenly.

"*Me?* Avoiding you? It was you who left, Your Majesty."

"I had a country to run. I'm only going to be here for a few days, then I must return home."

"I understand. A King's work is never done," I said, keeping my tone even, but avoiding his eye.

"I know things are different now. Your sister is settled as Queen here, and I have my own kingdom to care for. I wish things were simpler between us, like they were when we were at the cabin. Those were some of the happiest days of my life." His tone was wistful.

"Me too," I said softly, feeling slightly choked with emotion. I coughed to cover it.

A heavy silence stretched between us, taut as a bow string, before Henri finally spoken again.

"I know a lot has changed, but I still love you, Rose."

I stopped walking and looked at him.

"I love you, too," I said simply. "But you're right; things have changed. We can't pretend that they haven't or that we can just go on as we did before. I know that."

I plucked a rose from a bush as we passed and unconsciously began tearing away its petals.

"I know losing your mother was hard. I can't imagine how desperately unhappy you must feel, and I know I am, at least in part, to blame. You made a difficult decision to save me. It seems you're always in the midst of saving someone." He smiled a little sadly. "But even without all of that, all I want is you, as you are."

We had stopped walking and he took hold of my chin, gently tilting it so I was looking at him, and searched my face with his beautiful brown bear's eyes.

"You do, even after the things you've seen me do? You don't think in time you would come to fear me or wish I were different? I saw it happen with my mother and father. What I believe started as love turned to fear and hate."

"Never. You are and have always been perfect. Even your imperfections are perfect to me. You're stubborn and brave and independent. You're so competent it's a little intimidating. You're beautiful and kind and clever. There are so many reasons why I want you, and why you'll make an excellent queen." He released his hold on me, and I took a step back.

"Even though I'm a witch?"

"A witch who saved her kingdom, who saved her sister, the Queen, from a terrible fate. And, who incidentally saved me – several times, actually – as well. Or do I need to remind you that before I met you, I was quite literally a bear?"

"Don't joke, Henri, not now. I don't think you understand – I didn't mean to do what I did to my mother; I didn't cast a spell, I didn't have a plan or any clear thought in my head, apart from needing to save you. It just happened. It was like my power just acted on its own. I never meant to kill her."

"I know that," he said soothingly.

"Do you? Then you also know it means I can't control my powers. It means I'm not safe to be around. What if I hurt you? I couldn't live with myself if I hurt you. Oh god, what if we had a child?"

He took my hand and laid it on his chest, just over his heart.

"I don't think you will. I've seen you do a lot of magic, and almost all of it was for the good of others. You did what you did to save me, and I'm sorry you had to. I should have listened to you when you suggested I stay with my men. You were right, I wasn't any help to you. But I'm not afraid of your power. I'm not afraid of you. And even if there is some small danger, I think you are worth the risk. I was worried that you'd hate me for what happened, for not listening to you. If I hadn't been there-"

"No, I know it wasn't your fault. I did this. Which is why I need to learn more about my magic, about how to control it. I need to be safe, for your sake, for everyone's, as well as mine. And, if we had children, I'd need to know they're safe from me, too."

"We'll manage every hurdle and risk that comes our way. I've never seen you back down from a challenge; I don't believe you'll let anything bad happen to those you care for. I trust you, more than anyone. And if you need time and space to better understand your power, I'll do whatever I can to help. We'll find other witches to help you if need be. Whatever it takes to make you happy and safe. But I'm not going anywhere."

I reached up, tangling my hands in his lovely brown curls, and kissed him.

"So, we're still getting married?" I asked when we finally moved apart.

"Yes, as long as you want to."

"Yes, I want to," I laughed, and then I cried.

✸ ✸ ✸ ✸

Our wedding was to be held in Altenburg, and, in a break from tradition, it would be a wedding and a coronation in one. I arrived a few weeks ahead of the big day, to get settled in, be fitted for my wedding gown, and spend some more time getting to know Henri's family and the city. I was happy to be back in Bellin Stadt; I loved the vibrant, busy city, the bright colours of the town. I was also pleased to be reunited with Artemis; she'd been left behind with Sophie and Gisela when we had set off for Silvaner, and I'd missed her terribly.

"We've taken good care of her," Sophie assured me when Artemis bounded up to me the day I arrived at the palace.

*Perhaps a little too much care,* I thought, seeing that Artemis had grown fatter while I had been away. She yapped and jumped and licked at my hands when she saw me, and I was happy that she hadn't forgotten me after a few weeks of being utterly spoiled by my future in-laws.

All my things were brought across from Silvaner, and I was set up in the beautiful suite of rooms Lily and I had shared when we first arrived. Henri had also organised for my workroom to be set up more fully to meet my needs, now that it would be a permanent arrangement. Anyone who asked was told that I had a great interest in medicine, and would use the space to make healing preparations, which was in part true. I'd had all of my mother's books on magic brought over, along with all her potion-making equipment and supplies, hoping to discover more about the uncontrolled power I'd displayed the night she died.

The room couldn't have been more different from the space my mother had used as her workroom. Where her room had been small, dark, and cramped, the room Henri had gifted me was airy, brightly lit by large windows overlooking one of the gardens, and had numerous cases, cabinets, and cupboards to store the many materials I needed. The space was beautiful and welcoming, but what mattered most was that it had a secure lock, and I had the only key.

Not that I had much time for witchcraft or study when I first arrived; my days were taken up with planning for the wedding, lessons to help me memorise the names and houses of all the nobles who would be attending, and dress fittings. In addition to my wedding gown, I would have an entirely new wardrobe to go with my new role as Queen. I thought it was excessive, and said as much, but my future mother- and sister-in-law both argued that it was tradition and very much required, as though that settled the matter. Not that I minded; I liked the idea of beginning an entirely new life with Henri, and if that required an entirely new wardrobe, I was ready to capitulate.

Lily and Christian came for short visits in the lead up to the wedding, but they never stayed more than a week. This was the downside of having their own kingdom; they were too important to be absent for very long. Nevertheless, I liked being able to talk to Lily about being Queen and being married, and it was comforting to have her insights on what I could expect when I became Queen myself.

"The most important thing," she told me earnestly, "is to be very firm with your council. Listen to their views, but don't allow them to bully you."

"I don't think either Henri or I are at risk of being bullied. Do you have any other sage advice, from one Queen to another?" I asked, half-teasing.

"Just this; you and Henri are each other's best comfort, so you must be open and honest with each other. I suppose that's advice for marriage as well as ruling a kingdom."

I knew this already, perhaps even better than Lily did. Henri and I had been through so much already. We'd overcome obstacles of gigantic proportions, but we'd always done it together. Even when it came to my powers, to the fears I had about them, Henri was the one person I was able to be entirely honest with. Even Lily didn't know the full story, and I didn't want to tell her about my fear that I was dangerous, or the terrible dreams that still haunted me about my mother's death. No matter how worried I was, the knowledge that Henri loved me, believed in me, trusted me, made it all easier to bear.

I was less concerned about the marriage; we'd already lived together and knew each other so well. I thought back on our time in the cabin fondly and sometimes yearned for the peace and quiet, the solitude of our little retreat.

I wondered what it would be like to marry someone you had rarely, or never, been alone with. The thought terrified me, and I felt doubly lucky that Henri and I had the shared history we did. Still, the lead-up to the wedding was not without its awkwardness and trials of various kinds. For one, I had to endure an excruciatingly uncomfortable conversation with Henri's mother.

I was having tea in my sitting room with Queen Gisela and Sophie. After we'd finished tea, and I was just rising to go meet with Henri, Queen Gisela asked Sophie to excuse us. Henri's sister looked a little affronted, as she always did when she felt she was being left out of something. But obeyed her mother, who took a seat close beside me, patting me gently on the hand, and awkwardly began what I suspected was a well-rehearsed speech.

"As your own mother is no longer with us, dear, I feel that it is my responsibility to tell you about the, erm, marital act."

*Oh, dear God, please no,* I thought. My insides crawled with discomfort and I thought I might actually bring up the few small treats I'd just eaten with my tea. Gisela looked equally unhappy; her face turned very pink, and she kept glancing about the room, looking everywhere but my face. I wanted to tell her the speech was unnecessary, but I then I realised I'd have to explain why, and that was more horrifying than the alternative, so I let her go on.

She used words like 'duty', 'discomfort', and 'consummate'. It made me very, very glad I already knew what she was talking about, because if this was the explanation given to most young women, I wondered how anyone ever got them down the aisle. It also made me feel incredibly sorry for my future mother-in-law, if that was how she felt about her relations with her late husband.

✱ ✱ ✱ ✱

I saw little of Henri during this time – except in the evenings – as he carried out his kingly duties; but he would drop in on me during the day whenever he could. Sometimes, when he had an hour free and I managed to dodge dress fittings, dance lessons, and tea with the ladies of the court, we'd lock ourselves away in his room where no one would disturb us.

"It's not going to be like this forever, is it?" I asked on one of these occasions, when I'd manage to escape. We lay on Henri's bed after having taken our time undressing each other and making love.

"No, I promise, after the wedding and coronation, we'll have more time to ourselves."

"I won't have to drink tea with your mother and the other ladies every day, will I? If I keep it up, I'm worried I won't be able to face another cup of tea ever again."

Henri laughed.

"I'm serious! Every day there's someone new to meet and it's always over tea. When I'm Queen, I'm going to outlaw tea drinking in groups of two or more."

"When you're Queen," Henri said, running his fingers through my hair, which was loose and tumbled over my shoulders. "You can do whatever you want."

"Not *whatever* I want, or you and I would never leave this bed, then who would run the kingdom?" I asked with a mischievous smile.

"You're a terrible influence on me," Henri replied, moving closer so that our bodies were pressed together again.

"I know," I replied. "It's part of my charm."

# Chapter Twenty-Two

I stood before an enormous mirror in the seamstress' workroom, having the final touches and adjustments made to my wedding gown. It was the most gorgeous dress I had ever seen, and I felt spectacularly beautiful in it. The dress was in two pieces; the bodice, sleeves, and underskirt were all one piece, while another, fuller skirt sat atop the first skirt, giving the dress magnificent volume and making my waist look tiny. I hoped the doorways would all be wide enough for me to pass through.

The central panel of the bodice and the underskirt were a rich, golden damask, embroidered with crimson roses, while the sleeves, back, and outer skirt were a deep, vibrant, emerald green silk, which became streaked with gold when it caught the light at the right angle. I loved the way it combined the colours of Altenburg with the red roses, like a marriage of our two houses. I had always had beautiful clothes, but never anything as elaborate and utterly perfect as this. There is a saying that clothes make the man. This dress made me feel like a Queen.

I was admiring the dress in the mirror, turning this way and that, when Queen Gisela entered the room.

"My goodness, aren't you magnificent!" she exclaimed, her hands pressed against her broad bosom as she gazed at me with an expression of awe.

"The dress is marvellous, thank you so much for letting me use your seamstress." I'd already been effusive in my gratitude, as Henri and his mother had insisted that all the expenses for the wedding, and my new wardrobe, would be paid for out of Altenburg's coffers, not Silvaner's, as they usually would have been. Lily had argued at first, but Henri had insisted that it was the least Altenburg owed me.

"It's not just the dress, dear, it's the wearer as well," Gisela gushed as she scanned my gown and me from head to toe. "You really are a great beauty. But there is something missing."

I raised my eyebrows in a silent question, and just as she was about to explain, there was a soft tap on the door of the workroom.

"Come in!" Gisela called, and three servants entered the room, each carrying a sizable, ornately-carved wooden box, which they set on the table before us. The lids were removed to reveal the largest collection of jewels I had ever seen. A great many rings, necklaces, earrings, and a few tiaras, all beautifully detailed with different coloured gems, sat before me.

"I know you haven't chosen your jewels for the big day, so I thought you might like to see what looks best with your gown," Gisela said kindly, gesturing to the trove of finery that lay before us in an off-handed way.

My eyes were immediately drawn to a necklace formed by a circlet of rubies, each the size of my thumbnail and surrounded by its own crown of small diamonds. I tried it on, and it complemented the gown perfectly, accentuating the red of the roses on my bodice. Matching earrings and a tiara also embellished with rubies were added, until I felt weighed down by the jewels. Now I knew why the royal family so seldom wore their crowns outside of state functions.

"There," Queen Gisela said, standing beside me as we both looked appraisingly at my reflection. "Now you truly look like a Queen."

I was not permitted to see Henri the day before the wedding, but he sent me a note, which was delivered while Lily and I sat in my room, ready for bed, but still discussing the enormity of the following day.

The note said:

*My darling Rose, I am desperately excited to call you my wife, but even more desperate to be able to see you whenever I please. After tomorrow, all the time in the world shall be ours.*
*Love,*
*Henri.*

A broad, silly smile spread over my face as I read this.

"You two really are too adorable," Lily said, watching me. "I'm so glad you've found someone to make you so happy. I remember when you said you might not marry at all. Now here you are, only nineteen and marrying a King, no less!"

"I know, I *am* sickeningly happy," I said, trying to push away the darker thoughts that had been weighing on me. "But, well, I can't help wishing Mother was here," I added, giving voice to one of many things that were causing me grief.

Her death was still so raw, and my guilt was never very far from my mind. I still had nightmares about that night, from which I'd wake drenched in sweat and terrified I'd hurt someone else I loved with my uncontrollable powers. Sometimes I'd dream it was Henri on the floor soaked in blood, other times it would be Lily.

But there would be time to tell her about all that later, for now I wanted to think only of the wedding. Afterwards I would find a way to make sure I could control my magic.

"I know," Lily said, taking my hand.

"Not that she ever liked the idea of marriage. It was totally at odds with her ideas of freedom and happiness," I said with a small smile.

"Even so, I think she would be pleased to know that you are happy, and that you've made the choice for yourself."

I woke early the next day, having been so deeply asleep that I felt that my head had barely touched the pillow before I was being shaken awake by a swarm of maids. I'd had none of the fears and doubts that kept others awake the night before their wedding, only hope for my future with Henri. But first, I had to survive the wedding and the coronation.

First, I was forced into a bath of hot, steamy water that had been scented with fragrant oils. Little ribbons of steam smelling of lavender, jasmine, and geranium unfurled from the surface of the bath, filling the air with calming fragrances. This, at least, was relaxing, unlike the next two hours I spent having my hair tugged and combed and pinned into place, my rebellious curls fighting against the hairdresser at every step. Next came the wedding gown. Beautiful as it was, I wished putting it on wasn't such a long and involved process. Finally, I was decked out in the spectacular jewels I had chosen.

Then, I was being led to the chapel, where Lily and Christian had also been married. I was glad to have Lily by my side, giving me away in the absence of our parents. My hand clasped in hers, we walked down the aisle as a harpist played a delicate tune. The church was packed with hundreds of people, representatives from every corner of Altenburg and Silvaner, and the kingdoms beyond. I spotted Elsa in one of the pews, her face half-hidden behind an old handkerchief I'd embroidered so long ago as she mopped at the tears already streaming down her cheeks. But the hundreds of faces turned towards me, watching my every step as I made my way down the aisle, might as well not have been there at all; the only person I saw clearly was Henri, standing beside the bishop, his radiant smile making my heart melt.

The ceremony was long, and somewhat tedious, just as Lily's had been. We exchanged vows, promising to honour, love, and cherish for the rest of our days, before we exchanged rings. It was the first time I had seen mine; it was a tastefully set hexagonal emerald stone, surrounded by diamonds. At last, we kissed, a chaste little kiss that was purely for show, and were pronounced man and wife, and the crowd burst into delighted applause. The ceremony was not over, though; we still had to sit through the coronation.

After kneeling on the cold stone floor for the better part of an hour, we took our seats in the golden thrones that had been placed on the dais. Henri and I both held a rod and sceptre, recited the vow of sovereignty, which was not so different from our marriage vows, and finally had the crowns placed on our heads. They were terribly heavy, and it was a great relief to remove them when the ceremony was finally over.

However, we were still not free to be alone together; there was a long reception of our guests, followed by a feast. This, at least, I could be enthusiastic about; I hadn't eaten all day and the long, tedious ceremonies had sapped all of my energy. I practically moaned when I was finally able to eat, and had to force myself to take small, feminine bites instead of shovelling it all into my mouth as I longed to do.

The meal was followed by dancing, then a speech by Henri, then at long last the day was over, and we were allowed to retire. Once we were in the privacy of our room, I flung off my shoes and threw my arms around Henri, kissing him deeply, hungrily, as I hadn't been able to do with hundreds of pairs of eyes upon us earlier.

"I have been wanting to do that all day," I said, smiling.

"So have I, it's been maddening not being able to kiss you whenever I feel like it," he replied.

"And is that often, Your Majesty?" I teased, batting my eyelashes.

"At least a dozen times a day, Your Majesty," he said, kissing me again.

"At least we're together now, and always will be. I'm just relieved that we never have to do that again. I'm exhausted."

"Not too exhausted I hope?" he said teasingly.

"Why, what did you have in mind?"

"Well, Your Majesty," he said with a playful little bow. "As it's our wedding night, I rather expected you to make love to me."

"Naturally. But can we have a little nap first? I've been up since sunrise and am utterly exhausted."

"Thank God, me, too," he said, laughing despite the fatigue of the day.

Without undressing, we lay side by side on the bed, still in our finery, though I removed all the jewellery that had been weighing me down all day.

"Now that the wedding and coronation are done with, we can start looking for answers about my powers," I said, snuggling closer to Henri, his arm around my shoulders and my head pillowed on his chest as we lay together on the enormous bed in the suite of rooms we now shared. "I only hope we find them. I don't want to live in fear of my magic, and I don't want to give it up."

"You won't have to. I promise, we'll do whatever it takes to get the answers you need. When you're ready, we'll make a plan. But I'll never ask you to give up your magic."

I leaned in and kissed him softly, this beautiful man, who loved me, flaws and all.

"Well, how is this for a plan? We'll have a well-earned sleep, and then we'll find a way to make sure I can use my powers safely. Then we shall live happily ever after."

"Agreed," he replied, stifling a yawn. "I love a happy ending."

"Well," I paused, echoing his yawn with my own. "You know an ending is really just another story beginning," I said happily, closing my eyes and drifting off into a peaceful sleep.

# Acknowledgements

It's hard to believe how quickly this book came together, but I know it wouldn't have happened without the love and support of my amazing family and friends. To my mum, Joy, thank you for being my first and most enthusiastic reader. To Clare and Scott, thanks for your amazing feedback. This story would never have been what it is without your insights. To Tim, thanks for understanding my obsessive need to write.

To Michael Occhionero from Ace of Swords, thank you for believing that this story was worth telling and for supporting me through the whole process. Being a first-time novelist is hard, but you made it as easy as possible. To Julia Bifulco and Kirk Middlemiss, thank you so much for your attention to detail and care with this book.

Finally, thank you to anyone who reads this story, I hope it brings some small measure of magic into your life.